PERFECT
LIARS

PERFECT

Includes *Such a Good Girl* and *Secrets, Lies, and Scandals*

AMANDA K. MORGAN

LIARS

SIMON PULSE

An imprint of Simon & Schuster Children's Publishing Division
1230 Avenue of the Americas, New York, New York 10020
This Simon Pulse paperback edition June 2020
Such a Good Girl copyright © 2017 by Simon & Schuster, Inc.
Secrets, Lies, and Scandals copyright © 2016 by Simon & Schuster, Inc.
Cover photograph copyright © 2020 by Shutterstock

For information about special discounts for bulk purchases, please contact Simon & Schuster
Special Sales at 1-866-506-1949 or business@simonandschuster.com.
The Simon & Schuster Speakers Bureau can bring authors to your live event.
For more information or to book an event contact the Simon & Schuster Speakers Bureau
at 1-866-248-3049 or visit our website at www.simonspeakers.com.
Cover designed by Laura Eckes
Interior designed by Tom Daly
The text of this book was set in Perpetua Std.
Manufactured in the United States of America
2 4 6 8 10 9 7 5 3 1
Library of Congress Control Number 2019955803
ISBN 978-1-5344-7382-9 (pbk)
ISBN 978-1-4814-4959-5 (*Such a Good Girl* eBook)
ISBN 978-1-4814-4956-4 (*Secrets, Lies, and Scandals* eBook)
These titles were previously published individually.

SUCH A GOOD GIRL

For Ryan and Lindsay

Something to Know About Riley Stone:

• Riley Elizabeth Stone is just about perfect. Ask anyone.

ONE
Perfect

"What was it like being the homecoming queen as a freshman?"

Sydnee Grace Hill, a first-semester reporter for the high school newspaper, smiles across from me at a cramped table at Hartsville High's answer for a school café. She's writing a student profile on me for the next issue. Each month, a senior is chosen. They asked me back in August, but I was really busy with a fund-raiser for a local no-kill animal shelter, so they scooted me back a few issues.

"Oh." I smile at the reporter, a little impressed. She's done her homework. Well, she's tried, at least. "I wasn't exactly the homecoming queen, Syd."

Sydnee, a freshman herself, blushes at the nickname. "Yeah, but you got the most votes, didn't you?"

"Sure, but votes didn't matter. Freshmen didn't qualify. I think Madison Corrigan ended up getting it that year," I say, like I don't remember the exact moment they told me that I wouldn't be crowned homecoming queen and announced Maddie instead, a cold-hearted senior with white-blond hair who was known for publicly embarrassing freshmen in front of her senior posse. She made them hold her books outside the restroom and do her laundry (including panties and sweaty gym clothes) and even forced them to do her homework, like that was supposed to somehow increase their social standing.

It was definitely a travesty.

"You won this year, though," Sydnee points out. "And you've made homecoming court every single year."

I nod, smiling a little. It's humbling, knowing everyone likes you that much, and that you haven't intimidated your way into it. And scary. "It's an honor," I tell her, and I mean it. I really do.

She writes down my words verbatim. Her big red curls fall in her face and a couple of strands stick to her bubblegum-pink lip gloss.

"Can I fact-check a couple of things for the profile?" she asks. "Just to make sure I get everything right? I mean, if you have time?" Her voice wobbles.

I nod. "Sure."

"You've been accepted to Yale, Stanford, and Harvard, correct?"

"Almost. Not Harvard. Brown, actually."

I watch as she ticks off the names of the correct colleges and scratches out Harvard. She clears her throat. "Right. And you've been captain of the cheerleading squad for . . . ?"

"Two years now. Ever since Ilana Giavanni tore her ACL."

Sydnee nods and scribbles another note. I want to ask her to use her phone to record so the interview will move more quickly, but she seems so nervous I don't want to make it worse. This is probably her first ever interview for the *Harts High Beat* (and yes, that *is* the worst name for a newspaper ever) and I don't want her to think she's doing a bad job. She's actually doing pretty well. I once was interviewed by this boy who couldn't even write because his hands were shaking so hard. Poor thing.

"And you've had a 4.0—since forever?"

I laugh. "I think I got a lackluster grade in handwriting once. But yeah, my grades have been pretty good since—just say high school, okay?"

Sydnee's brow furrows. "Okay. Now, the fun stuff. Eye color, blue . . . height . . . five seven . . . hair color . . . blond?"

I fluff my hair. "Um, my hairstylist makes it look natural, doesn't he?" I laugh. "I'm kind of a dirty blond. Or a lackluster brunette."

She covers her mouth, like I told her some kind of dirty secret. "Am I allowed to publish that? That you're not a real blonde?"

"You can publish where I get it done, for all I care. Maybe he'll give me a discount for the free ad space." I laugh again, and Sydnee giggles, high-pitched and eager.

"Is Hartsville your hometown?" she asks.

"Born and raised."

"Okay. Now I need an embarrassing story."

"Hmm." I tap my lips. "I once got trapped in an elevator."

Sydnee's eyes widen. "What? How is that embarrassing? That sounds horrifying!"

"Well, it was. Except that I had just downed, like, an entire grande caramel brulée latte before getting on the elevator, and I was in there, alone, for almost four hours."

Syndee's eyes go super wide and round. "So what happened? Did you pee your pants?"

"Um, remember the empty Starbucks cup?"

"You didn't."

I nod, and Sydnee covers her mouth.

"By the time I got rescued, I had a full coffee cup with me. I just pretended it was, like, leftover latte, but you could totally smell it. It was pretty gross. The guy who rescued me actually made a face."

Sydnee chokes and then clears her throat. "Are you—are you sure you actually want this to be published in the paper, Riley?"

I laugh. "I don't care. It's funny, right?"

She nods. "Um, yeah. It's just crazy."

"You can't take everything so seriously, Sydnee."

Sydnee lifts a shoulder to her ear.

I stand up from the table. "I have to meet my family for dinner, but if you have any more questions, you can text me, okay?"

She blinks at me. "On your phone? I mean—you—are you sure?"

I smile. "Yeah, sure. Just let me know, okay?"

Sydnee unlocks her phone and hands it to me, and I enter my number as RILEY STONE !☺! 👄. I try to hand it back to her, but she's just staring at me, all trembly and owl-eyed, like I'm sort of a celebrity, so I swoop in and give her a hug and a pat on the shoulder and then I just leave her phone on her notepad.

"Don't hesitate to text or whatever, okay, Syd?" I put my sunglasses on, sweep my (dyed) blond hair over my shoulder, and leave the freshman alone at the school café. "I can't wait to see it in the paper. You'll let me know when it runs, won't you?"

"Next . . . next week. See you later, okay, Riley Stone?"

"See you, Sydnee." I smile big at her, trying to communicate that we're cool, and she's cool, and maybe she doesn't have to be so scared next time.

"This came for you," Mom says, handing me a neat white envelope with *Princeton University* emblazoned on the corner. We're all standing around in the kitchen, like we always do, but Dad's the only one really cooking. Mom's just getting things out of the refrigerator for him, setting them close by in case he needs them, like she's actually part of the process or something. She's pretty awful at it—cooking, baking, you name it. She can barely slap together a peanut butter sandwich without causing some serious damage. Dad has the talent, and right now he's stirring his signature red sauce while it simmers on the stove top, filling the kitchen with a warm, rich, garlicky scent that would put most Italian restaurants to shame.

"Do you want to try it?" my dad asks absently, not really expecting anyone to take him up on it. He knows it's good already. It's always good.

"Um, Mom, did you see what's on this envelope?" I wave it at her. Princeton. I didn't get accepted early decision there, but I don't really see any reason why I wouldn't have been. I know what's inside but I want her to just look at me, just for a second. "Mom."

I ease my finger under the envelope.

"Just a minute, honey." She's turned away and already talking to Ethan, my brother, and smiling down on him with her hands on her svelte hips. He's gotten into the garlic bread and has crumbs in the scraggly beard he's trying to grow. He brushes at them with the back of his hand, and they fall into his lap.

"How is she?" my mom is asking in a low voice, like the whole family doesn't already know that his girlfriend is six months knocked up.

With another man's child.

So scandalous.

I tear off a piece of the garlic bread for myself. "Yeah, how is she?" I ask, not because I'm being nasty or anything . . . but because I really want to know. His girlfriend's name is Esther and she's Mother Teresa, except six months pregnant, because she fell in love with the wrong guy, which was Not Ethan, before she fell in love with the right guy, which is Hopefully Ethan.

"She's good," Ethan says. "I'm going with her to her next doctor's appointment."

Mom glows at him. "That's sweet of you, honey."

I feel a little twinge beneath my breastbone. Here I am, getting greasy garlic-bread hands all over my letter from Princeton, and Mom doesn't really care. But get my brother to go to his pregnant girlfriend's doctor's appointment, and she's practically a living, breathing parental seal of approval.

I bite back my disappointment. Maybe all I need for some attention is something growing in utero.

I sit down at the kitchen table across from my brother while Dad takes the sauce off the stove and pours it into a white serving bowl. I stuff the garlic bread in my mouth all at once—Sydnee and everyone at school would *so* disapprove—and open my Princeton letter.

"Dear Riley E. Stone," I say through the mouthful of bread. I take a big drink of water and swallow it down. "We are pleased to inform you that you have been accepted into Princeton University's 2022 freshman class."

Dad turns toward me and favors me with a smile. "That's great, sweetie." He turns back to his spaghetti, takes it off the burner, and begins to drain the noodles. The hot water hisses as it hits the stainless steel of the sink.

Mom pats me on the shoulder sort of halfheartedly and Ethan fist-bumps me.

"Is Esther coming over for dinner, Ethan darling?" Mom asks my brother.

"She can invite her family," Dad says from the stove. "I've made plenty. Can you ask them to pick up wine, though, if her parents do come? I think a nice red could go well with this, but I haven't bought any in ages."

"Probably not. Her dad's on a business trip," Ethan says. "Dunno about her mom and sisters." He gives me a little smile. I think he feels bad. He's always stealing my thunder a little bit, without even meaning to. He's just that sort of person. Magnetic. Even when he's doing something utterly without merit.

He's the type of man who could lead an entire army into a meaningless battle and they'd fight with fervor.

In fact, in high school, he got suspended for two weeks when his Spanish teacher realized he was cutting class to host a twenty-man Call of Duty tournament (pay to play with a cash prize) in the school auditorium, and even after ten of the twenty players joined him (in less-serious punishments, obviously, as Ethan was found to be the ringleader) he still made out with, like, a thousand dollars. And then he just moved the tournaments to our basement when our parents weren't home.

My father sets the noodles in the middle of the table and follows it with the bowl of rich sauce, steaming from the stove. "I hear Purdue is really great," he tells me. "You're very lucky to be accepted."

I look down at the Princeton letter. I've left buttery yellow smudges all over it.

"Purdue is really great," I repeat.

No one bothers to correct my father, but I'm not entirely sure they know he was wrong to start with. They start passing around the noodles. Mom wants Parmesan cheese, so I run to the refrigerator and grate a little into a tiny red bowl.

"Food's perfect, Dad," I tell him.

TWO

Posse

There is nothing better in high school than being assigned to your own private study hall room with your two very best friends.

Of course, that's a bit of an exaggeration. I'm sure there are some better things.

For example, all-expenses-paid trips to Europe, or winning a brand-new Lexus with, like, heated and cooled seats and Wi-Fi, or an utterly perfect fake ID. But all of those seem far-fetched because (a) my mom swears that international travel is unsafe right now, (b) my dad says that my car is perfectly acceptable, thank you very much, and (c) honestly, I'm way too much of a rule-follower to purchase a fake ID, let alone *use* one.

I am a girl who takes acceptable risks.

However, as far as reasonably cool stuff, a private study hall isn't terrible or anything. Two years ago, the school got some sort of major grant and completely redid our library—which meant these little pods they added where students can study in a more private, soundproof environment where they're free to listen to music while they work (at an acceptable volume, of course) or collaborate in study groups. Best of all, the pods have actual doors, which means that for one hour, every other day, Kolbie, Neta, and I get (some) privacy to basically hang out.

Certainly, the doors have windows in them, so the library aides can make sure no one is making out or doing drugs, but other than that we're mostly safe to do as we please as long as we're not being ridiculous.

Technically we're *supposed* to be studying, but like the rest of the world, I am pretty sure in the history of high schools that No Student Ever has actually fully used study hall for its intended purpose, and that includes Goody Two-shoes like myself.

Liam, the college-age student aide who has a beard that would make lumberjacks jealous, pokes his head into our pod. "Are you all good to go for the day?" he asks with a goofy grin. His gaze pauses for a half second on Neta, and his ears turn pink.

Neta pauses from applying her lip gloss and spins around in her chair, crossing her legs. "Hi, Liam!" she says brightly. "How's your Comms project going?"

Neta has that effect on men, since she's basically a young Sofia Vergara. If she weren't so nice and if I were into that whole female-on-female jealousy thing (which I'm not, because I believe strong women like Neta and me should support each other), it would be so easy to hate her. Plus, Neta is more than just a bombshell. She was just awarded a huge scholarship for being a Future Business-woman of America, and my bets are on her to become the next CEO of a huge company. Or to build one.

Liam gives Neta an awkward thumbs-up. "It's great, Neta. Thanks for asking. Listen, if you ever need help with your papers, I'm here. And that goes for you two as well, okay?" He points at Kolbie and me, and then strokes his beard, twisting his fingers into the end. "Well, later."

Kolbie grabs Neta's notebook and doodles *LIAM + NETA = FOREVER* on the cover in bright purple pen.

"Seriously? Are we in third grade?" Neta snips, but her mouth sort of quirks up, like she's trying not to laugh.

"My penmanship is on point." Kolbie doodles a little heart after "forever."

"Pretty sure he's just into me because you wouldn't give him the time of day," Neta says, reaching into her purse and pulling out her own pen. "Besides, Liam is sweet in a plaid sort of way. A girl could work with that." She yanks her notebook away from Kolbie.

I stand up and peer over her shoulder. "Then why are you scrawling over your statement of your eternal and lasting love?"

Neta swirls around to face us both, and displays the notebook. She's scribbled out the heart and replaced it with *BFF*. "You know what I say. I like to take it slow. Give love a real chance to develop between two mature people."

"Not me," Kolbie declares. "When I met Jamal, I basically knew in, like, two seconds. We moved fast. Not like snail over here." She pushes on Neta's chair with her foot, spinning her in a circle.

"Hey!" Neta protests. "At least I'm not Little Miss Riley Stone, who makes Queen Elizabeth look easy."

"Don't drag me into this." I put a hand over my chest. "Besides, everyone knows Queen Elizabeth was a total badass. Don't hate. Besides, I'm like Neta. I would take it slow if I met someone anyway."

Kolbie bites on the tip of her pen and raises an eyebrow a little evilly. "Just saying. You don't like to take it at all is what I heard."

"I'm choosy!" I protest, but we're all laughing so hard, Liam knocks on the door.

"Can you girls keep it down a little? Or maybe turn on some music so the others aren't disturbed?" He smiles apologetically.

"Sorry, Liam." Neta pouts. "Don't let this come between us!" she calls after him as the door shuts.

Kolbie pulls a Bluetooth speaker out of her backpack and sets it on the desk. She puts on The Features and then kicks her red sneakers up on the table.

"Where'd you get that?" I ask, picking up the speaker and turning it over. It's definitely an upgrade from using an iPhone. I've seen it before. It's the newest model of a speaker that was just put out by a rapper turned mogul, and it's definitely out of my price range. "Damn, Kolbie. This is a nice one."

"Mom let me use a little money from the Zappos campaign." Kolbie makes a face. "She made me put the rest in a college fund."

She says "college fund" like everyone else says "poison" or

worse, "acid-wash jeans." Like she would never possibly have any use for a college fund.

Kolbie is also a supermodel. Well, almost. She's six one and was discovered at a coffee shop when she went to New York for the weekend with her mom. This man in what Kolbie calls ultra-skinny jeans and a long yellow scarf slipped her mother his business card, and the next thing you know she had an agent and was being jet-setted to photo shoots for magazines and stuff. And of course she's gorgeous, in this way that only magazine and runway models are that's a little bit seraphic. Her hair is always this huge explosion of curls and she has these perfect teeth that it looks like she had made and her outfits are always on point. It's all very effortless, like she just rolled into some clothes and they stuck on her and turned into art.

Needless to say, Kolbie is very glam and high fashion, and if she wasn't already a high school It Girl, a modeling contract would have made her one.

Anyway, as soon as she graduates from high school, her serious boyfriend, Jamal, is transferring to NYU, and she's moving straight to Manhattan to pursue her modeling career. She's already making some serious dough. She promised her mom to do college on the side, but honestly, I don't think she's serious about it. And who would be if they had a major modeling contract? Besides, she can go to college at any age . . . but how often can you go to Paris and be in the "Teens Who Rock" issue of *Claire*? Kolbie told us last week she gets a full-page spread and they're paying her five thousand dollars. When Neta and I found out, we planned Kolbie a full spa day to celebrate (totally on us, of course), and I bought her a two-year subscription to the magazine.

"So, Neta," Kolbie says, "now that RJ is out of the picture, who's up to bat?" She picks at a little thread on the edge of her jeans. She likes her jeans perfectly frayed and is always tattering hers with pairs of scissors or trying to get the holes shredded just well enough that only a tiny bit of skin shows through.

Neta sighs heavily. "RJ."

"What's so great about RJ?" I cut in. "Didn't he basically cheat on you with Lorna Chatsworth over the summer?"

"They almost kissed."

"Because you interrupted them," Kolbie points out. "And who knows how many other almost-things they did or didn't do? Or actually did? There were totally rumors about RJ and Simone. And RJ and Gabriella, too. Don't forget those."

Neta pulls her business book out of her backpack. "Please. It's not like I'm going to take him back. I just like seeing him grovel. And I'm just saying I'm not quite over him."

"Neta—"

I reach forward to touch her shoulder, but she pushes my hand off with a small smile. "We were together since middle school, you know? It's hard to get over someone like that. You just hope that . . . that you mean more to someone than that."

Kolbie chews on the end of her pencil thoughtfully. "I get that. But in the meantime, distract yourself with something. Or some-one, if at all possible. Let's see." She stands and walks to the window of the door, peering out at the library. "Who's the hottest guy in the school? Let's start there."

Neta doesn't hesitate. "R—"

Kolbie cuts Neta off with a look. "Don't even think about him."

She sits back in her chair and sulks. "I was going to say, 'Are you serious?' Can't I just concentrate on ROIs for once?" She flashes us her business homework, which I happen to know she's already aced.

"Really selling that, Neta." I pat her on the shoulder and join Kolbie at the window. "There's Donovan. The quarterback. I know it's cliché, but it's very all-American high school." He's sitting near the magazine section, but he's paging through a thickish book. He's a pretty smart dude. He did an extra-credit speech last year on James Joyce that earned him serious academic cred in my book, especially considering the rest of the football team did their speeches on stuff like MMA fighting and cafeteria food.

"Boring." Kolbie nudges me. "Ooh, what about November?"

I follow her gaze. November is a hipster type whose real name is Francis Hastings Lee, but ever since he took up the guitar he insists on being called specifically *November* and nothing else.

Which, I will admit, I thought was the most diva-ish thing I'd ever heard until I listened to him play his guitar. He's actually incredible. There are rumors that three separate record labels are courting him, but I don't know if that's true. Still, he has a track or two up on iTunes, and his YouTube channel has more than two hundred thousand hits. That's saying something.

"I don't feel like competing with groupies," Neta says. "Besides, you guys can stop looking out that window. If we're going purely by looks, it's really obvious, isn't it?"

Kolbie sighs heavily and turns toward Neta, resting her back against the door. "Yes," she says. "No contest."

"Uh, no." I look at Neta and Kolbie. "Who? Am I missing something? I think we've covered all the standouts."

"Mr. Belrose," they say together, as if it's the most obvious answer in the world.

Ah.

Mr. Belrose.

Our French teacher.

Our extremely attractive, jawline of a Greek god French teacher.

Key word "teacher."

He actually looks like he stepped off of a television show and just magically appeared in our classroom in a stylish button-up. I don't get it. There's no denying he's absolutely the most gorgeous man in a hundred-mile radius.

"I didn't know faculty was eligible."

"Oh," Neta says, giggling, "he's eligible, all right." Her cheeks get a touch rosy. "I mean, seriously, is there anyone that even compares?" She fans herself with her ROIs assignment.

"Nope," Kolbie says.

"Not even close," Neta says. "There's a reason why our school has the highest French scores in the state. And it's probably because every straight girl in the school—and some of the guys—sign up for his classes."

"And maybe because he's a really good teacher." I put my hands on my hips. "Besides, shouldn't there be some sort of age limit in place?"

Kolbie puts up a finger. "You are the biggest prude I have ever heard of, Riley. He's at *most* twenty-eight. Like, tops. We fangirl over celebs who are, like, eighty-six."

"That's pushing it."

She gives me a withering look. "You know what I mean."

She's not wrong. He is super young for a teacher. I'm pretty sure he only graduated from college four years ago. Or maybe less than that—not that long ago he was student teaching for the old French teacher, Mr. Andersen-Kraus.

"He's twenty-six," Neta says. "Same as your brother, Ri. They were in the same class."

She's not wrong.

"Regardless of age, he's mad altruistic," Kolbie points out. "Didn't he raise, like, ten thousand dollars for the cancer run last year?"

"And he volunteers at the hospital in his spare time, reading to children and, like, bandaging their little heads and stuff," Neta adds. "He's literally the perfect man."

I shake my head. "If only he wasn't married, right? You forget he's wifed up." I wiggle my ring finger.

Neta shakes her head, hair bouncing. "Come on, Riley. Loosen up. It's not like we're seriously considering a *teacher*. We're just fantasizing."

Kolbie thumps back in her chair and throws her feet up on the desk. "Seriously. You can't even admit he's fine, can you?"

"He's, um, a very nice-looking man."

"A very nice-looking man," Neta says in a high, squeaky voice, and they both crack up.

"For real? Are you trying to imitate me or Kermit the Frog?" I pretend to throw my chem book at her, and suddenly I'm laughing again too.

The door swings open while I'm fake-clobbering Neta and Liam stops, his eyes wide. "Um, excuse me," he says. "You know I think you girls are cool, but please, quiet down. And Riley, please don't assault anyone."

I clutch my book to my chest and suck my cheeks in to keep from smiling. "They should really put that in the library rules if they want it to be top of mind, Liam."

He nods. "I'll think about having signs put up," he says, completely dry.

We wait until he's closed the door to collapse in laughter again.

"This year," Neta announces, wiping away tears, "is the year of Hook Riley Up." She stands and holds up a bright pink pen and touches me on the nose with it, like she's knighting me or something. "You will get a boyfriend, or I will die trying. Or so help me God. Or whatever."

I back away. "Oh, no, no, no. I'm all set."

Kolbie clutches her hair. "That is so *boring*, Riley. Check yourself, girl. You're, like, incredibly smart, super funny, and mega hot." She checks off my dating qualifications on her fingers. "Like, one hundred and twelve percent of the guys in the school would date you. Not to mention Jamal's college friends. And you could use a college guy. They're way more mature."

I straighten my blazer. "I have priorities that are more important than men. Like *actual* college, not just the men who attend the institution."

"Haven't you already gotten in to, like, eight schools?" Kolbie says. "Plus, not sure if you noticed, but men are *fun*. And if you get a good one instead of a douche-wrangler like RJ—"

"Hey!" Neta scowls.

"You know I'm right. Anyway, it's the best thing ever. Jamal is a good dude, and he makes me happier every day, you know?"

Something in my chest twists a little bit, and I think about Ethan and Esther, and how weird and messed up and perfect they are together.

And for all of Ethan's mistakes, how much more my parents seem to like him than me. It's like whenever the two of us are around, both of them just gravitate to him. Like he is easier to be around, in spite of the fact I did everything right and Ethan . . . well.

Ethan is Ethan.

"Come on, Riley!" Neta urges. She puts her arm around me. "It'll be fun! We can double-date or something!"

I put my hand on Neta's shoulder. "Look. I appreciate you guys. I do. But as soon as I graduate, I'm out of here. A man will only slow me down. And since when do I need a man? I'm a strong, powerful woman. I don't need anyone!" I make a muscle like Rosie the Riveter.

Kolbie sighs and puts her chin on her fist. "I didn't ever say you needed a man, Riles. I just said you needed some fun."

"I'm way fun," I insist. "Buckets of it."

"Oh yeah?" Neta counters. "When's the last time you broke a rule?"

"Stick with me. I'm totally going to chew gum in class later." I wink.

Neta throws up her hands, reminding me of my mother when she's annoyed. "You're hopeless, Ri. But I'm not giving up on you. You'll go on at least one date this year."

For about two seconds, I play with the normal teenage girl hope that rises up in my chest. Maybe dating someone wouldn't be so bad.

Then I pinch it out like a candle.

I am more than all of that.

THREE
Lessons

"Bonjour, la classe," Mr. Belrose says from the front of the classroom. He is holding a stack of papers loosely in one arm, and smiles at his students as they file in.

There's something about his voice.

Something different from everyone else.

Something about *him*.

The something gives me shivers just under my skin.

I give my head a little shake.

Thea Arnold, a senior with a penchant for wearing entirely too much jewelry, pauses at the front of the classroom. *"Bonjour, Monsieur Belrose,"* she drawls, her words drawn out and slow and deliberately flirty. Her friends giggle beside her and all choose seats in the front row, nearest to his desk, where they cross and uncross their legs and make pouty faces and apply shiny lip gloss.

"*Bonjour*, Thea." He nods at her and she slides into her customary seat right in front of his desk.

Mr. Belrose is cool like that. He lets everyone choose their seats every day. He isn't like one of those teachers who has assigned seating. Of course, most of the girls choose seats in the front row. Except me. I think it's a little desperate. I do get it. They all know that they're never going to actually be with a beautiful married teacher, so they're just in it for the best view possible, but even so—I'm perfectly happy with the third row. Close enough that I can still see what's going on, but not so far back that I look like a total slacker.

As soon as most of the class is seated, Mr. Belrose begins handing out papers.

"What is this?" Thea asks immediately, her voice slightly accusatory. She might like Mr. Belrose, but she's not the most academic girl around. I've heard rumors, though, that her grades are strictly on account of laziness and she's been tested and is secretly a Mensa-level genius, which is how she made it into honors senior French.

"*En français,*" Mr. Belrose says. His voice is—interesting. He's demanding it, and we all know it, but it's sort of . . . well, soft. And inviting. And . . .

I am not into Mr. Belrose. I am not. I am into studies. And responsibility. And maybe a couple of celebs. Not teachers. Not educators. Not men who wear smart button-ups and have rich, clever voices and—

"Qu'est-ce que c'est?" Thea says, very slowly.

Mr. Belrose grins. *"Une interrogation surprise!"*

I perk up. I *own* at surprise quizzes. In fact, I've aced every single pop quiz that Belrose has ever thrown my way.

Garrett, a star baseball player behind me, pretends to choke.

His buddy Cay hits him in the arm. "Dude! Come on! *En français!*"

The whole class bursts out laughing. *"Un crédit supplementaire pour Monsieur Burke!"* Mr. Belrose grins and makes a flourish at Cay Burke.

That's just another reason why everyone loves Mr. Belrose. He's got a great sense of humor. Every other teacher probably would have been annoyed at Cay's joke, but Mr. Belrose actually gave him extra credit. Sure, it'll probably be only one point, but how cool is that?

A piece of paper lands on my desk and I glance over it. It looks pretty easy . . . just a review of verbs. Old ones too. Sometimes Belrose does this. He throws weeks-old stuff at us, just so we remember it. He doesn't want us to recall the language long enough for a test and then clear it out as soon as new material comes along. He wants us to retain French. He wants us to learn it as he has learned it, so we can stroll along the streets of Paris and order *macarons* and ride bicycles around with baguettes perched jauntily on our shoulders. Typical French activities.

I fill in the verbs quickly as Belrose walks up and down the aisles of desks and tsks at some papers and whispers, *"Très bien!"* over people's shoulders. He's rather distracting, all in all, during test taking. I finish with mine first and walk my paper up to his desk. He catches my eye as he leans over Teri Von Millhouse's desk and winks at me.

Pursing my lips, I turn my back to him and saunter back to my seat, keeping my shoulders square and tall. My eyes stray to the photos of the Seine he has on the walls; copies of the paintings hung in the Louvre; lovely aerial photos of the French Riviera, and one tiny, cliché photo of the Eiffel Tower, which is a requirement in any respectable French classroom. I do not look back at Mr. Belrose.

I do not care about my French teacher.

I don't. Not like *that*. It takes more than a pretty face and an infallible French accent to sway me. It does not matter that he winks at me and pays more attention to me than to other students.

I do, of course, care about my grade. And I care about *Les Mis*. Speaking of which.

I sit back down at my desk and pull my copy of *Les Misérables* out of my backpack. I try to read, but my eyes stray back to Mr. Belrose as he returns to his desk to grade the quizzes. He doesn't get to mine right away, because it was the first one turned in, and therefore on the bottom of the pile, so he makes a lot of strikes with his red pen before he reaches my paper, where he makes one mark: an A.

It's not like I can see it from here. But I recognize the three sharp strokes, like the Eiffel Tower.

I smile tightly to myself and bite on the cap of my pen.

A few minutes later, Mr. Belrose rises from his desk and passes copies of the tests back to the class.

"*Classe*, I'm going to switch to English for a few minutes while we review the quiz together, and you're going to tell me the verbs in French. Let's start with, ah, Thea."

Thea glows.

"'To make.'"

"Faire," Thea recites. Her accent is far from on point, but she does tend to have her French down.

I wonder why.

"Correct." Mr. Belrose rewards her with a smile, and she lights up like fireworks. He moves to the second word. "Uh, let's go with . . . Riley. Riley, how do you say 'to kiss'?"

Suddenly, I feel redness in my cheeks. Of course the word "kiss" is incredibly close to the word "embarrass," which he is currently doing. To me. *"Embrasser."*

"No one's surprised that Riley's correct!" He smiles even bigger at me than he did at Thea and then moves on to someone else, and my cheeks heat up even brighter. I duck my head, letting my hair fall in front of my face, praying that no one is looking at me.

I do not care about Mr. Belrose. I do not.

"You okay under there, Stone?" Garrett asks, poking me in the soft space just below my shoulder with the eraser end of his pencil.

I ignore him. I ignore everyone, even after the crimson in my cheeks has gone away and the bell rings and I've ignored about fourteen questions I definitely could have answered better than anyone else in the class. I shove my books into my backpack quickly and start toward the door, using my blond hair as a nice, effective curtain in front of my face.

"Mademoiselle Stone? *S'il vous plaît, attendez.*"

He wants me to wait. Mr. Belrose wants me to wait.

I think about the monks in Asia or somewhere who can control their bodies to a point where they can slow down their pulse simply by concentrating. I wish for that power now.

I turn slowly toward Mr. Belrose. *"Oui?"*

His faces softens from the normal teacher expression he wears—all the stern planes and angles smoothed out into something almost friendly. "I've been meaning to talk to you about something. Do you have a moment?"

I shift my backpack. I didn't position my books right, and the corner of my French book digs into the back of my right hip. "Yes?" My heart is beating unevenly with him so close. I am attracted to him.

I think of his hands on me.

My God. I need to get it together.

His eyes shift behind me. "Uh, actually, you know, I'll just catch up with you next class, okay? Great job on the quiz, though, Riley. You've retained a lot of information this year."

I squint at him, but he's still looking behind me. I turn—and see one of the new basketball players, a transfer from across town, waiting behind me to talk to Mr. Belrose.

Huh.

Whatever Belrose was going to say to me . . . he didn't want to say it in front of someone else.

Something in my stomach does an odd little jump, but I tamp it down.

Whatever he was going to say . . . it doesn't matter.

Not one bit.

I square my shoulders and walk out of the classroom.

I wouldn't flirt with him. And he couldn't flirt with me. I'm not like Thea. It's different with Mr. Belrose and me. We have . . . a history.

He is, after all, the same age as my brother.

I walk down the hallway to my locker, where I spin the combination without thinking and change out my books, which are all lined up neatly and have color-coded book covers for each class.

Mr. Belrose has helped me before.

He hasn't always been a teacher.

There was a time when he was just my brother's friend and I knew him as Alex and he was just the cute youth counselor helping out at the church, where we raised money each year to donate to domestic violence shelters. There was a time when I didn't think too much about talking to him, when his hair wasn't brushed so carefully and he didn't wear neatly buttoned shirts and khakis and he cursed a lot more. It was before he'd studied abroad in France his senior year of college and met Jacqueline and gotten married to someone who looked like she'd been painted by an impressionist.

I remember one time in particular.

With Alex. Not Mr. Belrose. Not then, at least.

I was volunteering. Because volunteering is part of me. It's more than just a résumé; if I really listed all my charity work on my CV, I'd have to cut down a good portion of a forest just for the paper.

That day, I was collecting clothes for domestic violence victims. My mother and I had gone through her overcrowded closet the night before, and I'd had fun trying on her high heels while she sorted through her old shirts and made startled noises about how she used to dress.

"Are you sure the women will even want these?" she had asked me, holding up a sweater with a tiny robin sewn onto the pocket. She wrinkled her nose. "We don't want to *insult* them."

And I wobbled over on a pair of her highest stilettos that she refused to donate but also swore were too uncomfortable to wear and added the robin sweater to her Donate pile. "It's fine."

It had taken hours, but I'd ended up struggling with a giant black trash bag of clothing. Mr. Belrose (Alex at the time) had seen me come through the door with it, my legs nearly buckling under the weight of it all. He tried to take the bag from me, but I held my hand out. "I got it." I walked unsteadily back to the booth we were both assigned to and heaved the bag behind the table.

He grinned at me the whole way, and I wasn't sure if he thought I was being silly by refusing the help or if he was sort of impressed, but I chose to believe the latter, and that I was one of those plucky sort of independent girls who people admired. It wasn't until I turned around and wiped my sweaty hair out of my eyes (I had some truly ill-advised bangs at that stage of my life) that his smile hit a false note.

"Looking a little rough there, Riley."

His eyes held mine—my left one, specifically, which was a messy watercolor of purple and black.

I let myself smile as much as my face allowed. The pain wasn't terrible, but it was always there, a constant reminder. The previous night, during a basketball game, I'd gotten elbowed by a girl who looked more like a female Thor than an eighth grader.

So I hadn't made the layup.

And only one of the two free throws, because I couldn't see through my eye for the second one.

(Shortly after, I'd decided cheerleading full time was more my speed.)

"Bad night," I muttered, pulling open the trash bag. "How are we sorting these, anyway?"

"Uh, shoes, pants, shirts. And then by size. What sizes do you have here?"

I pulled out a pink turtleneck. "This is a medium. I think my mom was, like, a six back then, though."

"Okay." Alex bent down to grab an armful of clothes from the garbage bag and began going through them, tossing them into piles without folding them.

A woman with an oversize banana clip clamped into her hair came to the table with a musty box. "I got clothes," she said. "Can I drop these here?"

"You're at the right place." I tried to smile at her, but she just sort of chewed her gum in my direction.

"Can you give me a receipt for my taxes?"

I stared at her. "Uh—"

"If you can't, I'll just take 'em back home." She put her arms around the box. "There's lots of good stuff in here."

Alex popped up beside me, one of my mother's paisley sweaters still draped over his arm. "I can take care of that." He tossed the sweater at me. "Riley, you're on sort duty." He grinned at me and pulled a pad of paper out of his back pocket.

I turned to my mom's garbage bag, and a minute later, Alex was back with the musty box. He opened it, and a puff of dust came off the top. "So," he said very quietly, so that no one at the booths on either side of us would hear, "can I ask you something really serious?"

I looked up at him and nodded, and for some reason, my pulse was going crazy. I could hear thudding in my ears, like pulling up beside a car with the bass turned up too high.

"Sure." My voice was barely above a whisper.

He reached down and grabbed an airy lavender silk scarf. He wrapped it around his neck and put his hand on my shoulder. "Is this—is this my color?" His lip quivered with a held-back smirk.

I cracked up. Pain shot through my face, but I couldn't help it. "Nope," I said, yanking the scarf away. It left his neck with a sharp *snick* sound as the fabric slid across his skin.

"What's going on here?" A familiar voice cut through my laughter, and we both turned.

Ethan.

Ethan, looking . . . all too familiar. His untidy hair was sticking up on one side like he had fallen asleep against something, and from the smell emanating off him . . . he had been drinking. Again.

A lot.

"You're early." My voice was frosty but calm. Very calm. "You weren't supposed to pick me up for another hour."

"Hey, man." Alex and Ethan did the sort of half-hug-and-hit thing that guys do. Only Ethan's half was wobbly. "You okay?"

Ethan shook his head like he was trying to clear it. "Uh, yeah. You got a chair or something?"

Alex and I exchanged a quick look. We couldn't really have a drunk dude hanging out at a domestic violence table. "Uh, yeah. Listen, how about you lie down back here for a minute?" Alex grabbed my brother's arm and guided him back, behind the largest piles of clothes, and put a couple of hoodies on the floor. Ethan stretched out on top of them and balled up a flowery blouse as a pillow.

"Think he'll pass out?" Alex whispered as he climbed from behind the piles of clothes.

I nodded. "He probably already has. Unless he snores, we're golden."

An older man with a cane approached the table, and Alex helped him while I snuck a look at my brother. His eyes were already closed, and his mouth had the slightly open look of sleep.

I grabbed a body spray from my purse and misted it in his direction, hoping no one close could smell the alcohol on him. I didn't want anyone to see my brother like that. Think of him like that.

He was better. He deserved better. Something was just going on with him lately, and I didn't understand. No one did. He came home late and he slept in late and he didn't talk to me anymore. But this wasn't him.

Still, he was definitely not going to be sober in an hour. Or anytime tonight. I was going to have to find another way home. And it wasn't just like I could call my parents. They were already pissed at Ethan. I didn't want to make it worse.

I sank down in a chair and slumped over, sighing. A few minutes later, Alex joined me, sitting cross-legged on the floor, below me. He looked up through his unkempt hair. "You okay?"

"Yep." The response was automatic and came out before I could think about how much of a complete lie it was. Maybe always was. It's one of those questions you're never really supposed to answer. Maybe it didn't count as a lie if you weren't ever supposed to tell the truth.

"Your eye—" He started to reach up, but then pulled his hand away, as if thinking better of it.

I nodded. "I know. It doesn't look good." I hesitated. "Things aren't . . . great."

I was misleading him and I knew it. He thought I was talking about my eye and I wasn't. I was talking about everything. Everything else. "I mean, this is fine," I amended, pointing at my eye. "Someone got a little aggressive with me during yesterday's game."

Alex just looked at me, the question in his face. But he was patient. He didn't push or prod, but he was still asking. I saw him asking.

"Things aren't always good at home." I looked back toward Ethan to make sure he wasn't stirring. "Ethan is always coming home blitzed. And my parents, they're angry, but he's just trying to make things easier. It's not like my dad doesn't drink too."

Alex's eyebrows shot up. "Your dad?"

I gave a tiny nod. "It gets a little scary. Sometimes I worry . . . he's not going to wake up. And my mom . . . she's just empty. She's hollow, like she's this perfect person on the outside and on the inside she's, I don't know, not even a person anymore. None of us really are. We're like these plastic people and we look so perfect as long as you don't see where we've been molded together so carefully." I stopped suddenly, aware of how bitter I sounded. I glanced at the booth to the right, where there were three women working, to make sure they weren't paying attention. "You won't tell anyone, will you?"

I was laying it on a little thick, but I relished his attention.

He reached up and linked his pinkie with mine, like we were girls together at a sleepover, sharing secrets. "No."

I gave him a smile with the side of my face that didn't hurt. "Thanks."

We were quiet for a while, and no one paid attention to us, set up in a booth in the big gymnasium, his hand linked with mine.

"I know it sounds stupid and everyone always says it," he said finally, "but it's going to be okay."

And even though it did sound a little stupid, it was exactly what I needed to hear. I let myself believe him.

So I let Alex hold my hand, and at the end of the night, he helped Ethan to his car. On the way home, with Ethan stretched out across his backseat, he took my hand again and squeezed it, and even though he didn't say it, I could feel it when he touched me.

Everything was going to be all right.

FOUR
Shame

"Rob!"

Rob Samuels, a senior football player I've gone to school with since preschool, stands at the end of the hallway, talking with Mr. Peters, the chemistry teacher and offensive coordinator.

Rob and I used to be really close. We used to play together at recess almost every day, and we'd usually stake our claim on the tornado slide on the east side of the playground, farthest away from any teachers on duty. When I fell down the ladder one day, Rob helped me inside and bandaged my knee for me without letting any of the other kids see I was crying. And when we got to be captains during PE, Rob would always choose me first for his football team, no matter what. But when Rob got really good, and

I started hanging out with Neta and Kolbie, that kind of changed. I kind of changed.

I don't follow the football team that closely anymore. I guess I sort of lost touch. I show up and cheer, sure, and I know who wins and loses, but my mind is elsewhere. I can reel off the players mechanically, and even the plays, if needed, but that's just it . . . it's automatic. I don't let myself love it.

Rob doesn't hear me.

"Hey, Rob!" I call again. I bounce on my toes and wave my hand, and half the hall turns hopefully. Mr. Peters hears me and says something inaudible to Rob, who turns.

His face splits into a wide grin.

Rob is glad to see me.

Always is.

Always has been.

That's how I knew I could count on him.

He waits on me at the end of the hallway, his backpack hanging on one shoulder, the goofy smile on his face. "Hey, Riley."

"Hi, Rob. Hi, Mr. Peters."

Mr. Peters nods and gives Rob a little punch on the shoulder, like, *Go get 'em, champ*, which I have no doubt has to do with me, before vanishing back into his classroom. The action makes me feel a little sick.

"What's up, Riley?" Rob asks. "What can I do for you?"

I cast a look back over my shoulder, at Belrose's classroom.

What can Rob do for me?

Because even Rob, smart, sandy-haired Rob, who a million girls like, who already has two football scholarship offers to good schools, respected schools, is a little suspicious of why I'd be talking to him.

Riley Stone doesn't date.

Everyone knows that.

So there has to be another reason why I'd be talking to him.

And there is.

It's because of . . . that night.

With Alex.

With Belrose.

What happened that night was most definitely not Riley Stone.

Not even a young Riley Stone.

It was stupid.

It was vulnerable.

And it's because of that moment in the classroom last week.

Nothing like that can ever happen again. After all, I have a future to think about. And if that means I have to put up some sort of obstacle between the two of us, even if it's just for my own sake, then that's what I'll do.

I link my arm through Rob's and draw him close to my side. "Well, we used to be friends, didn't we, Rob?"

"Sure," he says, slowly, as if waiting for the punch line, but there's something else in his voice. Eagerness.

"I was just thinking about you. That's all." I make my voice a little shy. A touch quiet. I was just thinking about him. I'm not promising anything. But if I can walk past Belrose's classroom with him attached to me, then maybe it will convince me that I am not actually interested. And that he is not . . .

Anyway.

It'll be enough for both of us. It will need to be.

"Yeah?" Rob asks, a little more air in his voice than usual, and his arm tightens around my own. "Yeah?"

He does that a lot. Or at least he used to. Repeat himself.

"Yeah." I let myself agree. "What class do you have?"

"World history. What do you have?" He looks down at me, his eyes filled with wonder, like he absolutely can't believe his luck, and all around us, I can feel people looking. For a moment, I feel like a starlet, and not in a good way—in a way that I feel like people are invading, ready to snap photos, ready to whisper, ready to take stock of my life and lay it all out for entertainment, and I'm exploiting it, mapping out the story and the characters and setting for my own gain.

"Walk me to the library. I have study hall," I direct. "Let's catch up."

"Of course," he says, and he's still looking at me as this great mystery, but there's happiness behind it. He turns up the stairs.

"Wait," I say. "Where are you going?"

"Library."

Oh. He wants to take the shortcut, straight to the study pod where Kolbie, Neta, and I always meet, which is on the second floor of the library. But I need to walk past the French classroom.

"Do you mind if I go to my locker first?" I say, blinking a couple of extra times. I think it's true what they say about eyelashes. They're endearing. All Neta has to do is bat her long black eyelashes and guys are practically dog-piling at her feet.

But that goes for anything Neta does. And has since basically fifth grade.

Rob walks with me to my locker, his chest puffed out and his shoulders squared. "Are you having a good day?" he asks me, and I realize, while I'm adding extra pencils that I don't actually need to my backpack, that he's waiting for my answer, his eyes wide.

He actually wants to know.

"Um, yes." It's automatic, like always. "Just the usual, you know? What about you?"

"Amazing." He looks at me, his gray eyes solemn, and I know he means it. "Just really great."

I smile at him, and my heart drops the tiniest bit in my chest. But I link arms with him again anyway, and he walks me toward the library, like he's supposed to be the man on my arm, and I feel the hallway buzzing around us, as if every single person is more interested in what's happening in my life than I am.

Except for the ten seconds when I walk past the French classroom. And in my peripheral vision, I see Mr. Belrose, in a cornflower-blue button-up, leaning against his door frame, talking to Lydia Andrews, one foot kicked up in front of the other.

And I think maybe, just for a second, he pauses when he sees me floating by with Rob. But I don't turn my head. After all, Mr. Belrose doesn't matter.

And maybe it's just my imagination, but I am almost certain I feel his eyes on my back as I walk away.

But I *don't* care. Not really.

"I have a football meeting tonight," Rob says apologetically as we reach the wide glass doors of the library. "Otherwise I'd ask you to hang out."

"That's okay, Rob. I'll just see you tomorrow at school." I give him a careful, practiced smile, and he returns it in full force.

"This was nice."

I nod. "I appreciate it." I am being honest. I do.

Rob pauses, working over something in his mind. I know the look. He's about to ask me something. Something I don't really want. "Listen—"

The bell rings, cutting him short.

I pretend to panic, checking my cell phone for the time. "I gotta go. I'll catch you later, okay, Rob?"

I touch his arm softly and disappear into the library, and when I finally look back, he's still there, watching me from the glass doors, not caring that he's late. It doesn't matter if I'm late to study hall, but I happen to know that football players who are late to class usually have to run extra in their conditioning practices.

But he's still there, watching me, his mouth a little slack.

I give him a wave, and walk up the stairs toward the study pod, where Kolbie and Neta are waiting.

"What the hell, Ri?" Kolbie says immediately, showing me her cell phone. "Are you hooking up with Rob on the down low?"

There, on the screen, is a picture of me, my arm linked through Rob's. I'm looking straight ahead, my gaze carefully fixed in front of me, and Rob is looking down at me, like he can't quite believe I'm there.

"It's nothing." I settle into my chair and pull out my French book, like I'm actually going to use the time to conjugate verbs or something. "Honestly, it's just old friends, walking to class together. And who sent you that?"

"I got two," Neta says. "This high school is disgusting. And you'd better be careful, Ri. That boy has got it bad for you. If you talk to him one more time, he might fall in love."

A short "ha" bursts out of Kolbie's throat. "Are you kidding me? Rob Samuels has been in love with Riley since preschool, when they built that Popsicle stick castle for art and Riley let him kiss her."

"Whoa, Riley. First kiss in preschool? Who would have thought?"

"It wasn't even her first," Kolbie says. "Riley kissed *everyone* in preschool. I mean *everyone*."

I start to laugh. "It was a serious problem. My dad had read me that story about that princess who kissed a frog and it turned into a prince, and I don't know, I got obsessed with kissing or something, and the next thing you know, both my parents were called in for a sit-down with the guidance counselor." I giggle. "It was an issue."

"Perfect Riley Stone, make-out maniac," Neta singsongs. "All I know is you better get a handle on this Rob situation. If it goes any further, he'll be hitting up your phone by the end of the week." Her phone vibrates on the desk, and she picks it up. "Oh look, another one!"

It's a picture of Rob and me, walking down the hall, with Belrose in the background.

He's looking away, obviously preoccupied with something else, failing to notice me walking down the hallway with someone on my arm.

Which is fine, of course.

"I'll handle it," I tell them.

And so that day, after school, I wait until the girls who have stupid questions about their French homework clear out of Mr. Belrose's classroom, and then I walk in. I stand in front of his desk for a moment, where he's sitting, a pair of black-framed reading glasses perched on his nose. They're very hipster and the frames are a little scraped, and I wonder if he needs them at all or if they're just for looks.

"Hello, Mr. Belrose."

He looks up, as if he's just noticing me, when I know for a fact the heels of my boots clicked very satisfyingly on the tiles when I walked in. "Oh, hey, Riley. Can I help you with something?" His forehead wrinkles, like he doesn't already know.

"I believe it was you who wanted to talk to me? Last class?" I keep my tone even. This is business. This is something that I need to have taken care of so I can stop thinking about it forever.

"Oh, right." He snaps his fingers, and pulls open his desk drawer. "I apologize, but I didn't want to do this in front of any other students. It might cause jealousy, you know. I'm sure you understand."

Mr. Belrose comes up a moment later with two crisp white pieces of paper, fastened neatly together with a tiny black binder clip. "You're the only student I'm giving this to, Riley. It's the Lou F. Durand Scholarship, and it's only for those who are interested in continuing their education in French in college. It's only for the most exceptional of students. Now, you don't have to major in it, but I believe you have to commit to taking at least two college courses, and this will pay for a semester of study abroad. Are you interested?"

My heart twists and beats and burns. This is everything and nothing I expected. A semester in France? More money for college? Of course. I would love a semester in France.

I force my face into a smile. *"Oui,"* I say. *"Merci."*

"Of course, Riley." He smiles back at me and takes off the glasses. "You'll get it. I knew as soon as I read it that this scholarship was for you. You'd make a perfect French teacher, you know."

"Would I?" I ask. I don't want to be a French teacher. I'm not sure what I want to do, honestly, but it's not that. I've made up a million different things and career paths in my college applications, but I'm not actually sure I mean any of them. Still, he paid me a genuine compliment. "Thank you."

Mr. Belrose extends his hand toward me, the papers clasped in it, and when I reach to take them, the skin of his hand brushes mine, just for a second.

It's not electric, like books say. It's not a shock. But it's warm, and nice, and there's—there's something there. A current, like there's already a bond. Something that I didn't feel when Rob intertwined his arm with mine.

"Have a good night, okay?" Belrose says, turning back to the papers on his desk.

Like he didn't feel anything at all. But he had to. A bond like that is felt between two people, not one. But he's playing professional.

"You too. Thanks, Mr. Belrose." I tuck the papers into a folder, slide it into my backpack, and I turn to walk away.

"You and Rob, huh?" he asks quietly, as I'm halfway to the door.

Bingo. I smile to myself. "Maybe."

And I realize maybe my little plan wasn't so fruitless after all.

That night, I dream of Rob. I dream of Rob and me and Popsicles, and we're talking and laughing and walking, and we're having fun, real fun, like I thought I never could have with him, and I'm thinking about how his eyelashes are sandy like his hair. But then when he leans in to kiss me it's not Rob anymore.

It's Alex.

Not Mr. Belrose.

But Alex, from the booth, who linked pinkies with me and held my hand in the car. Alex, who was nice and a little wild and fun. Alex, who was more a sleepy college student, half awake for class, than my teacher.

And he was nice to kiss.

Things to Know About Riley Stone:

- In second grade, Riley was the starting quarterback for the Pee-Wee football team. Her father was incredibly proud.
- Her mother made her quit in third grade and enrolled her in cheerleading and gymnastics.
- Riley won every spelling bee she ever entered. Every. Single. One.
- By age ten, Riley was so used to winning that she started making participation trophies for all the other students just so they wouldn't feel bad. She made special ones for her brother, because he never seemed to win at anything he entered.
- Riley always wanted to enter child beauty pageants, but her parents forbid it.
- They did, however, allow her to become a child model when she was discovered at an Applebee's while adorably covered in ice cream. She was even featured in a national ad at age four.

FIVE
Escape

"You're here."

Ethan steps back from his door, his brow furrowed.

"Yeah. Can I come in?" I peer inside his apartment, but it looks almost black inside, like maybe I'd woken him from a nap. The only light is a soft flickering, probably from the television. "I mean, is Esther here or something?"

He shakes his head. "No, she's at her parents' house. Come in if you want. Just . . . what are you doing here?" Ethan stands aside to let me in his apartment.

I walk past him. His modest TV is the source of the flickering, and the whole place smells like stale corn chips and Febreze. "I needed to get out of the house. It was suffocating me." I settle down onto the couch, next to a pile of laundry. I can't tell if it's clean or dirty.

"That's why I moved out so fast," Ethan says, grinning. "It's not like I'm not thankful for our upper-middle-class upbringing, but that house is sometimes the smallest place in the world."

He understands. My brother understands. I want to hug him. I nod instead.

"Do you want a beer or something?" he asks.

I shake my head. "Water is fine, if you have it."

Ethan disappears into the kitchen and comes back with a bottle full of grocery store brand water, which I accept gratefully. He flops back into his recliner. It looks about ten years old, which is saying something, considering I've never seen it before. And I've even been here once, when he first moved in after college.

"I would have straightened up if I knew you were coming," he says, twisting the top off his own beer. He pitches it in the direction of the kitchen, and I hear it clatter on the floor.

I laugh. "No, you wouldn't have."

He grins. "You're right. Still, I might have pushed the clothes onto the floor or something. Besides, it's not like you came over here in your Sunday best." He eyes my sweats and HARTSVILLE HIGH CHEER SQUAD T-shirt.

"Hey," I protest. "I came straight from cheerleading practice."

"And you smell like it."

I resist rolling my eyes. I know my ponytail is a sweaty mess that I've sort of pushed on my head and fastened with a hair tie, but he's my brother. It's written into the laws of family that unless it's Thanksgiving, and your great-granny Beatrice who you haven't seen in two years is visiting, you don't have to dress to impress anybody because they're genetically forced to love you. "Whatever."

"Do you want to watch something on TV?" Ethan offers, trying to be a halfway decent host. He makes to throw the remote at me, but I hold up my hand.

"Whatever is good." I don't really watch television. I don't have time for it, exactly, outside of a few juicy reality shows that you don't exactly have to keep up with to understand.

I am preoccupied with more important things.

My brother has a basketball game on, and we watch, together, in silence, for a few minutes in his strange-smelling apartment. He's just *happy*. Like fully got-it-together, all-the-time happy. It's not like his job pays him well, or that he's even figured out how the hell he's going to help raise another man's baby, but he loves Esther and Esther loves him back and he's pretty content with that.

He doesn't need anything else.

It's not like he hasn't screwed up a million times. He has. He's been in trouble with school, his grades, my parents, the police, but here he is, in his little apartment, with his secondhand (or maybe thirdhand) furniture . . . and he's completely got it together.

More than I do.

And if you're going by the book, I've got it together. Of course I do.

"Are you okay?"

"What?" I ask.

Ethan's not watching the basketball game. "You just . . . you look sort of . . . tense, Riley. Is there something going on?"

"I'm fine." I smooth down my already smooth hair.

"That," Ethan says, pausing to take a sip of his beer, "is a dead giveaway."

"Of what?" I demand, forcing my hand back into my lap. I am not fidgeting. I am calm.

"That something is not right."

"Everything is fine," I snap. "It's just, I don't understand how you can be so happy all the goddamned time with so much stressful shit going on in your life."

Ethan cocks his head at me. "What stressful shit?"

"A pregnant girlfriend? Not your baby? A job that doesn't pay enough? A record? I mean, does any of this ring a bell?"

Ethan shakes his head. "Riley. First of all, why does any of that actually matter? My job pays enough to cover my bills and a little extra. I'm saving for the baby. Second of all, my girlfriend makes me happy. And third, it's not like I was a real criminal. So honestly . . . what do I really have to be worried about, at the end of the day? What's in my life that actually, genuinely needs fixing?"

He says this all calmly, like I haven't just accidentally insulted his entire existence. He pauses for a moment, and the sound of the basketball game fills the room: the announcers, the cheering, and the buzzer for halftime and the traffic passing outside. The stop-lights shine faintly into the living room window: red, green, yellow, and red again. It's maddening and calming all at once, the way the lights hit the floor at the edge of the recliner.

Ethan leans forward. "Are you projecting, Riley?"

I lift a shoulder in a shrug, something I'd never dare do in a classroom.

Ethan continues, "Because I think you're worried you need fixing. And you don't know how to do it. And maybe you're not happy. And maybe that's because you're in high school, and high school's hard and it sucks and teenage angst and blah, blah, blah. Or maybe"—Ethan pauses, leans back in his chair, and takes a sip of beer—"you just need to practice not giving a shit for once in your entire life."

"Um, excuse me?" I say, very quietly. For some reason, I feel strange, and a little drowsy, and completely out of place. Maybe someone's going to pop out and shake me. No one talks to me like Ethan when we're alone. No one.

I wouldn't let them.

"There's this idea that you have to plan out your life perfectly before you go to college, and it's like this giant set of dominos: if you knock one over, you're totally screwed and they're all gone. But it's not, Riley. You need to relax every once in a while. And if you let something slide, so what? You've got a million other shiny gold stars on your résumé that'll back you up. They're not going anywhere."

I stare at my brother, in his sweats and holey T-shirt, sitting cross-legged on the old recliner. "Are you, like, moonlighting as an inspirational speaker? Or—"

"Shut your face." He throws a smelly pillow at me. "I'm trying to be your brother."

I grab his laundry and throw it back at him, mostly so I won't have to sit next to it anymore. And I ask about his new video game, which is the only luxury stuff he actually spends real money on, aside from things for Esther.

But inside, I think about what he's saying.

He basically wants me to pull a Sandy from *Grease.* But I can't just do the things that everyone else just wants to do. It gives me anxiety. I can't enjoy it the way other people can, and God, I wish I could. I wish I could just let go.

But my brother is saying it'll be the thing that'll make me happy.

But what if I did relax? Just the smallest bit.

"Anyway," he says, "how's everything else going? How's school?"

"It's kind of boring. Everyone's still there. Oh, an old friend of yours is teaching." I say this very casually, because it is, of course, a very casual conversation that I have no stake in.

"Really?" A commercial for detergent comes on, so Ethan switches to another channel. "Who?"

"Alex Belrose. He's teaching French."

"French?" Ethan snorts. "Really? I always thought he'd be more of the kindergarten type." He says it with condescension. Ethan clearly doesn't remember the Alex who threw him on old clothes because he was too drunk to function and then drove us home, and I'm not about to remind him. I don't want to chance him remembering—other things. Hand-holding things.

Past-things-that-need-to-stay-there things.

"Nope. I'm in his class."

Ethan chuckles. "I bet that's a goddamned mess."

"Um, what do you mean?" I keep my tone normal. I don't care. I shouldn't.

"He just doesn't seem like the academic type, that's all."

"Really? I mean, I'm in his honors senior French, you know. He doesn't *completely* suck. Of course, he's not exactly the best teacher out there." I feel a little bad saying that. Mr. Belrose is actually really good. He cares, I think, or maybe he's just not burned-out yet. He wants everyone to learn and grow and care about the language the same way he does. No one has done anything so horrible during class that it has irrevocably scarred him. Yet. And he's been tempted by about every girl in the school, and I don't actually think he's given in. He's a good guy.

Ethan laughs. "That's what I meant. In high school he was just a ladies' man. He had a new girl, like, every week. And in college he was always too stoned to worry about girls. I lost touch with him. I didn't know he graduated." Ethan stops on an MMA channel where two huge guys are pummeling each other. One has blood in his eyeball. "Whatever, I guess. He was just kind of a weird dude."

I want to ask more, but I stop myself. I cannot give my stake in this away. "Yeah." I take a sip of my water. The grocery brand is always a little oily and sits on my tongue even after I swallow, but it's better than tap.

"Side note," he says, "Esther's little sister says you're dating Rob Samuels. I think I should meet him."

I shake my head. "No," I say. "That, you're wrong about."

"Meeting him or dating him?"

I don't meet his eyes. "Both."

SIX
Bad

The bell rings, the sound dulled only slightly between the thick stacks of books in the library.

Not the first bell. The second one. And this isn't study hall, where Liam wouldn't dare mark me late, either. This is Shakespeare, where Mrs. Hamilton is well known for having a rather sizeable stick up her ass.

It won't matter, though. I'm never late. Ever. And I have to do this. I have to *try* it. To see if Ethan's right.

I steady myself against a bookshelf, both of my hands against a wooden shelf with the letter *S* emblazoned on them in Courier, my eyes straying over the titles, from the tops of the shelves to the books at the very bottom, where the most neglected books live simply by the disadvantage of being written by an author with an unlucky last name. I'm somewhere in fiction, and I've been strolling through the library, through the rows of computers in the labs, through the last of the paper periodicals, waiting for the students lolling about during their passing period to clear out.

Those students don't care if they're in trouble. They expect to be—they wait around on purpose, drawing out the time slowly, languidly. They know they're up to something and everyone else knows it too, and they're in the library to sop up as much time as possible away from class until they get in enough measurable trouble to have to return.

It's how they live: How much trouble is permissible? How much before it's too much and affects them in some meaningful way?

But they, the typical troublemakers, could never get away with what I'm about to do.

In the corner of the library, there is a nondescript wooden door that the faculty enter through and exit from throughout the day. If I simply stood near the door and peered inside, I wouldn't see much—mainly a white hall with two faculty bathrooms. Most of the students don't even know what it is. The teachers keep it quiet. It's better that way.

But I know what lies past the hallway.

I know a lot of things.

If one would walk through the wooden door and down the hall past the two faculty bathrooms, there would be yet another door, this one with a little brown placard that reads two simple, powerful words: TEACHERS' LOUNGE.

I adjust my backpack on my shoulders.

A library aide pushes a metal cart past me through the aisles, one wheel squeaking as she presses lonely books into gaps onto their shelves. She catches sight of me and smiles, hesitantly, as if she can sense I'm not a typical loiterer, and then pushes the cart on, the wheel complaining in evenly timed little bursts.

She wouldn't stop me.

I can do this. I can break rules too.

My heart thunders strangely and my palms feel cold. I don't do things like this.

But I will.

I start moving toward the small door, my steps measured, even. I don't pause for even a second—I push through it and disappear into the white hallway, where I immediately run into Mrs. Carter-Smithy, a freshman English teacher, a pile of student notebooks in her arms.

"Riley!" she says, smiling at me.

"Good afternoon," I say smoothly, no trace of a quiver in my voice. Normal Riley would offer to help her with her notebooks and make conversation about her classes this year, but today I am not normal Riley.

And Mrs. Carter-Smithy doesn't ask what I'm doing.

She doesn't even pause.

She leaves the hallway and walks back into the library, like there would be a perfectly good reason why Riley Elizabeth Stone is hanging out in the hallway outside the teachers' lounge, where students are definitely not allowed.

And there is.

I walk down the hallway, past the two faculty bathrooms and the faculty water fountain that looks like it has never been used (or at least, never had chewing gum stuck to the spout).

And then, I enter the teachers' lounge.

And it is *glorious.*

When the library was redone, apparently they spared no expense when they renovated the teachers' lounge. Art—good stuff, too, not just stuff that looks like it's been lifted from the walls of a Motel 6—decorates the walls in polished wooden frames. There are pudgy leather chairs squatting comfortably around a small fireplace, a couple of mod tables with cute little stools, and best of all, free food.

On a counter in the kitchenette area, a yellow bowl of fresh fruit sits next to an array of granola bars and packs of Skittles and M&M's. A refrigerator squats in the corner with a sign on it that says FREE DRINKS—LIMIT ONE PER DAY.

The teachers have it so much better than I *ever* thought.

They barely look at me as I walk in.

Mr. Wellingsby, the art teacher, is lounging in one of the chairs, legs up over an arm, staring bemusedly out the window, his fingers in a small bag of chips. Mr. Codsworth and Ms. Sidmore, both middle-age math teachers (unmarried, rumored to be dating), are deep in conversation at a table. And then there's Mrs. Garder, the geography teacher, who is arguing with someone on her cell phone.

They all sort of glance at me, but no one bothers to even say anything.

I take a deep breath.

If I look like I belong, then I definitely belong.

I cross the teachers' lounge, threading my way through the little tables, and then open the fridge, which is filled with sodas and juices and waters and lunches labeled with first names I never bothered knowing.

I grab a sparkling water and shut the refrigerator. Mr. Wellingsby looks at me quizzically, so I smile.

He smiles back, disarmed, and goes back to his window-gazing.

Someone robbing a bank wouldn't smile, after all.

And then I walk out, not bothering to hide the Pellegrino in my hand. I let the door close softly behind me.

And no one says anything.

No one stops me.

No one runs out of the teachers' lounge, asking me what I'm up to or why I've taken something.

I blink slowly, turning back to look at the door.

At the little wooden placard.

TEACHERS' LOUNGE.

I. Did. It.

I rush into the bathroom, blood singing in my veins, and lean forward, my hands resting on either side of the white sink, trying not to look at the hair trapped in the drain.

I stare in the mirror.

I, Riley Elizabeth Stone, just stole something from the teachers' lounge.

While being late to class.

In front of actual teachers.

And no one bothered to stop me because, well, I'm me.

I smile at myself in the mirror. Maybe Ethan's right. And maybe—maybe there's something more to this whole thing.

Maybe being a Goody Two-shoes is the best cover ever for having a little fun.

What is it like to get in trouble, anyway?

And suddenly, in an odd way, I'm excited.

I walk down the empty hallway, my heels clattering on the tiles, and it feels . . . oddly normal, except that usually I have a pass in my hand, a piece of paper proclaiming me exempt from rules. I open the door of the Shakespeare classroom and step inside, counting my breaths. One second in, one second out.

The Shakespeare oil painting hanging on the opposite wall stares at me accusingly.

"Oh! Riley! I thought maybe you were out today."

"Nope, sorry, Mrs. Hamilton." I give her my specially formulated teacher smile, with a lot of teeth, and she returns it.

And I sit down.

Just like normal.

And she goes on teaching.

Just like normal.

Like I'm not late. Like I haven't just been playing a thief in the teachers' lounge.

"Riley? Would you please read for Macbeth today?" asks Mrs. Hamilton.

This makes me doubly sure she's not mad. I love reading for Macbeth. It's my favorite. And I love Mrs. Hamilton because she will let girls read big parts—she's not one of those teachers who forces girls to read only the female parts and vice versa.

I smile to myself between lines.

It's almost like being good is the perfect alibi for being bad. I read my lines on autopilot, and I think about my next class. PE.

I actually like PE. And I have it with Kolbie and Neta, which means it's a chance to hang out with my buddies. And today we're supposed to just jog around the indoor track, which means it'll be pretty easy overall. Mr. Gladstone, the PE teacher, doesn't really care if you're giving a million percent as long as you're moving around a little bit and he doesn't have to do sex talks more than twice a year.

But I don't really want to change into my crappy gym uniform today, and I'm pretty sure I left my sports bra in the trunk of my car. Besides, Neta, Kolbie, and I were going to meet at Annie Up's, a cute little coffee shop and café a few steps off campus, for lunch. Would it be so bad if I just went there a little early?

So when the bell rings at the end of Shakespeare, I tuck *Macbeth* into my bag . . . but instead of going to gym, I slip out the side door next to the weight room and head over to Annie Up's, where I snag a table next to the window and order myself a caramel latte. I put my sunglasses on and pull a long, dark pink ribbon out of my backpack, which I weave into my hair in a messy ponytail in lieu of my normal straight style. For just a few minutes, I allow myself to feel very special and sort of grown-up.

Ethan would be proud of me.

My phone buzzes.

It's the group messaging thread with Neta and Kolbie.

From Neta: WHERE ARE YOU??? ARE YOU SICK OR WHAT?

I smile. I should have texted them, really. Of course they'd think that something was wrong. I sip my drink.

Skipped. At Annie Up's. Will you two hurry? I'm starving.

Kolbie texts me back. Are you insane?!?! Can you put Riley on the phone pls?? Seriously???

I giggle, thinking of them running around the track with their phones out. They're probably cursing.

See you two at lunch. Cover if Mr. Gladstone asks about me.

Neta: SERIOUSLY GIRL ARE YOU KIDNAPPED OR WHAT

I push my sunglasses up and send them a picture of myself with my latte so they're positive that I am not being held hostage or being forced to skip gym by hostile means. It would ruin my day if my two best friends put out some sort of Amber Alert on me. Then I might actually get in trouble for skipping.

Kolbie: ????? WHAT THE ????????

I text them back. Is there anything happening this weekend? This town is boring. Can we go to a party?

I finish my latte, feeling sort of—smug. A waitress brings me the lunch menu, and I order my salad early and a piece of Oreo cheesecake for dessert. I also order Kolbie and Neta's standbys: a grilled cheese, tomato soup, and lemonade for Kolbie, and a grilled chicken panini, french fries, and a strawberry smoothie for Neta.

Twenty minutes later, my friends burst in, and Neta's normally smooth hair is still in a lumpy gym ponytail. Kolbie is her normal perfect self. They both sit down at the table with me, and Kolbie looks super pissed.

"What the hell was that, Riley?" she asks. "Do you want to explain?"

I lift a shoulder, the same way I did at Ethan's. "Didn't feel like getting into gym clothes. Was Gladstone pissed?"

Neta heaves a theatrical sigh. "No. He said he thought you had some extra work in the library or something and marked you like you were *there*. But seriously. Is something wrong? And what are you doing with your hair?"

"Nothing's wrong." I see the waitress come out of the kitchen with our plates. "Oh, and I ordered your food for you so you don't have to eat so fast to get to class. Hope you don't mind."

Kolbie's face softens slightly when she sees her order. "Thanks. But you need to talk to us, Riley. We were *worried*. Like, legit, Neta was about to call 911. No joke, she had it typed into her phone and everything."

"I'm sorry," I say, knowing they want me to feel bad. I stir the ice in my drink with my straw. "I should have told you before. It was a split-second decision, though."

"But *why*? I just don't get you, Riley," Neta says. "One day you're having a total meltdown about losing a point on a test and the next day you're risking detention. What's going on?" Her lips are pinched with concern.

"I'm just tired of being me all the time. I wanted to do something—different." I sigh. I can't explain it to them. It doesn't make sense unless you've been . . . *me*.

"Well," Kolbie says slowly, "were you serious about the party this weekend?"

I kick my feet up on the chair across from me and shave off little bits of Oreo cheesecake with my fork. "If you guys will take me."

"Are you sure you didn't mean a fund-raiser? Or, like, some sort of event where you're, like, saving malnourished owls or feeding hungry children or something?" Neta asks.

I shake my head. She's kidding, but not really. I'm sort of known for fund-raisers and social events where I order clothes from, like, Rent the Runway and then accept awards on behalf of high school kids who care or something while pretending to be a teenage Oscar nominee.

But not this time. I want to go out.

And I'm going to drink.

Maybe even a beer.

Neta hits me playfully in the arm with the back of her hand. "Seriously, Ri? Have we or have we not been begging you to party with us since we were in, like, eighth grade?"

I let myself smile, just a little bit. "Maybe."

Neta grabs her strawberry smoothie and her phone. "It's so on this weekend. You have no idea. Carlos is having a pool party in the hills, which is going to be nice. His parents have an indoor pool, you know. Or we could go to the south side to Alice's, which is more of a chill hang. Or we could just go old school and drive around and we see what we run into."

"I'm in."

"Which one?" Neta asks.

I smile evilly. "All of them."

SEVEN
Almost

"Jell-O shots for the ladies?" Mario Anders asks, holding a silver pizza tray of multicolored Dixie cups. "I have cherry, lemon, grape, and I think maybe a couple of strawberries left, but you're going to have to act fast."

"Sure!" Neta squeals, taking a lemon. She grabs a strawberry and a grape, and hands the red one to me. "Only if you're comfortable," she assures me, and I sniff it tentatively.

We're all crammed on a fat leather couch on the second floor of a huge mansion up in the hills, and Neta and Kolbie seem like they're having an *amazing* time because they're on their third drinks already. The music is loud enough that the walls seem to be throbbing with it, and I am fairly certain the playlist has been lifted from the seventies or something because I have recognized only one song and that's because I heard it in a movie.

Kolbie and Neta are laughing and smiling at everyone, our legs are sweating and sticking to the couch, and I'm trying to imitate them and not think about how sweaty my butt is going to look when I stand up, or if I'm actually going to have something to contribute to a conversation at some point, or whether this is what they talk about every Monday in study hall when they talk about *fun* and what happened over the weekend and how I *totally missed out again*.

Someone brought in cheesy disco lights, and they're flashing around at the top of the main staircase in time with the beat, and there is a stocky blond boy in a cutoff T-shirt doing strange dance moves on the marble foyer downstairs.

It's not going well for him so far.

I try not to look out the window for the eightieth time that evening. The cops are not here. In fact, there are no cops. If the cops were going to come here, they would not even be here to bust anyone. Carlos Rodriguez's family is wealthy and well regarded, so no one would ever *dare* call the cops on a party at their house. In fact, if the cops were here, it would probably be to keep people from entering the party. That's how exclusive these parties are, in fact.

At least, that's what Kolbie told me. Apparently, Kolbie and Neta have been to a million of Carlos's parties, and it's always pretty safe and a lot of *fun*. And that's why they decided to ease me in with a fancy Rodriguez party before, like, taking me to a gas station to illegally buy forties or something.

"Do you know how to do a Jell-O shot?" Kolbie yells into my

ear, grabbing the purple shot. I can barely hear her, and she's right next to me.

"I don't have a spoon!" I yell back. I chance another look out the window, but I don't see any flashing lights. I glance around. They didn't hand out any plastic silverware, which seems like common sense, honestly.

"You have to use your finger to loosen it up," Neta says, running her finger around the edge of the cup. "And then you just tip it back." She lets all of the Jell-O fall into her mouth and swallows it. "Yum. And you can't even, like, taste the vodka. It's so good, Riley."

Kolbie just squeezes the Dixie cup into her mouth, which looks a little less neat, so I decide to go Neta's route. It's actually not bad. It's fruity and sweet and slides down my throat easily, but leaves just a slight bitter aftertaste on the back of my tongue. It's better than the wheaty beer I've been nursing for the past hour and a half.

"Are you buzzing?" Kolbie asks me. "Do you want anything else?"

"Um, no thanks," I say. I don't think I like drinking much, and honestly, I don't feel a thing.

"The more you drink, the less you'll worry about getting caught," Kolbie says. "I know that's terrible real-world advice, but it's actually true." She tosses her cup at some guy walking by with a huge garbage bag, who tries to catch it, but it bounces off onto the wood floor.

Neta pulls on my arm. "It's too hot on this couch. Let's go talk to more people! We can see if there are any cute guys here from Bellview, okay? Oh!" She releases me for a second and digs in her wristlet, producing a bright pink tube of lip gloss. "Try this on, okay? I think you need some."

I stare at it for a second. It's way too bright for me. I know it. But this whole party isn't me. The point of the night isn't me. So I unscrew the top of the lip gloss and dab a little onto my lips to appease her. "Right back, Kolbie!" Neta says, and drags me away to a group of guys that she just dives right into, introducing me to Zayne and Jordan and Benn (with two *N*'s, he tells us, which is apparently way better than a Ben with just one.).

"I've heard about you," Zayne says, taking my hand and holding it for just a second too long. "You're the one who never comes out."

Wow. Even other schools know I'm a shut-in goody-goody. Still, I rather like Zayne. He has a wide smile with even teeth. His hair is dark and curly and he's just tall enough.

"Don't I?" I ask Zayne. "Then what am I doing here?"

Zayne smiles. "Surprising me. That means something."

"Enlighten me, Zayne. What does it all mean?"

"You're about to be my . . . beer pong partner. Right?"

"Sure, but there are conditions. Two, to be exact."

"Anything." Zayne grins, anticipating my response.

I hold up one finger. "Only if you teach me how to play." I smile at him as I take another drink of my warm beer. What am I getting myself into? I pop up a second finger. "And only if we play against Neta and her partner of choice."

Neta slides her arm around Benn with two *N*'s. "You better be good at beer pong."

He finishes his beer. "I've never lost . . . tonight."

"You haven't played tonight!" she accuses, and they're laughing together and he's looking down at her like she's everything and she's looking up at him like . . . well, like he's a beer pong partner she's going to have to peel off later.

Zayne leads us downstairs, to a room near the pool where a Ping-Pong table has been set up with several Solo cups filled halfway with beer. He explains the rules—if the other team gets a Ping-Pong ball in your set of cups, you have to drink. It's basically a game that would be super lame if beer weren't involved. I turn to Zayne. "We have a problem," I whisper.

"What?" He looks at me, alarmed.

I grin at him and pull at the neck of his shirt. "I hate beer. So if we lose—"

"I'm stuck drinking most of it," he finishes, and laughs. "Some partnership this is!"

"You chose me!" I accuse. "So this is totally on you."

"I don't regret it yet."

Neta winks at me from across the table, and I resist rolling my eyes. It's like they think I don't know how to flirt. It's not like it's hard. You just have to appeal to the three basic drunken categories for party boys:

1. Beer

2. Sports (of some kind)

3. Sex

Boom. Flirting. Done.

It's not rocket science. It's not even a challenge. And

honestly . . . it's a little boring. Is this how all parties are? Slightly bitter shots with Ping-Pong balls in skunky beer?

Is this what Ethan wanted me to throw everything away for? Was this a domino even worth knocking over?

"Your throw," Zayne says, handing me a beer-soaked Ping-Pong ball. This is definitely not sanitary. "Make it count, Stone."

"Give me space, Zayne." I move him out of the way with my hip, which he seems to like, and line up my shot. I close one eye, and across the table, Benn and Neta jeer at me. Neta sticks out her tongue, and I laugh, but I don't lose my focus. This is Riley time. This is Zen and the Art of Beer Pong.

I toss the Ping-Pong ball.

It bounces off the first cup and lands in the second.

"Does that count?" I ask Zayne.

Zayne grabs my hand and forces a high five on me. "Hell yeah, it counts. Chug it, B team!" he shouts across the table.

Neta makes a pouty face and pulls the Ping-Pong ball out of the cup. She winks at me, takes a tiny sip, and then hands the rest of the cup to her partner, who downs it, two rivulets of beer leaking out over both of his stubbly cheeks. "Woo!" he says, wiping off his face with the back of his hand. "I feel good!"

"We get to shoot again!" Zayne says, grabbing another ball. "Go, Stone!"

I line up again, and this time the ball goes long, hitting Benn in the shirt. "Damn!" I say, but Zayne pats me on the small of my back. His hand lingers for a millisecond.

"Don't worry," he says. "We got 'em the next time. Now we have to distract them." He shouts across the table, and I join him, feeling stupid. Suddenly, I want to leave.

But this is a *party*. This is what I've gotten myself into.

They miss.

Our go.

This is what people my age *do*. Right?

I sigh. I watch Zayne toss the ball. It makes it into one of their cups, and I cheer and we high-five again, and then I miss and so the ball goes to the other team. This time Zayne tells me I have to drink, and so I down as much as I can from the Solo cup and then hand the beer off to him to finish, feeling a little queasy and strange, like maybe my vision isn't following quite right when I turn my head and my smile isn't matching up on my mouth the way it should be.

The Ping-Pong ball changes hands again.

How lame would it be if I used hand sanitizer on it? Would that make the beer taste better, or worse? Or would anyone even notice?

Maybe Kolbie has it right with her college boyfriend. College parties have to be better than this, right? They have to be more fun. More . . . sophisticated. More substantial.

Maybe there's talking. Like real talking, not just lame flirting over beer-soaked balls.

Or maybe it's just more of the same.

I feel a hand on my shoulder, and I turn. It's Kolbie. "How's it going, Ri? How much beer have you downed?"

I smile at her. "A cup. Or something."

She frowns at me. "Are you buzzing? You don't seem like you're buzzing."

I think I am, if this counts as buzzing. Beyond the eye thing, I have this strange warmth inside me, and I feel like I'm underwater, but just under the surface, where things are just a touch slower. But I'm just a little drunk, and somehow it's not the happy, fun place where everyone else seems to be.

"I'm good," I tell her, and she slings an arm around my shoulder.

"I think maybe I should take my friend's place here," she tells them. "So she can run to the bathroom. She'll be right back. Won't you, Ri?" She puts her hands on my shoulders and looks in my eyes, telling me in friend code to take as much time away from the stupid game as I need.

I tell her back in friend language that I'm grateful, and turn to Zayne. "Be right back. Don't screw it up, okay? We have a lot riding on this game."

It's strange how it all comes so easily to me. The words, with no feeling to back them up.

He fist-bumps me. "We've got this in the cup."

I smile widely at his lame joke and escape in the general direction of a bathroom. The first two I find are locked, but I finally find a small one, just off the pool, that's more of a changing room than anything else. I flick on the light, but then after I've closed the door, I flick it off and slide down to the floor and savor being alone, just for a second.

I want to go home. I want to be at home, in my room, on my bed. Alone. These people who are like me on the outside are not my people. It's not like there's anything wrong with them. Tonight I know the truth: there is something wrong with me.

I lean my head back against the door and close my eyes, but someone knocks.

"Ri? You in there?"

Kolbie.

I reach up and turn the lock on the door.

"What are you doing in here in the dark?" She walks in and flicks on the light. "Are you okay?"

I try to smile. "Yeah. Sorry. I just needed a minute. These guys—I don't know." I flutter my hand.

Kolbie looks at me. "Yeah. I get it. I feel that way too. I told your boy Zayne to take my turn and came to find you."

I sigh, and she sinks down on the floor next to me, and I lean my head on her chest. "These are not my people."

"No, they aren't. But that's okay." She pauses, and pretend silence fills the room, but outside, the music from the party pounds, the bass so thick and heavy I can feel it through the floor. "Maybe we shouldn't be pushing you to be with someone. Or maybe you just need someone older. I'm just . . . I'm sorry if we put too much pressure on you. We didn't mean anything, you know?"

I nod. "I know."

She gets me.

But then I wonder . . . is she talking about someone in particular?

Someone we both know?

No.

That's impossible.

Of course not.

"Do you want to go home?" she asks.

I nod. My head is starting to spin in a fuzzy, strange way, and my stomach feels odd and too full. I don't feel sick, but I am starting to feel a little out of control.

And what if the cops really did show up?

All my dominoes would really be knocked down then. That would sure show Ethan for trying to make me an actual teenager.

"Come on, Ri." She pushes herself off the floor, then reaches down and grabs my hand to help me up. "I think this is enough party for one night."

"You're a good friend," I tell her, leaning on her shoulder a little bit. She stumbles, then rights herself, slinging my arm around her waist.

She pauses. "Don't forget all the nights you've picked me up off the floor and held my hair and let me sneak into your house when I'm late for my curfew." She winces. "Actually, *do* forget them, please."

I smile and squeeze her a little. "I'm here for you, Kolbs." The words are slippery in my mouth.

She smiles back. "I know you are, Riley."

EIGHT

Bookstore

There is something about bookstores.

Something better about bookstores than parties or movies or pictures. There's something hidden in books; lives and secrets and whispers and little bits of truth you could never guess at, even if you'd known the author her entire life and then read the book and asked her all about it. I think there are little bits of truth in books that are probably never discovered, even by the people who write them.

And also I like to read.

Smart girl problems.

It is Saturday afternoon, and I woke up with a little bit of a headache. I poured myself a glass of filtered water and took two

Tylenol before wrapping up in a big, loose henley and a gauzy lavender scarf and twisting my hair into a long golden braid. I walked to my favorite bookstore: a small one in South York Village called Pockets, where people laze around outside with croissants on little tables and drink tea in clay mugs with milk and sugar.

Inside, the rows are all hunched very closely together, and the shelves are old and splintering under the weight of the books, often stacked two high and three deep. They smell wonderful, like aged glue and ancient paper, and I draw slow breaths as I walk in, savoring the quiet scent that is only noticeable to the type of people who truly love it there.

This is a place that I could not take Kolbie and Neta and have them understand it quite the way I understand it. It's not that they don't like books; they do. They're both quite intelligent. It's just that this store is something to me, and I'm something to it, and I'm not entirely excited to share it with my friends, who might not find the peeling wallpaper appealing, or like the fact that the tap in the bathroom only runs cold.

I walk through the poetry section, and I pull out a secondhand copy of *Burning in Water, Drowning in Flame*, when I hear the voice. The unmistakable voice.

"Darling, what do you want?"

"I don't know. Do they have magazines here?" She pouts, and I imagine her sticking out her lower lip just slightly.

"Maybe old ones. I don't know. Don't you want a novel or something?"

I peek away from my Bukowski poems, and there they are: Alex

Belrose and his beautiful wife, Jacqueline, on the other end of the row. Mr. Belrose has a lanky arm around his spouse, who is lithe and fair and lovely, like she's stepped out of the pages of French *Vogue* after being artfully arranged by a fashion photographer. I heard Alex met her while he was studying abroad in France. She's American, of course, and so is he, but apparently they had this great, wild love story that sounds, naturally, like something that never actually happened. She's long-limbed and gorgeous and has a nose like a lost pink button. Her clothes hang on her like wings on a grand sort of bird; they're jewel-toned and spread out around her like she's some sort of queen.

She's no ordinary woman. At least, that's what people say.

I look down at my book of poems, running my finger along the page even though I've stopped reading the words some time ago. I tuck myself farther back, wishing I could disappear. I don't want to talk to Jacqueline. Don't want to have to be measured next to her. I feel small and lesser and strange, and I wish neither of them were here and this little bookstore were still mine, just mine, and I didn't have to worry about interlopers, even pretty ones I've dreamed about running into.

I rearrange my scarf so it's draped around my arms and covering my back and turn away from the storefront so no one can see me, when someone taps on my shoulder.

"Hello."

I turn around so quickly I almost lose my balance. I stumble a little. It's Mr. Belrose.

"Oh. Hey."

He grins. "I'm sorry. Did I scare you? Am I not allowed to talk to you outside of school hours?"

I look to the left and the right, like I'm scouting for someone. "Strictly against policy," I whisper. "I actually didn't know they let teachers out of the school. I thought they lived there. Had to take showers in the sinks and all that."

He nods solemnly. "You know our secrets, then. But they do let us out, for two hours each weekend, to give the appearance of being real people."

I snap my fingers. "It almost worked."

He chuckles. "Damn it." Mr. Belrose's eyes drop to my hands, and he lifts the poetry book from them. "Bukowski, hmm?"

"Yes," I say. "He's my favorite poet."

"He's a bit dark for my sunshiny-est student," Mr. Belrose says.

"Perhaps there's more to me than meets the eye," I say, then immediately hate myself. *Did I really just say that? To a* teacher? *Am I stupid?*

"That," Mr. Belrose says, "I'm not surprised about. But I've never been much of a poetry fan, unless it's classic and French. I prefer a good novel in your cheap American tongue." He smiles, and runs his fingers over the spines of the books on the shelves fondly. "I come here on the weekends often. I've found a lot of my favorites in this very store."

"Really?" I fold my arms over my chest.

He glances back at me. "You don't have to sound so surprised. Take, for example, Stephen King." He plucks a copy of *The Shining* off the shelf. "I love a good horror novel as much as the next person." He slides it back with reverence. "Or maybe Hemingway. I love a sharply written book, you know? *The Old Man and the Sea* is my absolute favorite. But you . . . you're different. I can tell. Dark stuff. Stuff that you can't find in the high school library. Beyond a typical horror."

"There's other stuff too," I protest. "I love Jane Austen as much as the next girl. And I love romance novels. And I enjoy Shakespeare." I turn a corner and flick a copy of *The Complete Works of William Shakespeare* with my index finger and thumb, completely mis-shelved. "I love young-adult novels and picture books and anything I can read with chocolate-chip cookies and mint tea." I run my hands over the spines, just like he did, my fingers picking up particles of dust.

"Ah." He clasps his hands behind his back.

"Ah?" I ask. "What does 'Ah,' mean, then?"

"Can I make a suggestion?"

"Do I have a choice?"

I feel dangerous, flirting with him with Jacqueline so close by. I am warm suddenly, so I take my scarf off and tuck it hastily in my bag.

"Always." He just looks at me, no trace of a smile around his lips, his green eyes intense.

"Darling? Where are you?"

The lilt of the voice is unmistakable.

Unwillingly, my heart sinks a little.

Mr. Belrose turns. "Right here, Jackie." He whips back to me, and he presses a book into my hands urgently, and I realize I don't know if he's had it this whole time or if he's just pulled it from a shelf. "Read this," he says. "It'll do you good. And tell me what you think. Tell me what it makes you feel."

I find myself drawing the book in to my stomach and holding it tightly. Mr. Belrose walks toward the end of the aisle and waves at his wife. She comes toward him, a stack of magazines, which look like *People* and *Us Weekly* and *OK!,* balanced on her arm.

"Are you ready? I'm so bored." Her voice is a high-pitched whine, and I hate her a little then, for being bored in my perfect little bookstore and ruining everything.

"Sure," Mr. Belrose says. "Do you want all of those?"

"I'm bored," she insists again by way of answer. She thrusts the magazines at him, and he takes them under his arm.

"Okay." Mr. Belrose turns to me and lifts his hand. "Good-bye, Riley. I'll see you in class. Enjoy your books, okay?"

I wave at him, feeling a pang somewhere between my stomach and chest.

It isn't until I've paid the man at the cash register and I'm back at my house that I realize that somewhere along the way I've lost my pretty scarf.

It must have fallen out of my bag.

NINE
Untruths

School buses are genuinely the worst. I don't know what it is, but there's something about being underage that makes the bus designers say, *Okay, let's literally forgo every creature comfort in a traditional vehicle and just go with the absolute bare minimum. Like, let's just slap gray vinyl seats (no seat belts needed) into a metal shell and put a bunch of children on it and call it good. And if the engine sounds like it might explode at any possible moment, that's fine, it's not like the cargo is important in any way.*

Meanwhile other buses have plush seats and air-conditioning, heat that works without making the engine whine, and televisions.

"I always get my best sleep on a school bus," Neta says, yawning and leaning her head on my shoulder. "I love these seats. It's like

BO has permanently worked its way into the material. It's so sooth-ing." She takes a deep breath and coughs.

I fake-gag. "You're so gross."

"Don't be mad at me because I'm honest." She snuggles in deeper against my shoulder. "I'm just gonna sleep here, mkay? These gross buses are the best for sleeping."

She's right. There's something about the rhythm of a bus that's relaxing . . . maybe the lack of shocks as it bumbles over the road . . . or maybe it's, like, carbon monoxide leaking in and slowly poisoning us. It's possible.

I yawn, but I resist sleep. We're on the way to our mock trial meet. I'm playing a witness today: a psychiatrist who has to attest to the sanity of the plaintiff. I run over my notes for the meet, then I glance over at Neta, whose eyes are closed. She's breathing softly through her mouth. I lean over very slowly and feel around in my bag for something . . . one specific book, used, with a cloth bind-ing. With one hand, I slide it up my leg and into my lap.

It's the book that Mr. Belrose chose for me in the store. It's the one he pressed into my hands and told me to read. It's called *L'Amant.*

The Lover.

And it means something.

The whole book is in French, of course, so I'm working my way through it, slowly, carefully, looking up words on my phone and rereading passages and pages, but there is a message for me in it, I am sure.

There has to be.

L'Amant is the story of a young girl who meets a twenty-seven-year-old businessman. The girl is even younger than me. The man is just a year older than Mr. Belrose. I work through the pages painstakingly.

"What's that?"

Neta's awake.

I feel my face color. "Um, nothing." I let my hair swing down in front of my cheek, which is becoming a defense mechanism.

"Doesn't look like nothing." She rubs her eyes and sits up. "Where did you get it?"

"School." The lie comes easily, like I've had it lying in wait this whole time. "Just schoolwork." I say a silent prayer of thanks that neither Neta or Kolbie take French . . . and hopefully don't understand any of it, either. Both of them would have signed up for it had they not already been in advanced Spanish classes.

"Oh. Boring. I thought it would be, like, a sexy book, but you're reading homework?" She sighs. "Leave it to you to get all hot and bothered about an assignment. Give it a break, Ri. We practically have the day off."

"You could be prepping for your part," I remind her.

She pulls her hood up and yanks the strings on her jacket to bring it tighter around her face. "You are missing out on quality school bus sleep time," she points out. "You really need to put away your books and chill out for one second. What happened to rule-breaking Riley from the weekend who was, like, 'yay alcohol, let's take off all our clothes and get arrested'?"

I cock my head and rest my chin on my wrist, pretending to

think. "You're so right. Thanks for providing that direct quote. Except you left out all the stuff about the drugs that I think I yelled from a plane before I jumped out of it with a homemade parachute."

"I edited out the swear words." Neta giggles. She puts on a pair of black sunglasses and tilts her head back onto the top of the seat. "Now stop waking me up with your smart-people stuff."

I sigh and slip the book back into my backpack between my Shakespeare homework and a copy of *The Sun Also Rises*. I don't want anyone in my French class to catch me reading it either. They might actually translate the title correctly . . . and then I'd have to lie even better.

Everyone knows the best lies are the least complicated.

Besides, there's a part of me that wants to read the book alone, maybe when I'm about to go to sleep. There's something about it that feels . . . personal. Like maybe someone is whispering in my ear, telling me a secret that's meant to be heard only when no one else is around and I'm tucked in bed, under my covers, listening to the house breathing while everyone else is asleep.

Still, why wouldn't I tell Neta that Mr. Belrose gave me the book? She'd love knowing that I ran into him and his beautiful wife in the bookstore. There isn't really anything to hide with my French teacher. Everyone else has a crush on him, after all. Is it so odd that his star pupil does too? Neta and Kolbie would be terribly jealous and I'd get to tell them everything he said to me. And it would be sort of nice to tell them. Tell *someone*, at least. Would it really be so horrible to admit it? Besides, it's not as if there's something going on.

Is there?

I shiver suddenly and look out the window, at the passing trees and fields. There isn't. It's just a book that happens to be published in French, and I happened to be at the used bookstore at the exact same time as Belrose and his wife. I rest my forehead against the glass, and Neta snores softly beside me. I feel my phone buzz in my pocket and pull it out to check my e-mails. There's a few new ones . . . something from the shoe store at the mall, a 20 percent off coupon to Abercrombie this weekend, and . . . another e-mail.

Something unopened from an address I've not received a message from before. At least, not that I can remember.

And I would remember.

Because it's an address I can identify.

An e-mail that contains the names Alex and Belrose.

The e-mail itself contains one word:

Enjoying?

My veins flood with something like ice and then with a liquid burst of heat and then ice again. I know who it is without asking. I know immediately.

Suddenly, and oddly, I almost want to put my phone down. I want to delete the message and drop the phone and pretend the message never came to me at all, and that a teacher is not reaching out to his student about a rather naughty French book he gave her at her favorite bookstore and everything is normal, just very normal and fine, quite fine, thank you.

But I can't do that.

Very much so. Thanks for the recommendation. My finger hovers over the send button for almost thirty seconds, but then I touch it and the e-mail is gone.

And almost as quickly, one comes back.

It's a favorite of mine.

My heart pounds. I glance at Neta and angle myself away from her, drawing my knees up on the seat to put a barrier between us, so I have a small private space to send messages.

Any particular reason why? I ask.

Read it, and I think you'll know.

I am.

Good girl.

The last e-mail startles me. *Good girl?* The verbiage is highly condescending and too personal all at once, and I'm not sure how to respond. Because he's right. I am just a good girl.

I stare at my phone, but he doesn't send any more e-mails. I can't think of anything else to say, and I feel like there is a cement mixer in my stomach tossing around feelings like sick and happy and excited and horrible. I lean my head against the window and watch the blur of the asphalt through the glass.

Things to Know About Riley Stone:

- When Riley was ten, she started a fund-raiser to collect warm socks for the homeless. She engaged twelve schools and collected more than 1,500 pairs of socks for local shelters.
- Riley kept one super-cute purple pair for herself because hey, no one said ten-year-olds were perfect.
- At age twelve, Riley won the opportunity to make a speech at the local chapter of a veterans' organization. She spoke about what their service meant to her and her great-grandfather, who served in Vietnam. Riley received a standing ovation, and to date, the video has received 130,000 YouTube hits, which unfortunately is not quite viral by Riley standards.
- When Riley was in middle school, she set national records for most Girl Scout cookies sold by selling her wares outside of frat houses notorious for partying.
- At age seven, Riley, ever the type A, began to enter behavioral therapy because her parents worried about her taking on too much. Her therapists and psychiatrists agreed it was a good choice for a girl with her tendencies, but Mr. and Mrs. Stone were nervous about any social ramifications the therapy could have if Riley was ever found out, so she was never allowed to attend more than a few weeks of continual therapy at a time.

TEN
Secret

Good girl.

He's right.

He is.

That sums me up. Certainly, I was late to class. I skipped class. I drank beer and played games and went to a real party and did all the things that high school students are supposed to do for one stupid weekend, but that doesn't mean anything at all. It's not like it changed me in any real way.

I'm in the good-girl category. I live there. I am listed there firmly, my name printed, and a solid black checkmark next to it. My brother is still a bit lost, even though he's found Esther and he thinks he's in love, and we're all just stuck unless we do something drastic and wild that changes our hearts and tears up our souls a little bit.

Good girl.

I don't know why it bothers me so much, but it follows me. It tails me back to school. It follows me back into French class and sits curled on my shoulder and slides up my neck to whisper in my ear.

It's nothing, I'm nothing else.

Mr. Belrose doesn't look at me in any special way when he hands our tests back. He doesn't give me a special wink, or a specific smile. He treats me like he treats Thea . . . like someone holding on to something a bit distasteful, arm extended, away from the body. Like what you're holding is important enough that you can't drop it, but God forbid you let it near enough to actually *touch* you.

"Might I remind you all," Mr. Belrose says, "that essays are due today." He smiles at us like this is a special day, one we've all been waiting for.

About a month ago, he assigned us a monster essay. A huge one. Eight pages. Which would suck in any class, honestly.

Except that Belrose said it *all* had to be *en français.*

Which meant it was a *beast* of a homework assignment, and even the girls who were nursing huge crushes on Mr. Belrose were sort of grumbling about it because it was definitely not one of those things you could dash off the evening before in a Red Bull–infused rush of chemical energy.

Of course, I wrote mine on Julius Caesar conquering Gaul and had it done two weeks ago and made it *ten* pages long because

French history is really rich and interesting, and eight pages was just not enough to accurately cover the whole Roman takeover and how it was all about debt, but that's just me.

I pull my essay out of my folder and walk it up to Mr. Belrose's desk.

He is wearing glasses again today. Ones with thick black frames. They accentuate the deep green of his eyes, but I try not to notice. Deep green eyes are not my business.

He glances at me, and the corner of his mouth pulls up, just slightly. So slightly I hardly notice.

"*Merci*, Mademoiselle Stone."

His left hand moves to his side.

There is something gauzy and soft and lavender in his pocket.

Something—

Oh my God.

My scarf.

He watches as I notice. His deep green eyes—eyes that are suddenly my concern after all—fill with amusement.

His smile grows wider.

ELEVEN
Meanings

"How do you tell if a guy likes you?"

Neta and I are over at Kolbie's house, which is almost as nice as Carlos's. Her parents are super-overprotective and huge on family time, but they're usually cool about letting us hang out in the theater room in the basement.

Yeah. Her parents have a theater room. Her dad is some COO of an IT company, which means it's super-tricked-out, too, and there are speakers legitimately built into the floors.

"What do you mean?" Neta says. "And can you please pass me the Tiffany blue?"

I pass her the blue nail polish. We're all doing pedis while *Sixteen Candles* plays on the big screen. We're doing an old-school movie night. We try to do these at least once a month. Some are, like, super-old-school, à la Audrey Hepburn, and some are, like, *10 Things I Hate About You*, which is about a five on the old-o-meter.

"Did you not see Zayne at the party?" Kolbie asks. "Or the way he was drooling all over you and laughing at, like, every half syllable that fell out of your mouth?" She grabs a white polish and tosses it to me. I'm trying to give my toes French tips. "Trying" being the operative word.

"I know like that." I grab the tiny polish and spread out a newspaper under my feet. "But, like, what about when it's more subtle?"

"Subtle like how?" Neta asks. She started to paint her toes, but now she's distracted and diving into popcorn. Her fingers are covered in butter.

Like when he has your scarf in his pocket. And when he keeps looking at you and touching it.

And when he's your teacher.

"Like, what if instead of trying to get you to sink balls into beer pong cups and tongue your neck, he's trying to just be nice to you or something?"

"RJ licked my neck on our first date," Neta says defensively.

"Look how great that turned out." Kolbie holds her foot out. "Do I like this pink? I think I like this pink better than the blue."

Neta throws a handful of popcorn at her.

"You're cleaning that up later," Kolbie warns. "My mom does not play."

"Stop dissing RJ, then."

"Stop defending someone who treated you like something he put down the garbage disposal."

Neta throws another handful of popcorn because she knows Kolbie is right, and Kolbie stands up. "Seriously?"

"Can we get back to the point?" I ask. I smudge a little bit of the white on the bottom of my toenail. Damn it.

"It would help if we knew who you were talking about," Neta points out. A piece of popcorn falls onto her chest, and she licks it up with her tongue.

Kolbie raises her eyebrows. "You are so classy I can't even deal."

Neta winks at her. "More where that came from."

I giggle. "Seriously, though. It's not a particular guy. I'm just talking about mature, non-drunk dudes who are maybe a little bit past their beer pong stage of life. Like, what's the protocol?"

Kolbie points at me with a pastel-pink-painted brush, and a glob of paint falls off onto the newspaper. "As the only one here who has experienced an actual healthy relationship, I think I should speak to this. First of all, he will find an excuse to touch you. And not in a creepy, grind-on-you-in-the-club kind of way. In a sweet way. Like, he'll touch your hand or something. Or pick an eyelash off your cheek. Or whatever."

"You're telling me," I say, "that Jamal picked an eyelash off your cheek? And that you didn't steal that from *The Notebook* or, like, *Insert Cheesy Date Movie Here?*"

"It was an actual occurrence. And he also started leaving stuff around so I'd have to return it. And I did the same. Like, I left an earring at his house once. And he left his iPod at mine."

I think of my scarf, and feel my face color slightly. Maybe it *does* mean something that he has it. And he's holding on to it. It *has* to.

I think of the way he looked at me when he touched it, and I feel *something* in my lower belly.

"It might take longer," Neta adds, "but he'll let you know. And that's when you know it's a good one. Like Jamal, right, Kolbie?"

Kolbie settles back into her recliner, satisfied with her toes. "Just like Jamal."

"You're lucky," Neta says. "I'm still on the neck-lickers."

"More serious topic," Kolbie says, pointing at the screen. "Can we talk about how messed up this movie is? Like, could we have a side of humor with this load of racism, please?"

"I was still stuck on the massive amount of date rape." Neta reaches for the remote. "Because that is just exactly the kind of message any girl wants to hear."

"Can we veto this movie?" I ask. "I'm over it."

We binge dating reality shows instead, and while they aren't, like, completely *free* of sexism or anything, they're at least a little better.

The next day in French class Mr. Belrose announces that the class will have a lot of homework coming up.

"Why?" whines Thea, pulling on her hair. "I thought you liked us, Mr. Belrose. I thought we were, like, your favorite class. And didn't we *just* finish the giant essay of doom?"

"Well, I'll have a lot of extra time in the next couple of weeks," he says. His eyes shift to me. "My wife's gone. She's visiting her mother."

He holds my gaze.

I hold his.

He wants me.

He does.

My heart wants to beat its way out of my chest.

Around me, the class *oohs*. "How will you occupy yourself while she is away, Monsieur Belrose?" Teri Von Millhouse asks. She leans forward on one hand and flutters her eyelashes.

"Catch up on my Netflix. And give you more homework." Belrose shakes his head, and I realize, suddenly, his hair is getting a little long. He reminds me of Alex. Not a teacher.

Just Alex. The guy that I used to know.

"I'll comfort you if you're lonely," Thea says, raising her hand.

"And that's my cue to tell you to turn to page two seventy-six in your textbook, guys, before things get any more awkward. Questions about my personal life will now result in additional homework. With reasonable exceptions." His eyes stray to me again, and I press my lips together to keep my feelings from showing on my face.

And I wonder what it would be like to kiss him.

I wonder if he would be tender.

Or if he would be aggressive.

The truth is I've never had a real kiss before. Well, at least not one that I count. I suppose there was Erick Canders in third grade during the school play. He slipped me tongue because he was coughing really hard.

Which I don't. Count it.

And I don't count the little ones I snuck on the playground when I was a little girl. The meaningless ones with boys behind trees, just to see what it was like.

A real kiss is different. A real kiss is with someone who means something.

And so I have never had a real kiss.

I watch Mr. Belrose as if there is nothing out of the ordinary. I take notes in deliberate, even handwriting, highlighting the most important sections in three different colors, and I write down my homework in my planner, which is a bit more than usual. And I don't stick around after class to talk to him, because Riley Stone has no reason to stick around to speak to her teacher, not when she has absolutely everything under control.

But when I get home that evening, I find the phone book in the cupboard underneath my parents' landline (they still have both because they are stuck in the last century and don't trust cell phones in disasters). I make a mental note of Belrose's address.

And then I grab my keys.

I know the street, I think—it's about twenty minutes away, not far from a park on the other side of town. It's not a wealthy part of town, but it's not like it's horrible, either. It's a typical lower-middle-class neighborhood: chain-link fences, well-tended gardens with chipped gnomes, kids playing basketball in their driveways.

I drum my feelings out on the steering wheel, but I can't process them. I'm not sure if my heart is working quite right. Or at all.

Am I misreading all the signals? What am I doing? Did he even want me? Am I completely nuts?

I park three blocks away, pull on one of Ethan's old Denver Broncos baseball caps, and slip out of my car. I stare in the direction of his house.

This is bad.

This isn't late-to-class bad. It's not drinking-beer bad. It's actually *bad* bad. There is no going back from this bad.

He's a teacher.

He's over eighteen.

He's *married*.

And I am a good girl.

My mind ticks back to his e-mail.

If I go over to his house, then that's gone. I'm not just stepping neatly out of the category I've been shuffled in—I'm basically blowing it up with a nuclear bomb.

I can't go back.

But my feet start moving in the direction of his house. The street is friendly enough. There are tons of trees—old ones, with thick trunks, casting the trees in shadows. I glance at the little homes as I walk by. None of them are very big. Some have children and dogs in the yard. Some are empty. Some of the lawns haven't been mowed in a while.

My footsteps feel too deliberate and strange, like I've never used my feet before. Am I walking casually? How does one walk casually?

I pull the baseball cap farther over my head and push my hair behind my ears.

Maybe I shouldn't have dressed so much like myself—all

straight edges and J.Crew and neat. Maybe I should have worn a disguise.

I feel oddly cold, and it's a nice day. My fingers and toes tingle strangely. What am I doing? Is this who I am now? Am I really interested in Alex Belrose?

Shouldn't I learn to be happy with Zaynes, drooling over me while I play beer pong? With Robs? Rob is so sweet. Why can't I be happy with Rob?

Rob and I even have a history. I mean, we never really dated, but we were friends. We sat next to each other in fourth grade, and for my birthday that year, he gave me a pink unicorn pencil with a white heart eraser. Every year since, he's slipped the same pink unicorn pencil into my locker on my birthday, and every year he smiles at me because we both know but we never say anything about it.

My chest hurts.

Because I can't.

Not with Rob.

He's not for me.

I need something . . . else. Someone else.

And suddenly, I'm there. I'm at his house. It's a smallish brick thing with a barn mailbox. The yard is neatly mowed and there are yellow and pink tulips out front.

And Alex Belrose is sitting out on the porch in a hoodie that says PURDUE. He leans forward when he sees me.

My phone buzzes in my pocket. I pull it out. I have a new e-mail.

Go around back.

TWELVE
Bad

I know what he's saying.

Don't walk in my front door. Don't be obvious.

But come here.

My hands shake. I shove them into the pockets of my jeans.

I walk three houses down and cut through a lawn toward the alley, which is lined with trees.

And therefore hard to see from the homes on either side.

Good call, Mr. Belrose.

Alex.

Mr. Belrose.

I pause at the gate. It's white and wooden and badly in need of a paint job.

Stop.

I hear it in my head like someone is saying it, like someone is actually telling me.

This is it.

This is the line.

Right here.

And if I cross it, I become an entirely different Riley Stone. An entirely different girl. I will not be the good girl, the girl who loves bookstores, the girl who kisses boys because she has to because she's in a play, or the girl who is perfect because that's who she is and what she does.

I will have a secret.

I will have done something wrong.

Really wrong.

For one second, my body feels heavy, and I want to turn around and run. I want to sprint down the alley, as fast as I can, and cut back toward the street where Belrose can't see me and just leave.

But then I press my hands against the wooden gate and it swings open, revealing the backyard, choked with trees and an empty chicken coop and there he is. He is wearing khaki shorts even though it's too cold for them and his hands are jammed into the pocket of his hoodie.

And he's smiling.

Big.

At me.

Just at me.

It's not his teacher smile. It's the Alex smile.

"Wanna sit?" he asks, motioning at an Adirondack chair on his back porch.

"Um, yeah." I settle into the chair, sitting my purse down on the wooden planks. He sits too, opposite me, and we look at each other and look away and then look at each other and his eyes are so goddamn green and what am I doing?

"Do you want something to drink?" he asks.

"Sure."

He disappears into his house and comes back a moment later with two sarsaparillas.

"Do you like root beer?" He twists off the top for me, so obviously he doesn't expect me to say no.

It's not my favorite, but I take one anyway. "Sure." It's frosty and cold. I wonder if he has ice cream. We could make root beer floats.

No. That's immature. I'm an adult. I am grown-up. I am almost in college, and Mr. Belrose—Alex—is taking me seriously.

He could have offered me a real beer and I would have said, "Sure," and then I could have made a toast or something, but there isn't a lot you can say about root beer. Which is something you give a kid.

But a real beer—that would have meant something. If he would have given me a real beer, like an equal, I would have taken it, and I would have smiled at him, and that gesture would have said everything, just there, and I would have lifted my beer and said, "To you, Alex," and he would have said, "No, to you," and I would have known he was glad that I was on the same level as he was, and it would have been everything the party with Neta and

Kolbie wasn't. He would have been showing me he trusted me, and maybe I would have brought up something about *L'Amant*, and I could have told him how I really did understand the themes of repression and how we need to act on our desires.

We sit in silence for a few seconds.

He takes a sip of his sarsaparilla.

"So."

"Uh, do you want to talk about how great my essay is or something?" My joke feels weak and flat as soon as I say it, and I wish I could take the words back.

He laughs. "That seems like a safe topic."

I feel a smile working its way to my lips, and I don't know if it's because I am happy or because I'm nervous or because my stomach feels like something is alive inside of it. "We don't have to be safe."

His eyes catch mine. "No?"

I shake my head. "No. I'm not exactly the good girl that everyone thinks I am." I take a drink of my root beer, and a little bit dribbles on my chin. I wipe it off quickly, hoping he doesn't notice.

"I've known that for a long time." He looks away from me, into his backyard. "You're more than just a good student. You're better than that."

I cock my head at him. "Better?" What does that mean?

"I think that just sort of reduces you to a few grades and some scholarships. And people are scared of that sort of perfection, aren't they? They have to quantify you somehow to make you safer. So you're a certain sort of girl to them, and then everything is just—easier."

"Yeah? And who am I to you?"

He looks at me and presses his lips together. "I don't know yet. But if it's okay with you, I'd kind of like a chance to figure it out."

I feel a little warm. "I think I'd like that too."

I look up at the sky. The sun is starting to go down, and I can hear crickets starting up their insistent nighttime song. It's getting a little chilly, and goose bumps begin to prick up on my arms. "What sort of man are you, then?"

He shifts in his chair. "Would it weird you out if I said I didn't know yet?"

I set my drink down. "Not really. I think sometimes people spend their whole lives just trying to figure out who they are. And I don't know what the big deal is about having to define yourself immediately or even at all. Who says that you should have to discover exactly who you are by the time you graduate from college? I don't think anyone knows by that point."

Belrose leans forward, his elbows on his knees. "You're smart, you know that? And not like everyone has been telling you your whole life, either. But really smart. You see people."

I tuck my hair behind my ears and smile tightly in an attempt to veil how pleased the compliment really makes me. "Thanks."

And I realize that this . . . this is what it's supposed to feel like. Not Jell-O shots in damp Dixie cups. Not some guy who smells like cheap beer and sweat.

This.

I wanted Alex Belrose.

And not in a childish-crush way. Not in the stupid way that

everyone kisses in the high school hallways and fights about prom dates and makes out in their parents' basements.

I really wanted him. Truly. So much I can barely stand it. So much it hurts in my chest.

"I'd like to see more of you," Belrose—Alex says. He reaches for me, but then pulls his hand back, like he's unsure how I'll respond. Slowly, I reach out, and I brush my fingers against his. He catches my hand and holds it.

"I'd be okay with that."

"Maybe you could come over and . . . um . . . we could read. Or something. And we could catch up?"

I nod. "Yeah. Of course."

He smiles, and I stand up, and he stands too. He pulls my scarf out of his pocket and loops it around my shoulders, using it to pull me close to him, so our chests are almost touching and I can feel the heat of him near me.

My pulse quickens. I feel his breath on my face.

"I like you, Riley Stone."

"I like you too . . . Alex."

"I like when you call me that." He tugs me a little closer with my scarf. "Can I see you again soon?"

I nod. "Yes."

"Do you promise?" he asks.

"I promise."

He releases the scarf. "Good girl."

THIRTEEN

New

"Two suitcases? *Two?*"

Kolbie pants as she lugs the second leather suitcase into my room. "You could have helped."

I cross my arms. "Uh, I asked you to bring over a few outfits, not your entire wardrobe."

Kolbie gives me her sassiest hair flip. "Seriously? Don't exaggerate. You know it would take a moving truck to get all my clothes up here. Plus they wouldn't fit in your pitiful excuse for a closet." She casts her eyes toward my non-walk-in closet, which holds all my clothes quite nicely, thank you very much.

I hold up my palm. "Okay, can you tone down the sass, please? My wardrobe is actually pretty serviceable. I just want to try something new."

"Well, your wardrobe isn't pitiful. It just needs expansion. Oh, and I bought you makeup! I'm so excited to be able to make you over!" She does a happy little hop.

"I have makeup." I nod toward my little bathroom, where I have a couple of things I apply to my face every morning. It's very conservative, but it's adequate. I look perfectly presentable.

She unfolds a cosmetic bag across my bed. It looks like an artist's palette. "No, *I* have makeup."

I approach my bed cautiously. What is this girl doing? I asked for new style, not to appear on *What Not to Wear: Kolbie Edition*. I am looking for exploration, not a whole new Riley.

"It's okay," Kolbie says slowly, guiding me to a chair and sitting me down. "It's not a wild animal. It's not going to bite you. Besides, I owe you, don't I?"

"No," I say.

"Please. You were up with me until midnight going over my college applications with me, and I know for a fact you half wrote an entrance essay for Neta last week. The least I can do is fix you up." She tousles my hair, and I resist the urge to smooth it down.

"I'm not, like, fashionably challenged here," I say. "I don't want to go straight to Crazytown. I just want a little flair."

Kolbie begins sharpening an eye pencil. "Girl, I have got you a little flair. Relax, okay? This is going to be fun. And if you hate it, you can go straight back to J.Crew with the rest of your kind, okay?"

"What does that mean?"

"Nothing," she says innocently. "Now, what do you use for an eye primer?"

"A what?"

She groans theatrically and makes fists. "I have so much work to do with you. I for real need your foundation, though, because mine is not going to work on that pasty-ass skin of yours. Now stop squirming."

"I'm not even!"

"You are too!"

"Then stop pointing that eye pencil at me like it's a weapon!"

She puts it down and laughs. "Damn, Ri. Has anyone ever told you your room is too clean?" She leans over and unzips her other suitcase, and then pulls out the Bluetooth speaker she brought to study hall and turns it up. "Do your parents care if we have wine?" She pulls out a few little Sutter Home bottles.

I shrug. "If we don't drive, I guess."

The truth is, I don't know what they'd think. But as long as we aren't incredibly obvious I don't think they'd mind. Besides, the last time my mother checked on me in my room, I think I was, like, nine and playing with toy horses and had some sort of accident with red Kool-Aid that resulted in my mother having to replace my carpet.

I unscrew the cap on mine and try a sip. It's a little bitter and sugary all at once. "What is this?"

"Uh, chardonnay, I think." She tries a sip too. "It's good, right?"

"I guess. I don't really know anything about wine. My parents only let me drink a glass on holidays. And at communion at church."

"I thought that was grape juice."

I give her a withering look. "Please. The blood of Christ is *not* grape juice at my church."

She holds up a perfectly manicured hand. "Whatever. Hey, I was going to ask you. What's the deal with the sudden makeover request? And you wanting to go to parties and skip class all of a sudden?"

"Because I want to."

Kolbie gives me a look. I know the look. It's basically saying, *Come on, I'm not that stupid.* That is the problem with having smart friends who are not total clichés. In movies, the three popular girls are always, like, traipsing down the hallways at schools in tiny clothes and looking gorgeous and never actually doing schoolwork. But my girls are not just caricatures.

"It's not about a guy," I say. "It doesn't always have to be about a guy."

Lie number one.

"I know it's not."

"I'm just tired of being the same and looking the same. I'm bored. I want to have some fun, you know? Before high school ends? Isn't this supposed to be, like, the best time of our lives and stuff?"

Kolbie takes another sip of her wine and sits it on the end of my dresser. She begins laying the clothes out along my bed. "First of all, no. If high school is the best time of our lives, that's kind of sad. That means you're getting all the good stuff out of the way pretty fast, doesn't it?"

I smile at my friend. She really is brilliant. And of course she doesn't get enough credit for it on account of being super beautiful.

"I guess so. But still. Even that idea . . . doesn't that mean I should be having more fun than I'm having?"

Kolbie starts hanging her clothes along my closet doors. "If you want to have more fun, have more fun. Just do it, you know? Seriously. I'll tell you what. Jamal is going to be in town this weekend, he's bringing one of his good friends. And honestly, it's fun to date. So why don't you come along next time?"

"I told you this wasn't about finding a man."

Kolbie looks back at me over her shoulder. "It doesn't have to be. It's about getting out of the prison you call a comfort zone. So have fun. And if you like the guy, awesome. And if not, well, you hopefully had a good time and you ate some pizza or whatever. And I promise it'll be better than a lame party. Okay?"

I hesitate.

What about Belrose?

What about *Alex*?

But that's why I need to. I can't look like I have any attachment to him whatsoever.

I have to do this. For us.

"I'm in."

Kolbie beams at me. She pushes her hair back into a knot on top of her head, like a ballet dancer.

"Now, the look is professional chic. I am thinking this"—she pulls a pencil skirt off the bed—"with these and these"—she yanks a pair of patterned black tights out of her second suitcase.

"And I'm thinking maybe a cute V-neck, fitted, of course, with a scarf."

"I have the scarf. It's special."

I pull the scarf from the night before out of my closet and wrap it around my neck. It still smells like him—just a hint of his cologne lingers.

Kolbie taps a finger on her lips and juts her hip out, considering. "Why that scarf? You wear it all the time."

"This look has to have a little *me* in it, right? Besides, I got it shopping with you and Neta." I bury my fingers in it, daring her to make me take it off.

Kolbie shoves the clothes into my arms. "Okay, okay. Go. Try on. I have three more combos we can go through, and yes, you can borrow these. And I know you don't wear glasses, but it would be totally on point if we could get you some nonprescription frames. I'm thinking a round black plastic frame? Yes?"

I make a face. "I am not going to be *one of those girls*."

"There is nothing wrong with being one of those girls, Riley. Stop being judgy. Listen to the master." She points at herself. "Wear things because they make you feel good about yourself. Not because you think you should or shouldn't."

"Are you going to write a self-help book in the near future?" I ask innocently. "I think Oprah has it covered, but if you want to go for that, I mean, shoot for the stars—"

"Are you going to keep being a bitch to the girl who is going to do your mascara in about ten minutes?"

I laugh. I can't help it. I love Kolbie. "Point taken."

"Good. Now try on those clothes before we worry about the makeup, I guess. And then we're going to Instagram the hell out of this."

I smile a little to myself. Normally I wouldn't let her put anything on my Instagram. I reserve it for cute coffee mugs and perfectly round waffles and generally keep my face out of it.

But maybe, just maybe, someone important will be checking in.

FOURTEEN

Dinner

I cut through the alley again.

It's safer that way. I come from the opposite direction, and I wear a big black hat with my hair tucked up under it and a large coat.

I don't see anyone in the alley.

The door is unlocked, so I let myself in through the back door, into a den sort of room with a squishy brown leather couch and a fireplace. The décor is spare and a bit lowbrow, and not at all what I'd expect from Jacqueline Belrose—it's actually a little kitschy, all HOME SWEET HOME signs and flowers, like maybe it was lifted out of an outdated *Good Housekeeping*. A squatty little table holds a cookbook and a bouquet of dusty plastic flowers.

"Hey!"

I hear Alex's voice through a door. "Hey," I call. "It's me."

"Come into the kitchen!" he calls back, and I follow a red runner rug through the den and into a little kitchen with a small white table and yellow curtains. Two matching rooster salt and pepper shakers sit in the middle of the table, wings extended and necks out.

"Riley!" He sees me and grins, wrapping me in a quick hug, his arms around my body, and then releases me. "Sit. Please. I'm almost done." He pulls out a chair for me at the kitchen table, which is . . . set for two.

He pours me a small glass of red wine, then swirls it around, lifting it to his nose. "Do you like Malbec?"

I bite back a smile. I have no idea what Malbec is. "I love Malbec."

"I wasn't expecting you for a while," he says. "I thought you had cheerleading practice."

"I pretended I was sick and asked my cocaptain to take over," I tell him, and almost immediately regret it. Why was I so eager? Why did I do that? He's used to girls falling all over him. I should be different. I am special, after all. But instead of practice, I'd gone home to fix up my makeup exactly the way Kolbie taught me (well, a toned-down version of the way Kolbie taught me) and get pretty for Alex Belrose.

"That's sweet," he says. "You didn't have to do that."

"I just wasn't feeling it anyway."

He pours another glass of wine and takes a sip. "I'm glad you're here, Riley. I wanted to see you."

I want to smile and duck my head, but I force myself to meet his eyes. "Me too, Alex."

"God, I love when you say my name."

His voice sends shivers down my spine. "Yeah?" I grab my glass of wine and take a sip. "That's okay?"

"It's good." He turns to open the oven, and a warm, citrusy smell fills the room. "I think it's done."

"What did you make?" I ask. I can't believe he cooked for me. He must—he must actually *like* me. *Like* like me. I have the jitters. I busy myself with spreading the yellow napkin next to my plate across my lap. This is like a date. A real date. This is what couples do.

"Lemon-pepper salmon," he says, pulling an oven mitt over his hand. He pulls the tray out. "I hope you like fish."

"I do," I say, saying a silent thank-you that he didn't cook tilapia, which I personally think is too gross to eat. "Thank you so much for cooking."

"You're welcome." He takes my plate and hands it back with a salmon fillet and a few spears of asparagus. "My grandfather was actually a chef, so most of my family can cook really well."

"That's cool. Did he have his own restaurant?"

Alex sits down across from me with his own plate. "Yeah. It was called the Belrose. Creative, right? Anyway, it did really well until he died. My dad tried to take it over, but it wasn't the same without my grandfather. We were struggling to keep it afloat, so my dad sold it."

"I'm sorry."

"Yeah. Me too." He smiles, but it's missing some of the happiness that should be attached to it. "My grandmother, I guess, was the saddest. She is the only one of us who can't cook. Like, at all. She did all the financials for the restaurant because she would burn, like, *everything*. She tries to microwave something and it starts on fire."

I start to laugh. "That sounds like my mom, honestly." I take a forkful of salmon. It's delicious and flavorful, and it really does taste like something I would order at a fancy restaurant. "One time she tried to make my brother chocolate chip cookies and she started a fire in the oven. She forgot to add the flour."

Alex points at me with his fork, a piece of asparagus speared onto the end. "My grandfather actually kept an extra fire extinguisher in the kitchen specifically because of my grandmother. I mean, he forbid her from ever going in there, but every once in a while she'd try to make coffee or something and bring about world-ending fumes. Like, you could die if you went near. It was a hazard."

I giggle. "With coffee?"

He nods solemnly. "You have no idea. She's in a rest home now, and the nurses won't even let her try *tea*. To be fair, they probably don't let anyone, but they actually have good reason with her."

"Do you see her often?"

He pauses while he finishes chewing. "Not like I'd like. She's in Oregon."

"That's hard."

"Yeah."

We're quiet for a minute. I'm lucky. Even though my family feels remarkably distant sometimes, they're all close and here and alive. Most people experience death in some major way by the time they're in high school, it seems. But I haven't. I've been charmed.

Perfect Riley Stone and Her Perfect Life.

"This is really good," I tell him. "Like, really, really good."

"Thanks," he says. "It's one of my signature dishes."

"I'm glad you can cook," I say. "Because it's not one of my strengths."

Alex pretends to be shocked. He lets his fork drop from his fingers. It clatters onto his plate. "I thought you didn't have any *not-strengths*."

"I have several not-strengths," I confess, solemn.

"Tell me," he says. "Because right now, I sort of think you're perfect." He reaches across the table and brushes my hand with the very tips of his fingers, and it starts this strange sort of reaction in my body, beginning in my hand and then running through my veins and settling somewhere in my lower belly.

I bite my lip. "I sort of think you're perfect too."

"So give me a confession," he urges, his fingers still on the back of my hand. "Tell me something."

I want him to run his hand up my arm. I want more of those fingers. I want to tell him that.

"Well, I'm very bad at riding bicycles."

He smiles at me, anticipating a joke. "How can you be bad at riding a bicycle? Isn't that a rite of passage for kids everywhere?"

"I just suck. I think I have a bad center of balance or something. I just can't do it. It's stupid."

"You're lucky, you know." He stops stroking my hand, and I

long for his fingers back. I want to grasp at them, but I will my hands to stay still on the table.

"Lucky? How?" I look at his green eyes, the scruff growing on his cheeks.

His lips.

"I'm an excellent bicyclist. I could teach you."

"Teach me?" I ask. I smile even harder, smile from deep in my chest. I imagine his hands around my waist, steadying me. "When?"

"Maybe we meet in the middle of the night," he says. His hand slips under mine from across the table and squeezes. "Maybe we put the bikes in the back of my truck and go out to the country. And I can teach you there. And we'll get dusty out on the dirt roads and ride until the sun comes up."

I squeeze back. "That sounds perfect," I breathe.

"And you'll cook for me," Alex says.

I move back slightly. "Wait, what?" That was . . . a leap.

"Please?" he pleads. He blinks. His eyelashes are gorgeous. He's gorgeous. "Next time. Tell me what ingredients you need and cook for me. I promise to eat it even if it's terrible."

"The only thing I know how to make is, like, the little mini pizzas that Ms. Archer taught us to put together in Family and Consumer Sciences last year," I say. Which, of course, I got an A on. That and monkey bread, but I can't make Alex monkey bread and call it a meal. And I can make a mean plate of brownies, but that leaves me in the same place as monkey bread.

That's not to say I haven't had a yoga-pants-and-monkey-bread day or eight.

Alex releases my hands and stands from the table. He rummages through a kitchen door and comes back with a pad and paper. "Okay, Riley. Tell me what you need for mini pizzas. I'll bring back the ingredients, and you cook them for me. Okay?"

"Um, okay." I smile. "Will you help?"

He pretends to think. "A little. Maybe. If you're good."

I laugh. "I'm always good."

He watches me. "Are you, though?"

I duck my head, unsure of the answer. I am, but I'm not. I'm not. I am.

My heart does this strange twisty thing.

"Ingredients?" he presses, and I list them off the best I can remember, and promise to meet him again in two days.

This time, when I say good-bye, he touches me. His hands touch my back, and trace up and down. I stare at his lips and I tilt my chin upward, but he doesn't kiss me. My hands touch his shoulders tentatively and slide down to his chest. He is thin but all hard muscle.

"Soon," he promises.

I leave, full and starving at the same time.

Things to Know About Riley Stone:

- In third grade, Riley Stone was caught cheating on a spelling test. Because it was her first offense, she received a zero on the test but was not suspended or given detention.
- Riley's teacher suggested that Riley was under too much stress and called her parents in for a special conference. She was worried about Riley's personal development and wanted her parents to understand the amount of pressure their daughter was putting on herself to succeed.
- Riley never cheated again.
- Sometimes, even girls who do everything right make mistakes.

FIFTEEN
Italian

"I am going to make my pizza in the shape of a dinosaur," Alex announces. "And it will definitely kick your pizza's ass."

"Mine is definitely going to be cooler than that," I say, trying to roll out the dough properly. Honestly, I'm not even sure I've made the dough right, or if a pizza in the shape of a dinosaur would cook evenly. But I don't care. I'm happy in a strange, jittery way that I've never been happy before, and these pizzas will be perfect even if they cook black.

"How can you beat a dinosaur?" he asks, pretending to be offended. "You can't."

I grin at him. I grin at him all the time. It's hard in class, because all I want to do is grin at him, but I have to be studious and quiet and uninterested and sit in the same seat and do the work like I'm not going to his house at night. So I bite at the inside of my cheeks and grip my pencil a bit harder and think about later, when I'll be all his and he'll be all mine.

"I can," I say. "Easy."

"How?" he demands.

"A baby sea otter, maybe." I pull the dough into two pieces and toss him half.

"So," he says. "You're going to beat my dinosaur with sheer adorableness?"

I began shaping the dough with my hands. "It's a pretty fool-proof plan. You have to admit."

"It's so good I want to help." Alex abandons his lump of dough in the flour and stands next to me. Very, very close. I smile up at him. He's a floury mess, and I know I am too. His normally perfect hair has a dusting of the fine white powder in it, and there is just a smudge above his left eyebrow.

I'm not a very neat cook.

"How do you intend to improve on this?" I ask, gesturing at the vaguely otterlike shape that could also be a very good eggplant.

He steps behind me and puts his hands over mine. "Like this. Let the master work. I had a solid B in pottery, Riley."

I giggle. "Show me," I say.

"Well, you have to work with me." His breath is hot on my neck. His fingers interlace with mine, and we're both working the dough together. "How is this like an otter?"

"Like this," he says, and squishes it into an unrecognizable lump.

"Alex!" I cry, and spin around. I push at him with my doughy hands. "You ruined my otter-pizza!"

He doesn't laugh.

He doesn't move, either.

He's just there, close, looking down at me. He's not smiling. He's inches away, and he steps closer, so our bodies are touching.

We're touching.

I reach back, my hands trying to find purchase on his counter. "Um, Alex?"

He touches my chin, very gently. "Riley," he breathes.

And then he's all the way against me and his mouth is against mine and he's kissing me. He's kissing me nice and soft and slow, and I'm kissing him back the same way, my eyes closed, but my heart is doing something crazy, hammering like I'm going to die, right here, while Alex is kissing me.

He pulls away. "Are you okay?" he whispers, his lips next to my ear. His hand slides to the back of my neck.

"Yes," I whisper back. "I'm okay."

I am.

He kisses my neck. He kisses the bit of my chest that is exposed above my shirt.

And then Alex Belrose lifts me up onto the counter. He steps between my legs.

"You," he says, "are gorgeous, Riley."

And then he kisses me more. Pretty soon, I forget to think

about what I'm doing and his tongue slips into my mouth and he isn't so gentle anymore but I don't care because my hands aren't hanging onto the counter anymore either. They're on him.

And that is the story of my first real kiss.

Also, we ordered pizza.

SIXTEEN
Waiting

"You'll have to wait for me tonight," I tell Alex, my voice just above a whisper.

I've caught him in between classes, and I'm bending over his desk, frowning at a scholarship application. I point at a blank space, like I'm asking him a question.

He looks at me, his brows drawing together. "Wait?"

He's not used to waiting. He's used to getting what he wants.

"I can't skip cheerleading again," I murmur, moving my fingers to the next field, like this is just a normal discussion and we're just people, normal people. "I've already missed three practices. The girls are getting suspicious. So just hang on, and I'll be over after. Okay?"

He hesitates, and I know he wants to tell me no, that I should skip cheerleading practice and spend the time with him. But we're both sensible people. Sensible people who will do sensible things and not get caught.

Sensible people who know this is wrong by everyone else's standards.

But not by ours.

"I'll miss you," he murmurs. He casts a glance toward the doorway, but no students filter in. "What will I do without you?"

"I'll be fast. I'm head cheerleader, remember? I run the practice. Let me make sure we're good on our routines, and I'll be over before you know it."

Alex points to something on the application, and I fill in the bubbles above his finger without thinking, the marks messy and outside the lines. "Have your . . . has your family mentioned how late you're getting home?"

I choke back a short laugh. "They have not noticed. They don't ask where I am. I'm the good kid, remember? Ethan was the troubled one."

Alex smiles wryly. "You're *very* good." But the tone of his voice is slick and suggests something different and I suddenly feel warm and strange and I wish we were at his house and he was kissing me again.

That's all we've done. Kiss.

I think I'm getting good at it.

Alex clears his throat. "Just finish the second and third pages at home, and then drop it by tomorrow, okay, Riley?"

I glance up. Emilio Rivera has dumped his bag onto the floor and is digging around in it, throwing crumpled papers out on the tiles. Probably the extra-credit work that Alex assigned last class. Three points for writing a two-paragraph report on I-can't-remember-what. A-students weren't eligible, so I didn't bother to write it down.

I nod and gather up the pages, very neatly, taking my time. I wouldn't have hurried before "us."

I won't hurry now.

I tuck the scholarship pages into a folder, slide the folder into my bag, and don't check to see if Alex is watching me as I leave his classroom. I know it doesn't matter if he is.

Because he's mine.

All mine.

I head in the direction of the gymnasium, stick my backpack into my locker, and slip into my cheerleading gear. I'm the first one there, as usual, but before long Neta shows up, and then Bella Cooper, the cocaptain, who takes over when I'm sick. Mrs. Hernandez, the cheerleading coach, only shows up when she can, but she trusts me to run most practices. I've been in gymnastics and cheer since I was a really little girl, and I'm very good at it. And despite the fact that I have been avoiding it, I do love it. A lot.

"Riley!" Bella says, bouncing up to me as I stretch out. "Are you feeling better?"

I smile up at her from a frog position, taking her in. Bella is solid and perfect in about every way, and I try to stand her the best I can. "Yeah. Thanks for asking. Get stretched out, okay? I want a good, hard practice today."

She puts her hands on her hips and looks down at me. "Are you sure? Maybe you should ease into it. You've been delicate and all." Her tone is peppy, but I've been cheering with her since fourth grade, so I can hear the slight accusatory tone.

"I'm sure she can handle it." Neta plops down next to me into a butterfly stretch, pulling her feet in.

I smile up at Bella. "I've got it," I confirm.

Bella is the type of person who would run a cheerleading practice like we were in a daycare. I'm all for kindness and everything, but if it were her, we'd spend half the practice sitting in a circle on the gym floor holding hands and humming "Kumbaya" at a friendly volume. She thinks I push the team too hard, but that's also why we're good. If I left her in charge for too long, she'd petition to have us removed from competitions on the basis that she wants to be friends with everyone and doesn't like hurting anyone's feelings.

Of course, Bella used to be a lot more like me, but ever since her little brother was put into a juvenile delinquent facility three years ago she's insistent on being very amiable all the time. I personally think she developed the character trait as a coping strategy.

When the whole team is on the floor, I raise my voice a little. Everyone turns toward me. I know how to command power without yelling.

I feel a smile in the muscles of my lips, but I tamp it down.

"All right, girls. Get a stretching partner and count off, okay? As soon as you're done, we're in for some tumbling practice. I know it's basic, but we don't have room for sloppy stuff right now. Then, we'll do some jumps, and we'll take a short break and do some stunting. Okay? I want everything super clean today. We don't have any room for injuries. Everything *will* be tight for the games, and we're going to petition to get more competitions. We'll finish with some cheers and chants as usual, and I need to go over some final thoughts."

The group finishes their stretches and lines up on the black line running the length of the gymnasium, and we begin counting off cartwheels and handsprings. We always do this—start simple. Keep it clean. And then it gets more complex. I pull off a neat back handspring followed by a roundoff back handspring, and Neta whoops and gives me a high five.

"Looks good, Stone!" she says.

"Thanks!" I smile. "Give it a shot!"

She nods and bounces a couple of times and executes the roundoff-back-handspring combo perfectly.

"Gorgeous," I tell her, and she flips her ponytail.

There is no room for Alex in my head during cheerleading. One false move, and someone could be seriously hurt. He sneaks into my mind a couple of times, but I kick him right back out.

There is plenty of room for Alex *after* cheerleading, naturally. There is plenty of room for me in his house. In his arms.

"You're looking great," Neta tells me halfway through practice, when I give the team its second water break. She pats me on the butt.

I smile back at her. I feel good. "You too, Neta."

In fact, I barely even think of Alex.

At least, I don't until Fatima Patel pokes me in the arm after a single-twist basket toss. "Hey," she whispers. "Don't look now—but I think Mr. Belrose is checking us out." She giggles and throws her thick black braid over her shoulder.

I look toward the double doors that lead into the hallway of the high school, and there he is: Alex Belrose, in a T-shirt and shorts, like maybe he's been working out in the weight room or something, his arms crossed over his chest, a smile on his face.

And I can't tell if he's smiling because of me . . . or he's smiling because of everyone.

"Finish your jumps, girls!" I bark. "Toe-touches! Five, six, seven, eight!"

There is suddenly more giggling than necessary for something so simple. And then, of course, the team executes the jumps flawlessly.

"Okay. Herkies, then."

I join the girls, and we jump together. I don't look toward the doorway, but I can feel Belrose there, watching.

"Did he see?" Fatima asks, flicking a sweaty piece of hair that has escaped from her braid off her neck. Her pretty cheerleader smile is perched in place and she looks gorgeous, as usual.

That is Fatima, of course. She isn't a great student—she scores Cs, usually—is perpetually late to class, and always has a button in the wrong place or a shoelace untied—but she looks incredible doing it, and actually, quite secretly, puts in a lot of work on her I-woke-up-like-this selfies that she runs through at least three filters.

I feel hot, thick jealousy in my chest that makes it almost impossible to breathe. "Again!" I shout, and they're jumping again, and I know Alex hasn't left the doorway, and everyone is jumping extra hard, trying to look good for him, and they're *my* cheerleaders, so of course they do.

I want them to stop.

"Okay, everyone. Let's break for water." I clap, and they head to the bleachers—and then to the door.

Where Alex is standing, his arm outstretched, hand out, the *not*-Belrose grin on his face that's supposed to be for me.

Just for me.

And my entire team runs past on the way to the water fountain and high-fives him. Including Neta.

When they all have perfectly good water bottles in the bleachers.

Better water bottles, actually, because everyone knows that water fountains are disgusting places where germs go to live and breed and create mutant diseases than can take out entire populations.

Pathetic.

I walk to the bleachers by myself and grab my purple water bottle. Neta comes back to sit by me.

"Wow, Ri, you couldn't even line up for a high five?" Neta asks. She settles down beside me on the bleachers. "I mean, you have to admit he's hot."

"Whatever. Can we just get back to practicing?" I push away from the bleachers. "Stunting, please."

"That was barely a break," Claire Meadows mutters.

"Line up, please." I clap. "Now, let's go. No more distractions."

I don't glance back at the door, but I don't make practice

short, either. I make it long. Extra long. We go through stunts and cheers and do a second round of jumps. The team drags before the end of it. My legs scream with every additional movement, but I don't care.

When I finally let the team go and I'm taking off my shoes, my phone vibrates. It's an e-mail.

Are you coming over?

The jealousy curls around my heart and squeezes.

This is all too far. This whole relationship. Him and me. Everything is wrong. Everything. And I can't handle this. I can't handle him and me and the cheerleaders and the high fives and all this bullshit.

It's just *wrong* and it's been wrong the whole time and I've been an absolute *fool*.

No thank you, I e-mail back.

And then I turn off my phone.

I am done.

SEVENTEEN

To Play

French class is French class.

Alex is Mr. Belrose.

I am a student. A straight-A student and head cheerleader. Someone who made a mistake and knows it.

I am a student who does not put up with anyone flirting with other girls. Especially not right in front of her.

Mr. Belrose hands out our essays. I haven't let myself e-mail him or see him. I am good. I am the good girl everyone always thought I was.

He pauses a millisecond longer at my desk. A millisecond only I notice. I face straight forward. Thea giggles and tries to draw his attention.

He doesn't even look at her.

"Verb forms," Mr. Belrose says. "Let's start with, uh, Miss Stone. Riley—'to love.'"

"Oh. Hmm. I think it's *jouer*."

I fix him with an icy stare.

I have given him the French word for "play." Because that's what he's done to me.

Play. I am his little game.

"*Aimer*, Mademoiselle Stone. Incorrect. Surprising."

I stare at him, arms crossed over my chest, daring him to question me further.

He doesn't. He moves on to Keatra, and then to Cay, then Garrett, and Teri Von Millhouse.

He doesn't come back to me.

I don't meet his eyes.

And when the bell rings, I pack up my books.

"Riley, I'll need you to stay after class, please," Mr. Belrose says. He's not asking, either. His voice is a quiet command, and I want nothing more than to walk out the door with the rest of the students.

"Why?" I ask. My tone isn't the respectful one I save for teachers, either. But he isn't just my teacher anymore.

He doesn't answer, only watches as the students file out of the room. I watch them too, my backpack slung over one arm. I drop it on the floor as Mr. Belrose follows Thea to the door and closes it after her.

And then we're alone.

In his classroom.

During school hours.

Alarms go off in my head.

"You're ignoring my e-mails," he says.

I tilt my head at him. I had thought Alex Belrose was a smart guy. But he's not acting like one. Not at all. "Well, I haven't wanted to respond, particularly. Or see you."

"Can I ask why?" His voice is quiet. And a little dangerous.

"How many special students do you have?"

"Excuse me?" He leans in, his hand next to his ear.

"How many goddamn girls are you inviting over?" I ask. "One for every high five?"

He smiles, his mouth pulled up just a little farther on one side than the other. "Is that what all this is about?" He motions at me.

I stand up a little straighter. "What do you think it's about?"

"You think—you think there are others, Riley?"

"How am I supposed to know, Alex?" I snap, and then hate myself for using his name. Damn it. He's not Alex anymore. He's Mr. Belrose. My teacher.

Not someone who is fun to kiss.

He takes a step toward me, and I fight not to step back. I have to be strong.

"You're the only one, Riley," he whispers. "There's no one else. I swear to God. There's no one else in the world."

"How am I supposed to believe that?" I look at his eyes, but he doesn't blink. He looks at me straight-on.

"Because you're the only one I'd ever take this kind of risk for,

Riley. And I can't stop thinking about you. Not for one second. And it's driving me insane to know you're angry at me."

He reaches out and links his fingers in mine. I don't pull away. His hands are shaking.

"Will you come back to me? Please?" he pleads.

I feel my insides softening.

"I only came to your practice to see you. I'm sorry for upsetting you. Besides, I have something really special planned. Just promise you'll come see it tonight. If you hate it, you can leave." His fingers tighten on my hand.

I hesitate, dropping my head.

"Please, Riley." His fingers find the bottom of my chin and lift it, and he's staring into me. "I'm begging you. Please do this. For me."

I nod, even though my stomach feels cold and hard, like I've just had a gallon of too-cold water. "I guess. But this is for me. Not for you."

He smiles at me. "God, I want to kiss you so badly right now."

"Do it." I dare him. My words are hard and angry and I want him to but I don't. I want him to hold me and never let go and I want him to leave me alone forever.

I'm not entirely sure if I forgive him.

The classroom door swings open behind us, and he drops my hand and my chin like he was never holding me and jams them both in his pockets, like his skin has some residue left on it, some evidence that he was touching me.

"Due Monday," he reminds me, like that's what we were discussing all along. "And remember the bibliography."

I scoff.

What a terrible cover.

Like Riley Stone would *ever* forget a bibliography.

I walk out.

No looking back.

Riley Stone never looks back.

EIGHTEEN
Gifts

It is dark tonight, and unseasonably cold. I vary the times when I arrive at the Belrose house, but I don't think any neighbors have seen me. I dress quietly, and I wear hats pulled low over my face, but even so I change where I park, and my clothing, too. Tonight, I arrived well after the sun went down, and the cloudy night sky hid me well. Summer is barely gone, but the air already feels like winter. It's strange. Everyone says it's due to climate change, because normally at this time everyone would still be wearing shorts and running their sprinklers and lolling about on their lawns with glasses of lemonade on Sundays.

It's lucky for me that the early cold is keeping everyone indoors. And there was no one to see me slip toward the dark home.

There are no lights on in the Belrose house.

But when I push on the back door, it swings in, like he was waiting for me. And that is where I am right now.

I stand in the den, alone. I unwrap my scarf from my neck. Something is different.

"Hello?" I call, and I take a step inside. The house isn't completely dark . . . there's a faint glow coming from the hallway. I close the door softly behind me, my senses blinking on high alert.

My heart beats a little oddly. Is everything okay? I tiptoe toward the faint light. Why is everything off? Alex asked me to come. Did he forget? Is he gone?

Is Jacqueline somehow back and he wants me to leave?

I move toward the glow, my heart beating thunderously in my ears.

Oh.

Oh.

Several gorgeous, white, long-stemmed candles line the hallway. I follow the path down the hallway and through the little kitchen where we've cooked together, and finally, into his living room. And there he is. Alex. He looks at me, over his arm, which is on the back of the couch.

"Come sit with me, Riley."

No one has ever lit candles for me before. I thought it was something that only happened in movies. Silly movies. But he did it.

I walk to the front of the couch and curl into the crook of his arm, so that my back is against his chest.

"Hello," I purr against him.

"Hello," he says, smoothing my hair back. "I'm happy you're here."

"I am too."

And I am. The strange feeling in my stomach is all but gone. He wraps his arms around me and pulls me tight. "I have something for you," he whispers.

"You don't have to get me things," I murmur. And I mean it. I'm not the type of girl who needs *things*. But all the same, I'm excited.

"Close your eyes and hold out your hands," he whispers in my ear. He untangles his arms, and he places something in my palms . . . something light. "Okay. You can open them."

My eyes open. In my hands is a small rectangular box wrapped in light periwinkle paper, tied with a pretty white bow.

"A present! What is it?" I turn it over and look at the bottom, as if that will give me some sort of clue that I'm missing.

"You'll have to open it," he says. He touches my arm. "I hope you like it."

I slide my index finger under the paper, opening it neatly. He's given me something. Something special. He's lit candles and he's given me a real gift, something I can hold on to and keep. I unfold the paper, and there's a dark blue velvet box inside. Is it jewelry? I give him a quizzical look.

He smiles and nods.

I lift the top off the box.

It's a necklace.

He's given me a necklace. It is a tiny wooden chess piece on a delicate chain. A king.

My fingers stray to the hollow below my throat, where the little charm will hang when I wear it.

"It's gorgeous," I tell him.

He works the clasp apart. "Hold up your hair," he tells me, and I gather it all up while he drapes the necklace around my neck. The wood is cool against my skin. "I got this at a little shop in Paris," he says, "just along the Seine."

I let my hair drop and turn to face him, my fingers running up and down the little chain. "It's from Paris?" I breathe. I've never owned anything from Paris. Not anything from out of the country, until you count the little sand candle my aunt brought me from Puerto Vallarta.

"The man who owns the shop makes the charms by hand, and his vision is slowly failing, but his jewelry, it's all beautiful. It all has these tiny imperfections, you see, so they're all completely one of a kind. And I used to love chess when I was little. I played it against my grandfather at night after he closed the restaurant." He touches the necklace with a knuckle, and then leans in, his lips just barely grazing mine. "Do you like it, Riley?" he asks, his lips moving against mine.

"I adore it."

I'm not lying. I love it all. I love the candles and the necklace and his lips and his arms and being his. I smile, and I smile with my whole entire heart, in a way that I don't think I have ever smiled before.

I don't let myself think about how he originally bought the necklace for anyone else.

"Will you think of me whenever you wear it?"

I nod.

"I'm so sorry I made you feel insecure," he whispers.

Wait. Insecure? No one has ever—*ever*—called Riley Stone insecure.

I am *not* insecure.

I just have standards that do not involve whoever I am seeing high-fiving entire teams of girls who are doing cheers for him, that's all.

But then Alex's hands are on my back and his lips are on mine and I forget that maybe, just maybe, I'm a little insulted and I remember he has given me a necklace and we are us again and everything is going to be okay.

I know it is.

NINETEEN
Rules

Rules for dating your teacher:
- Don't skip multiple cheerleading practices. This goes double when you are the head cheerleader.
- Don't look at him any more than normal. Or less than normal. Don't smile at him.
- Ace your homework.
- Don't stab any of the girls who swoon over your teacher in the eye holes, no matter how tempting. This goes double for Thea Arnold.

He slipped a note in between the pages of my homework.

Life is better with you.

Tonight. I left my response beneath his grading binder when no one else was around.

We leave each other these little notes. We don't sign them. We don't write like ourselves. But we know who they're from. No one else would send me notes the way he does.

I sneak to his house at night. On nights when I don't have practice, I slip into my track tights and sneakers and walk over there, taking my time. My parents don't even care that I'm gone. I'm a busy girl, after all. I always have this fund-raiser or that volunteer event or this mock trial event or that.

Or *this* forbidden love affair or *that* forbidden love affair.

Or just the one.

Tonight, Alex is reading me French poetry. He isn't just paging through a book, though—he's copied his favorites into a worn-out leather-bound notebook, and the pages are a little yellowed and the penciled entries are smudged, like he's read through them a hundred times.

"You're like someone out of a story," I tell him, paging through the handwritten poetry. "You actually copied all these down?"

He nods. "It's what I did to practice my French, actually. And I thought that they were nice."

"They are nice," I tell him, and he smiles at me.

I prop my head on my hand, elbow resting on the floor. "Read me another. A love poem."

"A love poem? Are you trying to tell me something, Riley Stone?" He smiles at me over his notebook.

I roll over and look at him upside down. "Are you going to read me another pretty poem or not, Alex?"

He leans over and kisses me on the chin, then pages through his book.

"Aha! Here it is."

I turn right side up. He's pointing at a page with a corner folded down.

"It's called '*Les Roses de Saadi*,'" he tells me. "It's by this famous French poet—Marceline Desbordes-Valmore."

> *J'ai voulu ce matin te rapporter des roses;*
> *Mais j'en avais tant pris dans mes ceintures closes*
> *Que les noeuds trop serrés n'ont pu les contenir.*
>
> *Les noeuds ont éclaté. Les roses envolées*
> *Dans le vent, à la mer s'en sont toutes allées.*
> *Elles ont suivi l'eau pour ne plus revenir;*
>
> *La vague en a paru rouge et comme enflammée.*
> *Ce soir, ma robe encore en est tout embaumée . . .*
> *Respires-en sur moi l'odorant souvenir.*

"Tell me what it's about?" I ask. "Roses and the wind?"

"It's love being roses. And the wind tossing them about. This girl brings roses to her love, but the sash she has tied them with splits and they blow to the sea, and they turn the waves red."

"That's kind of sad."

"It is," he tells me.

"Why did you read me a sad love poem?"

He rolls on top of me and spreads little kisses along my neck. "So I can make you happy again."

Alex kisses me on the mouth, hard, so I can feel his teeth, and I wrap my arms and legs around him. I want him, and I want all of him, and I want my clothes off and to be in his bed, but I know that's not now. Not yet.

We've talked about it. A few weeks ago I hadn't had a real kiss, and now I'm talking about sex. Real sex, and not the giggly way I talk about it with Neta and Kolbie, but with someone who cooks for me and gives me jewelry and reads me French poetry.

"Are you ready?" he asks me, looking into my eyes, and I know what he's asking because his hand is on the button of my jeans.

I kiss him, hard, but then I turn and shake my head no into his shoulder. "Soon," I promise, but I'm lying because this is big and I'm not ready. I want to be ready. But that's a lot and that's moving fast and there's just a lot in this relationship that I haven't really thought through.

I feel him smile against my mouth. "I'm going to wait for you, Riley Stone," he says. "I promise. Do you know why?" His hip bones dig into mine, and I want him.

I do.

"Why?" I ask.

"Because I am absolutely falling in love with you."

I pull away and look into his eyes, but he's just looking down at me. I feel the weight of the necklace on my throat. "Do you mean that?"

He nods and kisses me again. "More than anything, Riley." He rolls off of me, and for a moment we're just next to each other on the living room floor. "Pretty soon, you're going to be eighteen. And you'll have graduated. And do you know what that means?"

"What?" I ask.

He smiles and touches my hair. "We can be together everywhere. Not just in secret. You won't have to sneak through the alley anymore. I can take you to the movies and to restaurants and visit you at school and you can sleep over and no one can say anything, ever."

"And Jacqueline?" I ask.

And then I hold my breath.

It's the first time I've ever mentioned Jacqueline.

Ever.

"I don't think Jacqueline's ever coming back. And if she does, we're as good as over." His voice is flat.

I want to ask him more, but the lack of emotion in his voice is strange. It excites me.

He's mine.

Really mine.

I don't think anyone in the history of the entire world has ever had a love like we have.

This is all going to work.

"Never leave me, okay, Riley?" Alex says. His tone is soft, and he tugs on a piece of my hair.

"I won't," I whisper. "It's us, forever." I put my hand on his heart, and he lifts my palm to his lips.

Things to Know About Riley Stone:

- Riley's parents were chairs of several local charities. Family outings often consisted of Saturday evening volunteer events, where Riley made several contacts.
- Riley's favorite charity is the Humane Society. However, Mr. and Mrs. Stone do not like the smell of the Humane Society kennels, so their daughter rarely had the opportunity to volunteer.
- Riley was never allowed to own a pet.
- Riley won several of her scholarships through very charitable organizations. Her entire college experience was paid off by the time she was a junior in high school, but she continued to apply for scholarships "for the experience."
- And, of course, the prestige.
- In spite of Riley's direction and planning, she has not yet chosen a major or path in life. Options include the following:
  + Doctor
  + Diplomat
  + Business owner
  + Event planner
  + President
  + Fashion designer
  + YouTuber
  + Cheerleading coach/entrepreneur

TWENTY
Fine

You're everything. Don't forget.

The note has been slipped into my locker.

I leave my finished scholarship application on his desk. "Section twelve B," I say. "I had a question."

He opens the booklet.

Tonight?

I have written the note on a bright green Post-it.

"Actually, I think we're all caught up, so nothing tonight."

I step back from his desk, stunned. Caught up? What about the note? What about us?

He looks up, but his eyes travel past me, to the door. He shuts the scholarship booklet. "This looks good, Riley. Can you turn it in before next week? That's the deadline."

"Yes, Mr. Belrose."

I turn around, and Mrs. Sanchez, the carpentry teacher, is standing in the doorway. "Alex! Will you and Jacqueline be coming to the faculty mixer next week? I heard she's back in town! I just adore her. She's so charming."

Slow flames start in my stomach and climb to my heart, and for a moment, I hate Mrs. Sanchez a little, even though I've always admired her before, based on the fact that she's dominating a male-dominated field. She's this total grandmotherly type and looks like she could turn around and pull cookies out of the oven at any moment, but instead she teaches carpentry and shows high school students how to build things. Of course, I also heard she has an insane temper and almost got fired five years ago when she threw a hammer against the wall when someone questioned her knowledge of table saws, but maybe you get that way from years of systemic sexism.

"I'm not sure. I'll ask," Mr. Belrose says, but his voice sounds normal, not like he's being torn apart inside like I currently am.

I force myself to calmly put my scholarship application in my backpack and walk to my locker, then into the bathroom near the stairwell on the first floor.

Slow.

Steady.

Calm.

I look in the mirror.

Jacqueline?

Back?

Not a big deal.

He's going to get rid of her.

The only reason he was cold to me was because he didn't want Mrs. Sanchez to see.

It's all very clear, of course.

Calm.

I smile at myself in the mirror, but it looks wrong—like I'm peeling back my lips to get a peek at my teeth.

I try again.

No better.

Of course he wouldn't want me to come over tonight. Of course. It all makes perfect sense, and I will deal with this calmly because this is what I got myself into, and I knew going into this that *complicated* was going to be an understatement.

I am very calmly sick in the toilet, and I wash my mouth out quickly in the sink before anyone catches me, then pop a stick of peppermint gum in my mouth.

Calmly.

Then I head to chem, which is a class I'm in with Kolbie. She's my lab partner.

I sit down at the lab table, brushing my hair back behind my ears and setting out my notebook and pencils on the table. I like the lab, usually. It's a change of pace from normal classes. I get to stand, move. The chemical smell of the classroom is strange and good and it makes me feel like sort of a mad scientist, in control of the whole world.

"Acid rain today, huh?" I say when Kolbie joins me. "Riveting stuff."

She snorts and ties her hair back. "If it were anyone else talking, I'd know they were being sarcastic. But knowing you—"

I smile. Already it feels better than the ones I practiced in the mirror, but still not quite right.

"What's wrong?" she demands. "I'm not pouring any acidy shit in here if you're not on your game." She puts on her safety goggles and makes an X motion with her fingers.

I keep my annoyance off my face. Of course I'm on my game. I'm always on my game. "I'm okay. I swear. I'm just a little overwhelmed."

"Maybe you should calm down every once in a while. Try to relax, and not just with dumb parties. Do something a little more you."

"What do you mean?" I ask suspiciously. What does Kolbie think is a little more *me*? Like, Science Club? Foreign Language Club? Smart People . . . Club?

"Like a book club," she suggests, completely earnest. "Where you read for fun. Or maybe—dating. But, like, just casually."

"Uh-huh."

Kolbie starts inventorying the supplies Mr. Peters has left on our lab table and slides them across to me for double-checking. "pH strips—do you think this is enough? This box is almost empty."

"We shouldn't need that many if we don't screw it up."

"And we won't. But anyway—do you remember how I told you I'd hook you up with an older guy?"

"Um, yes. I remember."

"So Jamal is coming to visit this weekend. And he's bringing his best friend since childhood, Sandeep. I have met him. He's really, really cute, and he's super nice. So anyway, I told Jamal that if you were down, we could maybe all go get dinner. Jamal really wants to try the Mexican place downtown if you're into it."

"You did that?"

"Yep." She studies me. "I think we're all good on supplies, don't you?"

I realize I've been running my hands over everything, counting them out for the third time without meaning to. But everything's here: the ammonia, the vinegar, the measuring tools. Everything.

"We're good." I know what I'm doing.

"And this weekend we're good too, right? Unless you have another fund-raiser or scholarship acceptance speech to give?"

I pause.

I think of Alex. I think of his wife.

I think of the way he spoke to me in the classroom today.

I need to do this. I need to be sure I am being a normal high school kid the same way he is pretending to be a normal husband. Besides, maybe Sandeep will be really nice.

Or maybe Alex will notice he's not my only option. He will notice I'm not pining away for him and that I am fine, just fine, just like always. Because I don't make choices I can't handle the ramifications of.

A sharp arrow of pain shoots through my heart. I try smiling again, and it feels strange and mean on my teeth. Weird how hard smiling has gotten lately.

"We're good for this weekend," I echo.

After all, I can always cancel if Alex leaves Jacqueline.

TWENTY-ONE
If

"You look super hot," Neta says. "In fact, I think you should shop in my closet more often." She twirls me in a formfitting red dress with a slightly flared skirt, and I smile. I actually feel pretty good about myself, too.

I try not to think about what Alex would say if he saw me. Would he like the dress? Would he think it was too much?

Kolbie and I are getting ready at Neta's house, because she said she wanted to live vicariously through our dates and was super pissed that Kolbie had not lined up some college-guy action for her.

"Like you couldn't get any without my help," Kolbie sniffed as she put on her eyeliner.

"Which means I needed your help?" I say, a little offended. I'm putting on my makeup by myself. I've gotten a lot better at it in the past few weeks. Of course, I could always do basic makeup, but now I'm rocking the smoky eye.

"Yep," Kolbie says.

"You don't even hesitate, do you?" I grin.

And I let her get away with it. Because she doesn't know better. And she can't know better.

My own secret gives me a little bit of mean satisfaction.

Except this week, I have barely heard from Alex.

Once, in class, I stayed a little late, and all he did was squeeze my hand and say, "Soon." But other than that, it's like we don't even know each other anymore, except as a student and teacher.

My e-mail inbox has stayed empty, although I did send him one. A simple question mark.

?

And nothing else.

But I am not pathetic. I do not stalk. I'm not going to show him how much he's hurting me.

After all, I'm *fine*.

I'm not hurt.

He said he was leaving his wife and that he didn't mind that I wasn't ready for sex, but it's fine. It's all fine.

And that's why I'm still doing this double-date thing with Kolbie and Sandeep.

"Try this, Riley," Neta said, thrusting a lipstick at me. "It'll match perfectly with your dress. Very va-va-voom."

"First of all, no one has actually said 'va-va-voom' since, like, the nineties. Secondly, I think that is just a little much for me. But thank you. The red dress is perfect, honestly." I smooth it down over my body. It really is. Neta and I are sort of the same size— except she's all curves where I'm more athletic.

Neta pouts. "Well, put it in your purse in case you're feeling sassy. Just be sure you don't get any on your teeth, okay? Mirror application *only*. Regular checks required."

"Promise." I find my black patent-leather clutch and let her slip the lipstick inside, even though I'm already committed to using the same clear gloss I always do. I already swept on a dramatic eye. The red lip would just seem like too much. I wouldn't even feel like Riley.

Although maybe that would be a good thing.

Kolbie, who is dressed in a flowy dark purple top and leather leggings, finishes her mascara. "Are you ready, Ri? The guys have been downstairs for ten minutes."

"We're late?" I ask. "Should one of us have gone downstairs or something?"

Neta giggles. "No, Ri. It's good for the guys to wait a little bit. Take your time, okay?"

Neta's right. The guys aren't even mad. Sandeep sees me and immediately kisses my hand, like we're in an old movie. "Riley, right?" he asks. "You're just as beautiful as Jamal promised."

I don't even blush, and Sandeep is actually really handsome— he has neatly cut dark hair, a sharp, strong jawline, and lovely eyes. "You're not terrible yourself."

He leans in conspiratorially. "New T-shirt," he confesses, and I laugh, because he's actually dressed in a crisp light purple button-up. "Shall we?" he asks. "I hear we're dining at a restaurant place where you actually have to *pay* for the chips and salsa. Very high-class stuff."

I take the arm he's offering, and we walk out to the car with Jamal and Kolbie, who are already kissing and cuddling. We let them have the front seat, and we climb into the back together.

"I have to tell you something," I tell Sandeep. "Something important."

"What?"

"The chips and salsa are free."

"Damn it. Are you telling me I could have worn an actual T-shirt?"

I nod solemnly. "Probably an old one. With a hole, even."

"Well, I have to be honest, then. I was trying to impress you. How am I doing?"

I tilt my hand, giving him the so-so sign. "You'll have to order guacamole. And then we'll see."

He laughs, and the sound is rich and kind. "You're funny, Riley Stone."

And I like Sandeep. When we arrive at the restaurant, he walks around the car and opens my door. And he actually pulls out my chair for me.

"Isn't he great?" Kolbie whispers in my ear as Sandeep orders extra guacamole.

And he is.

If my heart weren't all tied up in someone else, I'd really like him.

"What's your major?" I ask him.

"Engineering," he says.

"That sounds like a smart-kid major."

"It is," Jamal interrupts.

"It's Jamal's major too." Kolbie runs her hand over his chest. "His dad was an engineering major, and now he owns a construction company."

"And you?" I ask Sandeep. I grab a chip and opt for salsa instead of guacamole—just for this one.

"When I was little, I wanted to design the rockets that go into space. And I found out you had to have an engineering degree to do that, so I sort of just decided to get one." He shrugs. "So maybe someday I'll move to Texas or Alabama and work for NASA. And my rockets will be in space."

"That's pretty cool, actually," Kolbie says.

"Hey," Jamal interjects. "Mine is cool too. I'm going to take over the family business."

Kolbie leans her head on his shoulder. "I know. And you're going to build us a big house to live in, aren't you?"

Jamal runs a hand through her hair. "The biggest. With a pool and a tennis court."

"I love tennis," Kolbie says, leaning in for a kiss.

"I know you guys are relationship goals right now, but it's a little gross sometimes," Sandeep says, and I laugh.

The waitress comes to take our orders. I get fajitas, and Sandeep orders enchiladas.

And extra guacamole.

"Dude," Jamal says. "You have a problem."

Sandeep winks at me.

He's proving a point.

We all talk, and Sandeep slips an arm around the back of my chair. His hand brushes the bare skin of my arm, and I lean into it. I don't pull away.

My phone vibrates, but I ignore it.

"Don't look now," Kolbie says, "but our illustrious French teacher is here with his lovely wife." She giggles. "He must have heard me telling Sara about our double date when I was in class earlier and totally followed us."

My heart drops, but I force myself to giggle too. She thinks she's joking. "A teacher, outside of his natural habitat?" I force a laugh. "I didn't know they were allowed."

"Do I have something to be worried about?" Jamal asks, puffing out his chest.

Kolbie puts her hand on his cheek. "Of course not, baby. I like *older* men. Not old men." She kisses him again for emphasis, and I almost want to scoff. I happen to know Kolbie thinks Alex is more attractive than Jamal.

Pretending that I'm just flipping my hair, I turn my head—and there he is, sitting next to Jacqueline, at a table with maybe five others. His arm is looped around the back of her chair.

He catches my eye, but turns away quickly. I scoot my chair a little closer to Sandeep, but my heart is burning.

So much for him leaving his wife.

He's just a liar.

Which is fine. Just fine. I don't care.

Funny how much I've been telling myself that lately.

Because it hurts, deep inside me, like I've never quite had anything hurt before, and suddenly I want to be alone. But I can't do that. I can't let him ruin me like that.

When Sandeep excuses himself to go to the restroom, I pick up my phone, and finally, there's an e-mail.

Don't. Please. Don't.

What a joke. I glance back across the restaurant, and anger joins the hot jealousy burning in my chest. He's looking at me again, and his arm is unhooked from the back of her chair.

Then you don't, I type back. I look pointedly at Jacqueline, who is smiling and chatting with the rest of the table, oblivious.

"I don't think I like that guy." Jamal's still staring over at Alex's table. "He keeps looking down here. Gives me the creeps."

Kolbie snuggles into the crook of his arm. "Baby, you're being crazy. He's a weirdo teacher with a forever-young complex. Now, are you going to order me fried ice cream for dessert?"

Sandeep returns to the table and smiles at me. He's so handsome and sweet. "Do you want dessert?" he asks, noticing the open menu.

"Only if we share it," I say, trying to recapture the fun I was having before, but I feel Alex's stare on my bare shoulders.

The waitress comes back and we order two fried ice creams, and Sandeep feeds me little bites on a spoon, which makes me laugh. I feed him bites too, and one falls on his pants because my hand is shaking. He picks it off with his fingers and eats it anyway.

Sandeep thinks I am shaking because our situation is funny. But it's not anymore.

"Do you want to take a walk with me?" Sandeep asks when the bill comes. He pays it without asking, which is gentlemanly and sweet, and we don't have to do an awkward tug-of-war with the bill.

I don't let myself glance back at Alex. "Yeah. That sounds really—really nice."

He takes my hand and we walk out of the restaurant while Kolbie and Jamal are still eating ice cream at the table. I half hope Alex sees. I am no desperate girl. I am beautiful. I am desirable. I am not pining away in a puddle of tears while he goes home and makes love to the beautiful, empty wife he told me it was over with.

"I had fun," Sandeep tells me when we get outside. The night is cold, and the sky is cloudless. The moon is big, and nearly full, but the streetlights have washed away most of the starlight. I pull my coat tight around me, and the slight wind raises goose bumps on my legs.

"Me too. You're pretty cool."

He grins. "So are you. I have to admit, I was expecting someone who wanted to get drunk and party all the time. Not that there's anything wrong with that," he amends quickly. "It's just not my thing."

I sigh dramatically and put the back of my hand to my forehead. "Maybe I'm just not there yet, Sandeep."

"Work hard, and one day you will be." His voice is mock-serious. "Listen, I want to give you my number, if that's okay." He hands me a napkin from the restaurant, folded up neatly, which I stick in my coat pocket.

"Thanks," I say. "I'll text you."

And then we sort of get quiet.

We stop just under a streetlight. The stoplight under the corner casts his face red. Yellow. Green. "Do you think . . . can I kiss you?" Sandeep asks. He touches my cheek, tentatively, and his fingertips are cold.

I hesitate. "Um. Okay."

He leans in, and I lean in.

And then suddenly, all I can think of is Alex.

Please. Don't. Please.

I can't do this. I'm in too deep.

I pull away, and put my hands on Sandeep's shoulders. "I'm sorry," I tell him. "I'm so sorry. I just can't. Not yet. I'm, um, not feeling well."

And I leave him, on the corner in the streetlight, and hail a taxi to take me home. I text Kolbie that I got sick.

And I pull the napkin out of my pocket while I'm in the cab and I text Sandeep.

I'm so sorry. I had fun, but I'm just not ready.

I wish for a second I had never met Alex, because Sandeep is perfect for me: handsome and sweet and just a touch nerdy. But it's too late for that. I send one final e-mail, just after the cab drops me off in front of my house.

Keep your promise or I'll keep it for you.

He'll know what it means: get rid of Jacqueline, or I will.

TWENTY-TWO
Perfect

"Overall, I'm really pleased with this assignment," Alex—Mr. Belrose says as he passes the papers back. "There were a few of you who struggled, but I think that was probably more due to behavioral issues than anything else. Still, if any of you would like to see me after class, I'd welcome the opportunity to talk through your assignments."

We had submitted papers based on the first ten chapters of *Les Mis*. I know mine rocked, naturally. I have this whole Jean Valjean thing down pat. In fact, if we were ever to perform the play, they'd have to cast me as a lead. There would be no question, honestly.

I am more interested in my cuticles than my paper when Belrose tosses it down on my desk. The whole class, I haven't been making eye contact with him. It's his move, really. If he wants me, he knows what to do.

Rob Samuels, who conveniently moved from the back row to the seat next to me since I've sort of been avoiding him, gives a low whistle. "Damn, Stone. Slipping a little, huh?" He grins at me, and I automatically smile back.

We all know I don't slip.

Rob reaches out, and his hand grazes mine. Normally, I pull away when Rob does things like this, but today, I leave my hand where it is, letting Belrose see that Rob likes me too. That Rob has always liked me, and no matter how hard Belrose tries, he will never go back as far as Rob and I do.

He doesn't need to know that Rob isn't a real possibility for me.

"Are you okay, Riley?" Rob asks, his voice soft.

"Excuse me?"

He leans over and nudges my *Les Mis* paper with a knuckle.

I look down, and then do a double take.

What?

That's not possible.

Scrawled hurriedly across the top of the page is not the A I am so used to seeing in Belrose's handwriting. It's not even a B, or God forbid, a C.

It's an F.

On what I happen to know for a fact is a goddamned good paper.

"It's a joke," I tell Rob, but I flip through the other pages for comments. And there are none. Not one. And on a paper that warrants an F, there should at least be another red mark or two that explains *why*.

And the absence of said red marks can only mean one thing: Belrose is screwing with me. He's punishing me for Sandeep. He thinks he has the power here. But he doesn't.

Oh, he doesn't.

I look up at him and for the first time all class I meet his eyes, and I smile.

Challenge accepted.

I take my phone out of my backpack, preparing to send him a scathing e-mail, but Belrose yanks my phone out of my hand roughly.

"You know the rules, Miss Stone." His voice is cold, and he shakes my phone at me. His eyes hold mine, and they're hard. "If you want your phone back, you'll have to come see me after school."

The class is silent. And they should be. They're stunned. They've never seen Belrose be such an asshole. Especially not to a prize pupil like me.

"Fine," I say.

"After school, Stone," he repeats, and starts scrawling on the board.

So this is how he's going to get me to talk to him. Huh. He's going to embarrass me.

Is this his way of getting back at me? Or his weird way of saying he misses me?

I narrow my eyes. Either way, he has no idea who he's playing with.

TWENTY-THREE
Extracurricular

"Mr. Belrose."

I stand in the doorway to his classroom. We don't have cheerleading practice tonight, which is good, because I had to wait some time before all the girls who pretended to need help with their French homework cleared out of his classroom. It's almost four.

"Miss Stone. Please come in. Close the door."

I obey. I want to slam the door, but I know from experience the reverberation will rattle every classroom in the hallway and possibly break the thin glass paneling that exists so teachers *can* close said doors, so I close it softly. "I don't suppose I can have my phone back now."

He draws it out of his pocket, actually looking a little sheepish.

"Here. Um, also, you got an A on your paper. It's in the grade book."

I don't let him see that I was concerned. "I thought so," I say, keeping my voice stiff and professional. "Thank you for your time, Mr. Belrose. I'll keep my cell phone in my backpack in the future."

I'm almost to the door when he speaks again.

"I know you aren't serious with Sandeep."

Ah.

That means he somehow unlocked my phone.

And went through my text messages.

I turn back toward him and watch him from across the room. Rage rises up in my chest. So he can confiscate my phone and just—go through it? What gives him the right?

"Is that so?" My voice shakes, just slightly. I hate it.

"It is." He comes toward me, and I step away from the door.

"And what gives you the right to go through my phone without permission?" I ask, and he's advancing and I'm backing away and then all of a sudden I'm in the corner of the classroom with my back against the wall and he's looming over me.

The blinds on the wall are closed.

No one can see us.

"You've been ignoring me," he says, breathing hard. "I had to do something. You were being impossible."

I can't stand it. I hit him.

But before I can make contact, he catches my arm. "That's not nice, Riley," he says, and pushes my arm up against the wall. He captures the other, too.

And then he kisses me. He kisses me softly at first, and even though I hate myself, I kiss him back.

Soft.

Slow.

And then harder, and with more urgency.

He lets me go, finally, breathing hard. "I still care about you, Riley. I'm just taking care of some shit, okay?" His hand is behind my neck, cradling my head away from the cinder blocks that make up the wall. "The house will be empty tomorrow, so just come over if you can."

He releases me like he can barely stand it.

"I'm not just going to be your slut for when your wife isn't around," I tell him. "I thought it was over with her."

"It is," he says. "I swear to God."

I look into his eyes, and reach up to touch his cheek. "It better be," I whisper. "Because you don't want to find out what I'd do if you're playing me."

TWENTY-FOUR
Blood

"I cooked," Alex says. "I hope you're happy."

He's been waiting for me in the den, one leg propped up on the other, his foot wiggling. It's been raining since about five, so I take my boots off and leave them by the door. I couldn't skip cheer tonight. And I wouldn't. If he wants to be treated as a priority, he needs to show me I'm one too.

"What did you make?"

"Lasagna. My grandfather's recipe. And garlic bread." His voice has an edge to it. "It's been ready. I've been waiting." He doesn't stand. Just sits there and stares at me.

"I had practice. You know that. I can't just skip. People

would talk." I slip out of my jacket and hang it on the back of a chair. I took a quick shower in the locker room even though I hate the floors in there and there is an actual risk I'm going to get a raging case of athlete's foot. He should be grateful I got here this early.

Alex finally pushes off of the couch and takes my hand, leading me into the kitchen. "You're wearing the necklace," he says, and blood rushes to my cheeks.

"Yes."

I don't tell him I haven't taken it off. I'd almost unclasped it a hundred times, but I never had.

"You hungry?"

"Yes."

It's a lie. I'm not hungry. I'm nervous. He's acting weird— whether it's because he thinks Jacqueline will catch us or he's angry with me or he thinks this whole thing is a stupid mistake, I don't know.

I start to sit down, but before I can, he grabs me. His hands are rough, and he doesn't start gentle with me, like he normally does. He kisses me, hard, his teeth biting into my lips and his hands pushing up roughly under my shirt. I return the kiss, but he grows rougher, and before I know it we're on the kitchen floor and suddenly kissing him isn't fun anymore and I taste blood in my mouth.

I turn my head and shove him away. "Stop!" I push at him and climb to my feet. "What are you doing?"

He climbs to his knees. "I'm—I'm sorry, Riley. I just—I wanted you. I missed you." He runs both hands through his hair. "I didn't mean to scare you like that."

"You didn't scare me," I say. "I'm just not some whore you can screw on your kitchen floor, okay?" I pull myself into the chair. "We're not like that."

"Shit. I'm so sorry, Riley. I just missed you so much. It hasn't been easy to be without you." He ducks his head. He still needs a haircut. Parts of his hair, usually messy in a boyish way, are sticking up oddly, making him look a bit crazed. I want to smooth it down, but I restrain myself.

"Could have fooled me," I snap. I touch my lip to see if I'm bleeding, and my finger comes away with a small red spot of blood. "You've been acting like I don't exist."

He pulls himself up. "I—I just had to figure everything out, Riley. I didn't expect Jacqueline to come back. I thought it was over. I thought she was gone. And then all of a sudden she was back, acting like everything was okay and normal, and I was suddenly supposed to act like that too, and I just panicked and I'm sorry. Nothing about my feelings for you have changed. Nothing about our plans have changed. And I haven't touched her." He holds up his hands. "I swear, Riley."

"Well," I say, my fingers sliding over the silverware he's set out for me. They pause on the knife. "I'm not sleeping with you until you get rid of her. I'm not that kind of girl."

His eyes flash. "I never said you were."

I shrug, and I feel like the space below my collarbone is hollow.

"Okay," he says. "I will, so long as you never go on another stupid date while we're together."

"Fine." My words are sharp and they hurt even before they leave my tongue.

"Fine. Should we shake on it?"

I stare at him for a moment.

I need something more. Something bigger than a handshake. Something to make him remember who is really in charge.

"No," I say. I stand up and walk to his kitchen counter. "Take off your shirt."

Behind me, I hear the sounds of fabric as he slips it off. I take mine off and drop it behind me. His breathing quickens audibly.

I pull a sharp silver knife from the wooden block on his countertop. It comes free with a *snick*. I turn it this way and that to catch the light from the kitchen fixture.

Alex's eyes widen, but he doesn't step away.

I draw it across my chest in a neat line, opening a short, shallow cut over my heart. The flesh opens more easily than I'd imagine. The blood wells and collects and falls down my chest in well-ordered lines.

I hold it out to him, handle first, the blade resting loosely in my palm.

He stares at the blade for a moment, then takes it from me. He grits his teeth and makes an identical cut just over his own heart, and then grabs me and hold me tight against him. I feel the warmth of his blood against my skin, and for a moment I am angry and hurt and want to give in to him completely all at the same time.

"I promise." He looks down into my eyes.

"Me too." I don't blink.

"It's a blood bond, then. Unbreakable."

"It's forever," I tell him. I close my hand over his on the hilt of the knife.

Things to Know About Riley Stone:

- At age fourteen, Riley founded the Senior Friends Program through her church youth group. The group paired middle- and high-school-aged students with nursing home residents for companionship and fun. The group still thrives today.
- At age fifteen, Riley taught herself to read Braille in her spare time after volunteering at a camp for blind youth.
- Also at age fifteen, Riley briefly reentered therapy, but voluntarily quit after she realized she felt more intelligent than the therapist, attributing most of her issues to being overly type A.
- Her parents eagerly agreed with her self-diagnosis.
- Riley has standing prescriptions that she can call in for, however, and a therapist who will see her when needed. Of course, Riley thinks this is all quite amusing, as she has personally diagnosed at least twelve other people at her school who need therapy more than she does, one of whom is a teacher.

TWENTY-FIVE
Original

"So I heard you hit it off with Sandeep." Neta and I are in art, and she's pulling on her pink bubble gum with her fingers, which is something I really, really find disgusting, but I try not to bug her about. She does this thing where she pulls on it and wraps it around her fingers and then *chews* it again, then basically repeats the whole process, which is frankly just unsanitary.

"How are your watercolors going, girls?" Mr. Wellingsby, the art teacher, stops by our desk, wiggling his long-fingered hands at us inquisitively. He is a total bohem—he's very thin, with flowy, colorful clothes, and he's always talking about seeing love and pain and energy in art and going on about how we can channel our feelings.

"I'm conceptualizing." Neta grins up at him and pops her gum.

I don't respond. I've actually got a pretty good watercolor going. It's a waterfall. Which means about as much to me as a gold-fish. Or a red Converse sneaker.

Or nothing.

"Let your mind flow," he advises, opening his arms as if guiding Neta's creative energies personally. "Riley! I see so much inner turmoil in this picture! Gorgeous!"

I nod seriously. I know exactly how to deal with Mr. Wellingsby. "I'm glad you picked up on that. I really wanted it to show what I'm going through."

He strokes his goatee with his arachnid hands. "I get it. I do. Do you want to talk to the class about it when you're finished?"

I shake my head, keeping my face calm. "I want my art to speak for me. Please."

He touches his head and then extends his finger in an arc. "Yes, Riley. Yes."

And then he sort of wanders off to the next table, managing to look really high and sort of lost. Which he probably is.

He's strangely a great teacher, if you can get past his muddled exterior.

"So Sandeep," Neta reminds me. "Is he the cause of your inner turmoil?"

I snicker. "Oh yes. I'm definitely pining away for him. I think of him day and night. I write long letters for him and send them by the Postal Service. I got his name tattooed on my left breast."

I think of the cut on my chest where my fake tattoo is, and

feel the corner of my mouth pull up. If she only knew.

"Then why did Kolbie say you blew him off?" Neta is still messing with her stupid gum. I want to grab it from her and throw it across the room, only I don't actually want to touch it.

"Because I guess I did."

"And why would that be? If you were having a good time, why'd you ditch him?"

For a moment, I resent her. I resent my gorgeous, gum-snapping friend. I want to tell her to leave me alone. But if the tables were turned, would I ask the same question?

Yes.

I bend over my watercolor. "Please don't be mad at me, Neta."

She sighs heavily, the air whooshing out of her lungs, and finally, she stops playing with her gum and drops her hands. "I'm not mad. I just—I don't get it. If you liked him, what the hell?"

"I was scared, okay? And I'm not ready. If I get into something, I give up a lot of other things. And maybe in college I'll be ready to actually be with someone for real, and yeah, Sandeep is almost perfect, but right now, I'm just not."

Neta just sort of looks at me. "You don't have to do anything you don't want to do, Ri."

I paint green into my waterfall so I don't have to meet her eyes, which I know without looking are too kind right now. "I know."

"Hey," she says. "Look." She points across the room.

I follow her finger. "Um, what?" I see Anthony Waterford, half asleep on his arm, in the corner.

"No. Look at Kamea."

I glance at Kamea, who I sort of don't like, just on principle. It's not because she's a bad person or anything. Because she's not. And not because she's particularly irritating.

Of course, it's not like she's *great*, either. She dresses almost exactly the same, every single day, in these stupid button-up cardigans. Her closet probably looks like a cartoon character's closet, with just the exact same outfit, over and over and over and over. She couldn't get more boring if she made an actual effort.

And of course she's this cute, perky little girl-next-door type of blonde who is basically built to look good in any type of clothes. You know, the ones who fit into everything when you go shopping together and then look amazing in it?

Kamea has that body.

But she wears the same stupid cardigans.

And on top of that, she has one of those *voices*. Those high-pitched baby voices that belong on a girl, like, ten years younger that of course guys find attractive but is actually sort of disgusting.

And Neta and Kolbie both like her.

And she has been in second place for valedictorian for as long as I can remember.

"Look at the necklace," Neta prods.

My eyes drop to the gold chain around her neck, and my throat tightens.

Oh my God.

Holy shit.

A little wooden chess piece hangs from the chain.

A little wooden king that doesn't look one-of-a-kind at all.

"You and Kamea must shop at the same store." Neta giggles. "Awkward."

I don't answer her. My fist closes around my own necklace and I'm pulling on the chain until it digs into the back of my neck. And somewhere, deep in the recesses of my mind, I'm imagining pulling the necklace tight around Kamea's neck until her eyes bug out. And she doesn't even struggle. She just stares at me, like she does in class when she doesn't know an answer, like maybe, just maybe, I'll help her.

Because it looks like maybe, just maybe, Kamea's also getting a little French tutoring on the side.

"Don't freak out, Ri. It definitely looks better on you."

I whip my head back to Neta. "I'm not worried."

But I know that Alex has a free period not next period—but the period after.

And when he does, I march directly into his classroom and close the door, my arms behind my back.

"Hello, lovely." He touches the space above his heart where he cut himself. Mine barely stings anymore. I have two Band-Aids over my cut and I've religiously applied Neosporin. A blood bond is one thing, but I don't want a scar.

Inside, my temper rages, but I force myself to look at Alex. To study him. I thought he was smarter than this. I thought he would know better than to try to play two of us.

Especially when I'm one of them.

His eyebrows lower slightly. He's figuring it out. He rises from his desk. "What's wrong, Riley?" he asks, coming toward me. "Is everything okay?"

He doesn't touch me like he did last time we were alone in his classroom. That is a wise decision. I am not sure I could handle his skin. I would melt or I would attack. I am not sure which.

I put myself at risk for him, and he doesn't even care.

"Kamea Myers," I say, my voice a whisper.

"Pardon me?"

"Kamea Myers." I repeat myself. I look at him.

There is no response. Absolutely nothing. His face doesn't color. He doesn't look at his shoes. His eyes are trained on mine. "I don't understand, Riley. Would you mind catching me up here?" Finally, his eyes take on a small note of panic. "She doesn't . . . know about us, does she?"

Very slowly, I unhook the little necklace from around my neck. I hold it out to him, the chess piece swinging back and forth, hypnotic.

"This is what I'm talking about, Alex. This."

"Your necklace?"

His face is still a canvas of questions and innocence. He's good.

"She has the exact same necklace, Alex." I crush his name between my teeth, grinding out the two syllables. "Now, do you want to tell me how that's possible? Has she been getting extra French tips on the side, maybe? Some private lessons?"

He shakes his head, finally breaking eye contact. "No. Absolutely not. And that's impossible. The man . . . he told me those necklaces were one of a kind. She couldn't have one. It doesn't make sense." He lets out his breath, then looks at me again. "I swear on my life—on *your* life—that I didn't give her a necklace, Riley. I never would. That's not her. That's you and me. That's us, okay?"

He doesn't blink.

"Huh," I say.

"Trust me, Riley. I've never felt about anyone like I feel about you. Please, please, just trust me on this, okay?"

I don't.

Trust him.

And he's pleading.

His eyes stray now, from me to the window behind me, to make sure what we're doing looks PC. But he's desperate for me to believe him. Desperate. He looks disheveled, somehow, not the in-control teacher who I stopped by to see.

"Okay." The word I give him is tight and brittle and already splintering around the edges. "Fine."

His face relaxes.

I turn toward the door to leave him. I suddenly just want to go back to class.

"I'm leaving Jacqueline tonight."

It bursts out of him. I pause with my hand on the door, and I turn back to him. "Make sure you do. I'm not a mistress."

And then, without waiting for him to say another word, I walk back to class.

I don't even look back to see if he's watching me.

I know he is. Just like always.

It doesn't cross my mind that I might have underestimated him.

TWENTY-SIX
Mobile

There was a password on my iPhone, but it appears Alex knew it.

He knew *I knew* that he knew.

I lay in bed, staring at my ceiling, my cell phone resting on my chest.

My mom would yell at me for that. She says you can get cancer that way, by keeping your phone too close to your body.

I don't know why I'm even thinking about that right now.

Not after what just happened.

Not after what I just found.

I stare at it. I imagine it jumping with my heartbeat. I imagine it starting on fire so I never, ever have to find out.

Alex left me something on my phone.

Something in a photo album. One that I don't recognize. One that I don't remember being on there before Alex took my phone away from me. One that is titled *FORRILEY*.

A photo album that I definitely have never, ever seen before.

The first picture is the album—the thumbnail—and it's blurred. I can't tell what it is. No matter how long I look at it, blurred. I can't tell what it is. No matter how long I look at it.

But it's the color of skin.

I close my eyes slowly and then reopen them, focusing on the ceiling. What did he take pictures of while he was sitting at his desk all day? Am I even ready to see this?

Is this going to be gross?

No. Alex isn't like that.

I bite down on the inside of my bottom lip.

I click the album open.

The first photo is the blurred photo.

And the second photo is of me. Asleep. My right hand is tucked under my head, and my hair is wild, like I've been tossing and turning. My legs are tangled in the sheets.

My sheets.

In my bed.

Oh my God.

I flip through the rest of the pictures quickly. It's all me, in my white tank top and pajama pants, in various positions as I slept. In some, my arms are splayed out. In some, my top has ridden up, showing my stomach. In others, I've barely moved in my bed.

My bed.

In my own house.

Alex didn't take any pictures when he confiscated my phone during class. He broke into my house when I was sleeping and took pictures of me with my own phone.

And somehow, I had *no idea.*

Why would Alex do that? Why wouldn't he tell me he was there, or wake me up? Why would he chance getting caught sneaking into my room?

I think of Alex in my room at night, watching me, and my heart feels strange and scared and angry and excited, all at once. What is this, though? Is this some sort of insurance? Is Alex trying to *scare* me?

This is not normal boyfriend behavior. Even a girl who has never actually dated knows that.

It's been three days since he told me he was going to break it off with Jacqueline. Three days. And he hasn't done it. Jacqueline's teal-blue car is still parked out in front of their curb every single day, and every single day Alex tells me the same exact thing: *Soon. I swear. I love you.*

I tell him that I love him back, but a little hate seeps in around the corners. And then I let him go home to Jacqueline.

My room is strangely cold, but I don't want to go down the hall to check the thermostat. I just want to lay here. My heart hurts in my chest in a way that has become strange and familiar all at once.

And I think of Alex, standing over me while I slept, my phone in his hands.

My phone buzzes, turning the screen from my strange sleeping photos to Kolbie, smiling sweetly at the camera, her hands behind her back. I want to turn her off, to be wholly alone, but I force myself to answer.

"Hey, girl." I try to sound visibly cheerful, but I feel strange. My skin feels odd, like it's falling asleep over my muscles.

"Don't 'hey, girl' at me, Riley. Why haven't you been answering your phone?" Her tone is definitely Pissed Kolbie. I've heard her this way before, but never at me.

I cringe and hold the phone about an inch away from my ear. "Uh, what?"

"How many times did I call you? Don't you think maybe your friends need you? Or are you too caught up in Ri-Ri land to care?"

"I . . . don't know," I finish, because it's the truth. I suppose I noticed they'd called some, but I actually went home early on Friday and I've spent most of the weekend studying and organizing, with thoughts of Alex crawling around in the back of my head. Which was stupid. I always swore I'd never be one of those girls. And maybe, just maybe, I hadn't checked my messages all weekend. I pull my covers over my head but keep my phone to my ear. I deserve to hear her out. I know it.

"Well, you're being a shit friend, Riley, because first you walked out on Sandeep, and you wouldn't even talk to me about it."

"Yeah, well, I panicked, okay? I don't want him to get in the way of my priorities. I'm sorry." My words are defensive.

"I know, Riley, but if you were just going to ghost a good guy, I wouldn't have set you up with Jamal's best friend. You could have at least given him some sort of explanation."

"I'm sorry," I say again, and this time I actually do sound properly sorry.

"Just don't expect me to set you up with someone good again until you can actually handle it. Sandeep felt like shit, just so you know. And so did I. He really liked you, Ri." Her voice softens, just slightly. "I'm not saying you had to be with him if you weren't into him. And if he did something weird, you'd tell me, right? I won't be mad. I swear."

"I know. And he didn't. Please don't think that." And I do know. And I like him, too. There's a part of me that wishes I never touched Alex, so this Sandeep thing could happen. I shift beneath my blankets, my legs twisting up in the sheets. What would I be doing now if I hadn't ever gotten involved with Alex? Would I be talking to Sandeep instead of hiding out in my own house, feeling completely ignored and depressed?

"And you haven't answered Neta's calls, either."

"So you guys have been *talking* about me?" My voice is cutting. I can't believe they're hanging out without me, talking behind my back.

Kolbie is quiet for a few seconds, and then: "Well, more about her dead grandmother, but yeah, I guess so. She was worried about you. I was more pissed."

My body turns strange and cold for a half second. "Neta's grandmother died?" I say.

"Yeah."

"But she wasn't sick, was she?"

"No. She had a heart attack. And Neta's been calling you and calling you and so have I, but you haven't been there."

I swallow hard.

"Is Neta okay?"

"No."

Kolbie's furious at me. This isn't about Sandeep at all. Of course it's not. It's about Neta and the fact that I'm a completely horrible friend. Why couldn't I just check a text? Or return a call? Or do anything besides be completely stupid and self-involved?

"The funeral's Monday. First Trinity Church. The arrangements are in your texts, if you'd ever care to check them." She says it like I'll probably turn her down—like she expects me to. Like I'm the biggest disappointment ever.

"I'll be there, Kolbie."

"I should think so." Kolbie's voice is thin ice over a winter pond. Brittle and cold and hateful. And I don't fault her for it.

"Listen, Kol—"

But she's not there. She's hung up without saying good-bye.

TWENTY-SEVEN
Undercover

My dad has two pickups. There is one that he drives to work and treats like a baby; he spends his weekends washing it and waxing it and using a special cloth to clean it that he spent, like, thirty bucks on. Then, there's the other truck. The *real* pickup truck, that is actually used for pickup-type things.

He lets my uncle borrow it most of the time. It's faded blue and rusted and he uses it to drag around lawn mowers and hasn't properly cleaned it in almost twenty years. The windows are the kind you have to roll down by hand and they're smeared with years of fingerprints.

And so, the night before Neta's grandmother Pilar's funeral, I tell my dad I need to tote some stuff for the school food drive, and so it doesn't seem weird that I need to borrow the old pickup truck that basically no one ever sees my immediate family or me in, ever.

When I start the rust bucket, it takes two tries for it to catch, but the engine (or whatever) finally shrieks and turns over. I cringe. It's louder than I'd prefer, but it *is* ancient. I think it's actually from the eighties or something, so it's even older than Ethan. But I let it run for a minute, and the noise level evens out.

I start off toward the school, and then I turn in the direction of my destination: Alex's house. I know the way by heart . . . the names of the little streets, which intersections have stoplights and which have four-way stops. The sidewalks and trees and little painted mailboxes in his neighborhood have become almost as ordinary to me as my own street.

I park just down the road, in front of a squatty little orange house with all its lights off, and kill the engine in a spot where I can still see the Belrose home and Jacqueline's cute little teal car parked out in front.

She's still there.

Of course she is.

If he'd told her he wanted a divorce, wouldn't she have fled to her mother's or sister's or something? Isn't that what happens when people ask for divorces? One of them *leaves*?

It's not like I'm stupid. It means he didn't ask. It means he lied. It means nothing has changed and I'm just a fool who is wasting her time.

And I am not a girl to be made a fool of.

I grind my teeth and sink down in the seat. It's twilight, and soon, the streetlights will flicker on, but just now, the sun has sunk to the point where it's hard to see anything, which means no one will be able to see me in my dad's old pickup.

What is taking him so long to leave her? Does he still have feelings for a woman who totters around complaining and reading gossip magazines? Is he that shallow that he would choose her over me?

Yes. Being with Jacqueline is easier, certainly. But there is no way that she could be better.

Cold is beginning to seep in through the car, and I wish I'd brought along a blanket or a thermos of hot cocoa. I button my jacket up to my neck, and the streetlights come on, bathing the Belrose house in a yellow light that I happen to know comes in through the front windows and rests very softly on the beige carpet in the living room.

I blow into my hands and wrap my arms around my body, and then something happens.

The door opens on the familiar little brick house, and two people walk out onto the front steps. There is Alex, in a hoodie and jeans, not dressed enough for the cold of the night, and Jacqueline, in a red peacoat and high heels, a long wool scarf wrapped around her neck. They walk to her little car together, and he leans forward with a sense of familiarity.

They kiss, just for a quick moment, and his hand touches her arm in a way that means she is his.

And then she just drops her purse into the passenger side door, crosses to the other side, and drives away.

He waves at her, then walks back into the house, like he has done nothing out of the ordinary.

My fingers dig into the cracking vinyl of the seat.

They *kissed.*

It was not the kiss of a couple that is breaking apart. It was a worn-in, familiar type of kiss, the kind that's repeated for hellos and good-byes and maybe at night before turning out the bedside lamp. Something done out of habit. Not forced. Not unhappy.

He walked outside to see her off.

And then he *kissed* her.

With lips he promised were mine.

My heart rots from the inside out. I feel tears start in my eyes, but I blink them away. I turn the key in the pickup, but it only whimpers in a sad, ragged way. I turn the key again, and the truck groans and screams but finally starts, and in the house I am parked next to, a light goes on and the curtains are switched to the side.

I hit the gas and speed away, not caring, the truck rattling loudly along the little street.

Let them stare.

Alex doesn't care either. Obviously. He's certainly making it very clear he and Jacqueline are still very much a thing and I do not matter.

When I get home, I walk into the house through the mudroom and into the kitchen. Immediately, my mother hugs me. "Baby," she says. "You should have told me what was going on."

I untangle myself from her arms. I can't remember the last time we hugged. "Um, I'm okay. What?"

My mind jumps to Alex.

She steps back, leaning against the kitchen island. She looks concerned, for once. The lines around her face look deeper than usual, and her eyes are blurry and tired. Her blond hair, the same shade as mine, seems to have more silver highlights around her crown. "Neta's grandma. The funeral tomorrow. Have you been over there to talk to her? Have you figured everything out?"

"Yes."

That's a lie. I haven't been over there. Neta hasn't answered any of my calls, and her text had simply said, NO THANKS, EVERYTHING FINE. Which was code for LEAVE ME ALONE YOU SELFISH BITCH.

Which is fair.

So I let her know I was here if she needed me and then left her alone. And I texted Kolbie and extended the same offer, and of course she hasn't responded. In fact, she may have blocked me. I'm not sure. I'm scared to try to figure it out.

"That's good, sweetie." My mother reaches out to smooth my hair, then pulls back, as if thinking better of it. She's already hugged me once. That's our family love quota for the year, basically. Two touches in one day would just be ridiculous.

"I got into Princeton," I say, off the cuff, and she smiles at me, sort of sad.

"I know, honey. I remember. You told us at dinner."

Which is just weird, because I know for a fact no one at dinner was listening to me.

I leave her in the kitchen and go back upstairs to be alone, where everything makes just a little more sense. I lay out my black dress with thick black tights and black shoes, and I text Kolbie and Neta to tell them I'll be there, I promise.

And I fall asleep.

But the next day at the church, outside the chapel, things don't make sense either. Because where Kolbie and I should be standing, alongside Neta, there is someone else. Someone with a very similar GPA and a pretty chess-piece necklace.

Kamea Myers.

Standing right in the thick, with Neta and her entire family.

Holding Neta's hand while she cries.

I slip up to Kolbie, who gives me a grateful smile and slides her arms around me, pulling me into a big hug. I am stiff with surprise for a millisecond before I melt into her. I missed her.

"I'm so sorry," I whisper. "I've been going through some stuff, Kolbie, but I know that's no excuse and it's not about me."

She hugs me a little tighter. "I know, Riley. I'm sorry I was so hard on you. I know you'd never just ditch us without a good reason." She pulls away, and her eyes are misty.

My whole body feels heavy with the truth. Would Kolbie hate me if I told her? "Yeah." I clear my throat and flick my eyes toward Kamea. Neta hasn't even looked at me. She's just standing there, her pretty shoulders hunched over. "How's she doing?"

Kolbie shakes her head. "Neta's a mess. I don't know how to help her. She's so close to her grandma, you know?"

I nod. Pilar was almost a mother to Neta; she lived with her family. She helped Neta with her homework and dropped her off at school before she got her license.

"What's Kamea doing here?" I can't help but ask.

"I don't know. I think Kamea was, like, adopted by her cousin's brother-in-law or something. Some family connection. And they've gotten closer lately. So try not to hate her too much today? Please? I promise you can go back to full hate tomorrow."

"I don't hate anyone," I protest. But my eyes keep straying to the chain around Kamea's neck. And for some reason, the chain I'm wearing under my own dress feels cold. And heavy.

And wrong.

Like maybe I shouldn't be wearing it in a church. Or at a funeral.

Neta finally turns away, releasing Kamea's hand, and comes toward us. Her eyes are, for once, free of the dark makeup she normally wears, and she still looks stunning even though it's obvious she's been crying. She throws her arms around me. "I missed you," she whispers. "Are you okay?"

I stare at her. She's been worried about *me*? "Um, yeah. I'm so sorry I'm been gone. I've been . . . it doesn't matter. Are you okay?"

She wipes at her eyes with the back of her hand. "Sure." She tries to smile, but it's shaky and lasts only for a moment. "Thank you both for being here." She wraps her arms around Kolbie, and tears fall down her cheeks onto Kolbie's sweater. "I don't know what to do."

And I realize I don't know what to say to her. What do you say to someone when a most important part of her life is just . . . gone? "I'm so sorry, Neta. Please let us know . . . what we can do."

The words feel stupid and empty even as I say them, but she tries to smile again and cries even harder, and I just feel silly and lost.

"It's okay," Neta says finally, through her tears, and I feel like she's forgiving me. Her mother, who looks like her slighter older sister, comes to get her from us, and leads her daughter away, and they're buried in each other's arms.

Kolbie swallows hard, trying to keep from crying herself. "This sucks."

I nod. "Yeah."

We head into the church, and the usher seats us two rows back—close to where Neta's family will sit when they come in. Kamea walks up shyly and smiles at us, hesitant. She doesn't look particularly sad.

"Can I sit here?" she asks, looking back and forth between the rows of pews. Apparently she's not family enough to sit with the actual family.

"Sure," I say.

"Yeah," Kolbie choruses.

My eyes stray to her necklace.

I wonder again if she has French poetry readings.

"*Oui,*" I say.

"Huh?" Kamea asks, and wedges into the row right next to me, so she's the very last person in the pew. If we're singing today, we'll have to share a hymnbook.

I just smile like I'm baring my teeth and fan myself with the bulletin I was given when I walked in.

"This is so sad, isn't it?" Kamea whispers. "I feel so bad for Neta."

"Yeah," Kolbie says, and looks at me quizzically. Small talk at funerals isn't really my thing, but if I'm being honest, small talk with Kamea Myers isn't exactly my thing either. Still, I'll be kind, for Neta's sake.

"I like your outfit," I tell Kamea as more people file into the church. "It's very pretty." I eye her mauve pencil skirt and jacket combo with a tan silk top beneath. It's definitely probable that the jacket even has shoulder pads. It looks like she went straight to the mom section at Ann Taylor, but I suppose for that section, it's very nice. It probably cost a lot. Of course, I choose *not* to shop in the stores for people over forty, but that's my prerogative.

"Thanks," she says. "I don't wear a lot of black, so I had to buy it special for today."

"The necklace, too?" I ask innocently. My own necklace against my skin. *Why isn't it warming up? It's so hot in here. Why is it so hot in here?* I wave my bulletin faster.

She picks up the little chess piece off of her collarbone. "This?" she asks. "Oh, no. My own grandmother bought this for me from Costco. I know it's a bit silly, but it means a lot to me."

"Costco, huh?" Flames lick around the corners of my heart.

She smiles a little. "No judging! It's from my grandmother. It's special."

"Of course not." I smile at her. "I'm sure it *is* special."

I turn back toward the front of the church as the family is escorted in, my heart a dying lead thing in my chest. Could Kamea be telling the truth? Her grandmother got the necklace from Costco? What does that say about Alex?

"Now, was that so hard?" Kolbie mutters in my ear, her voice barely above a breath.

I want to laugh.

And then I want to turn to Kamea and tear her eyes out.

But it's a funeral, and I'm a nice girl above all, so I sit still and quiet and listen to the service and say my prayers for Neta and her family and her grandmother's soul.

When we all stand to leave, I stick my foot out and Kamea just happens to trip out into the aisle.

"What is wrong with you?" Kolbie asks.

I look at her, wide-eyed. "Oh my God. That was an accident, I swear."

I step into the aisle and help Kamea up and out of the way of the other mourners. "Are you okay?" I ask. "Did you twist your ankle?"

She shakes her head. "I'm sorry, I didn't realize you were trying to walk. I'm so clumsy."

"It's not your fault. Do you hurt anywhere?"

"I think I'm okay. Seriously, Riley, thank you so much." She is flustered and her tanned cheeks are pink with embarrassment.

I put my hand on her shoulder. "If you're sure, Kamea."

She's sure.

I return to Kolbie, and I wait until I have hugged Neta and her whole family and am alone in my car to Google the necklace.

There is a listing for it at Costco. There is also one at Target, and a very similar one on Amazon.

My lead heart grows heavier.

I type an e-mail to Alex.

I KNOW ABOUT THE NECKLACE AND I KNOW YOU'RE STILL WITH HER.

I send the e-mail in a mad rage.

TWENTY-EIGHT
Discussions

The classroom phone rang during Shakespeare.

That in itself was not a rare occurrence.

Nor was the fact that Mrs. Hamilton looked at me and said, "Miss Stone, would you mind stopping by the counselor's office?"

Everyone knows that when I'm summoned to the counselor's office, it's because I've just won another ridiculous scholarship or maybe some representative from some college wants to speak to me, or it's just some generally positive thing. So I leave everything on my desk (how long does it take to say, "Thank you!" and pose for a photo?) and skip down to Ms. Felcher's office to see how I can be of service.

But what I did not expect to see is what I am looking at exactly now, with a very frozen smile on my face.

Because my parents are on one side of the desk, with very stock-photography concerned parents looks carefully aligned on their deliberately parental faces. How pleasant of them.

More concerning is that on the other side of the desk is Ms. Felcher, looking a bit surprised (although perhaps she got just a tad too much Restylane at her last appointment) alongside none other than Alex Belrose.

And judging by the rosiness along the tops of his ears and the perfectly even set of his lips, he is angry.

No one could know anything, could they? Wouldn't the principal be here? Wouldn't it all be a bigger deal than just this?

"Hello, Riley," he says, his tone perfectly normal . . . for a teacher.

"Hello, Mr. Belrose. Mom. Dad. Ms. Felcher. To what do I owe the pleasure?" My tone is perfectly normal . . . for a student who has just been surprise-attacked by a meeting with her parents, a teacher (with whom she has zero romantic connection), and the school guidance counselor.

"Well," Miss Felcher says, "please have a seat, Miss Stone."

She has never called me Miss Stone before. Ever.

This is serious.

"There are no extra chairs," I point out.

"Oh!" she says, and runs out into the general office for one of the lumpy green waiting-room chairs, which she drags in slowly, bumping it against either side of her door frame.

Alex doesn't even offer to help her.

She leaves the seat sort of between my parents, but a bit behind, so that I when I sit down, crossing my legs, I don't exactly feel like I'm part of the whole conversation. I spread out the skirt of my little blue dress neatly around my legs just like nothing is wrong. Nothing at all.

Then I swallow my feelings down in one great lump and try not to throw them up all over my parents.

Ms. Felcher continues, adjusting her cat-eye glasses just a bit. "First of all, we'd like to share that nothing about this meeting will be documented at this point."

Something in my chest loosens, just a bit.

"However."

It tightens again.

"Mr. Belrose has called your mother and father in for a rather unprecedented conference. It seems he is very confused and a bit concerned about your recent academic performance in his class, so he set up this *unannounced* meeting with your parents. Without informing me." She shoots him a look, which he ignores. Instead, he steeples his fingers and looks at my father, then my mother, and finally, me.

"As you know, Riley is a smart girl. The most intelligent, I believe, in the school. Maybe the most intelligent and promising pupil I've ever had."

My father puffs up, like he's never heard this feedback before. "We're very proud of her," he says, and suddenly I'm actually a little embarrassed. Where has he been? Where have either of them been? He glances back at me and pats me awkwardly on the knee, his hand stiff and open.

What is the point of my entire existence?

"That's why I'm so alarmed right now."

My mother leans forward, both hands clutching her brown Coach handbag. "Excuse me? Concerned? About our Riley?" She shakes her head, like she must be hearing wrong.

"Yes, Mrs. Stone. Very concerned." He produces copies of my recent homework. Homework I know for an absolute fact I aced. Homework that was perfect and flawless and double-checked before I turned it in. He presents it to my parents.

C. D. F. D. F. C minus. D plus.

And of course, neither of my parents nor Ms. Felcher speak French, so there's no use telling them my French teacher is attempting to get back at me for trying to get him to leave his wife. There's no use asking them to check my French.

I am at his mercy.

I glare at Alex across the table and let my parents gasp at the false red marks and clutch at their hearts.

"Riley," my mother says. "What's going on? Is something wrong?"

I scoot to the very edge of my seat and look over at the homework, and flick my eyes up to Alex's face. I hope he's enjoying his little show. He knows he has me trapped. He knows every student likes him. He knows he's won Most Favored Teacher every second since he's been here, and does loads of community service, and is generally held in high regard ever since the *Hartsville News* did a piece on him last year.

And what am I going to say, really?

I look back down at the work. "Funny," I say lightly. "I thought I did a rather good job on these."

Alex peers at me from behind his steepled fingers, unshakable. "It appears you need to take another look then, Riley. I think that might be your problem; perhaps you aren't spending enough time on your homework."

"What do you recommend, Mr. Belrose?" Mom asks, using her Voice of Motherly Concern, the one she hasn't had to get out and dust off since the Ethan days, when parent-teacher-counselor conferences were a lot more frequent (and merited).

Belrose drops his fingers to my papers and moves forward conspiratorially. "Now, I wouldn't normally do this, but as a bad grade for the semester would move Riley out of her valedictorian standing, I'd like to see her just a little more often. Perhaps she should spend some time with me after school, when she doesn't have cheerleading practice. It will, I'm afraid, take a very serious time investment."

"Is cheerleading getting in the way of her studies?" Dad asks.

"I wouldn't pull her out of cheerleading . . . yet." Alex studies me like I'm not even listening, like I'm something in a zoo behind glass instead of a real girl. "But she should be very, very careful."

He's threatening me.

He doesn't want me to stop spending time with him. And he's willing to drag my parents into this mess in order to prove it.

He's willing to ruin my entire future just to keep me.

I feel my pulse quicken, but I don't move.

"Does that sound okay, Miss Stone?" Miss Felcher prods.

I let a smile spread across my face. "Absolutely, Ms. Felcher."

"Then I think we're done here." Mr. Belrose gathers my papers into a neat stack. "Unless there are any questions." He stands and tucks the papers under his arm.

My dad stands and takes his hand. "Thanks for caring about our daughter this much, Mr. Belrose. You're a good man."

Alex looks at me. "I'm just trying to do the right thing, Mr. Stone."

"Yes, thank you, Mr. Belrose," I say. I stand, straightening my dress.

It's only then that Mr. Belrose allows a flash of an emotion I can't quite identify cross his face, and I let myself smile. If he's going to play dirty, I'll play dirtier.

And that means I'll have to be more perfect than ever.

TWENTY-NINE
Love and Hate

"So you're not angry with me," Alex says for the thirteenth time.

I'm back at his house, and it's 6:42 a.m. I was supposed to meet him at school for an early morning study session, but since Jacqueline just happens to be in Vegas with her girlfriends, I surprised him at home, like I couldn't wait to see him.

"No. I'm not. I understand your reasons."

We're on the couch, and my head is in his lap. His hand strokes my hair slowly, softly, touching each strand like they are fine little woven bits of silk. I feel . . . special. Important.

"Your parents seemed nice," he offers, and I laugh. It's funny, in a weird, strange way, like this whole thing is screwed-up funny, and I don't even know what's going to happen next anymore.

And I used to have everything so smoothed out that I knew exactly what my next move was at any given time.

He leans down to kiss the top of my head. "You know I love you, Riley, don't you?" he asks.

I squirm around so my face is up, and he pushes my hair out of my eyes. "I need you to do something for me," I tell him.

"Okay."

"Be mine. One hundred percent mine. For real. I can't keep doing this otherwise."

His hand freezes on my forehead. "I will, Riley. I swear to God I will. I just can't right now. Not yet."

Alex kissing Jacqueline flashes across my mind's eye. "What's the holdup, then?" I try to pitch my voice to sound casual, but it doesn't. I don't. I sound jealous and catty and my voice has a harsh catch in it.

He lets out his breath. "It's just that Jaqueline's life is really hard right now, and I don't want to pile on, you know? As soon as she sorts everything out just a little bit more, I'll be able to talk with her, and we'll separate. Really separate, I mean. I won't let her come back this time."

I feel like someone has just put a vise grip on my heart. "Um, excuse me?"

He starts stroking again, but instead of his hand feeling good on my face, it's annoying me. I push it away and sit up next to him on the couch so I can look at him. "Why is now *not* a good time, exactly?"

He looks uncomfortable. "Well, her Fine Wines group, they're just being really mean to her right now. She's so beautiful, you know, women are always just mean to her, and she doesn't handle it all that well. She needs my help. She's delicate. I'm sure you get it. You're beautiful, too."

"Please don't compare me to her," I say coldly.

"But you understand, right?" He grabs my hands and holds them tightly in his.

I study his face. The wide jawline, the stubble, the deep green eyes, and I realize, on some level, I hate him a little bit. I hate the man who made me all the promises in the world and just won't keep them.

And I love him.

But I do hate him.

He leans in, slowly, closing his eyes, and I let him kiss me anyway. The kiss is slow and good, just like all of his kisses, and I hate myself a little too, for letting him kiss me like that. He starts lifting my shirt, but I pull away.

"You know the rules." I tap him lightly on the nose. "Is she gone?"

"For the weekend." He sulks, and I laugh because I know I'm supposed to give in, but I don't. "She's very depressed. I'm just worried about her. Really worried." He looks down.

I cock my head to the side. Is he confessing to me that he's worried about his wife? His wife who he said he wants to leave?

Does he want me to be *sympathetic*?

On what level is this—any of this—okay?

I fight the manic laugh trapped in my throat.

"We've been married for almost six months, Riley. I care about her."

Suddenly, I don't feel like I'm a part of him anymore. I feel like I'm in another room, or another house, and something's separating us. Maybe a curtain, or a window screen, or maybe I'm watching a fuzzy film of someone I used to know but don't quite anymore, and the communication is delayed, like I can see his lips moving but the meaning doesn't hit me until just a moment later.

"I'm so glad you understand me," he says gratefully.

He's wrong.

I don't understand him.

And clearly, he thinks I'm an idiot if he thinks I'm going to stand by and let me be a little pawn in his sick game.

Rage squeezes my heart. The veins burst and blood spurts and I die inside.

If Jacqueline were to just disappear, maybe it wouldn't be so weird. She is depressed, after all. And she is in the way. Of us. Of happiness. And she's clearly a horrible person.

If only I were a killer.

I squeeze Alex's hands. "I understand," I tell him. I touch his face softly. Kindly. I am there for him, he thinks. I am his silly little waiting-around toy.

"Can I see you tonight?" he asks, his voice low and gravelly, and I know he is dying to get his hands on me. They drop to my waist and squeeze, and I wiggle away and sling my backpack over my shoulders.

"Thanks to your surprise meeting with my lovely parents, I

definitely can't get out of any more cheerleading practices or study sessions or anything without looking suspicious." I kiss him lightly, but he furrows his brow.

"Huh? *My* meeting?"

I run my hands along his hairline and behind his ears. "Don't be ridiculous, Alex."

"I didn't schedule that meeting."

I smile. He wants to play. How cute.

I'm just not in the mood.

"I'll see you at school, okay, Alex?"

I lean over and kiss him one more time, hard and fast, and his hands are everywhere they shouldn't be, so I untangle myself.

"You need to be there soon yourself," I warn him. "And don't mess up my hair."

And then I walk out the back door into the cold morning sunlight. A few snowflakes are falling from the sparse cloud cover, and I smile into the odd weather and put on my hat before walking through the back gate into the alley.

Alex Belrose is going to be all mine, one way or another.

I am sure of it.

Things to Know About Riley Stone:

- When Riley Stone learned about the water crisis in Michigan, she began selling water bottles with the #HARTSVILLECARES hashtag–and ending up raising more than five thousand dollars. She spent the money on bottled water, which she sent to the impacted areas.

- Riley also began an anonymous gossip newsletter for the high school and employed her fellow students as models for the advertisements. The publication was eventually shut down by the school, but no one ever found out Riley ran the newsletter, and Riley made out with fifteen hundred dollars in profit, even after paying her models (who *did* get detention).

- Last year, Riley started a letter-writing campaign for the troops overseas. The effort gained statewide attention, and Riley ended up sending more than ten thousand letters and five hundred carefully selected care packages. She assembled a team of community volunteers and has since received multiple requests to run the campaign annually.

- At age fourteen, Riley's algebra teacher, Mrs. Corkstone, became very interested in her. While Riley passed her class with an A plus (as usual), Mrs. Corkstone did not trust Riley and kept an extra-close eye on her at all times, and often did not even let her leave class to use the bathroom.

- One of Riley's adopted grandparents in her Senior Friends program was convicted of second-degree murder–at age ninety-three.

THIRTY
Off

The morning after I visited Alex at his house, I have a doctor's appointment. It's just a checkup—nothing to worry about, of course—but since cell phones aren't allowed to be on in the doctor's office, and I'm not exactly the type of girl who needs social media 24-7, I don't bother to check it when I leave the doctor's office.

Or when I stop at Starbucks.

So it isn't until I pull into the parking lot that I notice something is different. *Off.* About fifteen students are clustered outside the glass door that leads to the gym corridor, and they are just *standing* there. Talking. Leaning in. And no one—not a student aide, or a teacher, or anyone, is telling them to get to class.

I check my phone. It is definitely class time. It isn't a passing period or anything.

And there are *thirteen* texts I've missed. I type in my passcode to open them.

Mom (1)

Kolbie (7)

Neta (5)

Mom: Can you stop at the grocery store before you come home tonight and pick up onion powder please? Hope your appointment went well. XOXO.

Kolbie: OMG DID YOU GUYS HEAR

Neta: YES. What is going on?!?!?!?!

Kolbie: I have NO IDEA

Kolbie: JUST GONE JUST LIKE THAT

Neta: Everyone is freaking out

Kolbie: Mrs. Tanner isn't even bothering to teach the lesson right now.

Neta: Is she crying, because there are girls in my class actually crying.

Kolbie: Yep cryers here too. It can't be that serious can it? I'm sure it's just a misunderstanding. Likeeee probably dentist appointment for wisdom teeth or something

Neta: yeah well I heard they called the police so . . .

Kolbie: OH SHIT WHAT

Neta: Yep. It's not like him, though. I would freak if I were his wife.

Kolbie: It's getting real. This is SCARY

I click out of my texts and slip my phone into my purse. I could ask Kolbie and Neta what is going on, but if they're in class, they won't be able to respond immediately. Plus, based on the current tone of their messages, they're likely to be more than a little dramatic.

So I stop by the students gathered of the steps leading into the corridor. "What's going on?" I ask.

A freshman girl with pretty braids detaches herself from the group, eager to share gossip with me. She looks both ways, like she's afraid someone might see her. "Mr. Belrose didn't show up for his classes this morning."

And then, everything inside of me falls apart systemically.

First, my heart seems to stop. Then my stomach curls.

And then my legs feel like they detach and my bones vanish.

"What?" I ask, very faintly. I want to rest my hand on her shoulder, to get my bearings.

"He just didn't show up," she repeats. "And no one can get ahold of him or find him or anything." She bounces a little bit, like this is very exciting news. "People are really worried. There are people praying in the library and other people trying to break it up because this is, like, a public school."

I think I say something back, but I'm not sure.

I fumble my way toward the locker room, which happens to have the closest bathrooms, and am promptly sick into the toilet, which is where Neta finds me twenty minutes later, still puking my guts out.

"Are you okay?" she asks.

I nod, wiping my mouth off with a clump of thin toilet paper that clings to my chin. "I think it was just something the doctor did."

She feels my forehead. "You're not that warm. Still, you should probably go to the nurse's office. I'll walk you down there."

I shake my head. I need to stay here. I need to figure out what is going on. If I'm home in bed, I'll have to rely on text messages, and I can't even be overeager about those or it'll look really suspicious. I wash my mouth out and grab a stick of mint gum from my backpack. "I'm okay," I insist. I try to pull my hair around my face a little bit, so I don't look so sticky and pale. I am not one of those crying girls in the hallway. I am not Thea, who is clawing at the wall, acting like her world has ended.

I am fine. Getting overly excited about a teacher failing to show up for class would be decidedly not Riley behavior.

"Did you hear about Belrose?" Neta asks, her voice low. "Weird, right?"

I nod. "Really weird. Have you heard anything?"

"He didn't show for a makeup test for Gabriella Hernandez this morning, but she just went to the office and reported it so they could mark that she hadn't ditched, you know? And they didn't think much of it. But then he didn't show for his first-period class. *Or* his second period. And he's still not here."

I swallow hard around my gum. My mouth still holds to the sick-sweet-sour taste of vomit, and my stomach feels like there is something living inside of it, thrashing and angry and vile and scratching at the lining, trying to get out.

Did he try to leave Jacqueline and she—did something?

Or did Jacqueline find out about me?

Or maybe . . . maybe he just slept in.

Maybe that's all.

It happens. People get tired. And Alex has been under a *lot* of stress lately. While we're walking, I pull out my phone and send him a quick e-mail.

Are you okay?

But I'm not the only one worried. The school is a mess. Students are in the hallways, along with teachers. But it's not loud. No one is yelling or running. Everyone is just staring around like they're looking for something and speaking to each other in hushed tones.

The minutes slip by strangely, like time is folding in on itself, too fast and too slow all at once.

And still no Alex Belrose.

"Let's walk by the office," Neta suggests. "I'm not in the mood for fifth period."

I nod. I'm not, either. I know I'm supposed to be toeing the line on account of my nonexistent French grade problem, but I don't really care.

Kolbie catches up with us in the hallway, and we walk to the office together, and that's when we see *her.*

"Holy shit," Kolbie says.

"What?" Neta asks.

"That's his wife," I murmur.

And there she is, in high-heeled boots and a big black hat, like she just stepped off a runway, just inside the glass enclosure of the main office. She looks like a pretty caged butterfly, flapping meaninglessly inside an enclosure. She's an homage to the reality star: all image and no substance, ready to be photographed, calm and put-together just in case there's some dramatic tragedy. What the hell would she be doing *here*? Shouldn't she be at the police station, if she's worried? I stare at her. How convenient that she's in all black. Already in mourning for her missing husband. She couldn't even wait a day to soak up the attention and pity.

"Does this mean she doesn't know where he is either?" Neta asks.

"I would guess so," Kolbie says. "A wife doesn't really have to be here to call you in sick, does she?"

I don't say what I already know: she's supposed to be in Vegas. Or at least she was, until last night.

I frown. Why *is* she back? Did she fly back when she heard her husband didn't show up to work?

Is she looking for him here? Did they call her in? Or is she just here to throw her own little pity party?

Jacqueline turns toward us, and Kolbie and Neta gasp, but I don't move. I lock eyes with her.

She pauses, her long eyelashes fluttering.

She doesn't even look upset. She looks normal, like maybe she's just dropping off something for him. There is no trace of concern anywhere on her radiant face.

And then she walks out of the office, like nothing happened, her heels echoing on the dirty tile. She stalks out the door and down the sidewalk, where her teal car is parked illegally in the loading zone.

But that's how I know.

She knows more than she's letting on.

And maybe that has something to do with me. Maybe she knows about Alex and me. Or maybe Alex had to run away to finally be free of her.

THIRTY-ONE

Nothing

He hasn't responded. Forty-eight hours and Alex Belrose has not responded.

I stare at my phone as I walk. It's not like this is new. It's not like he just supplies me with attention whenever I want it. I'm obviously not that important to him anyway.

I want to e-mail him again. But e-mailing someone who is potentially missing is probably not a great idea. I don't want them tracing anything back to me. I don't want them finding a hair on his couch and connecting the DNA or something.

I stick my phone in my purse and keep to my route: the Belrose house. And not my normal route. It's a long walk, but I don't care. I'm not parking a car anywhere close. I wore an old jacket from the back of my closet and tugged on mittens, two wool scarves, and a thick knit hat, and I even grabbed two hand warmers from my dad's hunting gear to keep in my pockets if it gets really cold. I haven't had to use them—I've been walking so much that I'm not particularly chilled beyond my cheeks, which are stinging a bit.

Normally, I'd be at cheer tonight, but with the hubbub, all after-school activities were canceled. Everyone's on edge. Everyone's a little scared. Any laughter in the school sounds strange and alien. And they've brought in Mr. Anderburg, a young, twitchy man, as the substitute French teacher . . . and he doesn't understand two words of the language, I'm pretty sure. He sort of stands at the front of the class in baggy clothes, stuttery and out of place, and the whole room feels pale and odd and scared without Belrose at the helm.

Everyone whispers. All the time.

I walk faster. I'm almost there. I think of the steps I am taking and my fitness wristband, but I don't want anything tracking me here. My location tracker on my smartphone has been off basically since I got it. I hate people knowing where I am at all times. It's creepy.

I like my steps untraceable.

I stop deliberately short of the Belrose house, and it looks just like it always has, like Alex is just waiting for me to slip in through the back gate and into the den, where he'll be waiting with French poetry and a kiss. Only he isn't. Only I've checked my e-mail ten thousand times and he's nowhere, and no one knows anything, especially not me, and it hurts somewhere strange and deep in me where I didn't know it was possible to hurt.

I study the house from as close as I dare, but I can't see anything of note. Just the same old house, looking the same old way, and nothing to show that anyone is missing or that anything has happened at all.

I feel strange and let down. Somehow I felt like maybe if I were in the neighborhood, he'd want to come back. He'd sense I was here and pop up, and be happy to see me.

If he could.

But there's nothing. Just the sound of the fir trees moving and distant wind chimes.

I swallow hard, resisting the urge to push through the gate and try the back door. I turn away instead, and walk through the trees, trudging back in the direction of my house.

When I get home, though, I force myself to concentrate. I sit at the desk in my room and finish my homework. I double-check all my answers even though I know I'm right. I double-check them even though I'm certain my teachers don't care right now either.

Everyone's mind is elsewhere.

Nothing like this has ever happened before.

Neta texts me.

COME OVER. I'M BOREDDDDDDDDDDDDD.

I'm not. But I need something else to think about besides Alex. Something else to do besides check my e-mail and pace the floor of my room, wearing a path in my rug.

"You came!" she squeals at me when I walk through the door, and hugs me. She looks good. A lot better since the funeral, actually, although I suppose that's not hard, since the funeral was pretty much the lowest I'd ever seen her. For a few days after the service she stopped wearing makeup because she kept crying it off so quickly, but she has it back on today and she's actually sort of smiling.

"You okay?" I ask cautiously.

"Just glad you're here," she says, but if I look hard I can see a little bit of sadness underneath her excitement. "Come downstairs. I have TLC on and I made brownies."

Neta is basically Martha Stewart (minus the jail time) in the kitchen, and I cannot resist her brownies. She also knows I'm not the type of girl to eat one bite of brownie and feel bad about it for a million years. I'll eat, like, twelve and feel pretty great about it, honestly. And then I might get a stomachache and decide it was a bad idea later, but I prefer to live in the moment. And in this moment, I need brownies in my life.

I am a girl who knows what she wants, after all.

"Do you have ice cream?"

"Rocky road."

"You're the light of my life, Neta Adriana Castillo."

She flips her hair. "I know."

We run downstairs like we're middle schoolers again. TLC is playing reruns of *Say Yes to the Dress*, which we both know is staged, but we don't care. The entire pan of brownies (minus two squares) are sitting, precut, on the floor in front of the television. Neta disappears for a moment and brings back two pints of store-brand ice cream—one fudge chocolate, one mint chocolate chip.

"Sorry, no rocky road," she says apologetically, dropping a

spoon in my lap, and we grab a bunch of old blankets and pillows and sit on top of them.

"Thanks for coming over," she says. "I needed some distractions."

"So did I," I say. "This whole thing at school with Mr. Belrose is nuts, right?"

She nods. "I heard, like, he got *kidnapped*." She pulls a blanket around her shoulders.

"What? From who?" I sit up a little straighter.

"Lilah Gilbert, actually. She said that he was taken by someone who was pissed about a grade. Isn't that insane?"

I sink back down into the pile of blankets. Nothing Lilah Gilbert says is likely to be anywhere close to the truth. In fourth grade, she pulled two hundred dollars out of a Cracker Jack box, claiming it was a prize, but she actually stole it from Mr. Jeppard's wallet, which he figured out during a spelling test when his wife came by to pick up the cash she was supposed to buy a used crib with. Of course, Elijah Piper pointed right at Lilah and mentioned her lucky Cracker Jack winnings, and Mr. Jeppard was so mad, he didn't stop at sending Lilah to the office. The cops actually arrested her for theft. She got suspended for two weeks, and when she returned, she was transferred next door to Mrs. Dones's class, which we were all pretty jealous about because Mrs. Dones let everyone call her Angelica and play music during reading hour.

"What do you think happened?" Neta asks. She's mashing brownie into her mint chocolate chip ice cream.

For a second, I want to tell her everything. I want to tell her about our nights together, and how Alex kisses, all of the meals he has cooked for me, and the French poetry, and the promises to leave Jacqueline, and how we were really going to be together. I want to tell her how he betrayed me and how somehow even though I sort of hate him a little, I think I actually love him.

But that's all ridiculous, of course.

So the moment passes. I grab a spoonful of her mint-and-brownie mess. "His wife is a little nutty, isn't she?" I ask. "Maybe they should start there."

Neta grabs the remote and starts paging through the guide, bored with the white-wedding-dressed women on the screen. "Maybe. Hey, did I tell you I'm talking to someone new?"

I blink at her. "No, you didn't!" I don't point out that I've been a pretty poor friend because I've very nearly been doing my teacher.

"His name is Chase, and he's friends with Jamal too, I guess. After the whole Sandeep fiasco, I suppose Kolbie thought I deserved a shot—so Chase just happened to be in town just after visiting his aunt and uncle or something. So we went to a movie with Kolbie and Jamal, and then, I don't know, I think we're a thing or something."

"You think you're a thing?" I ask, trying to emulate her level of excitement while my heart is dropping. "Have you talked about it?"

"Kind of. I mean, he's going back this weekend, and we're supposed to hang out. He's taking me to a nice dinner, and we've texted every night. See? We're texting right now." She thrusts her iPhone at me, showing three (3) new texts from Chase Abrams.

"You really like him." A little of the strange jealousy that rose when I realized that Kolbie and Neta have a life without me fades. Neta really needs a distraction right now. And if that's Chase . . . well, then, that's good for her. And I'm glad. She needs something positive in her life.

She wiggles a little. "Yeah, kind of. I just wish he were here, you know? So we could hang out as often as RJ and I did. RJ was always just—around when I needed him."

"Yeah. I get that."

I wish Alex were here too. Everything feels strange now. Before Alex, I would have been fine sitting here in the basement with Neta, eating ice cream and talking about guys and watching reality shows.

And now it doesn't feel like enough.

The doorbell rings upstairs. "Expecting someone?" I ask, but Neta shakes her head and chooses reruns of *Teen Mom* . . . but then Rob Samuels comes stomping down the stairs. One of his sneakers is untied and he's grinning and holding a liter of Dr Pepper and a big brown paper bag that says *SMILEY'S*, the name of the local grocery store. A big tear runs up the side.

"Hey!" he says. "What's up?"

I want to drag Neta in the bathroom and force her to explain herself, but she just points to the recliner near her shoulder. "What's up, Rob?" she asks. "Grab a seat."

He sits down. I shoot her a look. She could have at least told me he was coming. I feel slightly intruded upon. I thought it was girls' night.

"I heard it was junk food time," he says, and tears open the brown bag and leans forward to dump it out between us on the blankets. An array of candy flows out in a sugar waterfall: caramels, little packets of Sour Patch Kids and Swedish Fish, chocolate truffles, red and pink Starburst, and even fun-size packages of Skittles.

I relent a little.

"I'll get a little ice for the soda," he offers. "Are you done with the ice cream? I can put it back in the freezer if you want." He collects the ice cream containers and runs up the stairs, like he knows exactly where everything is.

"What?" Neta asks innocently. "He's *helpful.*"

I glower. "Helpful, huh?"

"This has nothing to do with you. I swear to God. He's just been sweet to me at school. That's all. So I told him he could hang out with us, and obviously he is cool because he is basically a girl, snack-wise. I mean, look at this. His sweets game is on point. There is not a Funyun or beef jerky in the mix."

She throws herself back on the pile of candy, doing a snow angel in the mess. I giggle in spite of myself.

"I guess. But I love Funyuns. And beef jerky."

Neta makes a face.

Rob stomps back down the stairs, three glasses filled with ice balanced in his hands. "Ladies first," he says without any trace of irony, and fills our glasses with cold Dr Pepper.

I observe him. He does seem sort of harmless, and if Neta's the one who wants him here, I don't exactly care. He sinks back into the chair and grabs a chocolate truffle off the floor.

"You can't tell my friends I'm here," he tells me, popping the truffle into his mouth. "I'd lose major points. Oh, hey, is this *Teen Mom*? I don't think I've seen this one." He leans forward and scoops up a couple of Starburst.

I watch him for a few seconds longer, but he sort of seems content just staring at the TV, so I nudge Neta.

"So, Chase this weekend, huh?" I ask, and she practically bubbles over with excitement. I let her talk over the television, which normally drives me crazy. Somebody needs a little happy in their lives, and if it can't be me, it might as well be Neta.

THIRTY-TWO
Fake

"Nothing."

My brother shakes his head. "This is bad. I just have this feeling, you know? It's in my gut. It feels like *shit*." He puts his hand on his stomach.

"Yeah," I say. I'm sprawled out across the couch in the living room, an old *People* magazine open under my arm, and Ethan is rocking back and forth in the recliner. It makes a small squeak every time he moves.

He won't shut up about Alex.

I give up on the magazine and pretend like I'm watching some stupid cartoon, only I don't know anything that's going on and I think I might be sick at any second. It rises up from the top of my stomach and sits at the base of my throat.

"There are search parties out, and they're just not successful. They're in all the parks and stuff, but they're not finding anything. I mean, *anything*. And the cops have questioned his wife, and I don't think she's a 'person of interest' or whatever. And maybe it's good that they haven't found him, but you know what everyone's saying, right?"

I don't want him to answer. I can't hear the answer. I don't want him to say it.

"They're saying that he's *dead*." He pauses, staring at the characters leapfrogging across the television. "Can you believe it? Someone I went to high school with? Just dead, just like that? Life is screwed up. I mean, I never knew anyone that *died* before."

He says it like it's final and done and inarguable and just a thing.

"I'm sure he's not dead," I say, but even as I say them, the words are tinny and false in my ears. I stand up, wishing I were numb, and walk to the little half bath by the kitchen, where I am very quietly ill before wiping my mouth and returning to the TV. I sink into the couch, my skin clammy, and pull a throw over my legs.

"I keep calling him, you know?" Ethan says. "I bet I called him twenty times. All of us have. It's like I expect him to answer, but he never does." He pauses, jiggling the remote. "Have you heard anything?"

"Nothing," I say, and my throat clams up a little. Are they going to start combing his house for DNA? Then what? Are they going to find me? Would it even matter? I'm sure I'm not in a database or anything, on account of never having committed any real crimes.

It's not like anyone would suspect me—anyone. No one knows I've ever been there. No neighbors have ever seen me enter or exit.

I don't think.

My blood feels oddly thick in my veins, and I run to the little half bath again, but there is nothing left in my stomach.

The next day at school, the mood is tense, and I can hardly get through my classes. The teachers feel pretty much the same way, and they barely give us any homework—which is a good and bad thing, because it means my mind has room to wander, and the only thing anyone can really think about is Belrose. Unless you're Neta, and then you're thinking about Chase.

Or Rob Samuels, blond-headed wonder boy, and in that case you're thinking about me.

"Hey, Stone!" He jogs up to me after school, as I'm headed out toward the parking lot. He grins at me, really big, in a way that nobody has really been grinning in the past week at all, and it's rather like shouting in a church.

In the middle of a funeral.

I cringe at the thought.

"Hey, Rob."

He falls into step beside me. "So, um, I had fun the other night chilling with you guys."

"Um, that's cool. Me too."

"Is it okay if I walk you to your car?" he asks as he walks me to my car, past everyone else still walking with their heads down, voices muted.

I frown. "That's fine." I stop at my car, feeling awkward. "Um, thanks, Rob. I appreciate it."

He still has that big, shouty grin on. "Sure."

"Um, thanks." I make to get in the car, but Rob sort of looks around and moves his feet over the ground, but doesn't leave.

"Riley," he says, "are you okay?"

I frown at him. "Why do you ask that?"

He kicks at the gravel in the street and leans up against my door, but he doesn't meet my eyes. "You've just seemed different lately. And not different like everyone else is being different, just, like, lately. But *different* different. Not to seem creepy or anything, but I notice you. I pay attention to you. You're a smart person, and you're a good person to take note of, but I can tell something is wrong, Riley. And I just wanted to see if I could, you know, help in some kind of way." His cheeks flush a little.

I bite the inside of my cheek to keep from tearing up. Someone noticed. Rob Samuels, out of everyone, actually *noticed*.

I hug him, right there, in front of all the students still walking out of the school into the parking lot. Let them think whatever they want.

I needed that.

"Why do you care?" I ask. My words sound mean, even to my ears, but I don't intend it that way. I really want to know. It's not like I've treated him all that well. It's not like I deserve it.

"I just do."

I look at him, just standing there, and his smile has lessened a little bit, so it's just . . . nice. Maybe I should have a boyfriend. It couldn't hurt. Especially not now. Maybe it would even keep . . . people . . . from looking at me suspiciously.

"Do you want to come over and hang out?"

The question is out before I fully consider it, and Rob looks at me, his eyes big and shiny and the loud smile back. "Yes."

I let him follow me to my house in his car and make him park at the curb instead of in the driveway, and when he follows me in I take him down to the basement, where we have a big-screen TV and an old L-shape couch that's perfect for long movies and cold days.

"I didn't bring any snacks," he says, and he looks miserable, like he has let me down in some unforgivable way.

"It's okay," I tell him. "I'll go get something from the kitchen."

My parents aren't home. I'm hoping if they see his car when they get off work they'll just think it's one of the neighbors being annoying or something. They hate it when someone parks close. I'm not ready to explain Rob to them just yet anyway. I run upstairs and grab a bag of my mom's Lite Butter Skinny-Woman Popcorn before tossing it into the microwave.

I watch it turn. The microwave hums and rattles where the plate isn't set quite right.

What am I doing?

Why am I doing this?

The bag slowly starts to inflate, the kernels cracking and popping. I make myself turn away. I am a hostess, aren't I? So why don't

I care right now? Why aren't I excited that there's a guy downstairs who really, really cares about me?

I grab two cans of Coke from the fridge and pull a couple of paper towels from the roll before grabbing the popcorn out of the microwave and walking it back downstairs. Rob has moved from the couch to the television, where he's checking out my parents' DVD collection.

"*Die Hard 2* and *The Notebook*?" he asks. "This is a tough choice. What do you want to watch?"

I lift a shoulder and open the bag of popcorn, my fingers burning a little from the steam that escapes from the top. I set it down and blow on them.

Rob stands and catches my hand in his.

"Let me," he says.

He raises my fingers to his lips and blows, very gently, but the air from his lips is warm. His fingers are rough on my palm.

It doesn't feel right.

Nothing feels right.

I pull away without meaning to.

"I'll just run them under cold water for a second, okay? Choose a good movie. Um, maybe an action movie."

I don't wait for his reaction. I run off to the bathroom and shut the door behind me. Maybe this was a bad idea. He wants me, and I know he wants me, and I'm just using him again. I have to hold him far away, because I can't make myself be with him.

I shove my fingers under the cold water even though they don't hurt anymore and count to twenty. And then I dry off my hands and walk back into the little den.

Where the opening credits for *Pride and Prejudice* are playing on the TV.

"I thought you'd like it," Rob says, looking a little guilty.

I sigh and sit on the opposite end of the couch. "It's fine."

He scoots a cushion closer, and I stick my feet out so he can't sit next to me.

"Do you want popcorn?" he asks.

I stand up and grab a handful from the bag and a can of Coke, then return to my seat. "I love this movie."

"Me too," he says.

But for someone who loves *Pride and Prejudice*, he spends more time watching me than Keira Knightley.

THIRTY-THREE
Struggle

"So tell us more about this Rob boy," Mom says. "He seemed so sweet! I don't know why you haven't brought him around before, honestly."

Of course Mom loved him. And I wouldn't have even had to introduce Rob last night if he hadn't stayed after the movie to clean, insisting that we'd left crumbs on the floor from the popcorn.

"Kernels are so hard to get out of carpet," he'd said, and then actually started opening closets and stuff until he found my Mom's fancy new Hoover she ordered off the Home Shopping Network, and even though I'd told him "please, no," he started vacuuming the floor and folding up throw blankets and putting the DVD into its case and doing stuff he most definitely did not need to do.

So of course my mom came downstairs to see what the hell her daughter was doing vacuuming so late at night (or at all), and saw Rob, who of course ma'am-ed his way into my mom's heart immediately, and I'm relatively certain she had him mapped out as my prom date and possibly as my husband before he'd left.

Rob does that to mothers.

I remember in fifth grade, he'd always be first to volunteer to help the class mothers hand out birthday cupcakes. Back then, he was stocky and cute and his blond hair was always getting in his eyes, and no matter whose birthday it was, he would always save me the cupcake with the most frosting.

Of course, now he's the kind of guy who would be cast in an after-school special. If I want to avoid being engaged by the end of the year, I'm going to have to figure something out.

Today is Saturday and the heat is broken. Apparently, while doing a major renovation on the house at the end of the street, the construction workers accidentally messed up the gas line, and now the entire neighborhood is waiting for the gas company to get it fixed. As a result, my mother got this idea that we should all have breakfast in the living room together under blankets and be a *family*. So she talked my father into making waffles and bacon and eggs and called Ethan and now we're sort of comfortable, weighted down under huge piles of old throws that smell just a bit dusty, with heating pads plugged in underneath. The sky outside is a deceptive blue, too light for the odd weather.

Even Esther is here, sharing a recliner with my brother, the swell of her stomach hidden under the pile of blankets. They have one plate of food between them, and her head is on his shoulder and he's smiling.

The TV is on, quietly, and for just a little bit, I feel happy, with me and my family and Esther, while we talk quietly and eat our waffles with extra butter and syrup and I realize I can't remember the last time I felt this content with them.

"Your mother says you had someone over last night," Dad says.

"He was very nice." Mom glows. "His name was Robert Samuels. He's a good boy."

Good boy. Good girl.

How *fitting.*

My dad opens his mouth to say something else, but Ethan interrupts, leaning forward and nearly spilling Esther out of his lap. He wraps his arms around her, and she grabs on to the plate, but the fork falls onto the rug.

"Turn that up, okay?"

The TV shows a picture of a pretty blond reporter holding a stack of papers. A picture of Alex, taken at the last school photo day, his HARTSVILLE HIGH tag clipped to his shirt, is shown in the upper right-hand corner. His smile is practiced and smooth, and his face is neatly shaven.

". . . possible signs of a struggle at the Belrose residence. Mrs. Belrose was taken into custody for questioning, but has been released. The police chief is asking that anyone with any information about this case please come forward immediately."

My heart feels like paper that has been lit on fire and is blackening and curling up from the edges.

It's a strangely familiar feeling.

She killed him. I *know* she killed him. But it's not like I can just go down to the police station and be like, "Hey, I just happen to know my sort-of boyfriend teacher probably got slaughtered by his wife."

Was it my fault she did it? Or did Alex actually grow the balls to ask her for a divorce and maybe she just flipped out?

Am I going to be brought in next?

"What about your grades?" my dad asks. "Now that he's out, who's going to fix them?"

Mom puts her hands on her chest. "You're right. I didn't even think of that. Should we call the school? This is bad, Riley, isn't it? He was going to help you."

Of course. Alex is missing and my parents are worried about my grades. They're not worried about him possibly being dead or the fact that he was most likely murdered by his crazy wife.

"Um, I did extra credit. So it'll be fine."

I don't mention that the bad grades were all bullshit anyway, and that I checked the grade book because the substitute is completely lame and bought my story when I said I needed to check that Belrose had recorded a grade for the essay I'd turned in before he'd disappeared.

He'd never actually recorded a single bad grade. Not one.

But I'd known that anyway. Of course.

"This is so fucked up," Ethan mutters. "What has it been now? A week and a half? And *nothing*?"

Esther pushes his hair back. "Were you guys in touch?"

Ethan mumbles something. Because they weren't. He is just one of those people, hanging on to an old connection, wishing he'd called or texted or something before his friend went missing.

And then everything is weird and quiet and I can hear my dad chewing his bacon, which he likes black and burnt.

"Rob is great," I say into the quiet. "He's really cool."

"Are you going to see him again?" my mother asks.

I nod. "Yep. Definitely." I take a sip of the coffee my mother made as her contribution. It's not very strong and could use sugar and creamer. Suddenly I'm hot. Too hot for all the blankets and the plate in my lap and waffles and coffee. I push them off and head for the kitchen.

"Where are you going, honey?" Mom asks, like I'm going out into a blizzard and not just a cold house.

"I need sugar."

Instead of going back to the living room, I stand in the kitchen. The floor is icy.

The cops obviously aren't taking Jacqueline seriously. And maybe that means I will have to.

And if Jacqueline isn't above killing, maybe I'm not either. And that goes double if Alex told Jacqueline anything about me.

Oh my God.

What if Alex told Jacqueline something about me?

I'm stirring sugar into my coffee, hopping back and forth on the cold tile floor, when the doorbell rings.

"I'll get it," I yell into the living room. The rest of my family is still likely cocooned into their blankets, so I run to the door, wishing I'd made it back to my bedroom for socks. I wiggle my toes into the softness of the rug and swing the door open, hoping it's the repairman, telling us our heat will be kicking back on shortly.

It's not.

It's Neta and Rob.

Neta bursts in without even saying hello. "Did you just see the news?" she asks. She lowers her voice. "We had to come over. Like . . . holy shit."

I wrap my arms around myself. "You chose the wrong house. Heat is out."

Rob smiles at me. "We don't care."

Neta fake-grins. "Yeah, we don't care." She imitates Rob and gives me this huge fake wink.

I lead them downstairs, away from the family meeting in the living room, and pull the remaining musty blankets out of the closet under the stairs. I find an old space heater and plug it in, and when I turn back Neta is on one end of the couch and Rob is on the other.

So I sit in the middle.

And cover up with the thinnest blanket.

"Do you want to share?" Rob scoots a little closer.

"I'm good."

The space heater starts to make an odd metallic noise. I hope it's not going to explode. My mom is always going on about space heaters exploding and starting stuff on fire and everyone dying.

"So do you think he's dead?" Neta asks. And she looks sad, actually. She wraps her arms around herself. "I just—I can't. I can't deal. But if there are signs of an actual struggle—"

"Then why are they just now finding them?" I interrupt. "This is all too weird. Why is this all just now happening?"

"Sometimes the cops don't release stuff right away." Rob pulls the blanket around his shoulders, and I turn on the television to a pop music channel to cover the sound of our voices. I don't want my parents to try to eavesdrop on our conversation, and since they're suddenly interested in Rob, they might actually try.

Weird that it took a guy for them to notice that their daughter was here, around, a sentient being instead of a picture to straighten on a wall. Weird that I wasn't enough on my own when I was being the perfect child and pinning awards and ribbons to my dream board and filling my bank account I can't touch with grants and my future with scholarships. It took a boy and bad grades to even get them to look at me.

Weird that being accepted to the right colleges wasn't enough. Weird that all my friends want to do is talk about men and what it takes to get them to look at you and what happens when they touch you and all the things you might have done wrong when they don't.

At the end of the day, that's really all that's important. And who are we without male approval?

And look what I have with Rob on my arm.

Approval.

Attention.

Weird.

Ethan was right.

"Why don't they release anything?" Neta asks. "I mean, that doesn't make sense. Nothing makes sense about this. Why would anyone kill Mr. Belrose? He was *perfect*."

"If they put everything out there and someone comes forward with information they haven't put out, well, then they know that person is involved with the crime somehow, you know?"

It makes sense.

Which means I can't say anything about Jacqueline.

Anything.

"Maybe there wasn't even a crime," I say. "What makes you so sure there was a crime? Maybe it was an accident. Maybe he just got stressed out. Maybe he just left his wife."

"I'm sure the police are investigating all of that. But they have to face the facts." Rob's hand appears from under his blanket and rests on my leg, and moves back and forth. "They haven't found a trace of him. And usually that means—something really bad is going on. The longer he's missing, the more likely it is he's dead."

I swallow hard. I want to move away. I want to push him away. I want to be anywhere but here. The blanket is thin enough that I can feel the pressure of each of his fingers. My skin feels strange and dirty.

"But it's Mr. Belrose," Neta says. "He's just—it's just—he can't be."

I stare at Rob's hand.

"He can't be," I repeat. "He's probably just lost or something."

Rob's hand moves.

I hate him.

I'm using him. I hate myself. And I'm using him. I need to end this, and I need to end this now, and I need to stop gossiping about whether Alex is dead, and I need to get him away from me and get him to quit touching me.

I am going to scream.

Neta draws her legs up on the couch. "How do you know so much about everything, Rob?"

"*Law and Order* addict. I'm an expert about this kind of stuff."

I stand up, and Rob's hand slides off my leg. "Do you guys want anything from the kitchen? Drinks? Coffee?"

"I can get it," Rob says, hopping up. "Do you want a Coke, Riley?"

"Something hot. A cappuccino, maybe," I suggest, knowing the machine isn't hooked up and it'll take him at least ten minutes to get it going.

"Me too," Neta says.

Rob runs up the stairs toward the kitchen and Neta focuses on me.

"You can't get rid of him," she says, reading my mind. "He's basically perfect. And you need a good guy, right?"

I stare at her. Of course. Women *need* men.

A good guy.

"Sure, Neta."

Weird.

THIRTY-FOUR

Brownies

Honestly, I didn't expect to learn a lot from the Senior Friends program I orchestrated, where I paired up students and cool senior citizens, but I have to say, Ms. Glenda did pass on the perfect brownie recipe. I happen to know her goddaughter, Dana, *really* had her heart set on the secret family recipe, but Glenda said that Dana had a real mean streak and she'd rather give it to someone who would appreciate it, and who am I to ignore the wishes of a dying old woman? Plus, Glenda said one day I'd need to make a decent pan of brownies, and I suppose she was right. I also suppose I didn't expect to make them for my ex-boyfriend's potential widow.

Baking is, after all, what you do when someone is grieving. Last time I went to my neighbor's house after her husband had died, everyone showed up with more pies and casseroles than she could have ever eaten. My parents showed up with a Jell-O salad with whipped cream and crushed pretzels on top.

I stir the batter, wash and put away the dishes, and have the brownies out of the oven before my parents can get home to ask what I'm up to. And then I head to the unhappiest house I can possibly think of.

A very familiar house.

The Belrose house.

I go with my brownies and my most perfect A-plus-student smile and a plan.

And I go because I can't stand it anymore even though there are a thousand reasons why I shouldn't.

I wear a perfect green sweater with a pocket on the right side of my chest, an A-line skirt that falls at just below my knees, and my National Honor Society pin. My hair is smoothed back into a careful ponytail, around which I have tied a dark pink ribbon that I've fastened into a neat bow so that two ends hang perfectly down on either side of my head. I in no way look like a harlot when I ring the doorbell with my plate of brownies. I know Jacqueline is home, because her obnoxiously bright car is parked at the end of the sidewalk.

For a moment, I don't hear anything, and then there are quiet little footsteps. The front door swings open, and then there's Jacqueline, adorned in a thin black dress, her makeup done with absolute perfection. A black fedora is perched on the top of her head and she has donned tiny little fingerless gloves. It's as if she's waiting to be photographed as the sad, sexy widow.

Like this has all been planned.

"I don't want Girl Scout cookies." Her voice is clipped, and she begins to close the door.

"I'm actually here on behalf of Mr. Belrose's French honors students," I say, my voice high and chirpy. "We just wanted to drop in on you to see how you were doing and give you these." I hold out the foil-covered pan.

"What are they?" she asks, turning her nose up a bit like maybe I'm trying to poison her.

Which wouldn't be a bad idea.

"Homemade brownies. From scratch. We're just so worried about you, Mrs. Belrose. We can't imagine what you're going through right now."

She gives me a long look, then cracks open her door, just a bit wider. "Well, okay then. Come on in."

I bite back a smile.

Excellent.

If the cops find my DNA in the Belrose house and someone traces it back to me, I want to say I've been in the house for a reason, even if it's giving brownies to a falsely grieving widow who doesn't look like she's been crying at all.

And if I happen to do a little detective work in the meantime . . . well. That's fine.

I sit down on the couch first, balancing my tray in my lap. "Maybe I should put these in the kitchen. They're still warm. Um, where is it?"

Because of course I haven't been here before.

"Just through there," she says, pointing to the doorway toward the cheery little kitchen. "Leave them on the table."

I do as I'm told.

"Those don't have any peanuts or anything in them, do they? I'm just terribly allergic. I mean, I would totally *die* if you gave me peanuts," Jacqueline says. Her hand raises her to throat. She speaks with an odd accent—maybe with the slightest French lilt, which is obnoxious, since I'm pretty sure she's originally from a small town in Texas.

"No," I say. Regrettably. I file away the knowledge. So Jacqueline has a severe food allergy. I could use that.

I sit back on the couch and cross my legs.

"How are you, Mrs. Belrose?" I furrow my brow, showing concern. I am a puppet.

So is she.

She wipes away a tear that isn't there.

"It's been so hard—uh—what did your say your name was?"

"Riley Stone."

I study her face. There is no flicker of recognition. Her eyebrows don't raise.

So he didn't tell her anything. If he said he was going to leave her, I wasn't a reason why.

"I'm going to be the valedictorian," I explain. "I am very good at French."

"Good for you, honey," she says. She reaches forward and pats me very lightly on the wrist, her palm flat and stiff. Is she always this weird?

For a moment, we're just silent, and I look out the picture window, trying not to think about all the other times I've looked out that very same picture window, and who was sitting next to me, and how much better I felt before.

"Is there anything—have you heard or found anything?" I ask. "We're just all so worried—I had to ask."

She smiles at me, but her teeth are hidden behind her lips. "There is a reason why I wear black, my darling."

"What?"

Her eyes flutter, like she's holding back tears that aren't really there. "A wife knows in her heart when she is widowed. And make no mistake. My husband is dead. I don't know how and I don't know why, but the other half of my heart has stopped beating. I feel it here." She presses her thin hand to her chest. "He is gone."

"How can you be sure?"

She looks at me sharply. "You would know if you ever really loved someone, Rayna," she says, forgetting my name already. "He is dead and has left me and all I can do is get used to it, and it's time for everyone else to do the same, and stop calling this a rescue mission. My love is dead. He's *dead*."

I stare at her. She's nuts. She's as much as confessing here. Why say someone is dead with so much certainty if you didn't kill him?

Why aren't the cops holding her?

"But how do you know?"

"I have premonitions about these things, my dear. It does no good to ask questions." She leans toward me. "Thank you for the snacks, sweet girl, but I think it's time for you to leave."

Right. Premonitions. How very intuitive of her. And that's a reason to give up on your husband if you didn't absolutely murder him in cold blood.

I stand. "Um, well let me know if you need anything else, okay?"

She takes my hand, and her skin is papery and cold and reminds me of an old woman. "Thank you for caring," she says. "No one else cares."

I try to smile at her. "I hope you're wrong."

"I'm not."

I leave as quickly as I can.

She's right, of course. She would know that Belrose is dead. Especially because I am willing to bet that she did it.

I blink away tears. Why can't they figure out what she did to him? Why can't the police understand that she murdered him? Why is it just me who can see it?

When I pull into my driveway, I realize that my parents are home . . . and so is Rob.

Rob Samuels.

Who is waiting in the kitchen with my parents, talking to them about God knows what, and my parents are just standing there, smiling, like I should be happy that he just showed up and is smothering me and won't leave me alone for a goddamn second.

"Look who's here!" my mom says, looking over the brim of her wineglass as she leans against the kitchen counter. My dad waves.

"Hi," I say.

Rob stands immediately. "Hey, Ri! Surprise!" He loops an arm around my shoulders right there in front of my parents, claiming me.

We're an *us*.

We're an item.

We're serious enough to show affection in front of my parents.

I feel sick.

He leans in and kisses me on the top of my head. "You okay?" he whispers in my ear, because he always notices things like that.

Why does he have to notice everything?

I shake my head.

No.

I'm not okay.

"Mm-hmm."

We leave my parents in the kitchen and go to my room, and Rob puts his hands on my hips and draws me into a hug. "What's wrong?"

I stare out the open window. The sun is setting on the street, and everything is falling into shadow.

"Just stressed," I whisper.

"I can make it okay," he says. "If you'd let me."

I want to tell him that stopping by unannounced is not okay. I want to tell him that being buddy-buddy with my mom and dad without my permission isn't all right, and moving in on Neta to get closer to me is really not going to work for me.

But I need him. And so I will make this work. So I let him hug me, and all I can think is that I don't fit right under his chin. Not like with Alex.

I feel strange and cold and for some reason, I feel like there's someone else out there. Someone else in the room. Someone watching.

"Can I kiss you?"

I tilt my chin up to let him, and then as he moves his face toward mine, I duck away.

"Do you want our first kiss to be when I'm this upset?" I say, burying my face against the blue cable-knit of his sweater.

"You're right, baby. We should wait."

He holds me tighter, and I feel like I'm dying in his arms. I didn't ever tell him he could call me that. I didn't tell him he could touch me. I shouldn't be in his arms. This isn't right.

My eyes flick back to the window.

"You're a good person, Rob," I whisper.

Maybe it's even true, but I don't mean it at all.

Things to Know About Riley Stone:

- In preschool, Riley actually got in trouble for kissing too many boys in the schoolyard. Her teacher threatened to use rubber cement on her lips. Of course, Riley does not count any of these as real kisses because they were (a) embarrassing and (b) in preschool.

- After Riley kissed boys in the schoolyard, she would push them. Hard. But she never actually got in trouble for pushing boys because the boys she kissed never wanted to admit they'd been hurt by a girl. Riley, of course, used their sexism to her advantage.

- Riley quit modeling at age fifteen when she won runner-up at the local modeling show she'd won every year since she was four. That year, a new judge, a Miss Brown, rated Riley low in every category.

- Kolbie won first place.

- After Riley quit modeling, she joined the Keep First Street Alive historical site fund-raiser, which was scheduled for the same date every year. The year Riley joined, the fund-raiser rented the modeling contest venue, and the annual modeling event was subsequently canceled. By that time, however, Kolbie was already signed to an agency in New York and did not see the cancellation as a slight.

THIRTY-FIVE
Car

As it turns out, a lot of geniuses were insomniacs. Groucho Marx, Vincent van Gogh, Thomas Edison—I'm in good company.

It's something about smart people, I think, being unable to turn their minds off.

Never mind that it's become a more serious problem recently, since Alex's disappearance. Never mind that I know every single little divot and crack in my ceiling, and how if I think too much about everything it all drives me a little bit crazy. Maybe I should take a Benadryl. The pharmacist told my mother to take Benadryl on any overseas flights instead of sleep aids.

My phone pings.

I roll over to answer it, pulling my already tangled sheets with me.

It's a new e-mail.

A new e-mail from Alex.

My heart almost explodes into a million pieces. He's alive. Alex Belrose is alive.

Unless it's someone else using his e-mail.

I click into the account, and there it is, plain as day: an e-mail from him to me. I can feel it. It's really him.

Meet me at the cliffs near Porter Lane at midnight.

He wants to see me. He wants to see me at the cliffs near Porter Lane.

Of course. It makes perfect sense. Everyone knows the cliffs near Porter Lane. Three years ago, it's where Paul Billson, the local mortician, got drunk and ran off the road. He almost ran straight off those very cliffs, but the fencing along the side saved him. The next morning, the police found him asleep in his car, one wheel dangling over the edge of the cliffs, about to plunge three hundred feet down into a river.

The fencing, damaged from Billson's accident, was removed and not replaced. The locals, spooked by the story, avoid the place completely.

Which is probably why Alex wants me to meet him there.

I check the time.

It's 11:46. I have to hurry.

Quickly, I pull on a hoodie, a pair of jeans, and sneakers, then slide open my window. I climb over the sill and push off, jumping clean of my mother's flowers that grow along the sides of the house, then I slip back between the flowers to quietly pull my window down. If I leave it open, the heat will kick on more often than normal, which might wake my parents.

I put my car in reverse and roll it out of the driveway without starting it, and then, once I'm in the street, I turn the key and pull away.

No lights go on in the rearview mirror.

I let out my breath, which fogs up the windshield. The night air is frigid. It's a bitter cold that settles deep into the bones of the earth on still nights, nights when birds and other animals tuck themselves away into nests and holes. The wind isn't blowing, not even a breeze, and the silence, even more than the temperature, makes me shiver.

I turn the heat on high and click on the radio, but for a moment, there is only static, and then a tinny old blues station comes in, like my car can't receive anything else. Then it clears up and the pop station comes through, blasting Taylor Swift too loud.

I turn it down, my skin prickling oddly.

Something is wrong. Something *feels* wrong.

But of course it does. It's the middle of the night and I've just snuck out of the house to meet my missing (and possibly presumed dead) teacher.

I reach the edge of town and turn onto the web of dirt roads that will lead me to Porter Lane. I hear the gravel crunch under my wheels even with the music on, hear it hit the undercarriage of my car as I draw closer.

I'm going to see Alex.

I'm finally going to see him.

The blood in my veins turns hot.

I turn onto Porter Lane, and my headlights fall upon someone: a tall figure, standing alone on the corner, in the tall weeds that the frost has been too stubborn to completely kill.

Alex.

I hit my brakes hard, my car jerking to a stop, and there he is, after so long, he's just there, looking like he's always looked, not hurt or lost or anything. I leap out of my car, leaving it running, the headlights on, and then I stop short, just standing in front of him, looking up at him, and it's him and he's there and it's just us after so long and he's okay.

"Alex," I whisper. His name, after so many days of uncertainty, feels good in my mouth. He gathers me up in his arms and kisses me, hard and long, my body against his, and it feels so, so good, like all the worry and pain from the past two weeks are just falling away, like they were never there in the first place, and I'm actually happy, just happy. He's okay. Alex is okay. I'm okay. He's back. Jacqueline didn't kill him.

"What happened?" I ask in his ear, and I realize I'm shaking. My body feels strange and tight and sore.

He pulls away, and the moonlight casts his soft features into strange, sharp places and valleys that I never saw before. "We're going to be together," he whispers, his voice a deep, long scratch. "We're finally going to get to be together."

My pulse quickens. "How, Alex? How is it going to be okay?"

"Do you trust me?" he asks.

No. The answer is in my heart, automatic and unbidden, but I squeeze his hand, and then he's kissing me again, and oh my God I have missed him and for just a second I feel like my life is back together but nothing is together and this isn't right.

I pull back for a moment, my head down but my hands still on his arms and his on my waist.

"Run away with me," he pleads. "Come on. Let's run away from here. We can start over and be together. And when you turn eighteen, we can get married. We can have a family. We can forget this whole stupid town and all of these horrible people and it can be just us, forever."

I stare at him. Is this what Alex thinks I want? Babies and a family? To miss out on everything I worked so hard for? To just give everything up for him? What was the point of all the secrecy if I was so ready to throw everything away? Doesn't he realize I want to go to college? To reap the rewards I've earned for myself? That I deserve?

Doesn't he know me at all?

I step back, away from him.

I stare at the man standing in front of me, holding his hands out, pleading.

"Alex, I can't. I've worked too hard for everything here. I can't just walk out on all of my responsibilities."

"I worked for my life, and look where I am—with a wife who cheats on me and leaves me for extended periods of time? With someone who loves her stupid wine club more than she loves me? In a job that doesn't pay me enough to cover my house and car payments? I can't live like this anymore, Riley. Please. Come with me. I'm begging you. I love you. God, I love you."

"I love you too, Alex. But *no*."

But then he's pulling me. Pulling me away from my car that's still idling, the door open and the headlights on. "Just let me show you something," he whispers. "Let me show you how it will all be better for us. Let me show you how I keep my promises."

"Can I turn my car off?" I ask.

He shakes his head. "It won't take long. I swear. And then we can leave here."

I cast a look back at my car, but I follow him, away from the light of the car, where there's only moonlight.

"Where are you taking me?" I ask.

"You'll understand when you see," he promises me, walking faster. He takes my hand and pulls me after him, and the cold is seeping through my jeans and into my bones. What is he doing? Where has he been all this time? Is he insane?

He's smiling. He's smiling so big, like there's something I'm missing, and I've been missing it this whole time and he's waiting to draw back the curtain and show me, but it's all off, and I shouldn't be here and I know it. But I don't want to leave him. Not when I've finally found him.

"What's going on, Alex?" I try to sound calm. I'm excited he's okay. I am. But I have a feeling that's like a vibration in my chest, and it's crawling up to the back of my neck. I feel like I'm watching a horror movie, and I want to scream at the girl on the screen to stop, to turn away, to just, for the love of God, not look around the corner.

But I don't.

He touches my shoulder. "I have a surprise for you, Riley," he says. "That's where I've been, you know."

"Where?" My voice is casual. This is just like any other conversation we've ever had, of course. Like we're talking about lasagna or cookies or poetry or how I won't give myself to him.

I feel mad inside, like there's something inside of me screaming.

"I've been planning."

"Planning?" My voice has a funny pitch to it.

"Just wait."

He speeds up, and I match his steps. The ground beneath our feet is hard and dry, and the cold air is full of dust. The earth has been begging for moisture, but it hasn't rained in weeks—just drizzled pitifully for a few minutes one day last week before giving up.

"There," Alex says.

And at first, I don't see anything. But then a shape emerges in the darkness, large and hulking, the moonlight glinting off the glass of the windows. It's a car, black, with rust around the wheel wells—and as we get closer, I see that it's moving. Just slightly.

Rocking in the darkness, at the very edge of the cliffs.

Alex turns to me and grins. He reaches into his pocket and pulls out a small Maglite. He clicks it on before handing it to me.

"I told you it would be worth it."

"What?" I ask.

But I'm scared of the answer.

"Come on," Alex says, and we walk toward the car together. I look back at my car, which is still waiting, the headlights two beacons in the night, the door ajar.

And at the black car. It's still moving, ever so slightly, in the darkness.

As I get closer, I realize why.

There are people in it.

People rocking back and forth.

But—why?

"Alex—"

He holds up a finger. "Wait," he says.

We reach the car, and he opens the door grandly. It creaks, loudly, and the familiar chemical scent of gasoline reaches my nose.

Alex takes the Maglite from me and shines it inside, and there they are, blinking against the bright light and struggling against thick knots of blond rope:

Jacqueline Belrose and Rob Samuels.

Jacqueline sits in the passenger seat. Her ropes have been knotted through the steering wheel. She's been gagged and a bloody purple bruise maps across her forehead, and she's making small noises behind her gag. Noises like she's trying to scream.

Rob is looking at me, throwing his head back and forth like a wild animal, his eyes wide and lolling. He's already in some sort of pain. Alex has hurt him badly, and I can't tell how. I can't see bruises or blood, but something's wrong. Something's really wrong.

I have to get them both out of here.

Jacqueline, perhaps, wasn't the crazy one. Maybe it was Alex all along.

He couldn't just be patient. He couldn't just do all of this the right way. He had to go psycho and put everyone in the car at the edge of a ravine.

I feel strange and ill. But I can't throw up. I can't. I have to be calm.

"What? Alex, what is this? What are you doing?"

"You wanted me to get a divorce, didn't you? So we could be together?" He laughs. "You know Jacqueline would never leave me alone. She would have bled me dry just for her designer clothes and her stupid wine. But if she's dead, she won't be able to." He laughs again, and it's short and mad.

"And you don't think blowing her up in a car is a little suspicious?" I ask faintly. "That doesn't look like murder at all, does it?"

"I'll be gone. They already think I'm dead, don't they?"

"And what did Rob do to you?" I ask. Given, he's not exactly my favorite person, and yeah, he's been really touchy and awful in ways I haven't appreciated lately, but blowing him up in a car?

Alex's face darkens. He looks strange and unfamiliar. "I saw you two together."

And that's enough.

"It wasn't really anything. I was just trying to make sure no one knew anything, you know? About us? Please, Alex. This is a little rash, don't you think?"

I pause and grab on to the sleeve of his jacket. "You don't need to kill them, Alex."

Alex blinks at me, his eyes closing. "I know I don't." He reaches into his pocket and tosses me a book of matches. "We do. Together."

I take the matches and pull one off. "So you want me to help you kill them? Is that it?"

He nods, his green eyes looking almost black in the deep of the night. "That's it. This is what binds us together. Not our blood." He touches his heart. "Theirs."

I turn the matches in my fingers, trying not to look at the way Rob is still thrashing in the car, at the way Jacqueline has her head strained toward me, her bulging eyes screaming all the things she can't. I think of all the times I wished Jacqueline dead. I think of all the times I actually started planning it.

And here it is, laid out before me, in one very messy car.

My hands start to shake from fear and pain and cold.

He's insane. Alex Belrose, my first and only love, is absolutely insane. There's no way around it.

"I'll get rid of Jacqueline forever if we can get rid of Rob, too," Alex pleads. He still has that smile on his mouth, and it's twitching and odd. Something about him has gone off.

And I'm in way too deep.

"About that . . . ," I say.

And I throw the matches off the edge of the cliff, into the water below.

"You're insane!" I say. "And I have the pictures on my phone to prove it. And I'll tell everyone you tried to fail me just so you could bring my parents in to threaten me. If you kill them, I'll show everyone just how goddamned nuts you are, Alex Belrose. You let them go and you don't come near me or them again."

He crosses his arms, and the flashlight lights up his face from below his chin. "P-pictures? What are you talking about? I didn't ask your parents to come in, either. And I don't know why you're attacking me like this." Very slowly, he starts unbuttoning his shirt, revealing a thin red line about his heart. "I can't lie to you, Riley. We're blood-bonded, remember? And they can test for that sort of thing now. They'll bring us in to the police station together, and they'll be able to tell we're part of each other, won't they?"

I'm breathing hard, and my heart is in my throat and my stomach and my head and everywhere all at once. I pull my phone out of my jacket and open the folder. "You snuck into my *bedroom*," I say, and my hand trembles.

He is quiet for a moment as he takes the phone, and he looks through the photos one by one.

I sneer at him. "You've gotten so good at lying you don't even realize when you do it to yourself. Do you remember now?"

He screams, then, and it's primal and animalistic, and he throws the phone down and starts toward the car.

"You did it!" he screams at Rob. "You were stalking her! She's mine! And you were after her, all this time! Fuck *you*!"

And before I can move or scream or stop him, he pulls another book of matches out of his pocket.

He lights them all at once, across the rusty side of the car.

And then he throws them in the door and slams it shut.

I grab my phone off the ground and run away as fast as I can.

I turn back, grabbing my ears, and the car is in flames, and Alex is just standing there, watching it, watching them burn, watching them die, and then it happens.

The explosion.

A giant orange fireball, bright as the sun, like a thousand guns going off at once, and I cover my ears and hit the ground.

But it doesn't stop me from seeing.

Alex, getting blown back by the force of the blast.

Toward the cliff.

Over the edge.

And gone.

Alex Belrose, presumed dead.

Things to Know About Riley Stone:

- When Riley Stone recounted her account of the events leading up to the murders to the police officers, her lawyer, and the DA, they were shocked that anyone could survive such a horrific incident with such grace.
- It was concluded, after an investigation, that Riley had been manipulated into a highly inappropriate relationship with her French teacher based on the threat of bad grades (and the promise of better ones).
- The photos on Riley's phone were found to have backups stored on Alex Belrose's e-mail account.
- Riley's grades had indeed been changed after the meeting with her parents, Ms. Felcher, and Mr. Belrose.
- DNA evidence from the Belrose residence corroborated Riley's story that she had, indeed, spent a significant amount of time at the Belrose residence.
- Throughout the process, Riley's bravery and fortitude were commended.
- When Riley Stone cried, the entire station cried, including the DA—who swore she hadn't shed a tear in ten years.
- The police station never knew that Rob Samuels, not Kamea Myers, had been Riley's real competition for valedictorian. He had been signed up for a special course that would have allowed him to significantly raise his GPA.

- Jacqueline Belrose had been a successful model since she was a teen. She had once been signed with a modeling agency in Paris, which was how she met Alex Belrose while he was studying abroad.
- Jacqueline's maiden name was Brown.
- Riley has a tripod in her closet specifically made to hold a smartphone. She bought it at the mall, on clearance. She uses it to make YouTube videos, or to take timed photographs of herself throughout the night.
- Riley knows the password to Alex's e-mail account, which connects neatly to his Outlook calendar and his cell phone. It's an all-access pass to everything Belrose.

THIRTY-SIX

After

I sit at my vanity, putting the final touches on my makeup while I wait for Sandeep to pick me up.

He's been so sweet through all of this, really. So supportive. So *perfect*. I couldn't ask for a better boyfriend. Tonight will be our fourth date, and I think I'll ask if he wants to make it official. Make Riley and Sandeep an *us*.

At first I wasn't sure if Sandeep would be into dating me again, especially after what happened last time we went out, but when he found out that Alex Belrose had manipulated me against my will and tried to ruin my life . . . he understood. And how could he not? *Any* good guy would understand.

I finish my mascara and blink at myself in the mirror. There's nothing there to show that a few weeks prior, I was a girl being mentally held hostage by an insane, delusional man who believed I really loved him. Nothing to show that I was helpless. Nothing to show that I was about to watch three people *die*.

Or that I was about to take a tour of several nationally syndicated talk shows to speak about my experience. Or that soon, I was going to be on the cover of *Clare* for their "Teens Who Rock" issue. They're calling me brave. They're calling me a *heroine*. And I understand why.

Anyone else would have broken under that kind of pressure. That kind of stress.

But not me.

I made it out alive. I made it out valedictorian. And it'll probably take me some time to heal, which is perfectly understandable, but I'll be okay.

Fighters always are.

Naturally, I had to figure some details out creatively to connect the dots, but it wasn't like it mattered. Alex didn't make it off the cliff and I did, and I needed, after all this, to be perfect, just like I always had been, in order to be okay. And if Alex loved me like he said he really did, he would have understood that.

I lean forward and touch the tiny red line below my eye, where a bit of metal hit me when the car exploded. I wince. It still hurts. It will leave a small scar. But it's nothing compared to what Alex did to me. Nothing.

It's too bad about the scar. And too bad so many people had to die. But so much good has come of all of it for me. I'm rising.

There is a knock at my door, and my father opens it, very slowly, as if he doesn't want to startle me. "Sweetie?" he asks.

"Yes?" I smile at him in the mirror.

"Your date is here." His voice is soft. That's how they talk to me now. They pay attention when I enter the room. They make sure I get enough to eat. They smile at me, albeit a bit sadly, when they think I'm not looking.

"Thanks, Dad. I'll be right down."

"I'll let him know."

Dad closes the door.

I tie a dark pink ribbon in my hair and then uncap a tube of lipstick.

I won't put on too much, of course.

After all, I am a good girl.

Something to Know About Riley Stone:

- Riley Elizabeth Stone is just about perfect. Ask anyone.

ACKNOWLEDGMENTS

Any author knows that the hardest part of the book is often the acknowledgments—there are so many important people to thank when it comes to creating a story!

First, to Michael Strother and Jennifer Ung: Michael, you are a fantastic editor who shared the vision for this book from day one, and that means the world to me! I had a blast creating it with you! Jennifer, I am so grateful to you for adopting this book and for helping to make it the best it could be. I cannot tell you how much I value your passion and commitment to this story.

To Melissa Edwards: thank you for being so amazing and supportive. I am lucky to have you as my agent!

To my parents, for always being there, for encouraging me, and for helping me every step of the way—thank you. I love you!

To Bethany and Suz, for being amazing, always. I couldn't do it without you.

To the musers—thank you for being there for me, especially this year.

To Tammy Gibson, my early reader—I appreciate it so much!

To Teresa Kirchner, for all of the incredible advice on cheerleading—you went above and beyond for me!

To Amy Ross, Carrie Straub, and Aldo Wilson: thank you for helping out with my French!

Secrets,
Lies,
and
Scandals

For my family

More Blood

There should be more blood.

He lay there, sprawled across the floor, his lips parted as if he were about to speak. But he wasn't. He wasn't even breathing. His left eye was partially open, revealing a half-moon of jelly-white eyeball.

Her breath caught somewhere deep in her throat and stuck there, a hard knot just below her vocal cords. She pressed her hand against her chest and swallowed, over and over again. She wouldn't be sick. She couldn't. Not here. Not now.

When someone dies, there should be more blood.

Ivy

Girls like Ivy McWhellen did not get embarrassed. And if they ever did happen to be embarrassed, it was in an adorable way. Like in an *Oh my gosh, I can't believe he thinks I'm cute* way, which was just ridiculous because girls like Ivy McWhellen *knew* they were cute. They were born knowing.

Which is why anyone would expect Ivy McWhellen to be doing something amazing with her summer. Like maybe sunning on the beach in Cabo. Or having some sort of whirlwind summer romance with the captain of the hockey team (if her school even had a hockey team). Or, at the very least, hanging with her best girlfriends/understudies.

One would not expect a girl like Ivy McWhellen to be trapped desperately on her back underneath a vending machine, slowly suffocating to death. Which happened to be where Ivy was at that exact moment.

It wasn't her fault. Ivy had been, until very recently, the queen bee. Then she made a really bad decision by following the advice of every terrible chick flick ever that told her to follow her heart.

What those chick flicks never told Ivy was that hearts are bad at directions, and that following her heart would eventually lead her into the high school over summer break and right up to a vending machine. And that her ex–best friends would tip it over on her and leave her there to die.

Stupid, stupid heart.

At least there weren't cameras. There had been some student council vote about using low-energy ones, and so the old ones had been taken out last week, and the new, not-yet-installed cameras were apparently on back order. The last thing Ivy needed was a stupid video getting stolen and going viral.

Of course, that wouldn't even matter, if she died.

Ivy took a deep, slow breath, and the vending machine crushed her ribs a little further. And then she lifted up as hard as she could.

The hulking monster of a machine moved two full millimeters.

Ivy lay back. Maybe she should just concentrate on breathing. And try not to think about the way Klaire—who had been her best friend since that time in kindergarten when Ivy convinced her to eat paste—had laughed while Johann, the quarterback, had held Ivy down. Then his two linebacker goons had slowly lowered the vending machine onto her body.

That bitch was going to pay. And so were Johann and the linebackers.

Ivy took another deep, slow breath, and pushed upward. The machine actually moved . . . maybe an inch. And then it teetered and slid, and pain rocketed up her arm as the weight shifted. Ivy sucked in as much breath as she could and tried to scream, but she hardly had anything left in her. All that came out was a pathetic little whimper, like a dying kitten, or like Marc Selver last year when he got sucker punched in the stomach.

"Ivy?"

Ivy tried to pivot her head. It couldn't be him. Please, God, say it wasn't him.

He took a step closer.

It was him.

Garrett.

Ruiner of Lives.

Kisser extraordinaire.

Also known as the ex-boyfriend who had cost her everything she loved when *he* had the nerve to dump *her* . . . and then the rest of the school had decided Garrett was the Cool One, as he had officially earned the status of the Only Guy to Ever Dump Ivy McWhellen.

And Garrett hadn't even been cool before that. He'd been, like, unseen. A nobody. But she had seen him, and gotten all of this Love Bullshit in her head, and he had ruined her entire life forever.

"Are you okay under there?" he asked, kneeling down, his stupid hipster Chucks way too close to her head. His face appeared above her, and he looked ridiculous and pudgy from this angle—like her face did when she accidentally forgot to flip the camera lens around and she surprise-selfied herself.

She wheezed throatily, and his eyes widened.

"Wait here a minute, Ivy girl. I'll save you. I promise."

He pushed himself up and she heard his Chucks tapping down the hall.

On one hand, yay, Ivy was probably not going to die. On the other hand, being heroically saved by the boy who had ruined her entire life was basically the cruelest thing in the entire world. Maybe even crueler than death, if she really thought about it.

"Don't call me Ivy girl," she tried to say, because what right did he have to use his adorable boyfriendy nicknames after basically pushing her off a social cliff? But all that came out was a strange whistling noise. The machine had probably punctured her lung.

Thank God she hadn't been caught under one of the *big* vending machines in the student foyer. It was just a half-size one that, until a week ago, when it was emptied for the summer, had been filled with all the healthy snacks no one ever bought anyway: $1.50 for some shitty rice crackers? No. Just no.

A few moments later, Ivy heard a click-clicking—the light, careful tread of girls. A lot of them. A whole pack.

She strained her neck around.

Freshmen. The type of girls that Ivy McWhellen would grind underneath her Louboutin heels and eat for Bitch Brunch.

They stared at her at first. At her dark hair with blond highlights tangled on the floor behind her. At her perfect little bag on the ground, with half its contents spilled out onto the dirty tile of the main lobby.

And then the front freshman—the smallest one—put her hand to her mouth.

That's when the laughter started.

Slow, at first, with a pathetic, high-pitched little giggle, and then evolving rapidly into heaving laughter as it swept through the group.

Those stupid little freshpeople were *laughing* at Ivy McWhellen.

One of them raised a smartphone and snapped a picture.

This was *not* how the world was supposed to work.

Ivy wanted to kill them. She would ruin her manicure to do it, and there was hardly anything she would ruin her manicure for. But this was definitely worth another set of forty-dollar gel tips.

"Ivy!" Garrett's stupid voice rang down the hallway. "Ivy, I found Janitor Epps. We'll get you out of here." He jogged up, like a Knight in Shining Lumberjack Clothes, and the old janitor lumbered a few steps behind, clearly not as concerned with Ivy's well-being.

The janitor knelt down close to her. "Better not have messed up my machine," he muttered, so close to her ear that she could smell the chewing tobacco on his breath.

Ivy wanted to punch him almost as bad as she wanted to get out, but not quite as bad as she wanted to kill the freshmen. Who cared about the *machine*? Ivy was dying here. The freshmen giggled louder, and Garrett turned to them.

"A little help, please," he said.

Ivy didn't have to crane her neck to know the girls were practically melting into puddles of goo just because Garrett, a senior, a *cool*, cute senior, spoke actual words to them. Suddenly, the little bitches were all Mother Teresa.

With Garrett and the janitor at the front of the machine (and said janitor standing at an angle where Ivy could see a suspicious stain near his crotch), they all started counting.

"One . . . two . . . three!" Garrett shouted, and together they all lifted until the machine was raised off of Ivy. She scrabbled frantically at the dirty tile until she was finally clear of the stupid machine, then continued to scuttle backward until her back was against the wall and she was clear across the room, breathing delicious lungfuls of air.

Garrett sat down beside her and handed her the little handbag.

"So," he said. "Want to tell me who did this?"

Ivy shook her head. "Machine wasn't secured," she said, her voice tight with bitterness. "So dangerous. I should sue."

"Oh, right," Garrett said. "Vending machines just randomly collapse on top of people. Happens all the time. Think it was haunted?"

Ivy smiled a little, in spite of herself. Garrett was funny. That was why she'd liked him at first. "Something like that. I never should have played with that Ouija board." She faked a shudder and pain lit up in her muscles. The machine had done more damage than she'd thought.

"So," Garrett said. "I'm here for a summer art course. And you decided to drop by the local high school because . . . it's such a grand place?"

Ivy didn't want to tell him the truth: that her parents had forced her to take a stupid, stupid psych class for credit, just because they wanted her out of the house. That she hardly did anything since Garrett dumped her.

That she'd lost every friend and follower she thought she had.

"Signing up for the summer psych course," she said. "I want to get a jump-start on college credit and they make you submit all this extra paperwork." She smoothed her hair out of her face. It was half true. Really, it was probably the last thing she wanted to do with her summer.

"Cool," Garrett said. "Is that the one that Dr. Stratford is teaching at night?"

Ivy nodded glumly. Stratford was supposed to basically be the devil incarnate. Exactly how she'd planned to spend her summer—being lectured by Satan himself. How fitting. Her whole life was going to hell anyway. Might as well get some face time with the boss.

Garrett put his arms on his knees and started messing with his wristbands, which is what he did before he said something serious. Ivy would know. It was what he did before he broke up with her.

Across the room, the freshmen watched, like eager little gossip vultures.

"Ivy girl, listen—about us. I'm sorry. I know things haven't been easy for you since we—since I—"

"No." The word cut through Garrett's fumbling speech. "No, Garrett." Ivy pushed herself up, wincing, and threw the bag over her shoulder. "Listen, it was great to talk to you, and thanks for saving my life, but really—I have to go."

He stared up at her with those pretty, soulful eyes he had, and for the first time, she turned her back on him.

And with that, Ivy walked away from everything she wanted.

Mattie

"Watch it!" Mrs. Byrne said, laughing, as Mattie dropped the very last box on her toe. "You're lucky that's just pillows. Otherwise you could have paralyzed me for life."

Mattie forced a smile. "Sorry, Mom." He knew she was trying to cheer him up, but there was only one person who could do that right now—and he wasn't here. He wasn't answering Mattie's phone calls. (Or his texts. Or his Facebook messages.)

"Look," Mrs. Byrne said, prancing to the huge window and throwing open the curtains dramatically. "The view! And you have your own balcony!"

Mattie followed his mom to the huge window, which turned out to be a sliding door. It opened onto a gigantic veranda. Next to an actual trellis, practically choked with crawling ivy. This room was basically made for sneaking out. He had to admit it wasn't totally bad.

His mom unlocked the door and stepped outside. His aunt's house was huge—the biggest in the neighborhood—

and located on top of a hill, so it had a perfect view of the trees and other immaculate homes. In the distance, the lights of the city twinkled like weak stars. It was beautiful.

"It's great," Mattie told his mother. She smiled and put her arm around him.

"It's not so bad, right, Mattie? I'm sure Derrick will visit."

Mattie wasn't so sure. Things with Derrick hadn't felt right. Not since . . . well. They just hadn't felt right.

"Or," his mother continued, "at least he will when he sees some pictures of your aunt's house. This place is great, right? Look at the pool!"

Mattie grasped the stone railing and looked down. He was directly over the pool, which was beautiful. It was an infinity pool, so the edge just seemed to stop, and you could swim up and enjoy the view from anywhere. There was a small, trickling version of a waterfall in one corner, and a bubbling hot tub in the other.

"Yeah," Mattie admitted. "It's pretty cool."

And it was. Mattie's aunt Janice had all the money in the family. She'd won the lottery in the late nineties (and not just a puny million-dollar jackpot) and she'd invested it. No one guessed that a weirdo art teacher who lived in a three-hundred-square-foot studio downtown would be able to triple her winnings in just ten years, but Aunt Janice had taken to numbers, to investments, to palling around with men in sharp suits, and she'd done it. And now, she was enjoying it. *Clearly.*

The house was incredible—a mix of ancient Rome and classic Southern style. Huge, but somehow not gaudy. It was pretty, actually. It was art.

Mrs. Byrne put both her arms around her son and pulled him tight. "I'm going to miss you, kid," she said, her voice suddenly misty and soft. Her blond curls tickled his nose.

"Then don't make me stay," Mattie pleaded. When his mother pulled away, she half smiled at him and rustled his hair, the same way she'd done when he was a little boy. "I wish I didn't have to, but you made a deal with your dad. You can't have an F on your report card."

Mattie grimaced. In a serious lapse in character, and for the very first time, he'd cheated on a psych test. Him. Perfect Mattie Byrne. His teacher had caught him with the notes in his lap and, well, in less than an hour, both his parents had been in the assistant principal's office for an emergency meeting, and Mattie was receiving two things he'd never received before: suspension and a failing grade.

Fortunately, Mattie's dad was good friends with the football coach, who was good friends with the principal, and, since Mattie had a perfect record, they'd agreed to let him retake the course during the summer. If he got a B, they'd pass him, and the F would be wiped from his record.

Unfortunately, in Mattie's tiny little town, summer courses weren't offered. (But three hours away? Of course!)

"Three hours isn't that far," his mother said. "And this will be good for you. To learn from an actual college professor? It's pretty cool." She grinned.

"Um, sure." Mattie tried to be positive. He did. But how was he supposed to? Everyone he knew was at home, spending their summer on the lake. Including Derrick. Who was to say Derrick wouldn't just forget him? Who was to say he hadn't already?

Who was to say Mattie didn't deserve it?

Mattie swallowed hard. He knew he was kind of being a jerk. Sure, he had to take another stupid psych course, but he got to spend his summer in a mansion so big, it had actual *wings*. And there was a butler to open the door, and a whole team of maids came three times a week.

Things could be worse.

But still . . .

Mattie's shoulders tensed.

His mom gave him a little squeeze on the arm and disappeared into the bedroom.

In his pocket, his phone vibrated. He pulled it out. A text from his dad: Have fun!

Mattie texted him back, and noticed a red *1* notification on his Facebook app. He opened it, and the first thing he saw was Derrick. As in his boyfriend, Derrick.

The next thing he saw was Aaron Rodriguez. (Who happened to be Derrick's ex.) Derrick's ex who definitely wanted him back. It was obvious, the way he was always following him around and sending him Snapchats of his stupid bull terrier (but hopefully nothing else).

The third thing he saw was Aaron's arm. Which was firmly around Derrick's shoulders.

We're just friends, Derrick had promised. *Aaron's totally harmless.*

Mattie sucked in his breath, and suddenly his chest hurt. If he'd never cheated on that test, he'd be home. And he'd know.

Kinley

Week one.

Third class.

Professor: tough, but fair. But really, really tough.

Chances of me getting an A: 100%

"What are you writing?"

Kinley jumped, just slightly. Tyler Green—who everyone he had ever met knew was bad news—was talking to her.

People didn't talk to her. They just . . . didn't.

Especially boy people.

She covered her paper with her hand, and she felt her face heat up. "Um. Nothing."

Tyler winked. "Let me see. I won't tell."

"I would," she said, "but see . . . you'd have to be able to read to understand." She shrugged and shut her notebook. "Sorry."

Tyler laughed. "You're sort of funny for a narc."

Kinley lifted a shoulder. Everyone said she was a narc, ever since the time she ratted on the middle school point guard for smoking weed on school grounds. But she didn't care. Kinley just did what everyone else was scared to do, and what was wrong with that?

She was always prepared to go further than everyone else. *Always.*

That was why she was here early. She wanted to get some face time with Dr. Stratford before class started again. The first couple of classes . . . well, Dr. Stratford clearly didn't understand who she was. He treated her like everyone else—with disdain, stopping just short of pure hatred.

He needed to realize.

She was the best student. Always. In every class.

She was Kinley Phillips. She had a reputation. A *good* reputation.

But Dr. Stratford was nowhere to be found. The only person she was getting face time with was Tyler Green, resident burnout. The kind of guy who did not give girls good reputations.

"Why are you in this class, anyway?"

Tyler flipped a yellow number two pencil through his fingers. "Trying to make up some credit." He shrugged. "I need to graduate."

Kinley raised her eyebrows. They made a crooked line across her forehead. "You're still eligible to graduate?"

Tyler smirked. "I'm not stupid. I'm a *delinquent.*"

"There's a difference?"

Kinley felt daring all of a sudden. She was talking to a guy. An actual guy. She was almost flirting.

She had never done that before. It wasn't exactly in line with her goals.

Tyler put the very tip of the eraser in his mouth. "Obviously. Stupid is easy. Delinquency . . . is an *art*. It's all about the things you do wrong versus the things you're caught doing wrong."

Kinley's lips pursed. It made an odd sort of sense, actually.

Around them, the other students started to file in. Because it was a course that could be taken for college credit, they'd been assigned one of the larger classrooms—one that could fit almost forty students. The administration had assumed that a college-level course would attract a few more students looking to pad their applications. With the added fact that the class was taught at the high school, thirty minutes away from the college campus, it was a win-win.

Almost.

There was a catch: it was a Stratford class. Everyone knew about Stratford, which meant only fifteen students had actually signed up.

Fifteen brave, stupid souls.

One—a tiny, mousy girl Dr. Stratford had picked on—hadn't shown up since the first day.

So fourteen. Fourteen total students.

Hardly any competition for Kinley Phillips.

Tyler scratched on the desk with his pencil.

"So your . . . lifestyle. You're saying you're a regular van Gogh," Kinley said. "Breaking rules as art." Her eyes followed his pencil on the surface of the desk. She couldn't tell what he was drawing. His arm was carefully angled in front of it.

Tyler grinned. "I'd say I'm more of a Pollock, really. I just throw shit at a wall and see what sticks. Oh, and I'm not opposed to copying others' work." He glanced purposely at Kinley's notebook.

Kinley laughed. Actually laughed. Here she was, the Goody Two-shoes of the entire school, and she was getting along with Tyler Green, who, upon closer inspection, was sort of cute. If you could overlook the stupid rock band T-shirt and ripped jeans. He could actually look good, cleaned up. She imagined him in a crisp blue button-down with a proper haircut.

He'd be perfect.

She bit into her bottom lip. She'd never had a boyfriend. Hadn't even had a boy show interest, unless you counted Marcus Canter in fourth grade, when he told her she was pretty before sneezing a bucketload of green phlegm all over her.

And it was weird, but . . . well, she kind of liked the attention. For something other than getting the highest test score.

"Kinley? Kinley Phillips? Care to join the class?"

Kinley's head snapped up. "Yes?"

Dr. Stratford stood at the front of the room, the full intensity of his focus upon her. He was not a normal professor type: his mess of hair, a tangled mass of gray with tinges of brown dye, sat atop his head like someone had placed it there. Half his face drooped. And his eyes were strange and too light. They were also staring directly at Kinley.

Kinley's head spun. When had he even arrived? How was it time for class already?

"I apologize, sir. What was the question?"

He cleared his throat loudly, and for the second time that day, she was reminded of Marcus Canter. "Roll call, Ms. Phillips. Now, should I mark you as present? Or absent, as you clearly don't seem to be here for class?"

Kinley didn't flinch. She looked him in the eye, ignoring the heat creeping up from her neckline. "Here, sir. I apologize." She bent her head.

Dr. Stratford just snorted. "Teller, Ella?" he asked. A girl in the front row slowly raised her hand, as if not to attract too much attention.

Kinley scowled. *Damn it.* She shot a look at Tyler. He'd been distracting her when she should have been paying attention. That was what happened to girls who got caught up with boys like Tyler. Or boys in general.

It was too bad. She'd liked talking to him.

Professor Stratford finished calling roll, and then stepped behind the desk—a desk that normally belonged to Mr. Tanner, a teacher with thick glasses who pretty much everyone liked.

He opened the desk and pulled out a huge tome that looked at least a billion years old.

"Today," he said, "we're going to talk about guilt. Specifically, Freud and his approach to guilt. Which I find to be a bit stupid and outdated—but then, so is Freud."

Dr. Stratford, Kinley thought, was definitely a teacher who was passionate about his subject matter.

"Now, last class, we discussed the psychic apparatus. Can anyone remind us what this consists of?" He looked around at the class. "Kinley? Do you remember, or were you too busy being desperate with that boy there?"

Kinley stared, her heart beating strangely in her chest. Desperate? This was the first time she'd ever spoken to Tyler.

"No? Okay. Well, then. Let's try Ivy in the corner there. Ivy, would you like to take a break from staring out the window?"

"I know," Kinley interrupted, her voice a pitch too loud. "The psychic apparatus consists of—"

"Stop," Dr. Stratford said, slamming his wrinkled hand on the desk. "Just stop. You had your chance. I wanted to know what you knew, not what you had time to google on your phone while I asked someone else."

Kinley's mouth dropped open. This was *not* how teachers spoke to her. Teachers *loved* her. She was a dream student. She was a pet.

Tyler leaned over and nudged her. "Don't worry about it," he whispered. "He's an asshole. Everyone knows it."

Kinley ignored him. She felt her face burn ever hotter. Her father would be so disappointed. He did everything right. He was a leader. He'd even written a book, and CNN had invited him in-studio to represent minority visions on modern culture. Her fingers reached for the ends of her braid—a nervous habit.

While Ivy struggled in the corner over the difference between id and ego, the door opened and a tall, sort of youngish-looking boy shuffled in and shut the door quietly behind him. Kinley couldn't remember his name.

Stratford's head jerked around, and he actually sniffed like he smelled blood. Hot, fresh blood.

Kinley said a silent thank-you. Stratford was going to lose it on this kid. He didn't tolerate tardiness. And hopefully, that meant he'd forget about Kinley's little mistake.

"Say, Mr. Byrne? Mattie, is it?" Dr. Stratford said, pulling his focus away from Ivy. "Listen, young man. Since you haven't sat down yet, I don't suppose you'd do me a favor?"

"Um, sure." Mattie waited at the door. The collar of his shirt was flipped up on one side, and his hair stuck up a little bit, like maybe he'd just woken up from a nap.

"Across campus, you'll find my office. It's temporary, and it has Mr. Tanner's name on it. I'm afraid I left my coffee over there, and I could really use it right now."

Dr. Stratford smiled, but there was something off about it. It was toothy and hungry and fell short on one side.

Mattie sort of smiled back, clearly relieved. "Sure, Dr. Stratford." He opened the door and stepped backward into the hallway.

Dr. Stratford stared after the student for a half second, and stroked the few stray whiskers he had growing out of his chin.

He crossed the room, pulled a heavy ring of keys out of his pocket, and locked the door behind Mattie.

Kinley chanced another look at Tyler, and she knew exactly what he was thinking: thank God it wasn't them.

There was something about Stratford. About the way he looked at you. It was condescension, sure. And no matter who he was looking at, there was a distinct and undeniable overtone of disgust. But beneath it all, barely lingering below the surface, was pure, unadulterated hatred.

It was clear to Kinley then. It was clear to all of them, really. Stratford hated students. All of them. In fact, it was pretty safe to say he hated teaching. He was probably only there because he enjoyed torturing students, one by one, as payback for some horrible way in which he'd been wronged in the past.

Kinley looked back toward Dr. Stratford, in case the professor thought she wasn't paying attention.

"I trust that will convince the rest of you that being late is something of a capital crime in my classes. Now, where were we? Ah yes. Guilt. What a beautiful, pointless thing. Let us discuss the struggle between the id and the superego."

And he went on that way for a few minutes, until suddenly

the doorknob rattled and Mattie's face appeared in the little window in the doorframe. He pulled on the door again, and knocked twice.

Kinley felt a little bad for him. She'd spoken to him, for just a second, outside the school on the first day, when he'd picked up a pen that had fallen from her notebook. He'd seemed nice enough.

"The id, of course, develops first, and, some argue, is humanity's natural state." Dr. Stratford crossed the room and, without so much as a glance at Mattie, pulled the shade down over the window. "The id is virtually incapable of guilt."

The doorknob stopped rattling.

And that was when Tyler Green made a mistake.

He laughed.

Tyler

A pen sailed at Tyler Green's face. He shifted, slightly, and it nicked him on the shoulder, leaving a faint blue mark on his Raging Idiots T-shirt.

"Laughing in my class, Mr. Green?" Dr. Stratford said. "Would you like to share what's funny?"

"Nah," Tyler said, casting a meaningful glance at the door, where that little punk, Mattie Byrne, was trapped outside. Mattie should have been smarter than that. Everyone who'd ever heard of Dr. Stratford knew he wasn't the type of teacher just to let shit go.

Students had to pay.

Tyler had a grudging respect for the teacher. He didn't screw around. He was a total asshole.

And he owned it.

Maybe Tyler would really try for Dr. Stratford. Maybe he owed it to him, and to himself. For once, here was a teacher who was a total D-bag, and he didn't pretend to be anything else. Tyler could deal with that.

Plus, there was military school. And there was his father's promise that if Tyler didn't get his shit together, didn't do something—anything—to show he was interested in his future, he wouldn't have to worry about living at home. Then they could focus on Jacob, Tyler's older brother. Jacob was a top swimmer at a local community college, and he was being recruited by three different Division One schools.

Tyler mainly got recruited to detention.

Stratford paused a second longer, staring at Tyler, and then resumed teaching. For once in his life, Tyler was actually sort of interested. According to Stratford's theory, people had too much id. They just did stuff because it felt good. The superego was the little angel on your shoulder, and the ego sort of balanced it all out.

Tyler studied Stratford as he lumbered back and forth across the classroom, shouting inane questions and theories. "When was Freud born?" he thundered at Kip Landers, a blond guy sitting in the corner. Kip stuttered and looked at his desk. He didn't know.

And then, once someone finally answered, Stratford would just come around to the same exact question a few minutes later.

The guy was weird.

There was something about him. Something about the way he limped, slightly favoring his entire right side. The way half his face drooped, just the tiniest bit. And there was something about his speech pattern—was that an accent? Was he from the far north? Maybe even Canada?

If he was Canadian, Tyler decided, he could go back to his home country. And take Justin Bieber with him.

"Tyler!" Stratford thundered suddenly. "The class's fate depends on your answer to the next question. Can you appropriately define recession?"

Tyler racked his brain. He knew Stratford had mentioned this last class. He'd actually been listening that time. "Like . . . holding back?"

Stratford stared at him. "Correct. Sort of. Not the answer I was looking for, which was to repress, which means to consciously reject ideas. Now, who likes my definition better than Tyler's?" He cast his eyes around the room.

A couple of hands raised shakily. Kinley raised hers and shot him a smug smile.

Stratford chuckled. The sound was like ice dropping into a glass. Cold. And sharp.

"Since we're all in agreement that Mr. Green's definition was inadequate, we're going to have a test exactly one week from today," Stratford said, rubbing his hands together. "I expect you all to study pages forty-seven through one hundred and ninety-eight in your textbooks. Be prepared to be tested on anything—and I mean anything—in those pages, as well as anything I've covered in class. *Capiche?*"

Tyler didn't say anything, but he felt his hands clench into fists at his sides. Stratford was blaming him for his stupid test? The guy didn't have the balls to say he wanted to torture them, so he was blaming Tyler?

He felt the little respect he'd held for the teacher being siphoned away.

"Now, out." Stratford sort of flipped his hand at them and then sat down, heavily, at his desk.

Tyler swung his backpack over a shoulder and followed Kinley out the door. She was really cute, actually. She definitely had a good, round ass. And great legs. Probably from hauling all those books around constantly. A long braid, as thick as a climbing rope, swung across her back. He wondered how she'd look lying on his bed with her hair undone and her dark skin peeking out from behind an unbuttoned shirt.

Maybe he'd hook up with her this year. Her or Ivy. Ivy was superhot, and after her fall from grace, maybe he'd have a shot with her.

In the hall, Mattie, the kid who'd gotten locked out of the room, was leaning against the wall, flicking his shoelaces. He scrambled up off the floor when he saw them leaving, his sneakers squeaking against the tile. "Hey," he said, keeping pace with Tyler. "Can I borrow your notes? I got locked out."

Tyler shrugged, pushing down the urge to make a smart-ass comment. "I don't take them." He sped up a step, catching up with Kinley, leaving Mattie behind. "Hey, Kin. Can I carry your books?"

Kinley stared. "My books?"

"Yeah." Tyler reached out and took them. "I'll carry them. Where's your car?"

Kinley tilted her head. Tyler was willing to bet that no guy had ever offered to carry her books before. In fact, she'd probably never even been kissed. He fought back a smile. This could be fun.

"Um. It's outside," she managed finally, like maybe she'd parked her car in the school cafeteria, and Tyler needed to know the difference. She ducked her head and bit her lip.

"What a class, huh?" Tyler said, ignoring her embarrassment. "What's up with that Stratford dude?"

She shook her head and looked backward, as if Dr. Stratford could be following them, waiting to pounce.

"He's tough," she said. "Really tough."

"Probably not for you, though," Tyler said. "Everyone knows you're one of those kids that win the National Spelling Bee."

"I'm not letting you copy," Kinley said suddenly, her eyes wide, like she'd just realized why Tyler was being so nice to her.

Tyler laughed. "I'm not stupid, Kin. I don't actually need to copy you, okay? I just want to, you know . . . talk."

The pair slowed outside, near the edge of the parking lot, which was nearly empty. Psych was the only night course offered this summer. The sun's rays had nearly disappeared under the horizon, and the street lamps hadn't yet flickered on.

Tyler shrugged off his backpack and set Kinley's books on the ground next to it. He pulled himself onto the low ranch-style fence that separated the sparse grass of the school campus from the asphalt of the parking lot. He patted the spot beside him, and Kinley hesitantly sat down—not close enough to be beside him, but not so far away that an onlooker would think they weren't talking.

"The class is stupid," Kinley said. "Dr. Stratford's terrible." She paused, and put a hand to her lips. "I think that's the first bad thing I've ever said about a teacher."

Tyler squinted at her. "Is it bad, though? If it's true?" He laughed. "You hold teachers up on some sort of pedestal, like they can't do anything wrong. But a shitty teacher is still a shitty teacher."

"You think all teachers are shitty," Kinley pointed out.

Tyler nodded. "You've got a point there." He dug into his pocket and came out with a slightly smashed box of cigarettes. He opened it and drew one out with his teeth. "Want?" he asked.

Kinley shook her head. Tyler knew she was probably mentally reciting school rules, and she likely knew that smoking on campus meant a three-day suspension.

"Come on," Tyler urged. "What are they going to suspend you from? Summer school?" He laughed again. "They'd be doing you a favor, you know." He offered her the pack, and she held up a hand, palm out.

Tyler frowned. Everything she did was so *choreographed*. Like she'd practiced it all a million times beforehand, and then performed with utter perfection.

"It's not even that," she said. "It's that I don't want yellow teeth." She flashed him a smile, showing a row of pretty, even teeth that could have been lifted directly from a toothpaste commercial and planted in her mouth.

"Oh," Tyler said. He rubbed his chin. "That's nice. Don't ruin those." He flashed her his own smile, which he happened to know was pretty great. People always said that they didn't know how someone with such a nice smile could turn out to be such a bad kid.

He'd heard that a hell of a lot, actually.

He lit his cigarette and watched Kinley blush for the fourteenth time. She really was cute. As cute as Ivy McWhellen, if you really thought about it. Maybe even cuter. Just more . . . understated. Like, you had to look at her to really get it.

He breathed in deeply, and blew out a thick cloud of smoke. "You're pretty, you know," he said.

Kinley smiled again. He liked that smile. "You're not so bad yourself."

They were quiet for a moment, and then Tyler suddenly stood and put his hand up, waving someone over.

An old purple Jeep—the kind that's been painted and repainted—pulled up to the fence. The engine made an odd chugging sound, like a rusty saw drawn over a crumbling slab of cement, and the back was covered in peeling bumper stickers. It wasn't exactly inconspicuous.

"Who's that?" Kinley asked over the noise.

Tyler stubbed out the cigarette on the fence. "It's no one you will ever need to know." He winked at her, then jogged up to the window and clasped hands with the driver.

"Is it coming in or what?" he asked.

The driver, Jer—a pale guy with almost no hair to speak of—handed him a small paper bag.

Tyler reached into his jeans and pulled out a finely folded stack of bills. He was good at this. No one watching would have even seen money, except maybe Kinley, and he kind of wanted her to see. To know.

The pale guy leaned forward and bumped fists with Tyler, and then he drove off, turning up his music as he went, like he hadn't just been dealing in a school parking lot.

No big deal.

"What was that?" Kinley asked.

Tyler grinned at her.

And even though he could see her fighting it, she grinned back.

Cade

Cade watched his father in front of his closet, flicking through his neckties.

Mr. Sano had quite the collection of neckties.

He was rather famous for it. Everyone always gave him ties — for work anniversaries, birthdays, holidays, anything. But his father only wore the best. Only wore ties out of his private collection, which was imported from all over the world — France, Italy, Spain — but most of the ties came from his father's home country, Japan. The brands were names Cade couldn't pronounce.

Someday it would all dry up. Cade heard people talking about it behind closed doors, in quiet voices. Everyone knew it. He knew it was why his father never seemed happy. Well, one of the reasons.

But until then, he would continue to import ties and buy expensive perfumes for his wife and drive the very best cars. In Cade's opinion, the biggest waste was the ties. Cade could think of better ways to go deeply into debt.

"I don't need you wasting your summer wasting my money," his father said, "or going down the same sorry path as some other people we know." He pulled a tie off, and it made a slick noise against the fabric of his shirt. Mr. Sano held up another option. "Do you like this?"

Cade stood up from his father's chair. "It's fine, Dad. And I know. That's why Bekah and I had this all planned out. We're going to do an old-school tour. Take Route Sixty-six—you know, the main street of America. Oh, and we were going to go see Centralia. You remember how I did a book report on it in sixth grade? How it's burning up from underground? Anyway, Dad, it'll be educational."

"Bekah, hmm? I think you're quite up to date on your sex education. She's a bit of a tart, isn't she?"

Cade crossed his arms, shoving his hands under his biceps. He wanted to defend his girlfriend. He knew what his father meant by "*tart.*"

Why was it that Cade could control anyone in his life with a few words, but he could never figure out his own father?

Cade ground his teeth. "I wasn't referring to Sex Ed, Dad."

"I know." His father selected a tie—a deep, dried-blood brown-red—and fastened it around his neck. He patted it all the way down his chest to his stomach, as if it were a living thing. "But I have a better way for you to spend your summer."

"You said this was fine," Cade said. "We talked about it ages ago." He leaned against the giant dresser, which held almost nothing—everything was relegated to the closet. "Bekah's been saving all year."

He wasn't sure why he was saying this. Bekah wouldn't care. Bekah always put up with whatever he threw at her. She'd probably just shrug and go, "Okay, next summer," and then they'd make out for a while.

Cade's father rolled his eyes, his fingers still attached to the bottom of the gruesome tie. "Poor thing, saving her money. You'd think she'd be used to disappointment, though, living the way she does."

"She's not a bad person, Dad," Cade managed, his jaw tight.

"Did I say she was?" his father asked. He reached over and pulled a bottle of cologne from the closet, which he dabbed delicately onto his wrists. "Anyway, Cade. I've gotten you into a psychology course for college credit. It'll be much better than frolicking around the country, getting into trouble."

"A psychology course," Cade repeated. His heart did this weird, droppy thing that he was too used to. He wasn't even sure why. It was just a course.

"With our history and your genes, I thought it might be useful." Cade's father turned, meeting his eyes for the first time. "It's already started, but I have a friend who was able to pull some strings. You won't have missed much."

Great. That meant Cade had to do extra studying. In the summer. While he could be with Bekah.

"I'd hoped to visit Jeni, too." Cade didn't meet his father's eyes, but he could tell the comment turned him to stone.

"And why would you want to do that?"

Cade shifted back and forth. "For every normal reason why you visit someone."

Mr. Sano's voice was like hot iron, hissing and angry and red. "I don't see any *normal* reason why you'd want to. Besides, you'll be very busy with this class. I expect you to excel, Cade. This won't be one of those summers where you just slack off and spend my money."

Cade wanted to be angry, but there was something else inside of him. Something deep and sad and strange, but when he felt it rearing up he killed it, fast. Then he walked out of the room before it could rise up again.

Bekah was waiting in the sunroom, drinking mint lemonade that the housekeeper had prepared. She grinned when he walked in and wrapped her arms around him when he was close. The scent of freesia filled Cade's nose. At least, that's what Bekah said it was. Cade had never smelled freesias.

"We leave next week," she said, swiping her red hair out of her eyes. "We leave next week, and I bought maps. Like, real maps. Not the ones printed off the Internet." She dug into her purse and displayed one. "It's way bigger than you'd think. Oh, and I bought an atlas, which has, like, all of these interesting facts about places to stop. I didn't even know they made atlases. I just thought they were a thing in all those old road-trip movies." She laughed and grabbed on to his hand and spun in a circle.

"You're excited," Cade said. He hadn't realized she cared that much. He watched her dance around, her hair trailing behind her like a lariat of fire.

"Of course," she said. "I already bought snacks. Like, movie-theater style. And my parents are actually cool with this trip, you know? It took months, but they're actually cool with it. I actually can't believe how cool they are. My mom thinks we need to see all of the nerdy stuff, like the biggest ball of yarn and largest wad of used chewing gum."

"Is that a thing? Used chewing gum?" Cade put his hands on her waist. She wasn't the smallest girl in the world. That was probably another reason why his father wouldn't approve. Her hips were wide and her ass was even wider, and Cade liked her like that.

"If it is, we're going to see it. And we're both going to chew actual sticks of gum and add to it." She giggled and hopped onto him, her legs around his hips. He felt his jeans slip down slightly with the weight of her. "This is going to be the best summer ever, isn't it?" She leaned back so she could see his whole face, and then leaned in to kiss him.

Cade kissed her back, and all of a sudden, the feeling returned, the deep and strange hurt that he'd felt in his father's room.

He shoved it away.

Cade unhooked Bekah and set her carefully on the floor.

"I have to tell you something."

"What?" She looked at him, her eyes shining and her eyebrows raised, like she was expecting a surprise. Like he was going to whip out a box tied in a big bow, and she was the one lucky enough to open it.

She was so naive. So hopeless.

"We can't go."

She blinked. "What?"

Cade turned his back to her and looked out the window, onto the lawns they couldn't afford anymore. The fountain in the higher lawn was running low—barely a trickle erupted from it, and then it ran slowly down to the base. A couple more days without rain and it wouldn't run at all.

"My dad says I should stay here and take a course for college credit. Get ahead, you know." Cade's voice was quiet, calm. Like he didn't mind staying. Like it didn't matter.

Because really, it didn't, Cade reasoned. There were worse things than missing a stupid trip, even if you've been planning it and looking forward to it and finally, finally getting away from your father, just for a little while.

"It makes sense for me to stay here." He shoved his hands in his pockets and leaned back against the couch.

Outside, the lawn crew had just started. There were hedges to trim and the grass was just a tad long. The faint hum of lawn mowers reached his ears.

"But we've been planning for this for ages! Don't you even care?"

Cade shrugged. It wasn't that he didn't care. It was that he didn't really want to care. "I guess I care." But he only said it because it seemed right.

"Did your father put you up to this?" Bekah asked, her finger in his face. "Was it his idea to cancel the trip? He said it was fine. He said he didn't mind. He can't go back on that, Cade. He can't."

"No. It was my idea. Dad mentioned the course, yeah, but it was my idea to call off the trip."

Cade hated himself a little for the lie. He tried to take it back, but his mouth wouldn't cooperate. The words weren't there.

Bekah stared at him, and her mouth dropped open, just slightly. "I don't believe that. You wouldn't just change your mind like that, Cade."

"I did. I'm being responsible."

"You're being an asshole!" Bekah shouted. "This trip was important to·us!" Her eyes grew large and wet, and she sucked in her lips.

Cade shrugged. "Sorry, Bekah," he said. "We can do it another time."

She shook her head. Her face was an angry red now, and the color clashed with the soft flame of her curls. The tears that had been welling overflowed onto her cheeks. "No. No, Cade, we can't."

Cade frowned. Where was the easygoing girl who let him do anything he wanted? Where was the Bekah who always laughed and told him it was fine? Where was the Play-Doh Bekah who would always rearrange for him?

"Why not?" he asked.

Bekah pulled at her hair. "Because those are the kinds of trips that you take with your girlfriend, Cade."

"And you're my girlfriend. So?" Cade reached for her, just like he always did, waiting for her to melt into him. But she stepped out of his grasp.

"So nothing." She pawed at her face with the back of her hands. "I'm not your girlfriend anymore."

And Bekah Clark, Cade's second-favorite person in the world, grabbed her backpack off the table and left, crying.

And Cade was alone.

Ivy

"Hey, Ivy. Do you remember that time freshman year when you had to take a pregnancy test? Wasn't that hilarious?"

Ivy's former best friend, Klaire, grinned at her from across the table.

Ivy's father coughed and thumped his chest.

"Ivy?" Mrs. McWhellen asked, touching her daughter's arm. "Is that true?"

Ivy glared at Klaire. This is what the hussy chose to bring up at a family dinner. The absolute worst thing that Klaire could have come up with.

But then, Klaire had never been creative. That was why she'd been Ivy's second-in-command.

Klaire shouldn't have even been allowed to set foot in Ivy's home, but Ivy's older brother, Daniel, was engaged to Klaire's older sister, Laila, and the McWhellens had decided to invite the Petrusky girls over to celebrate Daniel's recent promotion. Apparently he was a Big Deal down at the precinct.

The whole thing made Ivy want to vomit. Why did Laila have to invite Klaire? Certainly Klaire must have told her that Ivy wasn't her friend anymore.

Everyone knew by now.

"Sure it's true," Klaire poked, smiling at Ivy. "Remember? You used the girls' locker room. We skipped PE."

Ivy had underestimated her. Klaire was clearly willing to go further than she had ever imagined. Further than almost killing her beneath a vending machine.

She'd advanced to full-on character assassination. In front of Ivy's entire family. The last people in the entire city who believed that Ivy was worth something.

Ivy glared. She stared at the cheap horse-hair extensions that they'd bought together at a shop on Woodrow. She stared at her stupid, too-flat nose that Ivy had always lied and said was cute. She stared at her former best friend.

It was *so* on.

Poor, poor Klaire.

But really, Klaire should have known better. Ivy had been Queen for a reason.

Ivy turned to her mother and laughed. "Yeah. We were good friends back then. I actually peed on a pregnancy test just so Klaire wouldn't have to take one alone!"

Klaire's eyes bulged. A forkful of lasagna fell back onto her plate with an audible *plop*.

Maybe Klaire had thought that Ivy had some sort of desire

to be her friend again. Maybe Klaire had thought that since she was Queen Bee now, no one would dare touch her. Especially not lowly, fallen Ivy McWhellen, the easiest target of all.

"Klaire!" Laila said, turning to her little sister.

Ivy shook her head and began cutting her lasagna with her fork, like they were discussing grades and the weather. "Yeah. It's a pretty crazy story, Klaire. I guess I wasn't sure you were ready to talk about it. I mean, I told her that Eric Langforter was bad news, but no, she had to go under the bleachers with him during a basketball game." Ivy laughed and leaned forward, like she was recounting a fond memory. "Cut to a month later—poor Klaire! I had to cut gym with her just to get her to take the test."

Klaire flushed. "Well, Ivy—" she said.

Ivy paused to listen.

"Yes?" she asked. The entire family was silent. Laila stared at Klaire with disgust. Daniel became very, very busy with spearing lettuce on his fork. And Mr. and Mrs. McWhellen— they were statues in their chairs, waiting to hear what horrible crime Ivy had committed.

But Klaire didn't say anything.

Ivy raised an eyebrow. She knew Klaire had just realized how Ivy had kept her title as Queen Bee all those years.

She knew everyone's secrets.

But no one knew Ivy's.

For a few moments, the only sound was silverware clattering over nice plates.

"It was negative," Klaire said finally, her voice stuck somewhere between hysterical and wheezy. Her face was a blotchy red-white. "The pregnancy test. It was negative."

No one said anything. Laila pursed her lips.

Finally, Mr. McWhellen cleared his throat. "Girls, I think that's enough. Daniel, would you pass me the pitcher of water, please?"

Daniel handed over the pitcher. "So, uh, I get an office at the police station," he offered. "I mean, I have to split it with Detective Wilkes, but he's hardly ever there. And, uh, I'm just helping out on stuff for now. But my boss says he's letting me take the lead on the next big thing that comes up. He thinks I'm ready."

"That's wonderful, sweetheart," Mrs. McWhellen said, eagerly latching on to anything that didn't have to do with teenage pregnancy. "Are you working on any interesting cases now?"

"Yeah," Daniel said. He took a sip of water. "Honestly, you wouldn't believe what goes on around this city. People suck."

"What's the most interesting case?" Mr. McWhellen asked. "What's taking up most of your time?"

Daniel fidgeted. "I can't really talk about them, you know? It's all very hush-hush. Legally, I mean." He said this with Much Importance.

"We understand." Mrs. McWhellen tried to smile, her face still pinched from the pregnancy conversation.

Klaire was a mottled tomato. "I need to use the restroom." She stood up from the table, her chair scratching across the hardwood floor. Mrs. McWhellen winced at the noise.

"Certainly," Mr. McWhellen said. "Who wants dessert? I have cherry pie and ice cream."

"The cherry pie from the bakery on Fourth?" Daniel asked.

"The very same."

"I'm in." Daniel grinned. "Laila, baby, you have got to try this stuff. I know you're trying to lose weight for the wedding, but this is worth five pounds."

Normally, Ivy would have agreed with him. Her mother had been picking up the cherry pie for as long as Ivy could remember. But right now, she didn't want pie. Her stomach was turning.

"Can I be excused?" she asked. She stood up without waiting for a response.

Instead of going to her room—which is where she really wanted to be, but it was on the way to the guest bathroom and she didn't want to chance running into Klaire—she slipped through the kitchen and into the backyard.

She needed a few quiet minutes to herself. A few minutes to think about how in the hell her perfect corner of the world had gotten so irreversibly screwed up. This was not supposed to be Ivy McWhellen's Life, that was for sure.

The night air was sticky-hot and wet—strange for so early in the summer. It felt a little like rain—except that the sky was almost clear. She wished, not for the first time, that she had a pool, like their neighbor. Her family lived an empty lot over from a giant, rather odd mansion with one of the best pools she'd ever seen. It was gorgeous.

It wasn't that her house was small, or not nice. It was actually pretty big, and her mom was a great decorator. It was that living next to the mansion was like living in a Polly Pocket house in a Barbie's Dreamhouse kind of world.

Ivy wondered if she could sneak over for a swim. The woman who lived there usually went to bed early. Ivy crossed the empty lot separating the homes and wedged her feet between the slats of the fence surrounding the mansion. She hoisted herself up, just like she'd done a million times—but someone was there. Someone Ivy recognized.

The boy from her psychology course.

The one who Dr. Stratford had locked out.

"Hey!" she shouted, hoisting herself the rest of the way and dropping over the fence.

Mattie

Mattie had been working very hard trying not to think about the fact that Derrick had only texted him once in the past two days when he heard something scuffling about near the fence.

(Maybe someone.)

He sat straight up.

"Hey!" he heard.

He lifted his head, and there she was—a beautiful, tan girl scaling his aunt's fence like she'd done it a million times before. Actually, she looked familiar.

"You're in my psych class," she said, coming up to the patio as if she just trespassed all the time. "I'm Ivy McWhellen. I live next door. I didn't realize Janice had a kid." She smiled at him, wide and confident. She was the type of girl who was used to getting what she wanted. She expected it, in fact, and she made sure everyone around her had the exact same expectation.

She was the type of girl Mattie might want to date if he were someone else—someone louder and brasher.

Mattie shut his laptop and stuck out his hand. Maybe he could use a friend. "I'm Mattie Byrne. And Janice is actually my aunt. I'm staying with her while I take the class. So."

Ivy shook it. "It's nice to meet you. Actually, it's nice to know someone is actually going to get some decent use out of the house and the pool this year." She grinned, looking at the water, which was lit from underneath with color-changing lights. Right now, it was a vivid purple. "You swim in it yet?"

Mattie shook his head. (He'd meant to. He'd just been . . . distracted.)

"You should," she said. "I sneak over here at night a lot. It's seriously the best pool ever." She half smiled and sat down on the bricks of the patio, looking out over the water. "So what are you up to?"

"I came out here to see if it was easier to not think about my long-distance boyfriend from beside an awesome pool."

That was the thing about Mattie. He was honest.

Usually.

"And?" She raised her eyebrows.

"Not successful."

Ivy laughed. She took off her sandals and dangled her toes in the water. "If I lived here I'd never think about my ex," she announced. "It's a magical ex remedy, I'd think." She looked up at Mattie and patted the brick next to her. "There's room for two. Or two hundred."

Mattie left his laptop on the little table, eased out of his sneakers, and sat down next to her. He touched his toes to the water. It *was* nice—cool on his feet, a delicious contrast to the wet-hot air.

His phone pinged, and he leaped up to grab it from the table. But it wasn't Derrick. It was his mother.

Love you, the text said.

"Expecting a call from the president?" Ivy teased. "Or the aforementioned boyfriend?"

"The latter." Mattie sighed and sat down next to her again. "He's been so weird lately, you know? I think he's having trouble with me leaving for the summer."

At least, he hoped that was it. It was easier to think about than the alternative—that Derrick was over him. Had moved on to greener pastures. Didn't need him anymore.

"Where are you from, anyway?" Ivy kicked at the water, sending a spray across the pool.

"Pikesville. North side, by the reservoir."

"Pikesville!" Ivy said, sitting up excitedly. "My parents have a little cabin near there. What's your boyfriend's name? Maybe I know him! I know lots of people from Pikesville. It's totally weird that I haven't met you."

It was probably because Mattie wasn't the most social creature. But he didn't need to tell her that.

"Derrick Waters," he said. "We've been together, like, I don't know, six months?"

Only he knew exactly. Six months, eleven days. He kept a little calendar, and he put a neat checkmark at the end of each day before he went to sleep. It was one of those stupid little things he did that he'd never confess to Derrick.

Never.

"Oh, Derrick?" she asked. "Yeah, I've met Derrick. He's wild." She laughed.

Mattie's heart sped up a beat. "Wild? What do you mean, *wild*?"

Ivy shrugged. "I don't know. Whatever people mean when they say 'wild.' He goes to lots of parties. He's always out there, I guess."

Mattie's chest got strange and tight, like it did a lot these days. For some reason, he thought that maybe, just maybe, Ivy wasn't telling him the whole truth. There was something missing here.

"Have you, uh, heard anything about him lately?"

"No." Ivy kicked at the water again. "Not lately."

"At all?" Mattie pressed.

Ivy hesitated. "Well, sure. You hear stuff about everyone, right? Especially everyone in Pikesville. I mean, the rumors were crazy."

Mattie leaned in. "What did you hear?" he asked. He almost didn't want the answer.

Ivy stood up and brushed her hands off on her shorts. "Um, nothing for a long time. Nothing important, anyway."

"But—"

Ivy gave him a short smile. "I've got to get back. But I'm glad you're here, Mattie. I think we're going to be friends."

And then, before he could say anything else, she was back over the fence, leaving him alone with his thoughts.

Kinley

Wednesday, June 10

Kinley had never met a teacher she hadn't liked.

More important, Kinley had never met a teacher who hadn't liked *her*.

And despite the fact that playing bad with Tyler had been kind of fun, and yeah, maybe she'd spent the better part of a night wondering what it would actually be like to kiss a guy for once . . . that wasn't *Kinley*. She was going to get along with Dr. Stratford, and he was going to like her.

Which was why she was here early. Again. She stalked through the halls like a soldier on a mission.

She opened the door timidly, and poked her head in. Mr. Stratford was sitting at the desk, a pair of glasses low on his nose, paging through a book with the weird, uneven expression he always wore across his face. A large cup of Starbucks sat beside his hand. Maybe next time she'd bring him coffee. And what was he reading? Maybe she'd check it out so they could have something to talk about. She squinted at the title. *Fifty Shades of Grey*.

Okay. Maybe they wouldn't be discussing literature.

"Excuse me, Dr. Stratford?"

He looked up, not even trying to hide the book. "Can I help you, Elsie?"

"Um, it's Kinley?"

Dr. Stratford took off his glasses and massaged his temples, as if calling her by the correct name greatly pained him. "Class doesn't start for another half hour, Kinley."

"I know," Kinley said, forcing herself to be bright. She would not be discouraged. She would win him over. She hugged her notebook to her chest. "I just feel like maybe I got off on the wrong foot with you last class, and I wanted to stop by and personally apologize."

Dr. Stratford cleared his throat. "Frankly, I didn't even remember that until you reminded me, but now it's burned into my mind. I doubt I'll ever forget it."

Shoot. Shoot, shoot, shoot. This was not going like Kinley planned.

"Well, um, now that you do remember, I just wanted to see if there was something I could do to make it up? Like, maybe I could do an extra assignment or something. I'm a really hard worker, Dr. Stratford. I'd do anything."

He turned toward her. "Is that so?" He steepled his fingers beneath his chin.

"Yes, sir." Kinley let out her breath. Maybe this wasn't going so badly after all.

"Very well." Mr. Stratford turned away and pulled a fountain pen from the drawer in the desk, and he scratched across the paper for a minute. He folded the paper neatly into fourths and handed it to her. "Have these done by next week."

A tiny, whispery part of her told her that next week was the first test. And that he was asking a lot. But that wasn't something she should say, so she just took the paper. "Thank you so much, Dr. Stratford. I can't tell you how much I appreciate this." She put her palm on her chest. "Seriously, thank you."

"I'll see you in class." He picked the book back up. "I need to prepare, so please come back when class actually is set to begin."

Kinley eyed the book. "Oh. Okay. Thanks again."

He fluttered his hand at her. "Go."

"Yes, sir." She left and very quietly shut the door behind her, then did a tiny little victory dance outside the door.

She was back. Kinley Phillips was back. As soon as she finished these assignments, she'd be the favorite student. The teacher's pet. She'd ace the course and do her father proud.

"Uh, what are you doing?"

She whipped around. Mattie Byrne, the boy who had been locked out of the class last time, was standing behind her. Obviously, he'd decided to get to class early this time.

She grinned at him. "Winning."

And then she walked down the hall. She unfolded the paper that Dr. Stratford had assigned to her.

Please check out Psychology: 305 from the local library.

Read and report on chapters one, four, seven, and eight. Each report should be minimum of eight pages long, single spaced.

Please answer test questions 1–30 for each chapter.

Complete activities 7, 12, and 14 in chapter one, activities 1, 2, and 16 in chapter four, activities 3 and 9 in chapter seven, and activities 1–30 in chapter eight.

If these activities are not completed by the beginning of the next class, I will assume you are not ready to take your academic responsibilities seriously.

PS: Remember, we have a test.

Kinley crumpled up the note in her fist, her blood cold. Then she smoothed it out, carefully folded it up, and borrowed a piece of tape from the front office to keep on the front page of her notebook. She downloaded the textbook onto her phone, and then waited outside the classroom with Mattie until the rest of the students started to arrive.

She would not be daunted.

She was Kinley Phillips, after all.

And Kinley Phillips had made a reputation out of accomplishing the impossible.

She would do this.

Kinley followed Kip in and took a seat in the third row— not too close to the back, but not so close she looked like an Eager Edith, or whoever.

She tried not to pay attention as Tyler came in. Tried not

to watch as he chose a seat in the back. Tried to pretend she couldn't feel his eyes on her.

At least, she hoped his eyes were on her.

Sort of.

Okay, she did.

Maybe she had a small crush on Tyler Green. And yeah, maybe Tyler Green was pretty much the first guy who'd ever actually given her the time of day, and maybe that was pathetic, but she couldn't help it. She liked it.

But when Dr. Stratford started talking, she turned off the boy-crazy part of her brain and began taking notes. She didn't get annoyed when Dr. Stratford was rude about questions, and only got a little bothered when an attractive Asian guy named Cade was introduced to the class as "an over-privileged boy whom I was forced to admit to the class by merit of an obscenely wealthy father."

Cade, who was sitting back in his chair, sort of lifted his hand lazily, acknowledging this. "Here."

He did look like a rich kid, Kinley thought. Like he didn't have to try.

"We're aware," Stratford said drily. "Now, we're going to skip around a bit. Who can name Freud's stages of psychosexual development?"

Kinley could name at least three, but she stayed still. Today, she wasn't going to draw attention to herself. Maybe she could answer one question directly and then fly under the radar before gradually emerging as star of the class. She didn't want to be obnoxious.

Surprisingly, Cade, the new kid, raised his hand.

"Mr. Sano? Did your private tutor provide you with the answer?"

Cade smirked. "Oral, anal, phallic, latency . . . oh, and genital."

A couple of the kids snickered, but it was quickly stifled.

"Surprisingly correct. Would you care to expand, Mr. Sano, or is that beyond your abilities?"

Cade lifted a shoulder. "I'll let you take it from here."

As Dr. Stratford launched into a detailed explanation of the oral stage, Kinley felt her phone vibrate in her pocket.

She ignored it and kept taking notes.

It vibrated again.

And again.

Very slowly, without moving her eyes from Dr. Stratford, she slipped her hand into her pocket and pulled her phone into her lap.

She didn't recognize the number, so she tapped the message.

Hey.

Do you know who this is?

Look behind you.

Kinley glanced back.

Tyler was grinning at her. He winked and gave her a small wave.

She felt her face grow hot. She smiled and turned back around.

And found Dr. Stratford staring at her.

He strode forward quickly and reached out to grab her cell phone. Then, without looking at the messages, he walked to his desk, opened the top of his paper coffee cup and dropped it in. He replaced the lid and swirled the liquid around.

Kinley's mouth dropped open.

And then, without acknowledging that he'd done anything out of the ordinary, he moved on to anal.

Tyler

"Kinley! Wait up!"

Kinley spun around, her braid wrapping halfway around her neck with the motion. "I am not talking to you," she said, lifting a finger. "You got me in trouble!"

Tyler jogged up to her, his heart beating a little funny in his chest. "I know. I'm sorry. I didn't think you were going to check your phone right there in class." He gave her his best innocent look, which was actually pretty good, considering.

Kinley folded her arms and put her weight back on one leg, which Tyler knew as the international girl-sign for *I'm pissed but I'm also listening.*

"Let me make it up to you."

"How do you propose that? You ruined my phone! How am I going to explain that to my parents? 'I'm sorry, I was just texting with the school delinquent and the professor destroyed my phone in his evening latte!'"

Tyler shrugged. A shitty, guilty feeling rolled around in his stomach. "Well, that was a little extreme. I mean, most teachers just take it away until the end of class. Or dock you points. But I'll fix it."

"I've tried the cell-phone-in-rice stunt," Kinley snapped. "Guess what? It doesn't work."

Tyler raised his arm in the air and motioned over a vehicle—the same purple Jeep as last time. He was going to fix this. He had to.

Kinley held up her hands. "I'm outta here. I've been in enough trouble for one day."

"Just wait," Tyler said. "I swear if anything happens I'll say you had nothing to do with it."

Kinley groaned. "I don't have time for this. Please tell me why I'm supposed to trust you again?"

"I'm trying to prove myself to you right now!" Tyler pleaded. He clasped his hands together, his fingers interlaced like he was praying. "Please?"

Kinley shook her head, but she didn't move.

Tyler waved again, and the Jeep pulled in, a few spaces away since the parking lot was still full. There was some kind of drama club meeting tonight.

"Wait here," Tyler said. He walked up to the Jeep, and the same pale guy—Jer—handed him two bags. Tyler slipped him a fold of bills.

"What about the other thing?" Jer asked, scratching behind his ear.

"Not today, dude." Tyler cast a look back at Kinley, who was playing with the end of her long braid.

Jer shrugged, following Tyler's glance. "Whatever."

"Thanks, man." Tyler bumped fists with the guy and then turned back to Kinley. He tucked one bag into the waistband of his jeans; the other, he tried to hand to her.

She took a step back. "I don't do drugs!"

He laughed. "It's not drugs. Check it out." He ripped open the bag himself and pulled out a phone. A brand-new model.

"It's unlocked," he said. "Maybe it's not exactly like yours, but it's close." He handed it to her "It's the least I could do. I know you're still not Dr. Stratford's favorite, but—"

"It's . . . a lot like my other one," she said, almost grudgingly. She turned it over, judging it closely. "How did you get it so fast?"

Tyler lifted a shoulder. "I texted my connections while Stratford was taking your phone for a swim. They always come through."

Kinley's grip tightened on the phone. "It's the only thing . . . I mean, thank you." Her face was lit up. For some reason, he got the feeling that maybe, despite all of her success, nice things didn't happen for her all that often.

He grinned. She was so damn cute. A couple of hairs had come loose from her perfect braid and were in her eyes. He wanted to move them, but he was afraid to scare her.

"I appreciate it. I guess." Kinley smiled a little. "God, Stratford totally sucks, doesn't he?" she said, and laughed.

Tyler chuckled. "He's an asshole. You're right. He gets off on being mean. It's not you, you know."

"Yeah, but he really seems to hate me." She pulled her notebook out of her backpack and showed him the list of assignments taped to the first page. "This is what I have to do to get back into his good graces—if I even can, after the phone incident. All by Tuesday."

Tyler pulled the list off and whistled. "Okay, maybe he does hate you. But guess what?"

"What?"

"You're in good company," he said, grinning.

Kinley slugged him playfully in the arm. Tyler rubbed the spot, pretending it hurt. He sort of liked her. No, he actually liked her. Kinley was the most badass chick he'd met in a while. "You know," he said, "you aren't the narc they say you are."

She didn't smile. "Yeah, I kind of am, actually. But you aren't the delinquent they say *you* are."

Tyler lifted up his shirt, revealing the Baggie, and pretended not to notice when her eyes roamed. "Yes. I am."

Cade

Cade didn't *like* his dad, per se. He guessed that maybe he loved him, in that way kids were genetically inclined to love their parents, but that was pretty much it.

Everyone said that it was just his culture that made his father so rough and unsympathetic, but Cade knew enough Japanese parents to know the truth: his dad was just an asshole.

It didn't mean he didn't have some decent qualities. Just not many. His very best quality was that everyone was half scared of him, and so basically they always treated Cade with a certain measure of respect.

He was sort of banking on that today. He cleared his throat and adjusted his shirt, and then he rang the doorbell.

He fidgeted while he waited, listening to the movement inside the house. This was exactly the kind of house his father scoffed at—it wasn't that it was low income or anything, but there was a sign next to the door that said BLESS OUR LOVELY HOME, and an odd, slouched scarecrow was packed into a mini rocking chair. The whole place was a well-off woman's tribute to a Norman Rockwell painting.

The door opened slowly, and Mrs. McWhellen walked out onto the porch, her red-brown hair pulled back and a touch of flour on the bridge of her nose. When she saw Cade standing there, she gave him a big hug, like she was thrilled to see him.

"Cade! Sweetie! How's your father?" Mrs. McWhellen put her hands on her hips and grinned at him. "I haven't seen him since he got back from India."

"Great," Cade said, returning her hug and breathing deeply. Mrs. McWhellen smelled like cinnamon and apples.

"What can I do for you, Cade? I'm sure you didn't come by to see Ivy's old mom."

Cade chuckled. "Actually, is Ivy home? I wanted to talk to her about our psych course."

Ivy's mom half smiled. "She sure is. She's been having a hard time, Cade. I bet you know that." She reached out and patted his arm.

Cade knew. Just about everyone knew about Ivy's fall from royalty. It was the most vicious mutiny he'd ever seen. There was something sort of beautiful about it, actually—some strange, poetic justice. Ivy had taken down countless girls in her time, and when she finally showed that she had some sort of actual feeling, everyone turned on her. "Nah," he said. "Everyone still loves Ivy."

Mrs. McWhellen glowed. Cade always knew just what to

say, especially when it wasn't exactly true. "Well, come on in. She's upstairs. You can go knock on her door if you want."

Cade thanked Mrs. McWhellen and headed up the curving stairs. He knew where Ivy's room was from a giant party she'd thrown last year when her parents were out of town. He'd actually tried to hook up with Mal Owens in Ivy's bedroom, and Ivy had been pretty cool about it—she'd just directed him to a guest room.

He knocked on her bedroom door, and it swung open to reveal Home Ivy, in yoga pants (tight) and a T-shirt (loose). Her dark hair was pushed back into a careless, messy bun, and her face was clean of makeup. She was far from the evil tyrant queen who ruled the halls of the school, but she was still really beautiful.

Not good enough to date, though. Not in her current state. It didn't matter how hot she was. He thought of introducing Ivy to his father and repressed a shudder that started at the small of his back.

Of course, he had another plan. One that involved making his now-ex second-guess her decision.

"Cade!" she said, frowning a little. "What are you doing here? She swung her door open a little farther, revealing the expanse of her bedroom, and he walked in, shoving his hands in his pockets.

"We haven't talked in a while," he said. "I thought I'd just stop by." He smiled and grabbed a picture she had tucked in the corner of her mirror—Ivy and that weird kid, Garrett. His arms were slung around her, and Ivy's face was relaxed. Happy.

She hadn't taken the picture down. That said something.

Without as much as a flush, Ivy snatched the picture out of his hands. "I forgot this was up," she said. And then she ripped the picture in two and tossed it in her small silver wastepaper basket. "Funny how your room just sort of fades into the same old environment, right? It's like you don't notice anything about it until someone else points it out for you."

Cade stared at the pieces of the photo. Ivy McWhellen did not mess around.

But neither did he. "How are you doing, Ivy?" He sat down on her bed, knowing it would make her uncomfortable. It didn't matter who she was—all girls got a little weird with such an intimate gesture.

Ivy, though, sat down at her desk and pulled up Facebook on her laptop. "Fine. Listen, what are you even doing here? Can I help you with something? I really don't have a lot of time."

This was the new Ivy, then. She'd dispensed with her old games. She was smart enough to see there was no point.

"I thought you could use a friend."

She spun around in her chair and glared. The same glare that had cut so many of her peers to ribbons. "Really?"

Cade respected that. Clearly, he wasn't going to get far with his revenge-on-Bekah plan. And clearly, Ivy McWhellen did not care what his father could do to her. She was already destroyed.

There was actually a certain freedom in total destruction, and for a moment, Cade envied her. She was freer than he'd ever be. Freer than his father. His mother. His sister.

Of course, everyone was freer than his sister.

"Psychology class," he amended. He didn't move from her bed.

She didn't stop glaring.

"What about psychology class?" she asked.

"I missed a few classes. And we have a test coming up, right?"

"Yes," Ivy said slowly. She folded her hands and rested them on a crossed leg. "What about it?"

"I thought maybe you could help me?" Cade asked. "I feel like I missed a ton."

"You could be asking Kinley. She's smarter than me."

Cade knew that Ivy wasn't being self-effacing. Kinley really was smarter than just about everyone. She was probably smarter than Stratford. Her family was known for being brilliant. Her great-grandfather was actually rumored to be one of Martin Luther King Jr.'s key advisers.

But that also didn't make Kinley a suitable study buddy. Or any other kind of buddy either. Cade ran his hand over Ivy's bedspread.

"The *narc*?" he asked. "Really?"

Ivy looked up at the ceiling, exasperated. "What do you want, Cade? Do you want me to tutor you? Do you want to study together? Or, what, do you want to be pals? Do you want to be the first dude to have sex with the recently fallen? Seriously. Just spit it out." She turned back to her laptop.

Cade spotted her backpack leaning against her bed. It was half open, and notes were sticking out of the top. Her psych notes. They had to be. Ivy definitely wasn't taking another class.

"I'll go," he said. He stood up, slipped the notes out of the backpack, and stuffed them in his shirt.

Ivy turned to him. "Fine."

Cade paused at her door. "I like you, Ivy McWhellen. But you really should be careful who you're mean to."

Ivy smiled very tightly. "I like you, Cade Sano. But honestly? I don't give a shit."

Ivy

List all of Freud's psychosexual stages and a three-paragraph description of each.

Ivy bit the eraser on her pencil as she reread the question. It was something she hadn't done since she was little—the pencil-biting. Something she'd only done when she was stressed. Her mother had hated it. She claimed it was the reason Ivy's teeth had gone all crooked around fifth grade. And every time Ivy bitched about having her braces tightened, her mother would instantly appear and remind her that it was Her Own Fault, and that if she kept it up she'd just have to get braces again, and wouldn't that be embarrassing?

Right now, Ivy didn't care. If there was anything the past few months had taught her, it was that a little metal in her mouth was the least of her life issues.

And right now, she could only think one thing: she wasn't ready for this test.

In fact, the only thing she was absolutely sure she could

get right was her name. And the way she was going, she would probably screw that up too.

Oral, anal, phallic, latent . . . She scrawled the words on her paper. *Damn it. There were others, weren't there? Hadn't that jerk Tyler gotten all snickery about them last class? Damn it.*

If only she hadn't lost her notes. She knew she'd written this stuff down. And she *knew* she had been putting them in her backpack and labeling them for every single class. It wasn't like she didn't have the time to keep good notes.

But then yesterday, when she finally decided to start studying, they were gone. Just gone. They weren't in her backpack. They weren't anywhere in her room. And she'd torn apart the car her parents had bought her for her sixteenth birthday and found nothing (except a peasant-style headband that she was certain Klaire had stolen, like, a year ago).

She bit down harder on the eraser. What were the others? Were they physical? Did *latent* count as physical?

She cast a furtive look around the room. Stratford sat at the desk, looking happier than she'd ever seen him. One half of his weird face quirked upward, like torturing innocent students with a ridiculous test was how he got his jollies.

The other students looked just as perplexed as Ivy felt. Kip was rubbing his forehead, and even perfect, pretty Kinley—well, she looked exhausted, like she hadn't slept all weekend. Maybe she was sick. Her braid had fuzzed out around the edges, and she wasn't even writing—just rolling her pen on her desk, up and back, up and back.

Ivy scanned the questions on the first page, then flipped to the second.

Describe Pavlov and his canine experiments in detail.

Ivy frowned. Her mother would have scolded her for that, too. Frown lines. Did Ivy really want Botox before she turned twenty?

Ivy was 100 percent certain that Dr. Stratford had never even mentioned any Pavlov, let alone any dogs. And what had he done to them, anyway? Wasn't experimenting on animals illegal? Well, maybe it wasn't in the Deep South.

Or maybe, just maybe, she would have known *all* of this if she hadn't lost her notes.

Ivy cast a desperate look at the door, and locked eyes with Mattie, who shrugged. She'd borrowed his notes last night, but they weren't great. Mattie didn't keep notes like she did, and he was missing an entire class from the day he was locked out.

Ivy flipped to the third page. Guilt. She remembered this. This was the stuff about the different portions of the psyche — id, ego, superego. She repeated them to herself as she scrawled them down. Maybe she'd actually get one right.

Probably not, though. Stratford was definitely the kind of professor who ruined lives if someone misplaced a comma.

Ivy sucked at commas.

She bit down harder, and part of the eraser came off in her mouth. She plucked it off her tongue and put it in her bag.

She looked outside. Night was falling, but it was still too dark for the time of day. Strange gray-green clouds had been moving across the sky all afternoon, and on the way to class, she'd watched little bolts of lightning explode across an approaching thunderhead.

As she'd driven in, she'd prayed for the storm to come faster, to bring severe weather warnings that would force Stratford to cancel class. Maybe he'd get in a car accident, and everyone would show up and he wouldn't. Or maybe Ivy would, but even if she were bleeding out in a hospital bed somewhere, she doubted the professor would excuse her from the class.

She glanced up at her professor again, at his gleeful face, and he caught her eye.

He grinned.

She hated him a little then.

Maybe a lot.

In the back of the classroom, she heard a chair scratch across the floor as someone stood up. It was Kayla, who wasn't even that smart. Even so, she crossed the floor and set her test purposefully on Stratford's desk.

"Have a nice night," he told her, reaching for his glasses and his red pen.

Kayla nodded cautiously, but even before she made it through the door, he began making big, gleeful red strokes across the front page of her test. "Abysmal!" he murmured, bordering on radiant happiness.

Everyone hated him then. Ivy could tell by the way they

hunched over their tests, the way they gripped their pencils, the way their expressions folded in on themselves.

Outside, the beginnings of rain began to hit the windowpanes. Thunder echoed in the distance.

"This is bullshit," someone muttered.

Ivy turned around.

Tyler. He was leaned back in his chair in that way that only the real delinquents have mastered, and it looked like he'd almost finished his test—at least, his test papers were open to the fourth page and had been covered in his heavy-handed scrawl.

"Excuse me, Mr. Green?"

"We never even talked about a bunch of this stuff!" Tyler said, motioning at his papers. "How are we supposed to know about dogs?"

Ivy sucked in her breath. That was definitely not the way to talk to a teacher. Especially not Evil, Soul-Sucking ones like Dr. Stratford. She glanced at the Evil Soul Sucker.

"I assume you haven't cracked your textbook, Mr. Green?" Stratford asked.

Tyler didn't answer. He just slumped a little farther in his desk.

"Well, in that case, why don't you bring your test to me right now? It seems that if you're in a place where you have time to volunteer your opinions, you don't need any more time to take my test. Am I wrong?"

"Fine," Tyler said, lurching out of his chair. He dropped the test on Dr. Stratford's desk. He had plugged his headphones into his ears and was almost out the door when—

"Wait," Stratford called to his back. "I think we have some items to discuss after class."

"Items?"

Dr. Stratford was smiling again, the weird, hungry smile that didn't properly cover his mouth. Ivy shivered. There was something wrong with that man. Physically, for sure, and maybe mentally, too.

"Sit, Green."

Tyler stared longingly at the door for a second, and Ivy thought that maybe—just maybe—he was going to make a break for it.

But he turned around and stomped back to his desk. He dropped his bag on the floor and slid back in, his lips pressed tightly together like he was trying to stop himself from saying something else.

Dr. Stratford stood, suddenly, and with his hands clasped behind his back, began walking around the classroom, surveying the remaining students.

Kip took the opportunity to jump up and throw his test on Dr. Stratford's desk. He was out the door before Stratford even had a chance to speak.

Mattie followed him, casting a fearful glance back as he left, like Stratford might reach out and pull him back in.

Mattie didn't even notice he'd left his phone on the desk. Ivy made a mental note to grab it and return it to him later.

One by one, the test-takers dwindled as Dr. Stratford

observed them, looking over their shoulders and making disgusted noises deep in his throat.

Ivy tried to ignore him, but it was pretty hard when he chuckled as he passed her desk. He moved toward the back of the classroom, his right arm crossed over his stomach, supporting the elbow of his left while he stroked the scraggly remnants of his beard.

"What is this?" he asked.

Ivy turned around. He was at Cade's desk.

Cade shrugged.

Dr. Stratford leaned down and pulled out a few neat papers. Papers Ivy immediately recognized.

Her notes. Cade must have stolen them out of her bedroom. Her heart sped up as Dr. Stratford paged through the papers, the sheets crackling under rough fingers.

"Cade, I do believe you'll be staying after class with Tyler. We'll be discussing the zero you'll be receiving in my course, and the fact that you will never be welcome here again. Oh, and"—he paused, scanning the notes—"Ivy McWhellen? Seeing as how you were so very excited to share your wisdom, I feel like we should have a similar discussion."

Ivy's heart moved into her throat. Dr. Stratford couldn't do that. Cade had *stolen* the notes. It wasn't like Ivy was sitting next to him, feeding him answers.

Surely Cade would clear it up. He'd tell Stratford the truth.

But then, Ivy hadn't been very nice to Cade. Maybe he'd take the opportunity to let her burn right along with him.

"Sir—" Ivy said, standing up.

"Sit," Stratford said, pointing down. "There's no talking during tests, Ms. McWhellen. We'll all have plenty of time for a little chat when everyone else leaves."

The wind picked up as he spoke, rattling the branches of the trees and throwing wet leaves against the windowpanes. Somewhere, far away, a faint police siren began to sound.

The high, keening wail made the hair on the back of Ivy's neck stand up. Suddenly, more than anything in the world, she wanted to leave. She should have turned in her half-finished test and left with Mattie. She stared toward the door and back at her test.

She wasn't even close.

The sky darkened further. Thunder exploded and shook the room. The electricity flickered off for just a moment, and the room was utterly silent—no air-conditioning, no buzz of electric lights—save for the wind battering at the window, making the glass creak and click in the panes, and then the electricity came back on with a rush of sound.

There were four of them left. Cade, Tyler, Ivy, and Kinley, who was scribbling furiously, completely blind to anything happening around her. Every once in a while, she paused, flexed her hand, and then went back to writing furiously.

"I can't stay here all night." Mr. Stratford put his hands on his hips. "Kinley, you have five minutes."

Ivy put her head down. She wasn't sure if Stratford would even accept her test, but she was going to do her best, and she was damn well going to fight to stay here. She hadn't done anything wrong. And with everything else, the last thing she needed was to go down in a cheating scandal with Cade Sano.

"Time," Stratford called, tapping two fingers on his wrist. "Okay, please bring your tests forward."

Kinley's head jerked up, and her lip trembled. She put her hands on her neck for a moment, and then she walked very slowly to Dr. Stratford's desk, like she was visiting the executioner instead of just a professor, and, very deliberately, laid the test on the top of the pile.

She turned around. "Dr. Stratford, I don't suppose I might discuss some of those questions with you?"

He chuckled. "I'll tell you what, Kinley. If you can wait out Thing One and Thing Two here"—he gestured to Cade and Tyler—"and then let me finish dealing with Ivy, I'll let you ask one question." He tapped his forehead. "Use it well. Now, Mr. Sano." He fixed his eyes on the back of the room, and Cade came slumping out of his desk, never once breaking eye contact with the professor.

Kinley stood behind the desk. She pulled her test from the pile and crushed it to her chest, like Cade might actually be trying to steal her precious answers.

Ivy stood up too, hesitantly, and behind her, she heard Tyler's seat squeak across the floor.

Everything happened very quickly from there.

It started at Cade's neckline. The redness began as a slow

build from the top of his chest to his chin, and then blossomed over his face.

"Sir," Cade began, "my father—"

Dr. Stratford stood up, and looked Cade straight in the eye. "Son, do you think I give a flying fuck about who your father is?"

Behind Dr. Stratford, Kinley covered her mouth. Stratford, as if this conversation were taxing him more than anyone could imagine, took off his glasses and set them on the desk. He rubbed the bridge of his nose, like he was in some sort of great pain.

Cade's face reddened further. "You should, sir. Everyone else does. And I think he'd be very disappointed to find that you failed me for notes I wasn't even using."

Dr. Stratford's face didn't change. "So you regularly go around with notes in your lap that you aren't using? Did you wear them to dinner last night, Mr. Sano? Did they accompany you to the gym?"

"No, sir." Cade's fists tightened at his sides. "I was just studying right before class, and I forgot to put them in my bag. I'm sure you understand."

"I'm afraid I don't, Mr. Sano, as I noticed you looking down at your lap many times during the test. I'm sure that other things you have down there aren't all that interesting." He parted his lips into something like a growl, showing a crowded row of yellowed teeth. "I'm afraid that you will not be invited to return to class. Please leave."

Ivy's heart sped up in her chest. This was bad. This was really bad.

"I didn't give them to him!" Ivy burst out. She couldn't help it. She couldn't let Stratford do this to her, too. "I thought I lost them but he stole them out of my bag! I wasn't helping him cheat, I swear!"

Stratford cast a look at Cade, who was sucking in these deep, loud breaths. "Is this true, Mr. Sano?"

Cade looked at Ivy. And then he nodded. "Yeah, I swiped them. Ivy didn't know." Every word that came out of his mouth was like being dragged across broken glass.

Dr. Stratford looked at Ivy for a half second. "I suppose in this specific scenario, the best thing I can say is that you should have taken better care of your things. Perhaps you can retake my class next summer, Ivy."

For a moment, Ivy felt like she couldn't see anything. Her body went stiff and cold and her heart felt like it had turned to scar tissue. And then, what she said next was, quite possibly, the worst thing she'd ever said to anyone.

"I'll kill you, you bastard! You can't ruin my life like this!" she said, her voice coming out in a high, windless shriek.

Dr. Stratford smiled.

He didn't see Cade's fist coming.

But Ivy did.

She saw the way it collided with his face.

How it knocked him backward.

The way his heels caught the toes of Kinley's patent-leather shoes.

Dr. Stratford's face went slack and blank, like everything, all at once, had gone out in him.

His head hit the eraser tray on the chalkboard, and like a soft cloth doll, he fell to the tile floor.

And outside, the rain fell harder and louder, and on the floor, their professor lay, still and silent, with the tiniest trickle of blood coming from his nose.

There should have been more.

"Is . . . is he dead?"

All four of them turned toward the voice, and there he was—Mattie, probably coming back for his phone, staring at their still professor on the floor.

Tyler grabbed Mattie by the collar and pulled him into the room, and then shut the door and lowered the shade.

Mattie rushed to the professor's side and knelt down, his fingers searching for a pulse.

Ivy dropped to her knees. She held her hand over his mouth. There was no breath.

She looked up at Mattie. He looked back at her. And they both knew.

"He's dead," Kinley whispered, her test papers falling slowly to the floor. "You killed him, Cade."

A crash of thunder shook the room, and the lights went out.

Mattie

Mattie rolled back on his knees.

The lights flickered back on. His professor was in front of him. And he wasn't breathing. He had no pulse. He looked waxen already, and the small bit of blood that had leaked out of his gaping nostril was black-red.

Ivy tipped the professor's head back, trying frantically to give him CPR. She pumped at his chest and breathed into him. "You have to press hard," she whispered, half to herself, as she pushed down. The professor's body jerked under the compressions, but he didn't open his eyes.

Didn't take a breath.

Mattie stared. He needed to do something. Anything. He needed to fix this.

Stratford's blazer fell open, revealing an inner pocket of used tissues.

Mattie almost gagged. The professor had a cold.

"Cade," Kinley whispered again. "You killed him."

"We have to call 911!" Mattie said, pushing himself up. "We have to get help." It was the right thing to do. Where had he left his phone? They had to get help. They had to report this.

"He's dead as shit," Cade pointed out, motioning at the body. "No ambulance is going to help him."

"We can't just leave him! We have to try."

"You killed him!" Kinley's voice was now a whisper-scream. She pushed Cade. *You killed Dr. Stratford.*

Cade stared at her. "No. I punched him. You're the one who fucking tripped him. I didn't kill him—you did!" He turned on Ivy. "And *you* threatened to murder him! Everyone here heard you!"

Kinley's hands moved to her throat, as if it were choking her. Mattie put his hand on her back. "Kinley. It's okay. We just need to use the phone. We need to report this."

Kinley swung around to face him, and her eyes were wide and glassy. "It's not okay, Mattie. It's not okay." Her hands scrabbled at her neckline. "It's not okay at all." She clung to him, suddenly and hard, her arms around him so tightly he almost couldn't breathe. Mattie motioned to Tyler.

"My phone's on the desk. Get it and call the police. Now."

Tyler sprinted back to his desk and dialed the three numbers.

And then he stopped. His face froze, his panicked expression dropping slowly away.

"No," he said. "We can't."

He put Mattie's phone back on the desk.

"What the hell?!" Mattie cried as Kinley burrowed deeper into his neck. "Don't you want to try to save him?" He didn't understand. When someone got hurt, you didn't just pretend it didn't happen. You got out electric paddles. You called EMTs. You tried everything.

Tyler shook his head. "No. I don't. We all need to get the fuck out of here before we get blamed."

Ivy looked up. A vein pulsed wildly in her jawline. "You didn't do anything, Tyler. Neither did I. It was an accident."

"An accident? No way. You think Captain Wonderful here punching him in the face and then Kinley tripping him is an accident? No. At best, it's temporary insanity. And me? Do you think I ever get accused of something and get out of it?" He put both his hands behind his head and dipped forward. "Fuck!" he said. "We need to get out of here. Let's just leave him. No one's here. No one will find him until morning. Let's just get out, all right?"

Mattie bent down to look at Stratford. He *looked* dead. He didn't look like a body—he looked like a *thing*. And Mattie looked at Ivy, who was still kneeling beside him, wiping her eyes and smearing mascara across her face.

"Kinley," Mattie said pleadingly. Kinley was a good girl. She never did anything wrong. She wouldn't want to leave him. She'd help Mattie do the right thing. "We can't abandon him."

But Kinley just looked at him. "We need to go, Mattie."

Mattie stood up, his knees shaking. His whole body felt like he was running a fever—he felt hot and cold and hot-cold and strange, and he was half sure that the hot dog he'd eaten before the test was slowly edging its way out of his stomach and into his throat.

And without really feeling like he was making a choice at all, he was grabbing on to Ivy's hand and leading her outside, with the whole group behind them. They shut the door and walked down the hallway, out the double glass doors, and into the rain, and they stood outside in a clump, blinking through the wetness. The rain was still falling steadily, and it soaked through their hair and into their clothes. A clump of wet leaves stuck to Mattie's ankle. He didn't bother to shake it loose.

They stood together and stared back at the building. Through that entrance, through that hallway, in that class-room, was their dead professor.

Mattie looked at Ivy in the rain, beautiful and perfect and somehow completely ruined, and he felt strangely terrible for her, most of all her. Ivy had just tried to save him. He wanted to hold her, suddenly, wanted to put his arms around her and draw her to his chest while they were all the only ones in the parking lot.

Except—

"Hey, guys!"

Kip Landers jogged up, panting. His blond hair was matted into a dirty brown by the rain.

"What are you doing here?" asked Cade, his voice sharp.

"I realized I forgot to do the back of page four." Kip bent over and put his hands on his knees, breathing hard. "I came back to see if Stratford would let me take another look. Think he would?"

Mattie, who had never wanted to hurt anyone in his entire life, wanted to slug Kip. Hard. "When has Stratford ever done a favor for anyone?" he asked bluntly.

Kip stuttered. "Well—uh—well, what's the harm in asking?"

Kinley smiled at Kip, her upper lip stretching over her teeth like she was snarling. "I get it, Kip. But he's gone. He left a while ago. We were just late getting out because we were bitching about him."

Mattie frowned. Kinley wasn't the type to curse. Kinley, who had teacher's pet written all over her, was acting least like herself.

But Kip actually nodded. Apparently, he believed Kinley. And who wouldn't? Once, Mattie had heard people whispering about how Kinley would tell on just about anyone for just about any reason. (Thank God she was here.)

"I'll just try back in the morning. Maybe he'll be here."

Kip turned away, and Ivy grabbed on to Mattie. "We have to go back," she hissed into his ear.

"No." The word came out before Mattie could reel it back. The last thing he wanted was to go back to see Dr. Stratford, cold and dead on the floor.

But she was right. Ivy was right. They should leave everyone and go back right now. They should call 911 and try to get help and just deal with the consequences.

But now that they'd lied to Kip—well, what if Kip changed his mind and came back tonight? Or hell, what happened when he came back in the morning? Then he'd know that Kinley had lied. He'd know they all lied.

And they'd all be linked to Stratford's death.

Forever.

Mattie watched Kip vanish. Vanish like his biggest problem in the world was a page of forgotten test answers. And Mattie hated him a little for that. He hated him for not being pulled into a room. He hated him for not having to witness a death.

He hated him for not knowing.

And more than anything, Mattie hated Kip because he wanted to be him.

"Someone should go back," Mattie said, echoing Kinley. "We can't just leave Dr. Stratford in there to be found by whoever wanders in there. We have to go get him."

"I'm *not* going back in there," Tyler said. His face was almost as pale as the body. "Let the janitor find him and call 911 on *his* busted ass."

"And then Kip will know we lied, and he'll know that we had something to do with it," Kinley said. She reached out and rested her hand on Tyler's arm. "We have to go back, Tyler."

He looked at her. Really looked at her. And then he looked out at the parking lot. He swallowed hard. "Fine," he said. "But we all go. All of us. No one gets off easy here. If we do this, we do it together."

"I didn't have anything to do with this," Mattie snapped. "I got pulled into that freaking room, but I didn't touch the guy. Just let me go and I'll act like I was never here."

Cade's eyes glittered. "I don't know. You touched his neck. Don't play like your DNA isn't all over that man."

"I was trying to help," Mattie snapped. "I was trying to save him. That's all Ivy and I were trying to do."

Beside him, Ivy looped her arm into his and drew him tightly to her. She wanted to leave too. Mattie could tell. Her skin was gray and her lips were drawn.

"That's funny," Cade said slowly. "Because Ivy slobbered all over him doing mouth-to-mouth. So *both* of your DNA is everywhere. All I got in was one quick punch. So I'd say you two look the guiltiest of all."

"For trying to save him?"

Cade laughed. It was a low, ugly sound. Almost guttural, like it was torn from somewhere deep inside him. His eyes rolled in his head like blank marbles. "If either of you—no, any one of us—if *anyone* goes to the cops, then we will *all* hold that person responsible. Got it? That means if one of us narcs—the rest of us will personally ensure that person is held solely accountable for the murder of Dr. Stratford. Do you really want homicide on your record, Mattie?"

Something deep inside Mattie twisted and writhed and

went out. "No," he said, very quietly. Looking at Cade, at his flat, emotionless face, he knew that he'd do it. There was something *off* about him. Something soulless and strange. "No, I don't."

"Then help us. We're going in there, and we're going to move the body."

The hot-cold feeling intensified. But he followed the other four inside. Ivy kept squeezing his arm, but he wasn't sure if it was on purpose or not.

Kinley

Kinley half wanted Stratford to be gone when they returned. Just vanished. Or maybe he'd be fine. Maybe Mattie had been wrong about the pulse, and he'd be rolling around, groaning, clutching his head. Maybe he'd be up, walking around, and fail them all for almost killing him.

It was the first time in her life that Kinley wished for an F.

But he wasn't any of those things.

Stratford was still lying there. Only now his left eye was partly open, and half of the milky white was exposed. Kinley gagged when she saw him.

"There should be more blood," Ivy whispered into Mattie's shoulder. "If he's dead, why isn't there more blood?"

Mattie shushed her, and Kinley shot her a look. Some people just couldn't hold it together.

Kinley wasn't one of those people. She knew she was screwed, but in that knowledge she felt strangely okay. In control. She had the facts, and now she just had to figure out how to arrange them to her advantage.

It was how she lived her life. With facts. Finding the advantages. Making them hers.

Kinley straightened and took a deep breath. "I'll go keep watch. Tyler, Ivy, grab his arms. Mattie and Cade, his legs. We're going to get him out of here."

"What about cameras?" Tyler asked.

Ivy shook her head. "No." Her voice shook. "They're being refitted. The new eco-friendly cameras should be in by next week."

"She's right," Kinley said. "Student council voted on it. Now, let's do this. We're going to put him in my trunk."

No one argued. And if it was anyone's car, it might as well be Kinley's. No one would ever suspect perfect little narc Kinley to transport a dead body.

And Kinley knew that.

She forced away her revulsion at the idea. "I'm going to go out in the hall," she said, "and at my signal, you lift." She pulled her keys out of her bag. "I'm going to pull around."

She poked her head out into the hallway.

No one was coming.

No footsteps.

They were alone.

"Go," she hissed back into the room, and she took off down

the empty corridor. She didn't look back. She walked quickly out the double glass doors near the parking lot and into the rain.

The lot was still almost empty. She threw her backpack into the front seat of her Honda and crossed the car to the driver's side. She opened the driver's-side door and slipped inside.

Out of habit, Kinley flipped down her visor and caught her reflection. She looked pretty much the same as she always did. A little wetter, maybe.

If only her father could see her now.

She took a slow, deep breath, the same way she did before penciling in the first answer on a big test, and pulled the car up to the curb, as close as she could get.

The rain pattered across the windshield.

Kinley stepped out, leaving the front door open, and popped the trunk. It was empty. She wished, for a moment, that she had garbage bags or something to line the trunk with, so she wouldn't get *body* on it. But she had nothing.

And that included time.

She heard the clatter of the door opening, of the bar being pressed and released, and then the slow shuffling of her classmates. She looked up. There they were, carrying their professor's body over the sidewalk. The legs of his pants were sliding up, exposing the white skin of his calves, which were slick from the rain.

Down the road, in the distance, headlights appeared, two small circles of light.

"Hurry," Kinley urged. "Someone's coming!"

"Shit!" Ivy said, and Tyler tripped, dropping Stratford's arm. It dangled down onto the wet concrete, and the rest of the group grunted. Tyler stood up and grabbed back on to the arm, heaving toward the car.

"Faster!" Kinley said, raising her voice. The group was hardly moving, and the headlights were growing steadily brighter.

"He's heavy, Kinley!" Cade groaned.

The car was closer. Closer still. What if the car turned into the school? What if someone caught them there, hauling the dead body? Could they pretend they were taking him to the hospital?

She hurried toward the group and squatted down beneath the body, to position her hands under his midsection. "The car's almost here," she whispered. She remembered the stories about mothers who were able to lift cars off of their children in desperate times. Athletes who were actually able to channel their adrenaline to perform amazing, Olympic-level feats. She'd have to find that now. She'd have to be the one who got this body where it needed to go.

She had to be the one to save them.

Kinley bent down a little farther and took up more weight, her hands sinking into Stratford's doughy midsection. She couldn't think about it. She wouldn't.

Kinley chanced a look back. The car was near the school.

Near enough to see them with the rain? She wasn't certain. She could hear it now, the engine, the tires on the wet pavement.

"Now lift. One, two, three!" Kinley bent her knees and gave the body a shove, and, like a giant, soggy doll, Dr. Stratford fell into the trunk. "Get in," she commanded Mattie, who stood still, watching as she pushed the professor's limbs in and then reluctantly climbed in after the others.

She sprinted toward the front seat and threw herself into the car, and hit the gas. Hard.

"Not too fast, Kinley," Tyler said.

"I just want to get out of here." She checked the rearview mirror and pressed down on the accelerator. The tires hissed over the slick pavement and rain pitter-pattered off the windows.

"Drive normally," Tyler directed. "We don't need any attention, okay?"

He was right. Of course he was right. Tyler probably knew everything there ever was to know about crime. Kinley forced herself to breathe slowly. Like in yoga class. Channel her energy. Find her center.

And then, the car was there. It slowed down and put on its blinker.

It was pulling into the school.

Her pulse went crazy.

The car was pulling into the school.

It was old—probably more than twenty years—and it was so rusted and dilapidated that she couldn't even tell what color the car had originally been painted.

That was the kind of car you transported a body in.

It rolled past them, slowly. The night was too dark to see who was inside.

Why would anyone *be here this late?* Kinley gulped, and forced herself to leave the parking lot at a reasonable speed.

A few moments longer, and they would have been caught. If she hadn't helped them . . .

"Where are your cars?" Kinley asked.

"I rode my bike," Mattie volunteered. "I'll get it later."

Tyler shrugged. "Grounded. My dad told me to find my own way home."

"My dad's driver dropped me off." Cade yawned. Actually yawned. Kinley stared at him in the rearview. What was wrong with him that he could actually yawn at a time like this?

Ivy looked back. "My car's in the lot. Is it weird if I leave it there?"

"Didn't you always used to leave your car here?" Cade asked. "I mean, you're always making someone else pick your royal ass up, aren't you? I swear, your car spends more time in the school lot than the bus."

Ivy settled back in her seat and wrapped her arms around her body. "I guess we can say I made Kinley drive," she muttered. "And Mattie got a ride home too, since he didn't want to ride his bike in the rain." She yanked at a strand of her hair, running the tips of her fingers over the ends.

Kinley's heart did a quick double beat. How strange that she'd once envied Ivy McWhellen and her entourage. The girl who sat distraught in the backseat was nothing like the beautiful, confident queen Kinley had so admired.

"My uncle has a farm," Kinley volunteered.

"So what?" Tyler said from the passenger seat. He looked over at her, and all the wit and charm was gone.

Kinley looked at him. "It's far away from the town. No one lives there since my uncle passed two years ago. It's a place we can go to . . . figure stuff out."

"You mean stash the body." Cade almost sounded bored.

"I mean figure out where to stash it," Kinley said. "Listen, I saw this TV show, and they used chemicals to destroy the body. Do you think we could do that? Get some Rubbermaid containers—"

"It worked on *Breaking Bad*," Mattie murmured, his voice breaking. "Shit, I can't believe we're talking about dissolving a body." He put his heels up on the seat, tucking his knees into his chest.

"If you have a brighter little idea floating around, we'd love to hear it," Cade snapped. "Shit, Mattie, pull it together."

Mattie shut his mouth with an audible snap. He huddled closer to Ivy, and she put a hand on his knee. Kinley frowned. She'd keep an eye on Ivy and Mattie. The heroes of the equation, really. She could see them forming an alliance.

She almost smirked. She would never have imagined Ivy McWhellen doing something that would be considered *good*, but she'd been the only one who actually tried to save Stratford's life tonight. Even though he'd just told her she was going to fail his class.

The Ivy who Kinley knew—the same Ivy who bleached the tip of her braid white in seventh grade—would have ground a boot heel in the asshole's face and left him to choke on his own blood.

So who was this new Ivy?

Kinley narrowed her eyes. She didn't trust her.

The group was silent as they drove, and the lights of the city faded in the distance. They didn't mention how the washboards of the road and the thick mud rattled the car and sent it pitching left and right and nearly off the road and into the ditch. Kinley knew what they were thinking: if something happened, they all deserved it.

The rare farmhouse passed, and with it an occasional faint light, a reminder that there was life out in the deep country. Mostly, there was darkness. Thunder erupted from the sky, and lightning exposed the farmland: the fences, running along either side of the road, and the cottonwood trees that grew wild in the fields. The rain was carving deep ravines in the narrow dirt road. Normally, Kinley wouldn't have dared drive on roads so dangerously close to being washed out, but tonight it just meant that there wouldn't be anyone else to see them.

It was perfect.

And it was horrible.

The group was still silent when they pulled up to the abandoned barn on her uncle's property. And when they got out of the car. There wasn't anything to say. Not really. Kinley popped the trunk, and they wrestled the body out. The corpse's flesh was waxy and slick in the rain, but they didn't drop him this time.

Inside the barn, Kinley lit a couple of old gas lamps and hung them. The resulting glow was wholly eerie, as if they had faded into another century. The body rested in the corner, facedown. None of them could bear to look at Dr. Stratford.

"Mattie, Cade, and Ivy? Take my car. Drive slowly, and find the chemicals. Don't search them on your phone, just try to find the right things. Tyler and I will stay here. Stay in contact. If you aren't back in an hour, we call the cops. Deal?" Kinley tossed them her keys. They landed on the cement floor.

"Whatever," Cade said. "I'll drive. Let's go." He bent down and picked them up, and they were gone a moment later, leaving Tyler and Kinley alone in the barn.

Tyler

The rain stopped outside the barn, and the silence crept in, heavy and thick. In the distance, cows from a neighboring farm mooed balefully in the wet air and a train barreled over tracks, letting out a long, mournful whistle.

And the body of Dr. Stratford lay in the corner, his face buried in musty old straw.

Tyler watched Kinley. She looked almost normal, sitting there on an old hay bale, except that almost half of her hair had escaped from her braid. And she was shaking.

"Are you cold?" he asked her, more for something to say than anything else. It wasn't cold out.

She nodded. "I know I shouldn't be, but I am." Her voice held none of her body's quaver. She cast a look at the body in the corner. "I hate that he's in here."

"I know," Tyler said. He moved and sat next to her, and tucked her errant strands of hair behind her shoulders. "We're okay, though. And we're going to be okay, you know. They'll be back."

They would be. He'd been telling himself that since the car pulled away. Wouldn't it be easy for them to disappear? To leave them to dispose of the body and never return?

"I know." She would have sounded almost annoyed, but the desperation in her words gave her away. She was shaking harder now, and clasped her hands together like she was trying to stop it.

"Come here," Tyler said, and he wrapped his arms around her, drawing her tight to his chest. "I'm warm."

But the truth was, Tyler was as cold as she was, even in the warm, summer night air. Although his actions had every appearance of comfort, he needed to touch her. He needed to touch her more than he'd ever needed anything in his entire goddamn life.

And she melted into him. He had always thought of Kinley as hard and cold and haughty, but she was anything but. She was soft, and warm, and made him feel things he had no right to be feeling with his professor's dead body a few feet away.

Tyler held Kinley tighter.

"I can't believe we're here," he whispered, and his breath moved strands of her hair. "I can't believe we're—*this*." He didn't look toward the corner.

Kinley straightened and pulled away. She put her hands on his legs. "Can I say something?" she whispered.

"Anything." Tyler looked into her eyes. She was beautiful like this. She was actually really beautiful all the time. Her dark skin. Her impossibly light brown eyes, which were just a little too close set. It made her look too serious and he liked it. "Anything, Kin."

He felt his body respond to her. He shouldn't be feeling like this. He shouldn't. It was wronger than wrong. If he wasn't going to hell by helping to cover up a murder—well, he was now.

Kinley squared her shoulders and her hand tightened on his knee. "I'm glad he's dead."

Tyler stared, and drew back a little bit. "What?"

Kinley glared toward the body in the corner. "He was a foul, angry man who enjoyed hurting people. I'm a good student, Tyler, and he was going to fail me. He hated me, and for what? Talking to you? And it wasn't just me. He hurt everyone. You included. And so I'm sorry. I just can't feel bad that someone so horrible is dead. And yeah, I wish I hadn't accidentally tripped him. I do. But I don't care that he's not coming back. In fact, I'm glad."

Something flashed quickly across Tyler's mind and was gone just as quickly—had Kinley tripped him on purpose?

No. *Hell* no. Never.

"Do you think I'm horrible?" Kinley asked, peeping up through the loose strands of her hair that had fallen back over her shoulders.

Tyler took her hands. "No," he whispered. "No, Kinley. I don't."

He understood why she said it. In a way, he wanted to agree. But deep in his heart, he knew that he would have gone to military school to make this go away. He would have done a stint in juvie.

He wanted out.

But he wanted to identify with her too, so he said, "You know if I had failed the course, I would have ended up in military school."

Kinley frowned. "I can't imagine you in the army. You're too . . . free." She rubbed his arm.

Tyler smiled, but it was wry and dark. "I can't go. My brother needs me too much. He—relies on me."

Kinley drew back a little. "Your *older* brother? He needs you? Isn't he some golden-boy Olympic hopeful? He relies on *you*? I mean, no offense, but I thought it would be the other way around."

Tyler laughed, just one short "ha." "You'd be surprised, Kinley. Some people will do anything for a little success."

"Like?"

Tyler shook his head. "I just need to be there for him. I'm his brother, you know?"

"Sure."

But Tyler knew Kinley didn't get it. And he couldn't explain it to her. He couldn't explain it to anyone.

Outside, the rain started again and the thunder boomed in the distance. Kinley burrowed against him, her head on his chest, and for a moment, in the old, musty barn, lit by old-fashioned gas lamps, he felt a strange sense of satisfaction. He held her close and touched his lips to her hair.

If he never had to leave this moment, never had to deal with his parents or his brother or the screwed-up shit that was lying there, right now, in the corner, and he just had Kinley and she just had him, he would be okay.

Of course, part of him knew that wasn't true. Knew it wasn't even close to true.

But he wanted nothing more than to believe it.

And she lifted her head. She looked up at him, her eyes big and sorrowful and sexy, and he kissed her.

It just happened.

He didn't mean to. He didn't even want to. It just was. And the worst part and the best part is that it didn't feel wrong.

It felt good. Really good. Her lips were warm and soft and her hands on his back turned him on like crazy, and he put his hands in her hair and gently pulled her closer.

She moaned, softly, and moved against him, and he crushed his body against hers, needing her completely.

Cade

Cade tapped his fingers on the steering wheel. Everything was closed. Everything.

"I don't even know where to buy chemicals!" Mattie burst out. "Especially at ten thirty at night!"

He and Ivy were in the backseat together. Cade had insisted on driving.

"We have to figure something out," Ivy said quietly, her voice still choked with panic. "There has to be *something*."

"Mattie's right," Cade said. "Even if we find something, who knows how much it's going to cost? And what am I going to do, put the chemicals on my dad's credit card? And what happens if they're the wrong ones?" He hit the steering wheel with a fist. "This was a stupid plan, you guys." He lowered his voice. "Stores have cameras. The school might not, but any store nowadays has cameras. Like, all of them. And what happens if we buy the wrong chemicals, and someone finds the body, and we just happen to have that strange combination on our receipts?"

Cade knew. They couldn't go in there.

"So what do we do?" Mattie asked. "Just go back?"

Cade didn't answer. There was nothing else to do. He started the car and began to pull out of the parking lot. A faint bolt of lightning erupted in the distance. The storm was leaving, but the rain was still falling—not hard, but steadily.

"Yeah. I mean, what else are we going to do? Any genius ideas?"

He watched in the rearview mirror as Mattie and Ivy exchanged glances. Ivy had retreated into a corner of the car, her back against the door, like she could disappear into the upholstery if she tried hard enough.

"No," she whispered finally.

"No," Mattie admitted. "Let's go back."

"'How do you get rid of your dead professor's body?" Ivy laughed, suddenly, but it was harsh and grating, like a metal chain dragged over gravel. "I guess I should have paid more attention to the mystery novels my mom has." She laughed again, and Mattie reached over to take her hand.

Cade fought the sudden urge to yell at her. The truth was, he was barely keeping it together, and if someone went over the edge, he wasn't sure if he could handle it. What was wrong with him, anyway? He was the one who should be in charge here, not that brat Kinley. Sure, Kinley was from a well-known family, and her father was powerful, but they weren't rich. Not like his father.

But why the hell couldn't he think of one goddamn thing to do? He was the one who knew how to work people. He'd worked

Bekah for two years before she'd caught on and ditched him.

He fought a lump in his throat as her memory floated across his mind. God, he wanted her now. He could have never told her, but he wanted her. She was so serene. She just went along with stuff. She'd calm him down now, or maybe he'd calm her down, and all this would seem just a shade more okay.

They didn't talk on the way back to the farm, not even when Cade took two wrong turns and nearly fishtailed into the ditch. They got quietly out of the car, and Ivy and Mattie followed Cade back into the barn.

Cade clung to the quiet. Quiet meant no one was losing it. Quiet meant keeping it together. He counted his breaths. Concentrated on his steps. And then found Kinley and Tyler in full make-out less than twenty feet from their professor's body.

"What the hell?" Cade shouted. "Are you kidding me right now?"

The couple separated. Kinley scooted away and ducked her head, but Tyler just sort of shrugged. "You guys were gone for a while. Chemicals?"

Cade shook his head and explained the situation. "We need another plan. Can't we just bury him somewhere?"

Tyler stood up and began to pace. "With what? I think I saw a rusted pitchfork in the back. But that takes time. It's not like in the movies where you can just knock out an eight-foot hole in twenty minutes. It'll take all night. And with the mud? The rain? No way, man."

"You'd know," Ivy quipped, but Tyler ignored her.

"We could burn him," Mattie offered. "It would get rid of the DNA, right?"

"Two things, genius," Cade sneered. "First, how the hell would we get anything to start on fire tonight? All the wood is wet. Second, what if someone sees the smoke? It wouldn't be completely weird for someone to call in a brushfire. Do you really want the cops on the site of a fire that turns out to be a burning body? What happens then? 'Oh, sorry, officer, I accidentally set my dead professor on fire'?"

The group was quiet then. Cade felt a hot orb of rage rising in his chest, bubbling dangerously near the surface. It was the rage that ran in his family. That made his father so scary. He needed to do something before he blew up.

"The river," Kinley spoke, still sitting on the lopsided bale.

"What?" Tyler asked. Cade turned toward her, flexing his hands into fists.

"Let's throw him in the river. I think burning is frankly the best idea, but let's get rid of the body in the water. We'll throw some driftwood on him, and chances are he'll get stuck in it downriver. He'll get so bloated with water by the time anyone finds him that they won't be able to determine the cause of death." She bobbed her head. "In theory."

Cade glanced at the corpse and imagined it, fat and blue-purple with water, the skin loose and translucent. He let his breath out. The idea almost calmed him down, strangely.

He unballed his fists and scratched his head. It was throbbing, his pulse pounding in his ears. "Yeah, but how far is that? Are we going to have to throw him off the bridge downtown?"

"No." Kinley pointed to the east. "The river runs through the town. And then it runs through the farm. No one will ever need to know where, exactly, he was thrown in."

"But he'll be found," Cade said.

"Yeah. But he won't be found with us. It'll take him far away. Maybe so far that they won't track him back for a while. Maybe . . . maybe they'll think he drowned. Or something." Kinley rubbed her arms. "Any better ideas?"

The barn was quiet. The wind swept around the corners and made high, keening noises that sounded like crying ghosts.

Cade turned it over in his head. Right now, he wanted nothing more than to be rid of the *thing* in the corner.

"Let's do it," he said. "Let's throw him in the river. Can we get him back in the trunk?" Cade led the way to the corner. And when he turned Dr. Stratford over, a fat black beetle crawled out of the corpse's mouth.

Cade's stomach lurched. He turned away and vomited, very quietly, in the corner next to his dead professor.

"What?" asked Tyler. "What happened, dude?"

Cade cleared his burning throat and wiped his mouth with the back of his hand. "Nothing. Just . . . grab on to him. Let's get him out to the car."

They were better at it, this time. The corpse-carrying. It was something, unfortunately, that got easier with practice. They got Dr. Stratford back into the car in record time, and Kinley drove them to the river.

"He stinks," Ivy whimpered. "God, he already stinks."

"No." But Cade wasn't sure she was wrong. He felt like the corpse was invading his nostrils. The feel of Stratford's waxen skin against his hand was infiltrating every pore. It was like Stratford was already haunting him, and he had been dead only a few hours.

He remembered the last corpse he'd seen. Somehow, he assured himself, it had been worse than this.

He would get through this.

He would.

He'd done harder things. Maybe.

Kinley pulled up to the riverbank and pressed the button to pop the trunk. It was raining harder now. *Good*, Cade thought. It would wash away any tracks they left.

The five gathered at the trunk and lifted their professor out, his legs catching on the lip. One of his shoes slipped half off.

"Put it back on!" shouted Kinley. The river was moving quickly, and it roared in their ears.

Ivy stepped away, her hands in the air. "No!" she yelled. "I can't!" Rain streamed over her face.

"Holy shit, Ivy. I will, okay? Sue me if I don't want a dead man's shoe in my car." Kinley leaned one of Stratford's shoulders against the back of the car and pushed past everyone like they weren't even there. And she grabbed Statford's leg and shoved his shoe back onto his foot.

"Let's go." She grabbed on to a calf. "Come on!"

Together, they heaved the body down toward the edge of the riverbank, slipping and sliding in the mud. Tyler went down once, and popped up, half covered in the thick river sludge.

"Are you okay?" Mattie asked.

"It's fine, dude. Let's just do this."

Tyler grunted under the weight of the body. Cade's back strained. But together, they moved Dr. Stratford toward the river.

They paused at the very edge. The river had risen to the top of its banks, and it was rushing by with an intensity that Cade had never seen.

In town, there was a tiny bridge arching over the river, which was calm and lovely on most days. The kind of river people stopped to dip their toes in. The kind of river people spread picnic blankets beside and jumped into from giant rope swings.

But not tonight. Tonight, he imagined the water was nearly touching the bottom of the bridge. If the river flowed in the opposite direction, Dr. Stratford might even get caught against it, swept over the top, and found the next day, draped across the walking path with muddy clothes and leaves in his hair, by terrified lovers who were up for an early-morning stroll.

He shook his head, forcing the image away.

The rain and wind were coming in bursts now—for a

moment, the rain and wind would buffet them and then it would stop before it began again.

"Okay!" Kinley shouted. "On the count of three, throw him in!"

Cade looked around the group. Their faces were drawn and wet, and their hair lay over their faces in giant flat strands.

"One!" Cade shouted. "Two . . . and three!"

And then they heaved their professor's body into the river.

It barely splashed. He was there, on the surface, and then he was gone, into the stormy darkness, swallowed by the furious river.

They all stood there, together, for a moment, the wind and rain battering against them and the river rising steadily.

"We should have weighed him down," Ivy said suddenly.

Cade stared at the river. "Let's just go."

And he turned his back to the wet grave that hid their crime and climbed into the car. They did it quickly, their wet clothes trailing after them, desperate to be gone. They shut the doors, closing out the weather and the storm and the river and what they'd just done.

It was then they heard a voice, tinny and upset.

Coming from Mattie's pocket.

Mattie froze for a few moments while the voice echoed in the car. He grabbed his phone frantically and it dropped on the floor. Mattie picked it up and tapped the screen.

It was silent.

Ivy

Ivy's mouth dropped open. Had he just . . . had it just . . . had someone just heard them disposing of Dr. Stratford's body?

She would have bet any amount of money that her night could not get worse. She would have staked her life on it.

And she would have lost. Oh, how Ivy would have lost.

"How long was he on?" Kinley asked. Her voice was low and quiet. She hadn't started the car yet. The whole group was sitting, very quietly, but the energy in the air was palpably electric, as if one tiny spark would set the whole vehicle aflame.

Mattie just sat there, his phone in his fingers and his face totally slack. "It was Derrick," he whispered.

"Who is Derrick?" Tyler demanded.

Ivy stepped in and plucked the phone from his fingers. "His boyfriend," she said. She unlocked the phone and pressed *recent calls*. She held her hand against her chest and her eyes got huge. Mattie had screwed up. Mattie had screwed up big-time.

And they were all going to pay.

"What?" Tyler asked. "What is it?"

She pushed the phone back at Mattie. "He was on the phone for five minutes. Five fucking minutes."

"He didn't hear anything," Cade insisted. "It was raining too hard."

"Not the whole time," Tyler interjected. "Not the whole time." He lowered his voice. "We didn't say—did we say . . . ?" He trailed off.

They all sat, crammed in the little car, in complete silence.

"You shouldn't have hung up," Ivy whispered. Part of her wanted to make Mattie feel better. She knew he must be horrified.

But she was horrified too. Her heart was doing this rabbit-fast thing, and she hoped, for a second, it would just explode. Then they could throw her in the river too, and maybe it would really all be over.

"Wh-what was I supposed to say?" Mattie stuttered.

"You weren't supposed to hang up, Mattie." Ivy felt tears, for the first time that evening, welling in her eyes. If Derrick had heard anything, everything was lost. "You weren't supposed to hang up."

"What am I supposed to do now?" Mattie asked desperately. "What am I supposed to do?"

"How much do you trust your boyfriend?" Ivy asked, her voice quiet.

Mattie paused. "I—I trust him." But his voice was small.

Ivy knew better. Ivy could tell from day one that they had problems. And Mattie wasn't a good liar. He was too sweet. "You need to make sure he doesn't talk, Mattie. You need to make sure."

"He didn't hear anything," Mattie said. "He couldn't hear anything."

But everyone knew he wasn't sure.

"I'll text him," he said, and Ivy watched as he typed in Sorry, pocket dial, studying. Talk later.

And then he hit send.

"What are we going to do?" Kinley asked. She was facing forward, and her hair was curly and wild from the storm. "Seriously, what are we going to do?"

It was the first time Ivy had heard the real pinch of stress in her voice. And it made the feeling in Ivy's chest even tighter, made her sure that it was only a matter of time before this all blew up in their faces and they were rotting away in prison, their lives ruined. She imagined herself in twenty years, her face lined and aged, her hair a bunch of dried feathers against her orange jumpsuit.

She deserved it. After how she'd acted in her life, she deserved it.

"We make a pact," Cade says. "We make a real pact. Right here, right now."

"What?" Tyler asked. "We're not a damn babysitters club."

Tyler was right. But Ivy knew that it was bigger than that. More important.

It was life and death.

Ivy leaned forward in her seat. "He's right. No one can talk."

She looked back at Cade, and he began to speak.

"If one of us talks, we're all screwed. So we agree. No one does. And if anyone as much as says a word—not just to the cops, but anyone—your mother, your brother, your best friend—then we turn you in. The rest of us band together and ruin you. If any of you even considers telling anyone what really happened tonight, you're gone. You take the fall and the rest of us back it."

"Yeah," Kinley said breathily. She cleared her throat. "Yeah, that sounds fair."

"I'm in," Mattie said. His voice trembled.

"Shit. Yeah, me too." Tyler brushed his wet hair back from his forehead.

"Ivy?" Cade asked. "Are you in?"

Ivy stared at the faces of her classmates. She was mean. That was for sure. Everyone knew it. She was a horrible, horrible person. But to be part of hiding a murder and getting rid of a body?

She was every goddamn bit as horrible as everyone always said she was.

"I'm in," she said. She hated herself for saying it. But some things had to be done. "And we need a good alibi other than a barn and each other."

"And that's what?" Tyler asked. "Studying?" He shot a look at Mattie.

"No," Ivy said. She sat up a little straighter. "Hey, Kinley. Can you drive us to the movies? We can sneak in the back and it'll look like we've been there the whole time. If we hurry, we can catch the late show."

"What's playing?" Mattie asked, his voice faint.

"Who cares?" Cade asked.

"What about tickets?" Kinley asked. "They'll know we snuck in."

Ivy glared at her. "That's right. They'll know. And we'll be seen leaving. And at worst, we'll have to shell out ten bucks apiece or we'll get in trouble over seeing a free movie. But if anyone asks, people will know we were there. At the movie theater. *Tonight.*"

Kinley held up her hands. "Okay, fine. Got it."

They returned to the barn and used an old farm spigot to wash the mud from their shoes, and for Tyler, half his body. And then they were on the way to town, the air conditioner blasting to dry them off, cracking their windows whenever the rain slowed.

Kinley parked in the alley, and Ivy showed them what she'd only ever shown Klaire and Garrett before: the perfect, sneaky way to get into the theater without being seen. There were two doors that opened into a basement, and stairs from the basement that led directly into the back of the theater, right next to the rows that no one ever chose because they were too near the giant air-conditioning vents.

When Ivy and Garrett snuck in, they'd wear giant, fat sweaters and scarves and spend the entire show snuggling. Ivy would put her head on his shoulder and he'd wrap her up in his arms and she was happy, happy like she'd never felt.

This . . . this was different.

The group slid silently into the aisles, unnoticed. There was barely anyone in the theater. A lone man ate big handfuls of buttered popcorn in very middle, and a couple in the front row was already making out so heavily there was no way they'd notice if a bomb went off, let alone a few extra people slipping in to escape a murder charge.

Ivy stared at them. The movie was a stupid comedy, so she watched the man eating popcorn and the kissing couple. And she envied them.

A few months ago, she wouldn't have imagined going to a movie alone on a Friday night. Now, she wanted to trade places with the man. With anyone.

"Are you okay?" Mattie whispered.

"Great."

She realized she was crying again.

Mattie

Friday, June 12

"Make a scene as you leave," hissed Kinley, grabbing Mattie's sleeve. "We need people to remember we were here."

"I'm just going to . . . I'll be right back," Mattie said. He stood up from his seat. He'd been in the theater, next to the freezing vent, for almost thirty minutes, but his clothes were *still* damp from the rain. He was cold like he'd never been cold; like his heart had been frozen and was pumping ice through his veins.

He could feel all their eyes on him as he moved to the doors of the theater and then out, near the concession stand, where the only sound was the distant booming of a cannon (an action movie was showing next door) and the popcorn, the kernels exploding lazily now that there wasn't anyone in line. The concession stand girl watched him for a second, and then busied herself with making a Slurpee.

He called Derrick.

He listened to it ring. Twice. Four times.

Voice mail.

Thank God it went to voice mail. He slipped his phone back into his pocket.

It vibrated against his leg. He jumped, and the girl behind the counter took a large sip of her Slurpee and rolled her eyes.

Mattie pulled the phone out of his pocket.

Derrick.

He didn't want to answer it. He wasn't going to. He couldn't deal with talking to him right now. (But, he *was* finally calling.)

One tiny, joyous bit of his heart was thankful.

After all this time, Derrick was finally calling him.

"Hello?"

"Hey. It's me." Derrick's voice, rough and low, came through the phone.

Of course it was.

Mattie's stomach flip-flopped, and he felt a sick sort of happiness breaking through his pain.

"Hey! What's up?"

"Just returning your call. *Both* of them."

The temporary happiness that Mattie had felt faded away. "Oh. Sorry about that."

"It didn't *sound* like studying." Derrick's voice, usually so friendly, was accusatory.

"What did it sound like?" Mattie asked, before he could think better of it.

"I think we both know what it sounded like."

Oh God. Mattie's heart hammered. "What—I wasn't studying yet. We were on our way. And we stopped. It was storming."

"Stopped studying?"

"No. Stopped in the car."

"So are you studying *now*?" Derrick asked.

"Uh, no. We decided to ditch studying since we just had a test and we, uh, hit up a movie."

Derrick sighed heavily on the other side of the phone. "Really. You planned a study session after a test."

Panic rose in Mattie's chest, threatening to choke him. He cleared his throat. "The class is really hard, Derrick."

"Is it?"

"Yes."

There was silence—a thick, pregnant silence that pounded in Mattie's ears, smothering him.

"I think I'm tired of talking, Mattie."

"I'm sorry." The words burst out before Mattie could stop them.

"Oh? Why are you sorry?"

Mattie paused. "I—I'm sorry that you're upset with me."

"Yeah. Well, me too."

And then—nothing.

"Hello?" Mattie asked.

He was gone.

Mattie put his head in his hands. How much did Derrick know? How much had he heard?

What had they said?

Part of Mattie wanted to call him back, to beg his forgiveness.

But maybe . . . maybe Derrick was angry for another reason.

Mattie felt sick. Incredibly, invasively, deeply ill.

He had promised himself a million times he'd never, ever lie to Derrick again.

And he'd just done it.

"Here," said the girl at the concession stand. She slipped him a box of Swedish Fish. "Sorry about your girlfriend."

Mattie didn't bother to correct her. He tried to smile as he took the box, and he slipped back into the theater.

With the rest of the criminals.

Kinley

Kinley rolled over in her bed, her covers wrapped around her waist. She'd gotten up yesterday. She'd gotten dressed and braided her hair and talked to her mom and dad. Her dad had given her a couple applications for scholarships and smiled at her and she'd filled them out and given them back.

I'm going to be okay, she had thought. *Everything is going to be okay.*

But today was different.

She'd gone to bed last night and stared at her ceiling. She stared at the little stars her mother had glued there—one for every perfect test. Her eyes followed the crack that spidered out from the corner of the wall. She eyed the trophies and medals that glinted faintly, lining every empty space of the room.

She'd worked so, so hard for a perfect life. And she'd had it. She'd had everything.

Her father had been proud. She was following in his foot-steps. She was going to be just like him.

She wondered what her father would say now.

It was two in the afternoon and she was still in bed. Exhaustion dragged its heavy claws across her, but she couldn't sleep. She kept seeing it happen.

Why hadn't she moved her feet? She'd seen Cade throw the punch. She'd seen Stratford fall back. She'd watched his feet as he stumbled.

And she hadn't moved.

She'd just let him stumble. She'd let him fall.

She was the reason his head had hit the chalkboard tray. She was the reason he'd fallen to the floor like a rag doll.

And maybe that meant—

Maybe that meant she was the reason he was dead.

And somehow, amid all that darkness and pain and guilt, there was a fierce gladness.

No one had found the body yet. It would have been all over the news. Right? But sometimes cops held news back, if they thought there was foul play.

If they were trying to get someone to come forward.

Her phone pinged beside her. The stolen phone. The one Tyler had gotten her. She picked it up.

Tyler.

What are you doing?

For one fierce moment, she wanted to tell him the truth.

That she was miserable. That she was suffering. And that somehow, she was still glad she didn't have to deal with Stratford ever, ever again.

She glanced over at her notebook that held the extra work he'd given to her. The work she'd spent hours upon hours on. The work she'd been unable to finish.

She couldn't have succeeded with Stratford. Now, she didn't have to.

Nothing, she typed back.

Guess where I am

She smiled a little. Where did Tyler hang out? In purple Jeeps? In shady parking lots?

A dark alley.

Look outside

Kinley's chest did this crazy thing where it tightened and expanded all at once. For the first time all day, she pulled herself out of bed and went to her window.

And there he was, standing outside, his hands shoved deep in the pockets of his jeans. When he saw her, he pulled a hand out and gave her a salute, and then pointed at her window. The question was clear: Could he come up?

Kinley bit her lip. No. No, he couldn't. Girls like her did not have boys in their rooms. Especially not boys like Tyler Green. Boys were a distraction. She couldn't afford distractions.

Still, she slid open her window. The hot summer air kissed her skin.

"Come on," she said, and sighed, and before she could change her mind, an actual guy had pulled himself up on the windowsill and slung a leg over. He shifted and dropped onto the carpet.

"Tyler," she said. She was extremely aware of herself— mostly the fact that she hadn't brushed her hair today. Or her teeth. And that she was wearing giant flannel pants and a huge T-shirt with two crows sitting on a branch that said ATTEMPTED MURDER.

"That's funny," he said, pointing to her shirt.

She touched the fabric and smiled a little, impressed that he got it.

"Uh, can you give me a second? I just have to—"

And then she left him there and escaped to the bathroom that she shared with her two little brothers. She brushed her teeth quickly and dragged a comb through her ratted hair. She grabbed a pair of jeans, a tee, and most important, a bra from the hamper and pulled them on.

She looked in the mirror. There. She didn't look so bad. Today, she looked almost normal. Except there was something different about her face. She leaned on the counter, peering closer. Something strange and old.

Maybe that was what happened to you when you accidentally killed someone. Something changed, deep inside, and it changed the outside.

Maybe no one else would notice.

A knock on the door made her jump.

"Kinley, get out! I have to peeeeeee!"

It was Leon, her littlest brother. She groaned, shoved her pajamas into the hamper, and opened the door to where he was dancing, his hands clutching his privates.

"Thanks!" he cried, rushing past her, and was peeing before she was even out the door. She rolled her eyes and closed the door after him.

And then she went back into her room.

Where Tyler was sitting.

On her bed.

She'd never had a boy near her bed. In fact, other than her brothers, a boy had never even *seen* where she slept.

"Nice digs," he said. He eyed her outfit. "I liked the pajamas better, I think. Easier to get out of." He winked at her—actually winked, like a boy in a novel—and grinned.

She grinned back. She couldn't help it. She'd gone from complete innocent to having a boy in her bed in no time.

But there was a thing in the air that hung heavy between them.

Kinley could get past it, though. She could get past anything. That's what she told herself.

"How did you know where I lived?" she asked.

"Your parents are retro. They're still in the phone book." He pushed himself off the bed. "And besides, everyone knows who your father is, being a politician and all. I'm surprised he's listed."

Kinley wished they weren't. A few years ago, a group of activists had thrown eggs at their house, screaming obscenities until the police had finally shown up. One had thrown a rock, and it had crashed through the dining room window.

Her father had installed an alarm system after that. And a fence. As if it would stop people who wanted to throw worse things than eggs and rocks.

Kinley didn't know what to say. She shrugged.

"I've been thinking a lot about you," Tyler said. He began to walk around her room. He rubbed a purple ribbon between his fingers, and checked his teeth in the distorted reflection of one of her trophies. "I wanted to see you."

"I—I'm glad you're here." Kinley's voice wavered. What was wrong with her? How could she be so cool during what happened Friday and lose it during this?

It was like that hadn't been her. It was like a cooler, more suave, better Kinley had taken over, and now she was back to awkward perfectionist. Daddy's little girl.

Who really, really wanted to kiss Tyler again.

What was wrong with her? Had being completely devoid of a boyfriend made her totally desperate?

She moved toward him a step, tentatively, and he reached into his pocket and pulled out a pack of Marlboros. He flipped it open and drew a long, pale cigarette out with his teeth.

"You aren't smoking that in here," Kinley said. "I mean, are you?"

Tyler lifted a shoulder. "Does it bother you?"

It did.

"No. I just . . . I think that maybe . . . with all the trouble we're in . . . could we be . . . We should toe the line, right?"

Tyler smiled, and the cigarette pointed up in his mouth. "No."

"No?" Kinley took another step toward him, and felt her body heat spread from her chest to her neck. She thanked God she wasn't born white and pale. Her blush would have been *so* much more obvious.

"Don't you think we need to act like ourselves more than ever?" Tyler said around the cigarette.

Kinley reached out and plucked it from between his lips. "Why?" she asked.

"Well," he said, reaching out and sliding a hand along her elbow, "if you start dressing in black leather and doing hard drugs, you might get some extra attention, right?"

She nodded.

"And if I become a choir boy and swear off all the things I love the most, well, that'll make me look suspicious, right?"

A giggle rose in Kinley's throat. "You'd make a terrible choir boy," she said. "Can you even sing?"

"No," he said. "But I can do this."

What he did next had absolutely nothing to do with being a choir boy.

He slid one hand down the small of her back. And he

kissed her. He kissed her hard. And pushed her back onto the bed.

She bounced once, and she felt her hair spreading out around her, and suddenly he was on top of her, kissing her with such intensity, she could barely stand it. And then her hands were on him before she realized was she was doing, rubbing over him, reaching for the gap where his shirt had ridden up. His skin was smooth and warm, and she wanted to touch more of it.

And then she pushed him away and sat up quickly, wiping her mouth on the neck of her T-shirt.

"What?" Tyler asked, squinting at her.

She was panting, heavily, sucking in breaths like she couldn't get enough air.

"I can't," she said. "I'm sorry."

Tyler

He stared at her.

God, he wanted her.

He didn't want to stop. He wanted to jump back on top of her and rip her clothes off and make her beg for him. He wanted to kiss her more than he'd ever wanted anything in his life.

Tyler Green liked Kinley Phillips.

Weirder shit had happened.

"Is that okay?" Kinley asked, drawing her knees up to her chest like she was trying to put a barrier between them. Tyler stepped back.

"Of course." His voice was soft. He wanted her, but he could wait. "It's whatever you want to do, okay? No pressure here."

Of course, he'd just thrown her onto the bed and tackled her like a linebacker. Maybe that could be considered pressure.

But he'd needed a distraction. Something to turn his mind

off. He hadn't slept. He hadn't eaten. When his parents tried to speak to him, he couldn't even remember how to answer.

He couldn't think of anything but *that*.

He'd needed Kinley.

He sat down in her desk chair and watched her from across the room. Her hair was frizzed around her. It looked beautiful. She looked like a queen.

"You okay?" he asked.

She relaxed her legs a little. "Uh, yeah. Sorry. I'm not used to"—she motioned between them—"this."

Tyler rubbed the back of his neck. "I get it."

He didn't want to get it. He wanted something else. He wanted to be an asshole. His eyes traveled to her neckline, and then below, and then he looked away before he tackled her again.

Her room was like a museum. It was cluttered, sure, and kind of small, but it was absolutely perfect. Every trophy was perfectly spaced. The countless ribbons created a strange tapestry against the wall.

Where there wasn't evidence of Kinley's academic perfection, there were books. Lining every wall. Overflowing bookshelves. The extras were stacked, knee high, in perfect piles, largest to smallest, near her bed.

On her nightstand was her psych book.

He averted his eyes quickly. He couldn't think about that. If he thought about it too much—

"Are you okay?" Kinley's voice cut into his thoughts.

Tyler started at the question. It had pierced right through him. "Yes."

It sounded like a lie, even to him. Kinley cocked her head, considering him.

He couldn't let her see.

He turned away, his eyes searching her desk. His hands settled on wires, thin, spindly wires, and a small flash drive, all connected to what looked like a miniature earpiece. He picked it up, rubbing it between his thumb and forefinger. "What's this for?"

Kinley's eyes widened. "State secrets," she said. "Um—"

"No, seriously," Tyler said, unable to let it drop. He couldn't have her go back to talking about *that*. About Friday. "This looks high tech. I've never seen anything like it."

"You've never seen a flash drive?" Kinley asked, narrowing her eyes. "I knew you were a slacker, but I never realized the extent."

He forced a chuckle. "Yeah." He went back to looking at the flash drive. For some reason, he couldn't look at her. "This is weird."

He didn't know why he said it. He just wanted to say something. Anyway. He had to stay away from *that*.

"Tyler." Kinley's voice was sharp. "Put that down."

But before he'd even set it back on the desk, Kinley leaped off the bed and pushed herself into his arms. She lay her head on his chest for a moment, and he put his hand in her hair, holding her tight.

"It's okay," he whispered, but he wasn't sure if it was for her benefit or his. "It's okay, Kin." He breathed her in deeply. She smelled a little like sweat and the sharp-sweet scent of freshly applied deodorant. He liked it.

She burrowed further into his arms, and before he realized what was happening, she was kissing him again, pressing him backward with as much urgency as he had pushed her onto the bed. He half stumbled onto the chair, and she straddled him, her hair falling over him as her lips touched his. Her tongue, tentative, tasted his own.

She tasted good. Her body was lovely and warm against him, and his hands wandered without meaning to.

Slow, he told himself. *Don't scare her.* So he forced his hands to stay above her clothing, forced himself to kiss with tenderness, with patience.

She was so goddamn perfect.

And she filled his mind completely. She was everything and he never, ever wanted to leave the moment.

"What the *hell*?"

Kinley tore her lips away from his and froze. Tyler turned, his arms still around Kinley.

Her dad was framed in the entrance of the room, a look on his face like murder.

Her *dad*.

The famed politician. The bulldog of the current senatorial race.

Kinley jumped off of Tyler's lap, her hair everywhere. "Dad!" she screeched. "Do you knock?"

Her dad stared at Tyler, his eyes huge. His arms were making big, wild movements, like he was trying not to punch him. "You're that Green kid, aren't you?" he asked through his teeth.

"Uh. Yes. Yes, sir."

Tyler started to stand, but then thought better of it, staying stuck to the chair. Kinley retreated slowly backward until she hit the bed and wobbled, looking in horror at her father.

"Dad! Stop!"

Her father ignored her. "I never—*never*—want to see you around my daughter again. Got it? You could take some notes from that brother of yours, you good-for-nothing failure." He blew a hot breath of air out, and he reminded Tyler of a bull before it charged.

Tyler slowly rose from the chair, palms in the air, and slid along the wall. "Um, I think I'll be . . . I'll be going."

"Goddamn right," Kinley's father said, and then grabbed on to the collar of his T-shirt and hauled him, by the neck, out of Kinley's room and clear to the front door, his horrified daughter trailing after him and squealing, "Dad! Stop it!" every few feet.

"Stay away from my daughter!" Mr. Phillips said, his voice low and deadly, his breath stinking of onions and fish.

And then he gave Tyler a giant shove out the door. Tyler stumbled down the front steps, overbalanced, and crashed onto the cement.

Behind him, the door slammed shut, and he could hear Mr. Phillips yelling behind it.

Tyler slowly pushed himself up on scraped palms. Pain shot through his knees. His jeans were ripped and his skin was filled with a fine gray gravel.

Tyler gritted his teeth and brushed the gravel away, and pulled himself up.

He looked back at the little yellow home. The curtains in the front window were closed and he could still hear Mr. Phillips's voice, loud and angry.

Sticking around would only make it all worse.

It wasn't the first time he'd been tossed forcibly out of a house.

But it was the first time he'd really needed to stay.

He started to walk. He lived almost two miles away. It would seem even longer with scraped palms and a red, raw knee that stung like a bitch. Stupid Mr. Phillips. He'd needed her. He'd needed someone.

She was so beautiful. And soft. And smart. And so weird. What was up with all of that stuff on her desk, anyway?

Maybe she wore a wire. Maybe she was some sort of under-cover cop narc, like those kids who stood outside of liquor stores and tried to get unassuming adults to buy them beer and then when the adults brought it out—*boom*, arrested. He could see Kinley doing that.

He smiled to himself a little bit as he limped along. Somehow, Kinley was the realest girl he'd met in a while.

One thing was for sure: if she'd been wearing a wire last night, it all would have gone very differently.

For one second, he wished that she had been. He'd never tell. But maybe—just maybe—things would be better if he could.

Cade

Cade watched Mattie from his car.

The kid couldn't handle it. Cade couldn't help but think of him that way—a kid. Young. He was pacing, back and forth, up and back. His backpack bounced on his shoulders, and sweat beaded his forehead.

There weren't too many people there. This was the first class since . . . since that night.

And only five of them knew that Stratford wasn't going to show up. Their tests would remain ungraded. Their class would cease to continue as it was.

The students who had arrived were casting looks at Mattie. Cade groaned and pushed open the door of his Mercedes. "Dude," he called to Mattie as he crossed the pavement. He needed to get to Mattie before someone else stopped to ask what the hell was wrong with him. Cade wasn't sure what Mattie might say.

Mattie stopped pacing for a second, his eyes moving frantically around the parking lot as Cade neared. "Cade," he said, and his voice was tight, like he was on the verge of tears.

Cade patted his back. "Calm down, man. It's okay. Everything is fine. But you need to man up and walk inside with me. Sit next to me. We'll figure this out."

Mattie nodded. "Okay. Yeah. Okay."

For about a half second, Cade understood as he walked into the room next to Mattie. He wanted to freak out too. They all did, probably, except maybe Kinley. She was cold. Colder than he was, probably.

And then, he started thinking. His mind had started working again, after that night of being blank and scared. He felt like himself again. Almost.

Cade surveyed the classroom. The others were already here. The other three, at least. Kinley was sitting in the second row, her notebook and three colored pens laid neatly in front of her. She was a tough one.

Tyler was in the back again, as a slacker should be. He was in his trademark pose: ass scooted forward to the front of the chair, pen in his mouth, and a cap that he shouldn't have been wearing inside the school pushed down over his eyes.

And then there was Ivy. She looked . . . well, she looked a little rough around the edges, like maybe she'd done a couple too many shots the night before, but in that hot-girl way: her hair was perfectly coiffed, and her outfit hugged her curves in a way that said *Look at me*.

Cade knew how scared they all were.

But Mattie—Mattie was the only one showing it.

Mattie was the weak link.

Cade watched him from the corner of his eye. "Sit next to me," he said. He was going to have to watch him. Make sure he didn't go too crazy.

It was one thing to get a little stressed about test results. It was another thing to show something was really wrong. But Mattie was verging on a full-on breakdown, and Cade had to stop it.

This class wasn't going to be easy.

Cade glanced around the room.

Someone had been in to clean. Probably the janitor. The board had been wiped. The room had the sweet-sour smell of the recently mopped. And the tests, which had been left in a messy pile on Stratford's desk, had been straightened up very neatly.

There was nothing to show that Cade—with the help of his *friends*—had killed a man there.

Nothing to show that their professor had died on the floor a few days earlier.

Cade's throat suddenly went strange and numb. He cleared it and coughed.

Mattie shot him a look, alarm in his eyes. "Are you okay?" he asked. Mattie was kind. Easy to manipulate.

It would be his downfall.

"I need water, I think." His voice came out hoarse. Cade stood up, but Kip waved him down.

"Don't do it, man," Kip hissed. "Stratford's gonna be in any second. Do you really want to be in the hallway?"

Cade paused. If Stratford were really going to show up, would he risk it?

No.

No, he wouldn't.

Cade sunk back into his chair and reached for his book. "Hey, man." Kip leaned over again. "What happened after class? Did Stratford flunk you?"

Cade shifted, and he felt a strange warmth in his stomach. He hadn't been prepared to talk to people about what had happened after class. "Uh, I don't know. He was a dick about it. He said I'd figure it out when I got the test back and then he just left."

Kip whistled. "Cold, dude. Maybe it's a good thing I didn't catch him. I saw him in the teachers lot after I ran into you guys, but I just let him go. I froze. Dude is scary."

Cade frowned, and Mattie's head snapped toward Kip. Kip thought he'd seen their dead teacher in the lot? His stomach clenched. How long had Kip stayed after they'd told him Stratford had left, exactly? Had Kip seen something he shouldn't have? Or did he actually believe he'd seen Stratford walking across the lot? If Kip actually believed what he was saying, then he was their best alibi yet.

Or was Kip just messing with his head? Cade narrowed his eyes. If Kip had stuck around, maybe he had seen Cade and his little group too.

"Stratford was in a bad mood," Cade muttered.

Kip leaned back in his seat, a pencil flipping quickly between his fingers. "He's always in a bad mood. How do you think he's going to be today?"

Cade sighed. He could see Mattie still watching him. "I don't know. How is he always?"

"A tool."

"Then I'm going to go with tool." Cade turned away from Kip. He was tired of talking. He glanced at the clock.

Stratford was officially late.

Five minutes late.

"What's the rule?" Tyler asked. "Teacher isn't in after ten minutes, we all get to leave? Scot-free?"

A couple of the students glanced nervously around the room, as if Stratford was going to pop out from under his desk or emerge dramatically from the supply closet.

He didn't.

Another minute ticked by.

No one spoke. Cade could feel the others watching him. He could feel their eyes.

Mattie was sweating beside him. Cade shot him a look.

"What, dude? I think I screwed up the test, okay?" Mattie asked. "I blanked."

Cade nodded. At least Mattie was playing off his nervousness as test-related. He wasn't totally stupid.

"Me too," confessed a mousy-haired girl who sat near the

front. "I don't know how I'm going to pass this class." She paused. "Where is he, anyway?"

Cade stared up at the clock.

"Maybe he's dead," a freckled kid in the back joked. "Maybe we don't even have to worry about the test." He laughed, awkwardly. "Best-case scenario, huh?"

Kinley whipped around, her long braid wrapping around her. "That's not funny."

"Whoa," the freckled kid said, holding his hands up. "It was a joke. Calm down, narc. Don't go tell the principal, okay?"

Tyler bristled. He blew his breath out noisily, and then caught Cade's eye. He looked left and right, making sure no one was paying him any attention, and lobbed a crumpled ball of notebook paper onto Cade's desk.

He had good aim. Probably from years of passing dirty notes in elementary school. No one wrote notes anymore.

Cade quietly smoothed out the ball of paper.

Tell them.

He glowered at the paper, then the meaning hit him. Someone needed to tell the office Stratford hadn't shown up.

Cade glanced at the clock.

Their professor was twenty-five minutes late now.

Twenty-five minutes.

He chanced a look at Mattie. Poor kid. He might not even make it through class.

He stood up, and cleared his hoarse throat again. "I'm

going to tell the office Stratford didn't show. Maybe they'll let us leave."

Kip scoffed, deep in his throat. "If Stratford walks in while you're there, it's your funeral."

Funeral.

Cade hated Kip's choice of words. He made a show of hesitating. He sat back down at his desk, and then stood up again.

The mousy-haired girl stood up and walked to the desk. She picked up the stack of tests, casting looks at the door.

She turned back to the class, scowling, tests clutched in her hand. "He hasn't even graded them," she muttered. "We're all waiting to see what happened, and he hasn't touched them. Except Kayla's—oh, *Kayla.* Don't look, okay?" She slammed the tests on the desk and turned back to her seat.

"I'm not sticking around if he's not coming," Cade announced. He couldn't stay in the classroom any longer anyway. He couldn't take another second staring at Mattie, wondering if he was going to erupt. He shrugged on his backpack, left the room, and walked down the hall toward the office.

The evening receptionist, a black-haired girl with thick wire-framed glasses, looked up at him as she swung her purse over her shoulder.

"On your way out?" he asked. He wrapped his hands around the straps of his backpack and rolled up to his toes, then back to his heels.

Be cool, he told himself. *Calm.*

"Um, yeah. I don't stay until your class gets out. I was just cleaning up a little." She motioned at her desk, which was still covered in stacks of paper. A full mug of pencils sat to the left of her chair, which she pushed in carefully—a universal signal for *I'm leaving right now.*

"Uh, I just wanted to come by to say that Stratford never showed. We've been waiting for a half hour."

"That's weird. He lives two minutes from here. He's never late. He just walks over."

"Well, he's late today. What should we do?"

The girl shrugged. "I don't know. I'm not even the real receptionist. Maybe everyone should just go home."

"And if Stratford shows up after?"

"Your funeral." She grinned at him.

There was that word again. He forced himself to smile back. He hated that word. "Funeral." Would anyone show up to Stratford's? Did anyone even care that he was gone? He couldn't imagine Stratford had a family.

"Maybe I'll go back for a little bit just in case," Cade said.

"Cool. Have a good night, okay?" She smiled at him. "Fingers crossed that your professor doesn't show up. You look like you could use a night off."

Cade felt self-conscious. Was he wearing his stress so obviously? Like Mattie?

The receptionist winked at him. And then she was gone.

For some weird reason, she reminded Cade of his sister.

Ivy

"Mattie!" Ivy waved him over. "Hey!"

"Hey," he said.

The other students walked around them like nothing was wrong. Like there couldn't possibly be an evil explanation for why Stratford hadn't shown. Like their lives hadn't changed at all, other than a lucky break.

Ivy had heard them laughing on the way out. High-fiving. And she wished, more than anything, that she was one of them. That she could just be glad that Stratford hadn't showed. Like she hadn't been silently praying for him to impossibly appear in the doorway in one of his tattered blazers, angry and foul-breathed and ready to fail them all.

"Pretty cool we didn't have class, huh?" Mattie asked. She shot him a half smile. She knew what he was trying to do. Act normal. Fit in.

Be like everyone else.

"Cool," Ivy agreed dully. Together, they watched until the

other students had climbed into their cars or onto their bikes and left, filing out of the parking lot like ants.

The others—Kinley and Tyler and Cade—didn't so much as look at them when they walked out. Of course, Ivy didn't want to look at anyone. Except maybe Mattie.

"Where's *your* bike?" Ivy asked.

"I walked," Mattie said. He didn't quite meet her eyes.

"That's way too far, Mattie. Seriously?"

He shrugged. "I guess I needed to blow off some steam."

"Well, that's crazy. Let me give you a ride home, okay?" Ivy put a hand on his shoulder. "Come on, Mattie. Get in. I'm not going to let you walk all the way back."

"Okay." Mattie followed Ivy to her hybrid Honda CR-Z. He opened the back door and shrugged off his backpack, tossing it into the seat.

He settled into the passenger side and breathed in deeply. "If I had this car," he said, rubbing the dashboard, "I'd drive every single day."

Ivy shrugged. "I don't know. I hate driving. I don't want the responsibility." She turned the key. "I had this sort of nice Jetta, but my parents got tired of me relying on everyone else for a ride and leaving my car everywhere, and so they decided that if I had a better car then I'd want to drive, you know?"

"Did it work?" Mattie asked.

Ivy blew a strand of hair out of her eyes. "Well, I feel guiltier, but no, not completely." She looked back and froze.

Her stomach went odd and cold, like she'd drank an entire bucket of ice water.

"What?" Mattie asked. "What is it?"

He turned back.

"It's the car," Ivy whispered.

The car from that night.

The rusted, screwed-up one that had turned into the parking lot as they left. Ivy could see it was a faint brown at one point, but now was smeared with rust.

The car chugged into the spot next to them, and the window rolled down.

"Hey!" said the woman driving. She rested one wrist on the wheel and leaned out, and Mattie rolled down his window. Ivy watched his face go pale and ghostly.

"Hi," Ivy said, leaning over, pasting on a fake happiness. "Can I help you with something?"

The woman paused. She was older—perhaps sixty—and her hair was a wiry nest of brown and gray. Her teeth were a sick yellow color, like she'd been smoking all her life . . . and from the smell rolling out of the car through the open window, she had.

She was clothed in a gray-white tee that had been through the wash too many times.

"Maybe you can," the woman said. "I'm Delilah Stratford. I'm just stopping by on my way back from the grocery store. I don't suppose you've seen my husband?"

Ivy coughed. The ice-bucket feeling in her stomach surged and roiled. Stratford was married? Someone had actually looked at the man as they stood at the altar and agreed to love him forever? The knowledge was strange and powerful, and it struck her hard.

Stratford had family. A wife. He wasn't the solitary type she'd imagined.

"No, ma'am," Mattie interjected. "We're his students. We were supposed to get our tests back today and he didn't show up for class."

"Well, hell!" the woman said. "I tell you, we get in fights all the time. And some days he just takes off. Sometimes he comes back an hour later, sometimes, it's a damn week." She cleared her throat.

"Have you tried him on his phone?" Mattie asked.

"Doesn't carry one. Hates 'em, actually. He says he has enough phones with the ones his students carry." She laughs, and it is gruff and clogged with phlegm. "He wouldn't answer my calls now anyway, even if I knew how to reach the bastard."

Ivy watched Mattie's hand curl around the gearshift, his knuckles white. He was doing a good job so far, but he was about to freak out. Or maybe she was.

Maybe they both were.

"If we hear from him, we'll tell him you're looking for him, okay?" Ivy tried to smile at Mrs. Stratford, but her mouth wasn't working right. Nothing was going right.

Mrs. Stratford flapped her hand at them. "Don't bother, kids. He'll get home when he gets over it. Don't fan the flames, okay?" She chuckled. "Have a good night."

And just like that, Mrs. Stratford threw her rust bucket into reverse and backed out of her space.

"Holy shit," Ivy whispered at the steering wheel.

"I don't know what shocks me more," Mattie said. "That someone agreed to marry him or that that just happened. We almost got caught that night. Do you realize that?"

Her breathing shaky, Ivy began driving slowly, wordlessly, to her home. She'd realized something else, too.

There was already someone out there looking for Stratford.

Soon, there would be more.

Mattie

Monday, June 15

It was big and shiny and beautiful and it was sitting in the driveway with a big, glossy bow in the center of the hood.

He'd been staring at it with wide eyes ever since Ivy had dropped him off at the end of the drive. (She hadn't noticed. But then, neither had he, until he saw the giant red bow.)

Mattie put his hands on both sides of his head. Was it for him? No. It couldn't be. Guys like Mattie did not randomly get surprised with Audi A3s. They got ties from their overprotective fathers and kisses from their mothers, but definitely not *cars*.

Besides, his mother had just gotten him a brand-new bike, right before he'd come here. One he'd barely ridden.

One that was now gone. He'd looked everywhere. He'd combed the area behind the school. He'd even checked around his aunt's block, in case someone had taken it by accident and dropped it off nearby. But no.

Someone had stolen the bike. On the night of the accident, someone had taken the bike he had left there after they'd stashed Stratford.

"Do you like it?" His aunt stood in the driveway, her chubby arms crossed over her chest. She was grinning a wide, cheesy grin of pure happiness. It was making her glad to give him something.

"Is this . . . is this for . . ." Mattie trailed off.

"I already have enough cars." His aunt dug in her pocket and pulled out a key fob. It was black and smooth with silver buttons and a keychain attached that said *Mattie* in ornate lettering. "Take it."

He stared.

She laughed, and then she crossed the driveway and placed the key fob in Mattie's hand. He felt his fingers close around it.

It was warm from being in her pocket.

He couldn't stop looking at the car.

The gift would have made him uncomfortable on a normal day. Neither of his parents could afford more than a used Toyota, and now his aunt had unloaded a beautiful black car that his parents couldn't afford in a million years. And it was for him.

Of course, it wasn't a normal day. It was infinitely worse. Because on a normal day, he might have just said he couldn't accept such a valuable gift and felt guilty for declining.

But today? All he could think today is that he didn't deserve it. He'd helped cover up a murder. He was a criminal.

(And lost his bike.)

And so he got a fancy car. Sitting there in the driveway.

A physical manifestation of his guilt.

"I don't deserve something so nice," he said, voicing his thoughts. "I can't accept it."

His aunt stepped closer and squeezed his shoulders. "Look, Mattie. I've been watching how hard you've been working at this class, okay? You're killing yourself over it."

Or someone else. Mattie gritted his teeth. "Yeah," he managed finally.

"Plus, I noticed that your bike has disappeared. What happened, Mattie?"

This was so hard. This was all so hard. "I don't know. I forgot to chain it up at a convenience store the other night, and when I came back, it was gone."

It wasn't true.

It wasn't.

After class, when he'd gone to unchain the bike—he hadn't forgotten to lock it up after all—the chain was lying broken on the ground where his bike had been.

And he thought he was being messed with. Or punished. Or maybe someone had been watching them.

Maybe they'd stolen his bike while he and the others were busy loading Dr. Stratford into Kinley's trunk.

He'd been turning over the possibilities in his mind ever since. They'd sunk in, deep, and probed harder and harder until every thought hurt, deep in his brain.

His aunt put his hand over her heart. "Oh, you poor dear. Did you tell anyone?"

Mattie shook his head. "It was embarrassing."

"Should I call the police?" his aunt asked. She pulled her cell phone from her pocket. "The police chief adores me, you know. I donated a large amount of money at a fund-raiser last year."

"No!" It burst out of Mattie. "Please, I don't want the attention. Please."

She raised her hands. "Okay, okay. Then you're taking the car. I know you walked to class today. Your parents would never forgive me if something happened to you in my care."

Mattie looked down at the key in his hand.

It was too late for all of that.

"Take it out for a spin," his aunt urged, patting the hood like the car was a giant animal. "See what she can do."

Mattie nodded. At least it would get him away from her horrible, well-meaning questions. "Yeah."

He forced himself to hug her. And he found that once he was wrapped in her arms—someone really and truly grown-up, someone who loved him—he didn't want to let her go.

"Thank you," he whispered.

When she released him, her eyes were shiny with tears. "I know you appreciate it, Mattie. Now go have fun, okay?" She grinned at him and dabbed at her eyes.

Mattie climbed into the car. But before he had even started it, his phone vibrated.

Derrick had posted a photo.

He clicked on it.

It was Derrick, dancing with another guy. Derrick, in the shirt Mattie had given him for his birthday. Derrick, who was clearly forgetting all about Mattie.

#Danceitup #Lovemylife

Mattie put his phone into the cup holder and circled out of the driveway.

He waved at his aunt, and the gate at the edge of the property opened slowly in front of him.

Mattie turned out onto the road.

And he wondered what it would be like to never, ever come back.

Kinley

"The door is locked, right?"

Tyler was lying on the bed, right next to Kinley. One of his hands was playing with her hair, and the other was draped across her.

"It's locked," she promised. "Besides, my parents are at a fund-raiser. They have no idea you're here, okay?"

She'd made sure of that. She'd actually pretended to be a little sick earlier. Not that it was even necessary. It's not like Kinley ever had anywhere to go. Any friends. Though her father had looked at her a little oddly the few days since the Tyler incident.

"I think your dad might actually try to kill me if he sees me again. I used up one of my nine lives just trying to get away from him."

Kinley giggled and snuggled closer to him. "So you're a cat?"

Tyler meowed, and she laughed harder. She needed him. As long as he was here, she could be okay. She could go without thinking, without being. Everything would be fine.

Just fine.

And when she started thinking about *that*, thinking about Tyler was the only thing that could turn her mind off.

She knew this was all too fast. But she didn't want to stop. She didn't want to give it up.

"You're fun," he said into her ear. "I like you."

She turned on her side, so she was close to him. And her lips were close to his. "I like you too," she said. "And I don't say that to many people."

"Please. You love everyone. I bet you tell them, too. Your barista. Your mailman. The neighbors."

Kinley pretended to gag. "Please. I basically don't like anyone. You're a rare case."

Tyler raised an eyebrow. "Would you say I'm special?"

"Maybe?" Kinley said. "Would you say I am?"

"Maybe." Tyler studied her. "You're definitely pretty and smart, which is a lethal combination. And you're a very good kisser."

Kinley wanted to bury her face in her pillow, but she forced herself to look into his eyes. "I don't know. I think I could use more practice." Her eyes strayed to his lips.

"Oh?" he asked. "Need practice, do you?"

"It's very serious," Kinley said. She touched his mouth with her fingertips. "We have hard work to do."

"Are you trying to get me to kiss you?" Tyler asked. His eyes studied her face, and her mouth hinted at a smile.

Kinley squinted at him. "Is it working?"

He touched his lips to hers, slowly, softly. "How was that?"

She shrugged. "Try again."

He laughed this time, really laughed, so loud that if someone had been in the house they would have heard him. "Practice makes perfect, right?"

"I like practice."

He slid a hand behind her head, and he kissed her.

He kissed her right.

Even though she was lying on her bedspread, she felt the funny-knees feeling she'd read about in books, and her heart leaped in her chest.

She wanted to do everything with him. She wanted all of him. She wanted to get into a car with him and disappear. She wanted new names and new lives. She liked this Tyler Green.

But he drew away, and her body ached. She missed the way he felt against her, and suddenly all the bad flooded back in.

"We need to be slow," he whispered between kisses.

"Why?" she asked, her voice small and whiney. "Don't go."

"I won't." He pulled back and looked at her. "I'm here, okay?"

Kinley wondered if he needed her for all the same reasons that she needed him.

"Can I ask you something?" he asked. His hand moved down and cupped her hip.

She smiled, anticipating his next sweet gesture. She didn't understand why people tended to dislike or mistrust Tyler. He was so kind. "Sure."

"What's with the stuff on your desk? The flash drive and the wires? And the earpiece? Are you some sort of secret agent?"

He smiled, but she felt her insides curl in on themselves. "Um, why?"

He moved his shoulders up. "I don't know. I just thought it was sort of cool. It looks super high-tech."

"It's not cool." She jerked away from him. She'd spoken too quickly. Damn it. Why had she reacted like that?

"Hey." Tyler's voice was soft, but he didn't reach out for her. "What's wrong?"

Kinley didn't look at him. She couldn't look at him if she was going to tell him . . . this. She stared at the ceiling. At the little stars.

At the little lies that had built up, year after year, into an entire solar system of falsehoods.

Was she really going to tell him this?

She'd repeated the story in her head for years. But she'd never actually said it. Not out loud.

"Something happened to me," she said. "A few years ago." She paused.

"You don't have to tell me this, you know."

Kinley still didn't look at him. When she spoke, her voice shook. "Um, do you remember the May Day parade? Five years ago? Well . . . there was an incident."

"What?" he asked gently.

"I got to be on the float that year. You know the float at the front of the parade? Where the kids get to dance around the maypole? I was so excited. My dad told me I was old enough, and so I got to dance. My mother made me a crown of flowers—pink and white and yellow—and it itched like crazy when she pinned it into my hair, but it was so pretty I didn't care."

Tyler shifted onto his side and propped himself up on an elbow. "I remember the float," he said. "My dad used to take me to the parade."

"That year," Kinley whispered, "it was raining. Not much. Just on and off. They'd thought about canceling the parade, but I actually prayed that they wouldn't. I wanted my moment, you know?" A grim smile found its way to her lips.

"We all had harnesses on. But mine wasn't buckled right. There was a teacher there—Miss Heathers—but it wasn't her fault. I was wiggling and jumping around. She kept trying to check my buckles, but I didn't want her to. I hated the way the harness looked on my pink dress. I wiggled out of it when she wasn't looking.

"Then, about a third of the way through the parade, the float stopped short because a horse in front of us had reared up. And everyone was jolted. I fell off the float. I fell off and hit my head on the concrete. I don't remember much—I think it knocked me out. But when I woke up in the hospital, I couldn't hear right. Something happened. And"—she swallowed heavily—"I never could again. That stuff, that little earpiece, it's a kind of hearing system, okay?"

"And no one knows?" Tyler asked quietly.

Kinley shook her head. "No. I don't need it all the time. My hearing isn't completely horrible. But I didn't want anyone to know. I didn't want to be accommodated or treated differently."

"And that's why you work so hard."

Kinley chanced looking at him. He was still on his side, head resting on the heel of his hand, studying her. His face was unreadable.

"I guess so. And, you know, my family . . ."

"They put you under a lot of pressure. Yeah, I get that. Mine too."

Kinley frowned at him. "They do?"

Tyler lifted a shoulder. "There are different kinds of pressure, Kin."

Kinley felt her heart swell a little bit. He got it. He got her. He touched her chin with his thumb.

"I'm sorry I didn't tell you."

He studied her. "It's okay. I understand."

Her heart swelled. And she felt something a lot like relief that slowed her heart and made her feel, at least for a small second, happy.

She kissed him for believing her.

Tyler

Tyler lay in bed with Kinley. She smiled at him, her lips swollen from kissing. She was damn good at it. Especially for someone who'd done so little of it. Tyler was willing to bet all the cash he had that he was her first kiss. Girls like Kinley didn't kiss much.

Still, he couldn't help but think that maybe she'd suddenly been all about the making out because she was trying to distract him from something. Maybe he didn't have her grades, but he wasn't a total dumbass.

"Can I ask you a question?" he said finally. He studied her eyes. They were sweet and clear, but there was something in them. Something a little guarded. A little strange.

"Sure." She smiled, anticipating something sweet.

"Have you heard anything?" Tyler asked. He rolled away from her and out of bed. "Is there—anything? Yet?"

He felt like an asshole for asking. He didn't want to know. But he had to.

Kinley shook her head. "Honestly, no. But I haven't looked for it. I leave the room when the television is on. I haven't checked any social media since"—she paused, her hand motioning at something out of sight—"that night."

"So you think he hasn't been found." Tyler crossed the room and leaned up against her computer desk.

Kinley sighed. "Probably not. Sometimes cops hold stuff back to see if anyone will come forward."

"Why would anyone?" Tyler asked.

Kinley ducked her head, and very quickly, Tyler grabbed her hearing aid and flash drive off the desk and stuffed it in his back pocket.

"I don't want to think about this, Tyler." She looked up at him. "What good will it do?"

He rubbed the back of his neck. "I don't know. I just thought it might be better to have the facts."

Kinley's eyes turned hard. "If the cops come to question me, I don't want to know anything about what's happened. Anything at all. I want to be clueless."

Tyler squinted at her. "You? Didn't you place, like, first in a regional current events quiz bowl or something?"

Kinley shrugged. "So?"

"So maybe you should know these things. Maybe it's weird that you don't know at all what's happening in an area you'd be an expert on. Besides, if your professor randomly stopped coming to class, wouldn't you be curious?"

"I just don't want to know, okay?" Kinley said. "Tyler, I just can't think about it. I don't want to think about it."

Tyler shook his head. "Just try to process what I said, all right? We can't go quietly into the night on this."

"I'm not stupid."

"I didn't say you were," Tyler said. "I'm just saying it will look suspicious." He shifted, and felt the weight of the flash drive in his jeans. It was practically nothing, but it was hers, and he was stealing it. He had to.

"And you know this because, what, your many run-ins with the law?" Her voice was cutting.

"That's not fair." Her words hurt more than they should have— they burrowed in, just under his skin. It wasn't that he hadn't heard them before. Hell, he heard them all the time. But he'd hoped Kinley, of all people, had thought more of him than that.

"Isn't it?" she challenged.

She wasn't wrong. Damn, that stung. But she wasn't.

"I thought you were better than that, Kinley," he said, his voice quiet.

Kinley tilted her chin up, just slightly. "Are you saying I'm wrong?"

Tyler glared at her. Anger started, hot and burning. He had been so stupid to believe that Kinley could ever understand. Did she even like him? Or was he just some asshole she was using to get her mind off the murder?

After all, girls like Kinley didn't like delinquent guys. They were meant for douche-canoe guys who wore thick sweater-vests and had glasses pushed up too far on their noses.

"No. You're right. I guess you already know this, but I have regular meetings with a probation officer. So I know the law. I know how cops work, okay?"

Kinley stared at him, as if just remembering who he really was. "So maybe we should be acting more like ourselves."

"Which means I should be getting into trouble. Being risky. Right?"

"And I should be toeing the line. Which does not actually involve this." She motioned at Tyler and back at herself.

"So I'm a problem?"

"Are you?"

And suddenly, she was close to him, and he wanted to kiss her. He wanted to kiss her hard, and he wanted her to remember him and forget that she wasn't supposed to be with him.

But his anger was hot and painful, and there was something else there. Something beneath it.

He didn't trust her.

But he needed her. He needed someone who knew everything that had happened. He needed someone just to be there with him. In fact, he was pretty sure he'd never actually needed anyone or anything like he needed her.

He leaned in and kissed her. She melted underneath him and kissed him back, her arms encircling his neck as he pulled her against him.

"I need you," he whispered in her ear. It was the kindest, and the most honest, thing he'd ever said to a girl.

Kinley put her head on his chest. "I'm sorry, Tyler. I need you too."

For a second, his heart felt full.

But later, as he was walking out—walking, not being shoved—he pushed his feelings away. He reached into his back pocket and ran the flash drive between his fingers.

There was something wrong there.

Something very wrong.

His Kinley—his only friend in all of this—was full of shit.

Five years ago, *he* had been chosen for the May Day parade. Not Kinley.

And five years ago, there hadn't been a parade.

It had been canceled due to rain.

Maybe she just had her facts wrong. Maybe it happened the year after. Or the year before.

But Tyler didn't think so. His mother was on the parade committee, and he was pretty sure she would have mentioned a serious injury.

He wanted to believe Kinley. He told himself to believe her. But there was something wrong.

He couldn't stop thinking about it. Not on the walk to find the purple Jeep. Not when he arrived at home. Not until his brother confronted him in the front hallway, his voice hushed and urgent.

"Do you have it?" Jacob asked, standing close enough that Tyler could smell the wheatgrass smoothie on his breath.

Tyler stepped out of his shoes. His mother hated when people tracked things into the house. He reached into the waistband of his jeans and pulled out a small package wrapped in dark yellow paper and secured with careful strips of packing tape.

"Here." Tyler handed the packet to his brother. "Make it last, okay? I don't have access for a while."

His brother tucked it under his arm. "Thanks, man. Listen, you're resourceful. I'm sure you can handle it."

Tyler narrowed his eyes and followed his brother into the kitchen. "No, dude. I can't."

Jacob filled himself a glass of water and turned toward him, leaning against the sink. "You *will* find it, Tyler. If you don't, Mom and Dad might get suspicious."

Tyler stared at Jacob. "Is that a threat, big brother?"

"You'll figure it out." He laughed, like it was all some big freaking joke.

"You're not funny," Tyler told him.

Jacob dumped the water out in the sink. "I know."

Cade

Wednesday, June 17

"Doesn't look like you'll be having class tonight."

Cade looked up from his Wheaties. They were his father's favorite—he actually really believed that Breakfast of Champions stuff, and it was all they'd had at the house for years and years. Once, Cade had snuck Froot Loops in to share with his sister, and when his father found out, well . . . Cade may as well have been sneaking heroin.

"What do you mean?" Cade asked. His father was scrolling through his iPad, like he did every morning now. A couple years ago, he had declared paper passé and decided e-books and e-papers were the only things worth his time.

"Who was your teacher? Stratford?"

Cade's pulse sped up, until it seemed like little lightning bolts were speeding through his body. "Yeah?" he asked, forcing his voice to be level. Calm. He thought about what he'd normally say about Stratford. "He's such an asshole."

His father raised his eyebrows and cleared his throat. "Well, you might want to keep that opinion to yourself. It would appear he's missing. He was last seen"—he paused, scrolling through the paper—"last Friday. Probably after your class. It appears that he was headed through the parking lot, toward his home."

Cade forced himself to take another spoonful of Wheaties. They were dry and scratchy in his throat and a pain to swallow. *Wait. Hadn't Kip said he'd seen him after class? He must have gone to the police.*

"He didn't show at class on Monday," Cade said, chasing another soggy rectangle of wheat around his cereal bowl. "I told the office. We waited a little longer after that, but eventually the whole class just left."

"*You* told them?" His father pointed at him. "*You?*"

Cade suddenly was uncomfortable, like he was too big for his chair. "Uh, yeah. Just the receptionist. She didn't seem concerned. Stratford's a little . . . intense. I didn't want him blaming the class when no one was there."

Mr. Sano shook his head. "Just surprised you were the one to do the right thing. That's all."

Cade should have been used to it. He should have. It wasn't like his father didn't do this every time they were together. But still, the words burrowed their way through his skin and into his stomach, where they sat, weighty and sick.

Mr. Sano laid the iPad on the table and considered his son. He pointed at him with the spoon.

"Cade, if there's something going on, I need to know. You need to tell me." He paused. "Your sister talked to me, and I helped her, you know."

"Yeah, you helped her, all right."

Cade's father clenched his hand into a fist around the spoon and rested it very calmly on the table. "Would you have preferred she suffered the alternative?" he asked. His voice was quiet. Except for the death grip he had on his utensil, he was a picture of tranquility.

This was when he was at his most dangerous.

"No, sir."

"That's what I thought," Mr. Sano said. He dropped his spoon into the bowl, and milk slopped out onto the table. He didn't bother to clean it up. He never did. That was for maids.

Cade finished his cereal and began to stand up, but his father directed him back to his chair with a single look.

"What are you going to do with your day, now that studying is out?"

Cade knew the answer. "I'm going to see about a job. Maybe an office aide or something."

"Women's work," his father snorted. "Still, better than nothing. Want me to make a call?"

"No, Dad. I'd like to do this on my own, if that's okay with you."

His father nodded, and for a moment, he almost softened. "Give it your best."

Sweeping up his iPad, he left without another word. It wasn't until he was gone—far gone, into his car and backing out of the driveway—that Cade said what he had wanted to.

"I'm not my sister."

The only reply was the distant echo of one of the maids vacuuming down the hall.

But it didn't matter. His father would never believe that. Cade stood up and carried his bowl to the sink. He brushed his teeth and grabbed his keys. He was leaving.

But he wasn't going to look for a job.

He was going to get through this whole unpleasant situation and he wasn't going to ask his father for any help. What would his father really do for him, anyway? Get him a good lawyer? Have him turn himself in? Nothing that could really *fix* anything.

He climbed into his car and backed up out of the driveway. But he didn't go anywhere. He just drove. And drove. He drove by the school, and he drove nearly all the way to the farm before he turned around. And he stopped by the river to look at the waters, which were still higher than normal. He'd heard there had been storms up north, too. Flooding, even.

He hoped that meant Stratford's body was being carried farther away. He imagined it going all the way down to the ocean, where it would sink into the sea and be eaten by sharks or some other hungry ocean animal.

He sank down onto a half-rotted branch that had fallen from a tree during the storm.

He needed time to think. To plan. Because he had something in mind.

And it all had to do with the extra bike he had in the garage.

Ivy

It was Garrett. It was the guy she loved. It was who she needed.

Hey, Ivy girl! How are you?

She pretended that he had texted her first. She pretended that she had not sat in front of her phone for thirty minutes, deep in indecision, her heart radiating an incredible, thick pain, needing someone who understood everything, before she typed out a pathetic, incredibly needy three-letter text: Hey.

And he'd texted back. She'd been sitting on the couch, channel-surfing through cartoons (her guilty pleasure). Her mom, who was sitting in the corner, was paging through an old issue of *Martha Stewart Living*, and hadn't even complained.

Best of all, Garrett texted back in less than ten minutes. With her nickname.

It was almost like he still cared.

I am great, she texted. Taking the summer class. How are you?

She pretended to watch *Gravity Falls* until he texted back.

Awesome. Just left the pool. Are you recovered?

Ivy winced. Of course the last thing he remembered about her was her body splayed out beneath the vending machine like a half-squashed bug.

Still. It was better than him knowing—

She cut her own thought short. Wait. What was he doing at the pool? The Garrett she knew hated pools. He preferred video games, and for an occasional exercise session, he made a fool of himself at the skate park, pretending to be a punk.

All healed. Thanks for your help.

No prob, he texted back.

She hesitated, biting her lip. Would he see her? Did he want to see her? She took a deep breath and watched the minutes tick by, ever so slowly, until an appropriate amount of time had passed that she wouldn't seem overeager.

Maybe we could get coffee and catch up.

His reply was almost immediate.

Just let me know when.

And for the first time since everything happened, she smiled. Actually smiled, in a way that reached her eyes and down to her heart.

If Garrett came back to her, if everything just went back to the way it was, then maybe she could pretend that this horrible, sick little section of her summer was just a dream.

She put her phone on the coffee table in time for Daniel to come crashing through the front door into the entryway.

"Mom!" he said. "Hey, Mom!"

"She's in here," she called to her brother. It was weird—
even though he was almost thirty, she was definitely the more
mature one. Whenever he showed up at home, he just wanted
SpaghettiOs and his laundry done.

He walked into the living room, beaming. "Hey, Mom.
Hey, Ivs."

Ivy smiled at her brother. "What's up? You look like you
just got laid."

Daniel grabbed a pillow off the chair and threw it at her,
but he was still grinning. "Don't be nasty, sis."

"Ivy!" her mother said, appalled.

"Come on, Daniel," Ivy insisted, muting the TV, "what's
got you all excited?"

"First case." He made a fist-pumping motion with his arm.
"And it's a big one!"

Her mom jumped up from the chair, and *Martha Stewart
Living* landed on the floor, the pages splayed out. "Oh, honey!"
she said. "I'm so proud of you! Sit down and tell us all about it."
She pointed at the couch next to Ivy, and her brother thumped
down, rattling the whole living room. She never understood
how he got to be so tall—the rest of the family was in the upper
half of the five-foot range, but Daniel was almost six-six.

"Well, it's actually Ivy's professor," Daniel said. "Ivy, I'm
sure you heard, he disappeared last week. Just *poof*, and he was
gone. No one can find anything. It's like Keyser Söze shit." He
chuckled.

Ivy's heart stopped. Just stopped. Her blood was in her ears.

"Keyser who?" her mother asked.

The bottom fell out of Ivy's stomach. "So you don't know anything so far?"

He shook his head. "His wife's batshit and they got in a fight. He might've taken off for a few days, but his car never left the driveway. I guess the dude loves walking, so we're going to search the parks. See if something happened."

"The parks?" Ivy asked. Did the river run through the park? Oh God, she didn't know. What if his body washed up *in the park*?

Daniel turned to her. "Yeah, apparently the dude is into hiking. The fight was a blowout, so I wouldn't be surprised if we found the dude way up there, just waiting for his wife to cool off. Still, we're treating it like a real case, and the boss is letting me really take a big role here." He paused. "So, Ivs—any way I could question you?"

"What?" Ivy asked. "No!"

"Come on, please?" He put his hands together. "You'd be doing me a huge solid here. I could use the experience so when I question someone real I won't sound like an amateur. Besides, you know Stratford. You can tell me about him."

"Stratford's a jerk," Ivy said. "And no. I don't want to play cop with you, Daniel. You're old. Can't you handle your own job?"

"Ivy!" Mrs. McWhellen said. "Really! Don't you want to help your brother? He'd do the same for you."

Daniel gave her his dorky, too-sweet smile, the one he saved for when their mother was around, and she felt like she might throw up. But what was weirder—throwing up during fake questioning, or declining it altogether?

"Fine," Ivy said. "But not today. I'm super PMS-y."

Daniel shook his head. "I noticed. Call me. Mom, you can sit in too, if you want. It'll be fun."

"Sure, sweetie."

Their mother smiled, delighted.

Ivy felt her lunch writhe in her stomach.

"Great," she said. "Can't wait."

Daniel snorted. "Cheer up, sis. It's not like you killed him."

Mattie

Dr. Stratford was everywhere.

Everywhere Mattie looked.

His picture was on the news three times a night. His face was pasted on telephone poles. He was on the radio of his new car as he drove it around the neighborhood, trying to fill his mind with something else.

He was on at least three posts on Facebook so far, and two of those were from people who didn't even live here. They were from *home.*

That meant news of Stratford's disappearance had traveled. It wasn't just here anymore.

Mattie'd even posted it on his own page, thinking that if he didn't he'd looked callous and awful. (And he wasn't.)

(Only, he was.)

Just last night, his mother had called, worried about the effect that Stratford's disappearance was having on her son. And she didn't even protest when Mattie told her his aunt had purchased him a brand-spanking-new car. She seemed relieved that he wouldn't be riding his bike anymore.

He didn't tell her it was missing.

"Just be safe," she pleaded. "No one knows what happened to your professor!"

"Can I come home?" Mattie asked. "I don't want to be here anymore."

"But what about your class?"

"Who knows?" Mattie said. "The next few classes are canceled while they look for him. It'll probably just be canceled altogether if they can't find him. Or if they do, maybe he won't want to finish it."

"Don't sound so hopeful," his mother said, and laughed. The sound had made Mattie want to die.

Mattie felt that way a lot. The wrong word, the wrong sound, even, set him off. He felt that way right now, as he sat outside on his balcony, one leg dangling off the stone balcony.

If he fell, would he die when he hit the concrete below?

He looked across his aunt's property toward Ivy's house, crouched lower on the hill. He wanted to talk to her.

But he deserved to be alone.

His phone buzzed and for the first time since he'd moved, it was Derrick calling *him*. And not because Mattie had called him first, or because Mattie had texted him two thousand times.

He was just calling.

Mattie answered the phone and sat down on his window seat. The screen was warm against his ear. "Hello?"

"Hey, Mattie? Is that you?"

"Yeah," Mattie said. "Hey, Derrick."

The name sounded funny to him. Unused. *Felt* funny, in the way that although they hadn't broken up, maybe they didn't belong to each other anymore. But that didn't matter to Mattie. He was thrilled to be talking to Derrick. He had a pins-and-needles feeling all over his body and he wished, so badly, that his mother had let him come home.

"What's up?" Derrick asked.

"Not much. I missed you." Mattie stood up and opened the door to his balcony. The air was still and hot and thick, and the faintest breeze ruffled the leaves on the trees.

"Yeah. Anything else going on? I hear your neck of the woods is pretty weird right now. Like, creepy, *Texas Chainsaw Massacre* weird."

Mattie looked around the room, pretending not to know what he was talking about. "Yeah, it's crazy. And I'm living with my aunt. You should see her house. It's huge! And I got this new car. It has—"

"What about the murders?" Derrick interrupted, impatient. "I heard it's like murder central up there."

"Murders?" Mattie repeated.

"You know. Your *professor*."

Did he know? If he knew, why didn't he just say it?

"Um, he disappeared, I guess." Mattie hated talking about it. Hated. It. He was afraid he was going to agree with the wrong thing, or use a wrong tense, (like *was* instead of *is*) and give everything away.

Not that he didn't deserve it. He hadn't said anything. He was as much a part of the murder as Cade and Kinley.

"That's all you've got?" Derrick sounded disappointed, and Mattie knew he was pouting. Suddenly, he wanted to give him more.

"It was after class one night," Mattie offered. "A Friday. This guy in our class was the last to see him. Kip. He was walking across the lot."

That scared Mattie. He had lain awake every night since, wondering what Kip had really seen. If he knew anything. Or if he just wanted to be the one to talk to the cops.

"And then what?"

"Um. That's pretty much it. We all went to class on Monday, and he just didn't show up at all. We waited, and one of the guys told the office. We just went home." Mattie leaned his elbows on the railing. For a second, he wanted to pitch his phone into the pool, so he'd never have to talk to anyone again. But he clung to Derrick's voice in his ear.

Derrick sighed, like Mattie was boring him. "So. What do you think happened? What are people saying?"

"Well, apparently he likes to hike. They're combing some of the wildlife areas to see if he had an accident. Or they're thinking maybe he got sick somewhere." He wanted to give Derrick more. He wanted to talk to him. He just didn't want to talk to him about *this*.

"Do you know his wife?" Derrick pressed. "I heard she was crazy with a capital *C*."

"I met her once."

"Ooh, tell me everything."

Mattie's chest felt funny. "Can we . . . can we talk about something else? I'm . . . I don't know. I'm worried about it."

Derrick was quiet for a second. "Yeah. Sure. Can I choose, though?"

"Sure." Mattie was happy to spill his guts about anything but Stratford. He just wanted to get away from it. Pretend like everything was fine. For just a little bit. He felt his insides unclench, just slightly.

"How about you tell me where you were that night when you accidentally called me."

All the sickness came rushing back. It slammed into him with the force of a tidal wave, and Mattie clenched his teeth, trying to regain his composure. "I was with some people from class. We were going to study, but we snuck into a movie instead."

"Anyone special there?" Derrick's tone was a precisely designed sort of lightness.

"No."

"Did you do anything you're not telling me about?"

"No."

Derrick was quiet for a second. And then another. And still, another. And quite suddenly, Mattie couldn't stand the silence anymore.

"Who were those guys you were all over in your Facebook photos?"

Derrick didn't say anything.

But then he cackled. Mattie recognized the sound; he'd just never heard it applied to *him*. It was angry. It was the sound Derrick used when he was cutting someone down. Making them feel worthless. "You know what, Mattie? How about I tell the truth when you decide to."

And then he hung up.

Kinley

Kinley panted, her hands on her knees, in the middle of her room. Every drawer was hanging open. She'd pulled almost everything out of her closet. She'd looked under her bed. Checked every corner.

And still, it wasn't there.

It wasn't anywhere.

Her earpiece. And the flash drive. They were gone. They were gone and she couldn't find them anywhere.

And a girl like Kinley didn't lose things. She just didn't. She put her head in her hands and gathered up big handfuls of her hair.

Her father would kill her for losing it.

No. Even worse.

Losing it would kill her father.

Her whole life, she would never, ever be forgiven for doing this to him.

She knew what had happened. She knew exactly what and how.

Tyler. He hadn't believed her story. He was too smart. And he'd taken it. She dug out her phone from under a pile of sweaters she'd ripped from the bottom drawer and called him.

She counted the rings. He answered on the fourth.

"Hey, Kin."

Any other day, she would have smiled at the nickname. But not today. "I need you to come over right now," she said. "Please. I need you."

"Are you okay?" he asked. His voice was soft.

"No. Please, please come. My parents are gone again. Just come."

And within ten minutes, Tyler had pulled up in his car—even though Kinley knew he was grounded from it for the entire summer—and was vaulting through her window.

"Holy shit," he said. "Kin, did you get robbed?"

She shook her head. She tried to paw her hair back from her face, but gave up. She wanted to give in to sobbing, too, but she couldn't. She had to be strong. She had to get the flash drive back.

"What happened?"

She looked up at him through her hair. "I think you know, Tyler. You took it."

"Took what?" he asked, but he looked guilty.

She looked up at him. "Why, Tyler? Why did you have to take it? Couldn't you just have left it alone?"

He paused. She read the truth in his face.

"Couldn't you have been real about it? Or just told me you didn't want to talk about it?" Tyler asked. He cleared a spot next to Kinley and sat down. He put his hand on her shoulder. "Did you really have to make up an elaborate story? I thought we trusted each other, Kin."

His voice was small. Hurt.

She'd never heard him sound like that before.

"If I tell you the truth, will you give it back?" Kinley put both of her hands on either side of his face.

He lifted a shoulder, not meeting her eyes.

"Look, Tyler. No one—and I mean no one—can ever have that flash drive. They can never know that it exists. They can never *see* it. Okay?"

Tyler frowned. "Okay. But why?"

She released his face. "Because I'm not partially deaf, okay? I lied. I made the whole thing up." She ducked her head, and her cheeks burned. She was so stupid. Why had she ever lied to Tyler, the one person she felt close to in all of this? Why had she put this between them?

"I know," he said quietly.

"You did?"

He nudged her with his shoulder. "There wasn't a May Day parade five years ago. It really was canceled. I guess I should have told you that my mother's on the board. She would have mentioned if some adorable little girl sustained a grievous injury in her parade."

Kinley still didn't look up. "Do you hate me?"

"No," Tyler answered without hesitation. "But I wish I understood why you lied."

Kinley felt a tear start in her eye, but she blinked it away quickly. She could not cry. She couldn't. "Because I'm not as smart as everyone thinks I am."

It was the first time she'd ever said it out loud. The first time she'd admitted it, even to herself.

She just wasn't that smart. Not really. She wasn't the genius. She wasn't the prodigy.

She was just like everyone else.

Except worse.

Tyler's expression didn't change. He just watched her, waiting.

"I use them to study. They're a trick. It's a sophisticated recording-and-playback system. Sometimes, during class, I record the lectures to listen back to them. But honestly . . . I have the answers. And I listen to them during the tests." She paused and swallowed hard.

"You have the answers," Tyler repeated, very slowly. "How?"

Kinley pulled on her hair. "I used to volunteer in the office, you know. With standardized testing, teachers have to submit all sorts of crap to the front office and the state and stuff, so most of the teachers turn in copies of their big tests. I make copies of the Scantron forms and record the data onto the flash drive, which is, as you know, almost imperceptible. I just listen and fill in all the answers as I go."

Tyler shrank away from her, almost imperceptibly. She almost didn't notice.

She wanted to not care. But she did. There was some part of her that needed him.

"Say something," she pleaded. She reached out and put her hand on his arm, and he didn't pull away.

"You're cheating," he said, and his voice was a little dull around the edges. "You're not even . . . You're not making all those scores that you're known for."

"Yep," she said, and suddenly, she was bitter. "I'm a big old cheat. I'm too stupid to make the grades that my family expects for real, and so I have to be creative. So if you listen to what's on that flash drive, you'll just hear almost exactly what was on Stratford's test."

"Why not use notes like everyone else?" Tyler asked.

Kinley half smiled. "Teachers check notes. Remember Cade? If they ever happened to notice I was wearing an ear-piece . . . well, what teacher in their right mind would make a student remove a hearing aid? Talk about a lawsuit."

Tyler laughed, but Kinley couldn't tell if there was any humor in it at all. "I don't believe it."

"Don't believe what?" Kinley drew her knees up and rested her elbows on them.

"That you're not smart enough to get the grades on your own." He began to laugh again then, a little more. "You're kind of an evil genius, aren't you? God, this is so messed up. This is like a movie: the perfect girl with a dirty secret." He laughed harder, and she shoved him, and suddenly she was laughing too, even though her heart hurt and she wasn't sure if she found anything funny. It came from a strange place deep inside of her, where something was coming loose.

"Will you give it back?" Kinley managed finally, when her gut was aching from so much laughter. "Please?"

"Yeah," Tyler said. "I think I can do that."

And they sat together amid the mess for a while. When they moved, they didn't talk much, but Tyler helped her fold all of her clothes and straighten the trophies and rehang the ribbons that had fallen in the search. That night, they didn't kiss at all.

And Kinley wasn't sure she wanted to.

Tyler

Guilt was a funny thing.

Tyler sat on the couch in his living room. The TV was on—more for company than anything else, since neither of his parents were home—but he didn't even know what channel it was. The remote was on the coffee table, unused.

It was screwed up, Tyler thought, how the principal emotions were considered to be love and hate. Love and hate controlled everything. Except they didn't.

Guilt did.

Guilt, like they'd discussed the first day of class. Guilt, for what they'd done to Stratford. Guilt, for tossing his body in the river like so much shit.

For causing his wife so much worry.

And now, for stealing Kinley's earpiece. Beautiful, clever, cheating, lying Kinley.

He couldn't stop thinking about her. And he wanted to. He desperately wanted to.

He reached forward for the remote and began clicking through. Blindly. Watching a man demonstrate a blender. A woman on an obstacle course, climbing an impossible wall. An old man, dying, while a young man watched him.

Another news report about Stratford. It flashed to a picture of his family—Stratford, actually smiling, and not in the angry half way that he did in class. The bastard was really smiling, with his arm around his wife.

And his daughter, blond haired and gap-toothed, sat in front of them.

He had a daughter.

Tyler felt his heart collapse in on itself.

He'd helped cover up the murder of a man with a daughter. A wife. A family. He'd been more than the crotchety old man who despised his students. He'd had a life. He was a real person, not the mean-teacher caricature that Tyler had been erecting in his mind.

"Hey, Ty."

Tyler jumped. He hadn't realized anyone was home. Jacob held out his hands, palms up. "Whoa. Calm down, buddy."

"I'm fine," Tyler said. He tossed Jacob the remote. "I'm going to bed."

"Bed?" Jacob squinted at him. "Dude. It's seven thirty."

Tyler didn't look at his brother. He just walked past him, toward the stairs that led to his bedroom.

"I need more."

Jacob's voice was cold and clear and desperate. Tyler turned around, halfway up the stairs. "Sorry, bro. I told you to make that stuff last. My probation officer is putting the pressure on. I have to keep my nose clean."

It wasn't a complete lie.

Jacob jogged up a couple stairs to face his brother. "Please? I need it." His face was tight and pleading; his lower lip jutted out.

Tyler stared through him. "Find it from someone else. I'm not your guy anymore."

"Shit, Tyler. No one gets the shit you get. I can't risk it showing up in a drug test. I'm begging you, dude."

Tyler leaned back against the wall. "Don't you want to actually win on your own for once without steroids?"

"Just enough to get me through the summer," Jacob begged. "I have a scout coming to a summer meet next week to watch me. I need it for that, and then I'll stop."

"And then what? You get recruited and screw up your sophomore season because you quit?"

Jacob hunched his shoulders, and Tyler could see his anger growing. "I'll figure it out, okay? Just get me more. I need you to get me more."

And Tyler, who had always been in the shadow of his brother, had had enough. He couldn't be a part of this for one second longer. He couldn't be a part of one more shitty thing.

It couldn't happen.

"You're done, Lance Armstrong." Tyler punched his brother on the shoulder playfully. "Good luck in your next meet, though." He jogged the rest of the way up the stairs.

"I'll tell Mom and Dad," Jacob said.

Tyler froze. He turned back to stare at his older brother. "What are you going to tell them? That you're juicing?"

Jacob met his eyes. "I'm going to tell them that you made me. I'm going to tell them I didn't know about it at first. I'll tell them you got me addicted."

"That's stupid, Jacob."

"Who will they believe?" Jacob smiled nastily up at him. "Me or you? Don't you know all the cops on a first-name basis?"

Tyler studied his brother. Jacob was right. They'd believe his brother over his word any day of the week. They never believed him. If anyone ever, even once, believed Tyler, he would never have gone along with all the Stratford bullshit.

But he knew better.

"Get my shit, Tyler," Jacob said, his voice unusually high. "Figure it out." And Jacob ascended the stairs and pushed past his brother.

Tyler resisted the urge to punch him. He resisted the urge to lay him out, right then, and to scream at him. But who was he kidding? His roid-rage dick of a brother would kill him. He was bigger. Stronger.

Angrier.

He let him go.

He swallowed hard.

Kinley would have to wait on her flash drive. And he was going to have to take the car out again. He knew that his guy, Jer, was at home right now. And Jer probably had some.

And before he'd even made the decision, Tyler was in his car, behind the wheel, driving. He was leaving the relatively good part of town and he was going toward . . . if not the bad, then what his mother would call the *less fortunate*.

He drove slowly. And he hated himself with every mile his car crept forward. He should have told his brother no. Not just tonight, but the first time, when his brother had come to his room, crying, and begged him for help. Any kind of help. Anything.

Now his brother—his perfect, sweet brother, who charmed every old lady he'd ever met and had a secret Pokémon collection—was an addict. He was a mess and he was ruined and he was staking his entire swimming career on a drug that Tyler had gotten him started on because he'd just wanted to help. A drug that—maybe unfortunately—broke down really quickly in the blood. A drug that didn't show up in standard tests.

He wanted to run away now more than ever. But what would happen if he did?

He pulled up across the street outside of Jer's house and put the car in park. But he didn't shut it off. He rested both his hands on the steering wheel and put his head down. He didn't want to go inside. He didn't ever want to see Jer again, not even for a joint.

They'd been friends, at first. They'd smoked together. They'd tried new shit together. And then Jacob had gotten involved and it hadn't been fun anymore.

Tyler put his hand on the door handle. The shitty Jeep was in the driveway with the hood popped. Not surprising. The thing was always breaking down, but Jer refused to replace it.

In his pocket, his phone buzzed. He glanced down at it. A text from his mom. Either she was coming home soon, or she already was there, and she'd noticed his car missing. He wasn't exactly supposed to be driving.

He opened the door, just a crack, and that was when the car pulled up.

Tyler froze, his senses tingling. He very softly, very carefully shut the door. He did not look at the car directly.

"Damn it," he said under his breath.

It was a light blue car with an extended mirror and state license plates.

A cop.

Shit.

A *cop.*

The officer opened the door of his car, stepped out, and walked around to Tyler's door, where he paused. Tyler's heart went frantic. For a moment, he was sure he was going to die.

In the two seconds it took for the cop to reach his car, he saw it all laid out before him. Being thrown over the hood. Arrested for murder. Charged, while his parents and his brother watched from the back of the courtroom. Jailed for the rest of his life.

The cop pounded on Tyler's window with an open hand.

Tyler sucked in his breath. His fingers shakily pressed the down button, and the window rolled downward with a quiet hum.

"Can I help you, sir?" Tyler asked. He thanked God it wasn't a cop he knew, not anyone who'd arrested him or ticketed him before.

The cop eyed him. "What are you doing here with your car running?"

Tyler held up his cell phone. "My mother told me if she heard I was texting and driving one more time she'd take away my phone. So I pulled over."

"Can I see the phone, son?"

Tyler bristled inwardly. He hated when cops called him *son*. Like they actually cared.

He quickly unlocked the phone and showed the officer his mother's text message—which, thank God, said simply: Home soon. Lasagna ok?

"Is your mom's lasagna good?"

Tyler shrugged. "It depends on if she decides to put spinach in it, sir."

The cop guffawed, and Tyler smiled tentatively.

The officer patted the side of his car twice. "Get home. This isn't a good neighborhood."

"Yes, sir."

Tyler said "sir" like the police said "son," usually. He didn't mean it. But if a cop, for once in his life, was letting him go, he could "sir" all day.

"Have a good night," he told the officer.

Tyler watched the officer get back into his car. And then he drove back to his house, staying exactly at the speed limit the entire way.

He was done with Jer. And his brother could tell his parents. He didn't give a shit.

He was just done.

Cade

Dear Cade,

Everything is good here. I'm keeping busy, and I'm working at the restaurant now. Mom visits some. I think she worries, but she doesn't need to. I'm fine.

I hope you're having fun with school. I miss school sometimes!

It's hard being so far away from you. Don't let Dad get you down. I think he had a lot of do with how everything turned out.

Anyway. Write me back this time.

I love you, Cadey.

Jeni

Cade didn't cry very often, but his sister could make it happen. Sometimes it just took her name and he felt weird and fogged over.

He folded the letter up and set it on the patio table.

He missed her.

There was no use lying about that.

They'd been best friends. They'd hated each other, in the way that only siblings do, but at the end of the day they'd told each other everything.

Cade would never admit it, but when he was little, his father had taken away his night-light. Jeni had let him sleep in her room so he wouldn't be alone.

There were a lot of little things like that—like when Cade's father took the training wheels off Jeni's bike and told her to "figure it out," Cade, who had learned early and easily, had helped her.

And they'd sort of bonded over hating their father together.

Cade slipped the letter into his pocket carefully. He didn't hear from her often, and it was important when he did.

Maybe he'd write her back.

But maybe he wouldn't.

One thing was certain: he wasn't going to end up like her. Never. They might have been alike in every other way— something their father loathed—but he wasn't going to follow in her footsteps. He was going to be okay.

No matter what.

Cade tucked the letter into his pocket, grabbed his phone from the cushion on the patio couch, and dialed a number he'd pulled off of Facebook. This wasn't a call he could have while people were listening. While the phone rang, he let himself back into the house and jogged up the stairs, toward his room.

"Hello?"

It was Mattie's voice on the other end.

Mattie. The weak link. The opportunity.

"Hey, Mattie. It's Cade. I just wanted to chat with you, if you have a minute." Cade shut the door to his room and locked it. He tried the knob, just to be sure.

His father wasn't home. One of the maids was probably here, somewhere, but normally at this time they weren't upstairs. He flipped on some low music to drown out the conversation, just in case someone walked by.

"What's up?" Mattie asked. Cade could read the suspicion in his voice.

"I need to have a straight conversation with you, man."

"Okay."

Cade could hear the dread in Mattie's voice. He could hear the rising panic.

"That night . . . what did your friend hear?"

Mattie was quiet on the other end of the line. "Nothing . . . I don't think."

"How well do you know this guy?" Cade asked. "Is he someone who would keep the secret with us?"

"I don't know." Mattie's voice was quiet and tight. Seeping with bitterness.

Cade recognized the emotion. He knew it well.

"Well, you need to figure it out. I've been thinking, Mattie. I've been thinking a lot. Because if he figures it out, and he sees this stuff on the news, do you know what's going to happen?"

"Listen, I don't think he knows, but—"

"But you're not sure." Cade cut him off. "You're not sure, and he's going to go to the police. And the cops—*know* stuff, Mattie. They know how to trace the call. Trace your phone. Trace your exact location, and where you are at all times. Did you know that?"

Mattie stayed quiet.

"Have you talked to him since, Mattie?" Cade asked.

"Yeah."

"You need to find out what he heard. I'm calling because *you* need to be careful."

"What?" Mattie's voice raised. "What are you talking about?"

"The call was made on your phone, Mattie. He heard your voice more clearly than any of ours, if he heard ours at all. And do you know what that means?"

"I'm not stupid." Mattie's voice was cold.

"It means it's going to get traced back to you. You. Maybe us, but definitely, definitely you. Are you ready for that, Mattie?"

Mattie was silent again.

"Hello?" Cade asked. "Listen, I want to help—"

The line went dead.

Mattie didn't want to hear it. Cade understood. He didn't want to believe what Cade was saying. That Mattie could be blamed.

So he'd hung up.

Cade smiled and tossed his phone onto his bed.

It had gone perfectly.

He had watered the seed of doubt that was already there. And now it was taking root, deep and thick and irremovable.

Cade was not going to end up like his sister. Not ever.

Ivy

She was supposed to be in class. But she wasn't.

She was supposed to be surrounded by friends. But most days she spent alone, trying to think of new ways to occupy her time that didn't involve her friends or her minions.

And Garrett wasn't supposed to be at her house, sitting next to her on a couch in the loft, drinking the weird espresso that he always had, smelling the way he did, like spicy deodorant and just a hint of patchouli.

But he was.

He was finally, finally, with Ivy, and her heart was beating a Crazy Hummingbird-Wing Rhythm, and she had a tiny tic of her eyelid that wouldn't go away.

But he was *here*.

Ivy wasn't sure who was happier: her, or her mother, who fluttered around them, offering them homemade toffee-chocolate balls and even alcohol before Ivy had finally shooed her into the backyard.

Mrs. McWhellen clearly thought she was getting her daughter back. Her real daughter, not the sullen homebody who'd shown up this summer.

"I'm glad you suggested this," Ivy said. Garrett raised an eyebrow. "Coming to the house," she amended. "It's much more . . . personal than a coffee shop." She sipped on the latte she'd made with her mother's Keurig. It wasn't as good as Starbucks, but she didn't care.

"Well, I wanted it to be personal," Garrett said slowly. His left foot was tapping on the hardwood floor super fast—*tap, tap, tap, tap*. It was a nervous habit, and Ivy was dying to know what Garrett had to be nervous about.

"You did?" Ivy asked, her breath catching. "Why?"

He took another sip out of the tiny cup of espresso. "Because I think I owe you an apology."

"Do you?"

"Don't I?"

Ivy's hands felt sweaty, like they had the first time she and Garrett kissed.

"Why don't you try it, and I'll tell you how much I deserved it after?" Ivy asked sweetly.

Garrett laughed. He set his espresso on the side table and rubbed his hands over his jeans. "I'm sorry for what I did to you. I kind of ruined your life, didn't I?"

Ivy tilted her head. She wanted to say yes, to agree, but she wasn't sure. In some weird way she felt *better* now, like she wasn't expending all her energy on nastiness and hate.

Instead, she was plotting all her energy on getting away with being part of a murder pact. Which was arguably worse and more stressful.

But nothing had made Ivy reevaluate her entire life like giving CPR to a dead man.

And stuffing his body in a trunk.

And proceeding to throw said body in a river.

"I'm . . . okay," Ivy managed. "Really. I am."

It was a lie. But it needed to be.

Garrett took her hands in his. "It's not okay, though. What I did wasn't okay. You were the first girl who really took the time to look past my exterior and really like the real me, you know?"

Ivy nodded.

"I didn't do the same for you, Ivy girl. I thought you were gorgeous, and you are. I thought you were perfect, and you are. But I realized . . . I realized that I never once tried to look past your exterior like you did mine. You looked past Garrett the hipster dork, and you liked him. But all I could ever see of you was a pretty, popular girl who I could never identify with."

His words left tiny lacerations on her heart. Ivy stared at Garrett. She stared at his messy hair and his unshaven chin and the lips that had belonged to her. She stared at his band T-shirt and his un-ironic Converse sneakers.

"What are you saying?" she said finally. "Garrett, what are you trying to get across here?"

He took a deep breath, and squeezed her hands a little harder. "I'm going to try. I want to try. I want you to give me a chance to give you a chance."

Ivy leaped into his arms, hugging him. She hugged him so tight she thought she might disappear into him. She held him like she'd never held anyone before.

And Garrett held her back, his arms encircling her, and he turned to kiss the side of her face.

That's when she heard it. A rough, rumbling sound, like a chain saw drawn across concrete.

She knew that sound.

Ivy pulled out of her ex-boyfriend (current boyfriend's?) arms, and rushed to the window that looked out over the street, where the sound was coming from.

It was the rusted car from the school.

The one that had entered the lot as they left in Kinley's car.

The one that had stopped Ivy and Mattie outside the school.

"Who's the old lady?" Garrett asked from behind her. He put his chin on her shoulder and peered out.

It was Mrs. Stratford. Her window was down, and her elbow rested on the door.

And now she was sitting outside. Watching. She put a hand above her brow and peered up toward the window, like she knew Ivy was there.

"I don't know," Ivy lied.

Another car pulled up. An older black Explorer, boxy and too big to be good for the environment.

Daniel.

"Shit!" Ivy said.

"What?" Garrett asked. He grabbed her arm and leaned over her from behind. He felt too close, and Ivy wanted to shake him off.

Daniel got out of his truck and frowned at the car parked at the curb.

Did he recognize her? Ivy's mind whirled. He had to, didn't he? This was his case. Of course he would know who Mrs. Stratford was.

She watched as his head moved, as he followed Mrs. Stratford's line of vision to their house.

"Your brother will take care of it," Garrett said, squeezing Ivy's shoulder. "Good thing he's a cop."

Ivy shrugged out of his hands and watched while Daniel leaned over the car and addressed Mrs. Stratford. She opened the window, just a crack, but their voices were far away and muffled.

"Ivy—"

"Give me a minute, Garrett, okay?" she said. She felt, rather than saw, Garrett step back. But it didn't matter. Daniel was already waving as Mrs. Stratford drove away. *Shit. Shit, shit, shit.* Ivy put her hands on her forehead. What the hell was she even doing here?

She turned her back to the window.

"Do you even want me here?" Garrett's voice was small and hurt.

Ivy put her hands on the back of his neck and pulled his mouth to her lips. She kissed him hard and deep and with all the passion she could muster. She drew all of the pain and hurt she'd experienced since they'd broken up, and all the love she had for him, and every emotion she thought she'd forfeited since she lost him, and she kissed him, and he kissed her and his hands were on the small of her back and in her hair and everywhere.

"I love you," Garrett whispered in her ear. "Let's try again. Please."

Ivy clung to him, feeling his body against hers and trying to remember the way it used to warm her.

But even Garrett, who she thought she had wanted more than anything in the world, could not push all of the horror out of her mind. It could not remove the rusted car. The way Dr. Stratford looked in the trunk. His half-open eye that watched them as they moved his body.

Garrett was a complication.

An unnecessary one, no matter how much she had loved him.

She buried her face in his shoulder. It took all of her strength to stay there, for just another minute.

But she pulled away. And she felt like she was peeling off

her mask, the one distant shadow of her Former Self that she had been clinging to.

She touched his shoulders, her fingers barely brushing his shirt. "I think I need more time, Gar," she said. "I'm so sorry."

When she saw the hurt in his eyes, she added it to her Chest of Horrible Memories. The ones that weighed on her, that made her feel like she was dragging the whole world behind her with every step she took.

Horrible memories, she had learned, always outlast the good ones.

Mattie

"Iced soy chai, please. Extra large."

Ivy stared at him. "Um, you already told her that."

Mattie jerked out of his reverie. The barista (a pretty girl with a big hoop in the middle of her nose) stared at him, her hand out.

"Oh, yeah." Mattie dug in his pocket and produced a couple of bills before handing them over. She tossed them in the cash register and gave them a little card that featured a dog named Murdoch. "We advertise for the local shelter," she told them. "Our cards save over two hundred dogs a year."

Mattie took the photo of Murdoch and followed Ivy to a table near the back of the little shop. Ivy had just sort of shown up again while he was vegging on the patio, thinking all sorts of grisly things, and told him to follow her. So he had, and they'd ended up in this odd coffee shop with oscillating fans running everywhere and music that was just a little too fast for relaxation.

It was better, Mattie guessed, than sitting in his bedroom, watching the ceiling fan turn. Or sitting on the back porch, listening to the reluctant lapping of the pool whenever the breeze kicked in.

It was better than all the waiting.

He couldn't turn his brain off. He couldn't stop thinking about Stratford and the police and Kip thinking he had seen Stratford and the little line of black-red blood under Stratford's nose and how his dead skin had been slick in the rain.

Ivy and Mattie sat there for a moment, looking at each other. Gone was the easy back-and-forth from when they'd first met. They both knew what was between them, impenetrable and dark, like toxic smoke—too thick to breathe through.

She was beautiful, Mattie thought. The kind of girl he might go for if he were single and good enough for her. But he wasn't.

"Have you heard from your boyfriend at all?" Ivy's voice, a little strange, jerked him out of his thoughts.

They both knew what she was asking.

"Um, a little. I guess . . . nothing seems new. But I'm not sure."

Mattie watched Ivy's face, and for a second it looked like she was going to say something—something real—but the barista brought over their drinks, Mattie's iced soy chai, and a green tea frappe with extra whipped cream for Ivy.

Mattie frowned. Ivy was not the kind of girl who asked for added whipped cream. She was the kind of girl who asked for foam, just foam, and then scooped it out with a plastic spoon while watching happy full-figured girls gulp down chocolate-chip lattes. (It was how Nicole Kidman did it, he'd heard.)

"So let's talk about you and Derrick," Ivy said. "Tell me about your relationship."

(Translation: tell me if we can trust him.)

"He's the best," Mattie said. "We spent, like, every minute together. We told each other everything."

"Past tense?" Ivy asked. "So things haven't gotten better?"

Mattie shook his head. "Worse." He swallowed hard and looked across the table at Ivy. She was so beautiful and miserable. He knew what she was asking. She wanted to know if Derrick knew anything *dangerous*. "Can I just say it?"

Ivy nodded. Her lips clasped onto the straw and she took a long drink of her frappe. "Just give it to me straight." She looked left and right. There were people everywhere. "Are orange jumpsuits going to be a good look this season?"

Mattie laughed even though there was nothing funny at the heart of it. "I don't know, Ivy. I wish I did, but Derrick and I haven't been good since I moved here. Since maybe a little before I moved here. And we haven't broken up, but"— he paused, finally voicing a deep, silent fear—"I don't know if we're still together."

Ivy reached across and clasped his hands in hers. His hands shook slightly, and she squeezed them hard, trying to still them, but he realized that she was shaking too.

"Look, Mattie. I'm sorry if this is insensitive, but I have to know. Do you think he heard anything, or not?"

Mattie paused. "I think he did, Ivy. I just think he doesn't know what that was right now. I don't think he's going to say anything. At least not immediately. Because I know what we had—have, whatever—was real, and we both still value that. He just doesn't completely trust me right now, and I don't want him to realize . . . I can't let him figure out exactly what he heard." He dropped his voice, his eyes searching the people around him. No one was listening. "It's like he wants me to confess. He knows something is off."

"But he doesn't know exactly what?"

Mattie shook his head. "I mean, I don't think so. Really, if he knew, wouldn't he have said something? Wouldn't you have, if you were Derrick?"

Ivy's hands tightened around her frappe. "I don't know."

Mattie looked down at his own drink. He had barely touched it.

"You know," he said, his heart strange and thumpy and calm all at once, "I don't know why we're involved."

"What?" Ivy asked. Her eyes were jumping around frantically, taking stock of her surroundings.

Mattie leaned in, looked into her eyes, and said in a low voice, too quiet for anyone else to hear, "Why are we even here? What did we do to deserve this?"

He'd been thinking about it since Cade called him. He'd

been pulled in. He hadn't been the one to punch Stratford. Or trip him. Or the one to beg everyone not to tell. He hadn't done anything. And Ivy had just wanted to save him. But according to Cade, Mattie looked the guiltiest of all. His phone was basically evidence. Well, not technically, but Cade was right—the call was made from the river on that night to Derrick, and chances are, Derrick had heard Mattie more clearly than he'd heard anyone else. It made him look guilty.

Ivy shook her head. Her eyes got glassy, and she let her bangs fall into them. "Maybe it's punishment, Mattie. I didn't used to be . . ." She trailed off for a second, like she was watching the past unfold. "I'm not a good person."

Mattie's phone buzzed with a message from Derrick.

He unlocked it, and the message took all the air out of him, like he'd been socked in the stomach.

I think I deserve an explanation. Fess up, Byrne.

He handed his phone to Ivy and covered his eyes, trying to slow his pulse.

Maybe Derrick didn't know exactly what happened. But one thing was certain: he knew Mattie had done something wrong.

Maybe Cade was right.

Derrick wanted a confession. Maybe he knew what he'd heard that night.

If someone was going down for this, it was going to be Mattie.

Kinley

No.

NO. No, no, no, no, no.

Kinley's mind repeated the word, over and over and over, an endless cycle of pain and denial. It ran through her blood and stuck in the lining over her stomach and worked its way into her throat.

Kinley bent over the toilet and vomited. Her mother held her hair back and knotted it with a hair tie. "Baby," Mrs. Phillips whispered, rubbing her back. "Oh, sweetheart. Should we take you to the doctor?"

The idea of setting foot outside the house put her stomach in motion again and she heaved into the bowl, the vomit burning her throat and her mouth.

Her mother disappeared for a moment and returned with a box of Kleenex and a glass of water. "Here, sweetie. Wash out your mouth." She helped Kinley take a drink, like she had when she was a little girl, and after Kinley had spit the water into the toilet she dabbed her mouth with a pink tissue.

Kinley's mom flushed the toilet, sending her sickness into the plumbing. Kinley wished all her pain and guilt would go with it.

"Did you eat something funny?" Mrs. Phillips asked. Her dark brown eyes, almost black, were filled with concern, which Kinley rarely saw in her mother. Mrs. Phillips was a perfect politician's wife. Everyone called her the second coming of Michelle Obama—with better dresses. Which was hard to do.

It also made her hard to be around. She was determined. She was intelligent and poised. And she had no idea that her daughter wasn't equally intelligent. In other words, she didn't know about Kinley's little secret.

"I haven't eaten much lately," Kinley murmured. Her voice was scratchy from getting sick.

Mrs. Phillips put a hand to her daughter's forehead. "You might be running a fever, sweetie. Are you worried about your professor? Is that making you sick?"

Kinley's eyes filled with tears. Her mother had hit the nail on the head. She had no idea.

Just like Tyler had no idea.

Kinley had thought he'd just lifted one of her study recordings—probably the psychology one, or maybe even the Russian literature one she had been reviewing for a college course she had taken last summer—but no. He had taken one she thought she'd hidden away in her desk.

One that no one should hear unless the circumstances were incredibly, incredibly dire.

One flash drive that could ruin everyone and everything.

Kinley had tried to call him. But since she'd seen him last—since she had confessed—he had all but disappeared, save for a few one-word texts here and there.

He had disappeared with her deepest and darkest. And who knew what Tyler the Delinquent would do with it?

And to think she'd trusted him.

She started to cry, harder now. The kind of crying that made faces swollen and red.

And right there on the floor of the bathroom, Kinley's mother gathered her up in her arms and held her, just like when she was little.

Kinley, who preferred proud and cold and perfect to weak and shallow and useless, let her mother hold her. She closed her eyes and was dozing off, when there was a knock at the bathroom door. It opened, just a crack.

Her father stuck his head in. "Kin, are you okay?"

She lifted her head. Her skull pounded.

"Great, Dad."

"Okay, good. Do you think I can talk to you?" He cast a look at her mother. "Eleanor, she's fine."

Fitting that her mother was named for a great president's wife.

Her mother helped her slowly to her feet, and Kinley

smiled weakly at her. "Take it easy," her mother warned, and Kinley collected the words and stored them as close to her heart as she could.

It wasn't something her mother said often. In fact, Kinley couldn't remember the last time she'd said something so soft and kind. She wanted to fall back into her mother's arms and be a child again. But there was no room for that.

Her mother followed her into her bedroom with her father in tow. Mrs. Phillips tucked her tightly into her bed and left a fresh glass of water and a box of tissues on her nightstand, then moved the trash can close to the side of the bed before leaving.

"Are you really sick?" her father asked once they were alone. "Should I get a doctor?"

"I'll be fine," Kinley said, coughing. Her throat was raw, like she had swallowed a handful of nails. Part of her was angry at her father for the question, for dismissing her obvious pain, but the rest of her was grateful. Deeply grateful. She wanted to be normal again.

Her father sat stiffly at the foot of her bed. "Kinley, my dear girl, do you realize you have missed three SAT study sessions? Just because you've taken a break from your psych course doesn't mean you can take a break from your life." He paused and drew a package from his jeans. "Here. A little gift. Enjoy." Mr. Phillips patted her on the head and rose from the bed. He paused at the door, for just a moment. "By the way, they're getting a friend of mine from the college to finish the professor's course. It will resume next week. Remember to prepare."

And then he was gone, without any well wishes. He was just gone.

He just wanted his perfect daughter back.

So do I, Kinley thought bitterly. She tore open the little package and dumped the contents onto her bedcover.

It was a tiny, tiny earpiece. The smallest she'd ever seen. State-of-the-art, really.

And another flash drive.

As if anything could replace the information on the one she had lost to Tyler.

Tyler

Jacob slammed his hand into the wall. "What do you mean?" He breathed heavily, his face turning a mottled red.

"Calm down," Tyler whispered. He grabbed his brother and pulled him out of the kitchen and into the backyard, away from their parents, who were watching old reruns of *America's Next Top Model* in the den.

"What do you mean you can't get it?" Jacob was standing close, and obvious panic was lurking just beneath his skin.

"I tried, dude," Tyler said. "There was a cop staked out." He lowered his voice, glancing toward the neighbors' house to make sure no one was outside. "He freaking walked up to my car and asked me what I was doing there. I barely got out."

Jacob paced back and forth in the backyard, trampling a pair of their mother's prized yellow tulips. "Shit. *Shit*, Tyler. What are we going to do? I have the St. Andrews meet coming up." He clasped his hands together and blew into them, like it was cold instead of midsummer.

"There's nothing to do," Tyler said gently. "Jacob, we're done. We can't get it, okay? You need to stop."

Jacob sat down on the grass and started rocking, and before Tyler realized what was happening, his older brother was crying quietly on the lawn, picking up little threads of grass.

Tyler squatted down. "It's okay, Jake."

Jacob glared at him through his tears. "It's not okay. I can't swim without them."

"You're not going to tell Mom and Dad, right?"

Jacob looked up at his older brother, and for a second, Tyler was reminded of when Jacob really *was* his brother. When they'd ride through the neighborhood together on matching bikes until their mother called them in for supper. When they played Crazy Eights on Jacob's bed until Tyler was tired enough to fall asleep. When they would sleep on the floor of the den and watch scary movies after their parents had gone to bed.

How had everything gotten so screwed up?

Jacob wiped his nose on the sleeve of his T-shirt. "You have to figure out a way, Tyler. I won't tell Mom and Dad, though."

Tyler nodded. "Thanks, bro." He reached out and clasped his brother's shoulder.

"I'll tell your probation officer."

Tyler's whole body felt like he'd just been covered in hot, wet cement. He let his hand fall.

Jacob would tell . . . Jacob would do . . . *what*? He'd send his own brother to juvie? Into the military? For a drug? Because he was pissed off?

Tyler felt sick.

"You'd do that?"

Jacob returned his gaze steadily. "Well, you'd ruin my life like that. My whole career. My chance to transition out of community and into a Division One school. So yeah. I guess I would."

Tyler's blood went hot-cold and then hot again. "You know, they drug test a little more hardcore in D-One."

Jacob jumped up. "What are you saying?" He lurched closer, his breath warm on Tyler's face.

"I'm saying that it's a lot harder to be an addict when everyone's watching. No one cares when you're the big fish at a stupid community college. But when you're competing at a high level? It's just a matter of time."

Jacob smiled. "Then you better get me the good stuff, little brother. Because when I go down, you're going to go down right along with me."

"Why wait?" Tyler asked, raising his voice. He felt strange and reckless. "Let's just do this now. Let's tell everybody." He laughed, and it hurt in his stomach. "My dickhead brother's a cheat, everyone! And I help him do it!"

"Shut up," Jacob said.

"What? Why?"

"Shut up or I'll kill you."

Tyler stopped. He stared at his brother. Into his eyes, which were cold and hard and unfamiliar.

A lot of killing going around these days. Some deep, sick part of Tyler wanted to laugh again, but he couldn't.

"You're going to do this for me, Tyler," Jacob said. "You're going to call your little friends and you're going to figure this out. Don't test me again."

"Fine."

The word hurt to say.

Because he couldn't. He wouldn't.

Jer was being staked out by the cops, the number-one people he wanted to avoid on account of being involved with Stratford.

But if he didn't return, and his brother actually told, then he'd end up in the exact same position.

Unless he could get the drugs, he was screwed. He was done. But Jacob wasn't his brother right now. He was someone else.

But Tyler knew what to do.

He left Jacob in the backyard and went up to his room, where he locked the door.

His mother had gotten him a bookshelf back when she was trying to influence his tastes. It was filled, mostly, with a set of encyclopedias she'd insisted on buying, even though Tyler's father had sworn up and down that nobody ever used encyclopedias anymore.

No one knew, but Tyler did use those encyclopedias. Some nights, when he couldn't sleep—which was most of them—he'd choose one and look up faraway things until his eyes got tired.

Tyler reached under the top of the shelf, just above the D and E tomes, and unpeeled a tiny Ziploc bag.

Inside, there was an earpiece and a flash drive. It was what Kinley used to record her answers. He'd erase her psych notes, and then use it to record his brother, threatening him. He was going to get to his probation officer first.

He doubled-checked the door, then plugged the flash drive into the computer. His media player popped up, and Kinley's voice began in his speakers.

Her voice was rich and deep and full. Just like her. He hadn't talked to her much in the past couple of days, and suddenly he was filled with a strong yearning. She was so damn gorgeous.

He wanted to see her.

He wanted to kiss her.

He wanted to see her naked. To touch the soft velvet that was her skin.

Tyler wished he'd answered her calls. Her texts. He hadn't wanted her involved in the shit with his brother. He hadn't wanted anyone involved.

And he hadn't wanted anyone to know. His brother was supposed to be perfect. Tyler had wanted to keep him that way.

He'd wanted to give his parents one child they could really believe in.

Kinley's voice went on in his ear about psychosexual stages and Freud and pain, and it reached some strange, latent part of him. He lay back on his bed and shut his eyes, and he wished that she was there with him. Beside him. In his arms.

And then she stopped, midsentence. There was scuffling. Mumbling.

He sat, bolt upright, his body cold.

He could hear rain.

There was *rain* on the speaker. Like rain falling against a building.

He knew that rain.

It went on for a minute, maybe two, before fading into the silence. Thick, heavy silence, the kind broken only by uncomfortable shifts and pain.

And then—

"Are you cold?"

It was Tyler's voice.

"I know I shouldn't be, but I am. I hate that he's in there." Kinley.

And then Tyler, again. "I know." There was some shuffling of straw. "We're okay, though. And we're going to be okay, you know. They'll be back."

Tyler listened. He listened as the whole horrific scene was

played out again. Some parts he couldn't hear, but he could hear enough.

More than anyone really needed.

And yet . . . Kinley had been quiet that night. She didn't come off innocent, exactly, but good enough that if she ever decided to turn in the tape, she didn't look as bad as the rest of them.

A cold rivulet of sweat ran down Tyler's face.

The whole time they had been worried about a fuzzy phone call that had been made from Mattie's pocket.

And the thing that could doom them all had been sitting on Kinley's desk like so much homework.

He ripped the earpiece out. He had to get rid of this. He had to ruin it before anyone else could hear it. It couldn't go back on his bookshelf, where it had been, hiding next to a bag of good weed and a stolen cell phone.

He unlocked his door and walked, very quietly and calmly, down the stairs. His parents were still in the den, and Jacob wasn't anywhere to be seen.

He would call Kinley, and he would talk to her, and, somehow, he would find out if she had made any copies.

Tyler rested his hands on both sides of the sink and tried to keep his head from spinning. He clenched his teeth until his jaw hurt and the dizziness subsided.

Then he dropped the flash drive in the drain, and flipped the garbage disposal on.

Cade

Cade always thought that a shrink's waiting room should be interesting, but he'd been coming here for years and nothing ever happened.

The towering green houseplant in the corner always smelled like stale water and rotting roots. The receptionist popped bubble gum and made long, drawn-out calls to her boyfriend, Harry, usually about his mother interfering in their relationship ("Your mother shouldn't still be dressing you, Harry. Those sweaters aren't meant for men in their thirties."). And the other patients weren't any of the freaks Cade always hoped to see.

In fact, they always seemed pretty normal. So normal that since Cade had been little he'd made up stories about them that he'd whisper back and forth with Jeni. There was Annabella Axeworth, a beautiful teenager who had killed her parents with nothing but a pair of chopsticks. There was Nigel Knickerpants, who suffered from a fear of mosquito wings.

And then there was their favorite, Gerbil Hamburger, who had recently developed superpowers and was just having a lot of issues dealing with the responsibility of it all.

Cade's sister had been great.

Had been.

Without her, the place was pointless. But he was here because of his father, the esteemed Mr. Sano, who kept peering at Cade over his iPad and measuring his mental wellness with just his eyes. According to Mr. Sano, Cade was failing. Cade seemed "unbalanced" and was "hiding something," and needed professional help of some sort.

His father wanted him tested. He wanted to make sure that both of his children didn't suffer from the same horrible affliction.

The idea scared Cade.

Sometimes, it was like his father could see through him. Or see into him.

So, now, Cade was back with his shrink, Virgil Ainsworth. He loved Virgil's name. It was almost as ridiculous as the ones he'd made up with his sister. They were great names, but, Cade reflected as he glanced around the room, they were probably for boring people who were only seeing a psychologist to whine about how they made too much money in their otherwise empty, successful lives.

"Cade Sano?" A guy who barely looked older than Cade had appeared in the doorway that led to Dr. Ainsworth's office.

His name tag said TED. "The doctor is ready for you."

Cade pushed himself out of the chair and followed Ted. He hated this. He really, really hated this. He'd thought he was done with stupid, probing questions.

Apparently he wasn't.

Dr. Ainsworth smiled when she saw him. It was her doctor smile—practiced and smooth and completely inoffensive, just like her sensible pants and her too-loose blouse. Her hair was drawn back into an efficient bun, and not a single strand of hair was out of place.

"Cade Sano!" she said, a small note of professional pleasure in her voice. "Come in. Sit down. It's been too long."

Cade tried not to frown. Was that something that your shrink was supposed to say? If a patient wasn't there, maybe it was because he was actually doing *well* for once.

But then he had to mess up and accidentally kill someone. And his stupid, all-knowing father just had a gut feeling something was off. And now . . .

"Hi," Cade said. "You got new chairs."

They were brown and poufy, unlike the old black leather chairs that had graced her office. Cade had picked at the peeling bits of the black ones when he hadn't wanted to answer questions.

The chairs were the only pieces of her office that had changed. Her Harvard degrees still hung on her wall. Her collection of small glass kittens decorated her bookshelves—

although maybe she had few more, now. And the same ceiling fan still spun lazily overhead.

"Do you like them?" Dr. Ainsworth asked.

He sank into one. It was nice, actually. "Sure."

"So, Cade. Since it's been so long, why don't we start by you telling me what you've been up to lately. Tell me about your family."

"No." Cade's reaction was immediate . . . and a little too loud. He softened his voice. "I don't talk about my family anymore." He wasn't going to let her run this show. He wasn't a child. And no matter how many degrees she had on her wall, he was smarter than she was.

He was in charge.

Dr. Ainsworth considered him. She had to know what had happened. Everyone knew. "Maybe just your father, then. I think it would be good for you to talk about him. How is it, now? With just the two of you?"

"You know my dad." Cade lifted both his hands. "He's a dick. Not much has changed in the past few years. Maybe *he* needs therapy." He smiled, just a little. Let her believe he was engaging.

Dr. Ainsworth laughed, a "ha-ha" that was a little less therapist and a touch more human. Rare, for her.

"From what you've said, I could recommend a few sessions for him. But Cade, you're the one who's here. Not your father."

"I know that."

Cade remembered why he hated therapy so much. What was just talking ever going to change?

Dr. Ainsworth took a leather folio from her desk and opened it. Her eyes searched the page, but her face was smooth and expressionless. It betrayed nothing. She was good. But he was better.

"I understand you're taking a class this summer?"

"Psychology." Cade smiled again, ignoring the way his heartbeat quickened. "Ironic, right?"

"Important." The doctor looked at him for a moment, her eyes big. "How is your class going?"

"Why is that *important*?" Cade started to cross his arms over his chest, but stopped. Dr. Ainsworth would say it was a defensive gesture, and he couldn't act defensive right now. He was in control. Not her.

Dr. Ainsworth paused. "It seems like a significant part of your life, Cade."

"School isn't as big of a deal as everyone says." Cade looked away from Dr. Ainsworth, but then focused back on her. He didn't want to seem shady. And he couldn't avoid questions about this. He shouldn't.

"Some people can be a little overly obsessive about school and grades," she admitted. "But indulge me. How's the professor? Are you getting along?"

Of course she'd remember that Cade didn't have the best record with his former schools. And maybe there'd been an incident where he'd spat at someone. Or an incident where he'd followed his teacher home and recorded her dancing to the *Frozen* sound track in tube socks and a corset.

So this question was natural. Normal.

He flinched inwardly, but forced himself to speak. "He's missing."

Dr. Ainsworth leaned forward. "Missing?"

Cade lifted a shoulder. "One day, he just didn't show up for class. Now, we have Dr. Angelo, who is this super-old lady. She doesn't make us do anything, and she didn't even grade the tests we took." Cade forced a smile, and it felt funny on his mouth and stretched his cheeks. "So much for learning."

Dr. Ainsworth tapped her pen against her lips. "Tell me your thoughts on why he disappeared."

Cade didn't hesitate. "Wherever he went, he was in a hurry."

"Interesting. And why do you say that?" The shrink leaned forward in her chair.

She was so calculated in her movements. Her actions. Unlike Cade, she knew what everything meant.

He wished he could see into her head.

"Because he didn't take our tests with him. Kip Landers says he thought he saw him walking across the back parking lot."

"Did you see him?"

Cade frowned. Why was she asking so many questions? Was she cross-examining him?

"No."

"Do you . . . *care* for the professor, Cade?"

"Hell no."

Dr. Ainsworth seems startled. She pushed at her glasses. "Would you care to expand on that?"

Cade laughed. "The guy is a total douche bag. I've never seen anyone crueler, or take more delight in failure. And that includes my father."

"Really?" The doctor scribbled something else in her folio. "Does he have many enemies?"

"Do you want me to name them?"

"Please try."

"Let's start with everyone who ever met the guy, period. He was a straight-up horrible person. If someone out there actually liked Stratford, they'd have to be a masochist." Cade leaned back in his chair. He could talk about Stratford all day. That was the trick: stay as close to the truth as possible. That way, you had fewer lies to remember. "If one single person legitimately enjoyed his company—well, they could use some quality time in your new chair." He patted the arm.

"So he is someone who does not enjoy his job as a teacher? Interesting." Dr. Ainsworth paused, and she took off her glasses and carefully set them on her hulking wooden desk. "What do you think happened to Dr. Stratford, Cade?"

Cade hesitated.

He'd never expected to be asked this. He wanted to seem honest. He *needed* to seem honest.

"I don't know. Maybe he just left. Just peaced out. He was weird. I mean, he *hated* everyone. But then, everyone hated him, too."

"So you think something bad happened."

"I just told you, I don't know." Cade gritted his teeth. He couldn't let what his therapist called his "anger issues" show. He'd worked on those. He was supposed to be better.

Dr. Ainsworth stood and circled around her desk. She sat down next to him, and did something he had never seen her do before.

She reached out and put her hand on his arm.

"Cade," she said, her voice quiet and low, "I need you to listen, and I need you to be very, very honest with me. Okay?"

"Okay." Cade drew out the word. "What is it?"

Dr. Ainsworth took a moment to collect herself, smoothing out her already perfect jacket. She reached over the desk and retrieved her glasses.

"Cade," she whispered. "Did you have something to do with his disappearance? Because if you did, you need to tell your father and me now. You need to let us protect you." She gave his arm a little squeeze.

Cade stared at her hand. At the perfect cuticles. At the pearlescence of whatever translucent polish she was wearing. At the pinkie nail on her left hand, where she'd chipped it, just slightly.

"Did my father put you up to this?" Cade asked. His throat felt cold and dry.

Dr. Ainsworth, for the smallest sliver of a second, dropped her head. And then she was back. She removed her hand from his arm and sat, still and straight, like a guilty animal.

In the background, Cade listened to the same sound he had since his childhood: the clock on the wall above her bookshelf. Ticking his session by. Audibly slow.

But never more painful than today.

"I'm doing my job, Cade. I need to figure out what's bothering you. I need to figure out how to reach you."

Translation: guilty.

"What if I don't need help?" Cade snapped. "What if I'm perfectly normal, but my father keeps trying to put a finger on the pulse of what sick, psycho shit is lying in wait? And what if, sooner or later, it makes me snap?" Cade clenched his hands into fists and leaned forward on the desk.

Dr. Ainsworth sat very still. "People want to help you, Cade. That's all. They just want to help."

"I can't believe him. I'm done." Cade pushed out of the chair and strode heavily toward the door. His father knew. Or at least suspected. But how? And why? Was it just based on what his father had known for a long, long time?

Cade paused and looked back at Dr. Ainsworth, who had not moved.

"Next time my father calls, do me a favor?"

Dr. Ainsworth didn't say anything. Both of her hands were on either side of his folio. The same one he'd had since he'd started seeing Dr. Ainsworth when he was just a boy.

"Remind him I'm not my sister."

And then Cade was gone before Dr. Ainsworth said a thing to stop him.

He walked through the waiting room and pushed out the glass door onto the sidewalk.

His father was onto Cade. He knew he had something to do with it.

Cade looked up and down the street, and back, over his shoulder. Was his father having him followed? Was that how he knew? Or had he seen it in Cade since the incident?

Would his father go as far as turning him in? Cade wasn't so sure. He wouldn't put anything past the man.

Cade was suddenly hot-cold, like dry ice had been pressed against his chest.

He couldn't go out like this.

He needed to pin this on someone. Someone who actually could have committed the crime. Anyone but him. Kinley was probably too smart, but Mattie . . . he was kind and soft-hearted. That meant weakness. And for people like Cade, and his father, that meant triumph.

But there was also Tyler. And Tyler . . . well, he'd been in trouble for everything else. Would it be a leap for people to believe he could be capable of murder, too?

If he could frame Tyler, his work would be done for him. They'd never suspect Cade again, even if Cade had been the one who . . .

He hadn't meant to kill him. Cade was usually more subtle than that.

He wasn't going to go to prison for accidentally offing the most evil man in the universe.

Someone else would have to do that for him.

Ivy

"Why did you kill him?"

Ivy stared across the kitchen table at her brother, her eyes wide. "What?" she asked. Her hands gripped the wood, her fingernails bending against the hard surface.

"Dr. Stratford. Why did you kill him?" her brother asked, very calmly. Very matter-of-factly. As if they had already established that Ivy was a murderer.

As if he'd known the entire time.

Ivy's whole body started falling apart from the inside. First, her heart began to slow. Then she felt her stomach shrinking in on itself.

She was going to die. She was going to die right there at the kitchen table.

The corner of Daniel's mouth quirked up, and he started laughing. "Geez, Ivy, chill out, okay? I told you! I'm just practicing! I'm going to ask the hard questions, okay? Plus, since you actually knew the guy, you're good practice." He winked at her. "You'd be surprised how many supposedly minute details have led to arrests. *Real* arrests."

That's what Ivy was afraid of. She took a slow breath and hoped Daniel didn't notice her shaking. She moved her hands from the table and wrapped them around each side of her chair, like she was trying to hold on.

Maybe she was.

"I don't have much time," she told her brother. "We have class tonight, and I'm trying to get in good with the new professor."

"But you already had class with her," Daniel said, confused.

"Yeah, twice, but basically all she has done is introduce herself and talk about how sorry she is about Dr. Stratford's disappearance. Last class, she sipped on an actual glass of prune juice. Seriously, Daniel, if I make her wait she might actually die. She's that old."

The words sounded callous in her ears, now, but they were words the Old Ivy would have used easily. Flippantly, even. So New Ivy had to use them too.

She hated herself.

"Hey, I should hook you up to the lie detector sometime. We have an old one down at the station. We're not really allowed to use them since they say you can fool them now."

"Boring." Ivy pretended to yawn, but her insides were jumping. She could never go there, never do that, because then he'd know. "Is it over? Can I go?"

"Just sit tight, okay?" Her brother pulled a crumpled piece of paper out of the pocket of his khakis.

"Really? That's how you interview a criminal? With a love note from high school? Did someone toss that to you after they got their cell phone taken away?"

She hated herself even more. But she needed him to leave her alone.

"Ivy, seriously? I'm trying here." He smoothed the paper out on the table and cleared his throat. "Okay. You have to state your name. So, please state it."

"Ivy Katherine McWhellen."

Her stomach hurt. Big, sharp stabs of pain. Was this karmic payback? A sign from God, telling her to confess?

Or just more punishment? Her fall from grace hadn't been enough. Maybe Ivy had been so terrible to the people in her life that hers needed to be ruined. She imagined herself as Piper in *Orange Is the New Black*, carving a shank out of a toothbrush and trading Cheetos for shower sandals.

"Your relationship to the deceased?"

"Deceased?" Ivy said. "I thought he was just missing." Her muscles tensed.

Daniel sighed heavily. "No, Ivy. Seriously, we're just playing here, okay? Just bear with me."

Ivy harrumphed. "Fine. Just hurry up, then."

"What is your relationship to the missing man?"

"Um, he was my professor for my psych class. That's it." Ivy studied her brother, but he was hardly looking at her. His eyes were glued to the paper. His hand fumbled for the soda can in front of him, and she pushed it into his outstretched palm.

"Thanks," he muttered. "Um, let's see. When did you last see Dr. Stratford?"

A flash of Stratford disappearing into the river lightninged across her mental vision, and for a moment she was back at the river, carrying him, her arms straining with his weight.

Helping to throw him into a watery grave.

"Um, during the class when we took the test."

"The date was?"

Friday, June 12.

Ivy scoffed. "Seriously? You expect me to know the date? I don't even know what today is."

Ivy wished she were kidding about knowing the current date. But the more she tried to keep it together, the more everything swam together in a mix of colors and sounds and ideas and nothing made sense anymore. Nothing.

Not even Garrett—the one person she'd thought she still wanted—had made it right.

Not for a second.

But Friday, June 12.

She remembered that. She remembered it in perfect, clear detail. Every last bit. It replayed in her head, over and over, like a film. It followed her into sleep every night, and was there when she woke up. A shadow that clung to her.

Her brother stood up from the table and started pacing.

"Are you Good Cop or Bad Cop?" she quipped.

"I'm asking the questions." He clasped his hands behind his back. "Okay, Ivy. Here's a real question for you." He stopped. "Why is Mrs. Stratford outside our house again?"

"*What?*" Ivy pushed away from the table and hurried into the living room. She threw aside the curtains and looked out the front window.

There Mrs. Stratford was, her car idling in the street. Ivy turned back to Daniel, frantic. "Daniel, why is she here?"

He frowned at her. "That's a question for you to answer, isn't it?"

She peeked out the window again. Mrs. Stratford was just sitting in her car, the engine running and the windows down. Her elbow was perched on the door, and she was smoking a cigarette.

"I am so done with this!" Ivy shrieked. She tore open the front door and marched out, stopping by the driver's-side door. "What are you doing here? What do you want?" she shrieked.

Mrs. Stratford jumped, her cigarette falling from her fingers onto the sidewalk, showering sparks on the cement. She cursed, and then looked up at Ivy. "I wanted to talk to you." She pointed at Ivy with a trembling finger, swollen and thick with arthritis.

"Well, I'm here. Say what you want to say."

Mrs. Stratford stared at her, her eyes crinkled. "I think you know more than you're letting on. You and that boy next door. You know something."

"Yeah, we know our professor hasn't shown up to class. We know he's missing. It's everywhere. I know my brother's working on the case to try to help you find your husband. Is that enough?" She put her hands on her hips and narrowed her eyes, daring Mrs. Stratford to say anything else.

Mrs. Stratford glared at her. "Why were you so weird in the parking lot?"

Ivy threw up her hands. "Well, the world's toughest teacher didn't show up to his own class. Doesn't that seem a little weird to you, as his wife? I would think that you were the one who wasn't saying something. What did you do to him to make him leave, huh?"

Ivy was shouting, but she didn't care. She couldn't do this. She couldn't.

Mrs. Stratford's face crumpled, all the anger and suspicion gone from it like air from a popped balloon.

Daniel, who Ivy hadn't heard come out, grabbed her arm. "Go inside, Ivy." His voice was firm. "Mrs. Stratford, I need you to leave my home. Immediately. And I understand that you're going through a difficult time, but if you spend one more moment talking to my sister, then I have no problem filing a report at the station."

Ivy took a couple steps back, letting Daniel put himself between her and the car.

Mrs. Stratford spat out the car window and drove off, her car backfiring as she went. It sounded like a gunshot, and Ivy jumped.

Daniel turned to his sister. He rubbed his forehead.

"Having your brother as a cop doesn't mean you're above the law, you know." His voice was quiet, somber. It was like he'd drawn into himself.

"I know," Ivy said. "I don't know why that old bitch is following me!"

Except she did.

God, she knew.

It was because Mrs. Stratford, somehow, could see what everyone else was missing: Ivy's guilt.

Daniel considered her for a moment. "I think we really need to talk about this, Ivy. I think we should see you down at the station."

Mattie

"Bet you thought you killed me, didn't you?" Stratford pushed at his glasses, made foggy with moisture. "Bet you thought throwing me in that river was the last time you'd see me." He laughed, and a trickle of muddy river water escaped the corner of his mouth.

"You died," Mattie whispered.

But he hadn't. He was standing in front of Mattie in soggy loafers, with mud and leaves stuck in his sparse hair. "Wake up, Mr. Byrne. Next time you take part in a murder, make sure you do it right. You should have dismembered me. Just a few swings with an ax—"

Mattie sat bolt upright in bed, drenched in sweat and breathing hard.

There was no one in his room with him. Early-morning sun streamed in through his window, leaving long, bright rectangles on the floor. But, still, it was empty. No one else there.

Not Stratford, not anyone.

Except a cat. (His aunt's favorite cat, Macbeth.)

Mattie groaned and clicked on the lamp sitting on his bedside table. The cat mewed at him, and Mattie picked him up and set him on the bed.

The cat purred his approval and rubbed his head against Mattie's hand. Mattie pet him obediently, willing his heart to slow.

Stratford was still dead. Still in the river, probably, since no one had found him.

And no one knew Mattie had anything to do with it.

No one except the others.

(And maybe Derrick.)

Mattie's whole body hurt. He hadn't been sleeping well. The night before, he'd tossed back some NyQuil, which had finally, finally forced him into sleep.

And into dreams.

Dreams worse than waking thoughts.

Mattie realized he was shaking. He was shaking with the same fear he'd had in the dream, with Stratford trailing mud all over his room, reaching for him, shaking like there was a dead person still with him.

The cat purred louder now, arching his back and kneading Mattie's shoulder with his paws, pulling him just a little further away from his nightmare. Mattie realized he didn't want the animal to leave.

"I should do something," Mattie whispered to the cat. "I should confess, shouldn't I?"

The cat mewed at him.

"I need to," Mattie said. "I'm talking to a cat, which has to mean something. I'm . . . I don't know. But according to Cade, this is all going to fall on me. And I can see how he's right. Can't you?" He hesitated. "What if . . . what if I just took the blame? If I confess early, the police might be more lenient. . . ."

The cat didn't respond. Instead he circled and found another soft spot on the bed. He curled up and mewed softly.

Mattie didn't say what he was really wondering: that with Derrick hating him, with his parents sending him away, with no friends to speak of, would anyone really miss him if he went to jail for the rest of his life?

Maybe not.

And maybe that's where he deserved to be.

Mattie pushed himself out of bed and showered quickly. He needed to get out of the house. He needed a walk, or something. Anything. To see that the world outside was still the same. Still some semblance of normal.

After dressing and wandering through the almost-silent house, Mattie walked down the driveway and clicked in the code that would open the gate. That was when he saw it.

His bike. Just inside the gate. Hidden partially by the climbing plant that concealed the grounds from prying eyes.

The bike that had gone missing after the . . . event.

The bike he hadn't seen since that night.

But here it was, tucked away, like it was waiting for him.

Someone had left it here.

Someone who must have taken it that night, or soon after.

Someone who must have been there.

Suddenly, he couldn't breathe. He couldn't take a single breath. He sunk to his knees, sucking in deep gasps of air that hurt his lungs. Someone knew. Someone knew what he was hiding. Someone knew and was screwing with him.

Was it Derrick? Would Derrick have driven all this way? Was it Mrs. Stratford?

It was someone. Someone who knew him, or knew of him. Who knew where he lived. Who had watched him long enough to know it was his bike.

His head spun. It spun him around and around and around until he wasn't sure which way was up or down or where he was or where the bike was and his chest hurt like he was dying. He knew what was happening: he was having a panic attack. (Could he die from a panic attack?)

He couldn't do this. He couldn't live like this. Not anymore.

He was going to confess.

Mattie left his bike in the bushes and half walked, half crawled back up to the house and made it to his room. He closed the curtains, blocking out the sun.

He lay back down in bed and pulled his covers up to his chin. The cat climbed on top of his stomach and closed its eyes.

But Mattie kept his eyes open and listened to his heartbeat. It sounded like a thunderstorm in his ears.

If he confessed, everything would fall on him. But then he wouldn't have to worry about it any longer.

Kinley

"Nice pad," Kinley said approvingly as she walked through Tyler's house. It was surprisingly normal. Kind of like her own, only a little bigger and a little less plagued by politicians.

"Thanks." Tyler grinned. "What did you expect? Posters of creepy hard-rock bands and a temple where I worship at the altar of delinquents past?"

She laughed. "Something like that." She was happy Tyler was talking to her again. After almost completely ignoring her for a couple of days, he'd finally texted her. He'd wanted her to come over to his house. She didn't know why, but was willing to find out.

"We're so pleased you're here!" Mrs. Green had said when she answered the door. "I'm Ariana Green, and this is my husband, Jared. We've been begging Tyler to bring home a good girl since, I don't know, he was born!" She'd laughed, but in that weird way where Kinley could tell she was actually completely serious.

Then his father had actually hugged her, and suggested that Tyler and Kinley become study buddies. As if he didn't know that being study buddies was something students only pretended to do as a pretense for making out.

"I think your parents are planning our wedding," Kinley told Tyler when they were finally in his room with the door firmly closed (and locked). "They love me." She looked around the room, which was surprisingly neat and clean. The bed was made carefully with a neat blue bedspread tucked in on the sides; a desk, clean of papers, squatted beneath the window. There were no posters on the wall, and only a single picture of Tyler and a boy who looked like his brother taped on the bedroom mirror.

"Don't be too flattered. They love anyone without tattoos." Tyler smirked. "Speaking of which . . . I haven't been able to thoroughly check you for those." His eyes roamed over her body, and she felt warm and nice for a half second. But she was here for a reason, and she couldn't get distracted. No matter how cute he looked right now in his ripped jeans and Metallica T-shirt.

"So," she said, running her fingers over his chest. "I sort of came over to get that flash drive we talked about. It has some college prep materials that I need."

Tyler put his hands on her hips, and one of his thumbs dipped below the waistband of her jeans, sending delicious little chills through her body. He cleared his throat. "I kind of . . . well, I lost it. I know it's around here somewhere. I put it aside to do some cleaning and now I can't find it. But I'm sure it'll turn up. Eventually."

Kinley sucked in her lips. She couldn't let him see her panic. She breathed very, very slowly, willing her jackrabbit heart to follow her lead. He could not know what was on that flash drive. He could not.

"Well, I need it to record the psych classes now, so could you please look for it?" She kissed him once, very lightly, and then looked up at him through her eyelashes. "It's very important. I'd . . . reward you." She purposely cast a look toward the bed.

This was so weird. And so not Kinley. She didn't seduce or flirt her way into things. She outsmarted people. And when she couldn't do that . . . well, she cheated.

Was Tyler even buying it? Would he really believe that a virgin like Kinley would be bribing him like that? Maybe she should draw it back a notch. She didn't really know what she was doing, anyway.

Tyler kissed her then. He kissed her hard, and his arms tightened around her. "Anything for you," he whispered in her ear. "Anything." He put a hand on her chest. "Why are you so scared, baby? It feels like your heart is going to explode. Is there something you want to tell me? Maybe something you forgot?"

Kinley flinched. He knew. Didn't he? Why would he steal

the flash drive, anyway, if he wasn't going to immediately listen to it?

Pressure built inside of her chest. Kinley wanted to push him away. She wanted to scream. But instead, she covered his hand with her own. "It's just being around you that does this to me."

"Mmmmm," he said.

She was a liar.

Maybe he was too.

Maybe they were perfect for each other.

But how would he know what was on the drive? Maybe he'd heard the first portion of study notes she'd recorded and turned it off. She knew she'd be able to tell if he had listened. After all, Tyler was always in trouble. That had to mean he wasn't that great at hiding his crimes. That he wasn't a great liar. And Kinley was smart. She would know if he was hiding something. He wouldn't be able to kiss her if he knew. And he definitely wouldn't be touching her like this if he realized what she had done to him.

To all of them.

If he realized what was on the flash drive that he'd "lost," he'd hate her.

And if he'd really, truly lost it . . . well. She couldn't think about what that meant.

"I really need it, Tyler. Please? Please find it for me?" She pouted, sticking out her lower lip.

"Don't you make copies?" he asked, trying to kiss her again. "Or save the information on your computer . . . for safekeeping?"

She moved her head slightly, so his kiss landed on her cheek. And then he was kissing her neck.

"Not this time," she said. She put her hands on his chest. "Look, Tyler . . . they weren't just study materials, okay?"

He stepped back a little bit and took a look at her. "Then what was on there?"

She looked down at her shoes. "I spent two hundred dollars on the Internet for what this guy promised was the answers to the SAT test. I recorded them to the device."

Of course, if Tyler bothered to study for the SAT, he'd know you couldn't just buy the answers. But since he wasn't the most promising academic, Kinley was counting on him not exactly knowing the ins and outs of serious test-taking.

"So just re-record them."

"I deleted all communication after I recorded them," Kinley said slowly. "I didn't want to leave a trail."

It sounded *somewhat* sensible when she'd recited it on the way over.

So why didn't he look like he was buying it?

"I'll tell you what," Tyler said. "I'll look extra hard if you promise to do something for me."

"Anything."

"So, my brother's been . . . threatening me a little." His

face changed slightly. "He's trying to get me in trouble for something he did. Something that could really put me in the spotlight with my probation officer, and ergo, the cops. Which would clearly be a bad idea right about now."

"What is it?" she asked. Tyler could *not* be in trouble with the police right now, especially not if he had the flash drive somewhere, lost or otherwise. If they got their hands on that—they were all doomed. She played with the end of her braid—a nervous habit she'd been trying to quit. Lately, her fingers found their way there more and more often, and the tips of her hair were fraying into split ends.

Tyler winced, and walked to his window. "Do you mind if maybe we don't talk about that? It's personal. And I don't want to change the way you think of me."

Kinley's heart did this funny swelling thing that felt good and hurt all at the same time. Was he being honest with her? She hesitated. "Can . . . can I help?" She crossed the room and touched his shoulder. She wanted to trust him so bad. She wanted to be his and for all of this to be behind her. Like really his . . . a real girlfriend who would go out on real dates and kiss him in public and wear his sweatshirts home at night.

But she also wanted to shake him until all of his secrets spilled out.

"I want to record his threats. So if he ever does anything with them for real, I can bring the recording to my probation officer and show him I had no choice." He flexed his fingers into fists and then stretched them out. "I always get blamed, Kin. But I can't be that guy anymore. Not now."

"I'll help," she whispered. "I promise. Just do one thing for me, okay?"

He grabbed her hand and kissed her fingers. "Of course."

She studied him, wanting to give into his touch.

"Find the flash drive."

Tyler

"Wait, Kin," Tyler said. He stopped her at the door.

Tyler's parents looked up. They'd both been giving Kinley these big, huge hugs, and saying things like how they hoped she'd be around more. They were basically adopting her as a third child. They didn't want to let her go, and neither did he. He couldn't let her leave just yet.

He had something else he needed to talk to her about. Listening to the flash drive had given him an idea, and he wanted her help.

At least, he told himself it was her help he wanted, and ignored the weird little part of him that wanted to protect her, even after everything.

"Do you want to run to the Dairy King and maybe get shakes?" Tyler asked.

Kinley blinked, and Mr. and Mrs. Green exchanged hopeful looks, like they were hoping Kinley and Tyler had potential. It was the kind of look they usually gave each other about Jacob, when they were happy or proud, like, *Look at our amazing favorite son and all the amazing, fantastic things that he does.*

It drove Tyler crazy.

In any case, it had been a long time since Tyler had seen anything like it directed at him.

And all it took was the hottest, most manipulative, smartest girl that he'd ever met. A girl he was secretly afraid he was no match for.

Kinley ducked her head a little bit. "Yeah, sure," she said, her voice small.

"I think that would be fun," his mom said, glowing so much she was practically blinding everyone in the room.

Jacob made a choking sound behind them.

Everyone ignored him. For once.

"You two have a great time!" his father called, and his parents did this weird giggling thing and shut the door behind them as Tyler and Kinley walked out and climbed into Kinley's car. For a second, Tyler felt like his life had transitioned to a 1950s television show. Milk shakes and dates that were practically parent-chaperoned.

And murder.

"I take it you don't have girls over often?"

Tyler actually felt his face heat up. "I don't really have anyone over. Life of a delinquent and all."

Kinley smiled.

He loved when she smiled.

Ugh. What was wrong with him? He knew she wasn't the shining star of an individual that she pretended to be. She was what his grandmother called *slick*. She was an evil genius.

And she never, ever got caught.

And that, he had to admit, was sort of hot.

"Do you really want to get milk shakes? Or is that some lame metaphor for making out or getting high?"

Tyler laughed. "Nah. Let's indulge my parents' fantasies about how good and wholesome we are and get milk shakes." He smiled, a little deviously. "I want chocolate mint."

"No way!" she said. "Chocolate mint is my favorite!"

"Seriously?"

She turned onto Main Street. "Ugh. No way. I like strawberry. Are you kidding me with the mint? That's like saying, 'Ruin my chocolate with a side of VapoRub, please.' Gross."

Tyler laughed. Under any other circumstances, he could really have fun with her.

Under any other circumstances, they could rule the world. With his underworld knowledge and her badass intelligence? They'd be unstoppable.

A few minutes later, Kinley was licking strawberry ice cream off of her straw and Tyler was scooping out messy spoonfuls of chocolate mint, and he felt almost normal. Like someone who really did these things with no ulterior motives.

Except he had one.

"Kin," he said. "It wasn't our fault."

"What wasn't?" She dipped her straw back into the shake.

"You know what I'm talking about."

She hesitated. "I—I could have moved, Tyler. I saw him falling and I could have moved. But I just let him stumble back and trip over my shoe. I didn't move." She swallowed hard. "Why wouldn't I move?"

"It all happened really fast, Kinley. You didn't mean to kill him. But he was a jerk to you, right? So yeah, you let him trip over your shoe. But that wasn't you trying to murder him, was it?"

She shook her head, and her eyes were a little wet. "I'd never hurt anyone."

He put his hand, cold from the milk shake, on hers and gave it a squeeze. "I know, Kinley. And that's why you and me . . . that's why we're going to get out of this."

"How?" she asked. She rubbed her eyes, smearing her mascara.

"Your little recording devices gave me an idea of how we can actually fix this. For real."

"I'm listening." Kinley paused. Strawberry ice cream glopped from her straw back into her shake.

"We're going to get everyone together. And we'll record them. Bait them, if we have to. And then we get their confessions. Their spoken, no-bullshit confessions."

"And, what? We just send it in to the cops and that's it?" she asked. "You don't think that'll put us into the spotlight too?"

"We can get them on tape confessing and send it in anonymously. But we won't be the ones saying we did it. We'll know the recording is on. They won't."

Kinley shifted uneasily. "So we're just being silent during the whole thing? Is that it? Don't you think they'll just accuse us, too?"

"Kinley, do you want to be the ones associated with the crime or the ones on a tape confessing to actually killing him? We'll have their voices on tape saying they killed him. Don't you think that'll stand for something?"

Kinley was quiet. A drip of melting shake landed on her tank top, but she didn't seem to notice.

"So . . . what? We do this? And if the heat gets turned up on either one of us, we use it?"

Tyler nodded. "Exactly. It's insurance. If we get pushed too far—if it all seems too close—*that's* when we turn it in."

Kinley sucked on her straw. He could guess what she was thinking: Hadn't she already done that, to Tyler and the others? But he was counting on one thing: the fact that maybe, just maybe, she would want to save him, too.

"Okay," she said finally. "I'm in."

Cade

It had taken Cade a long time to find it.

A pay phone.

One that actually worked.

One that was far away from everything. It was on a corner, near a gas station that had long been shut down. The station's glass windows had been broken and replaced with plywood, which was now covered with graffiti. The Dumpsters out back were never emptied, and on days with a breeze, the smell was so strong it carried for blocks.

The phone booth itself was narrow and tall, the kind that Cade hardly ever saw anymore, outside of vintage photographs. There were remnants of hard pink bubble gum on the earpiece, and fingerprints all over the glass sides, like people had been trapped inside, trying to get out.

Cade was wearing gloves.

Gloves, and a long coat, and boots. Boots he'd throw away after he made the call, somewhere far from his house. It was an old pair he had found deep in the back of his closet, boots no one would have seen him wear in ages, so they couldn't be traced back to him if anyone were to try. He was dressed like it was winter, but somehow, he wasn't hot.

His body was a cold, hard block of ice.

He missed Bekah. He missed her more than he'd ever missed anyone, ever. He missed the way she cuddled up tight to him when they watched movies together, and the way she talked to fill the silence, and the way she just knew how much he missed Jeni without ever having to say it. He missed the sound of her laugh—low and husky and full of feeling—and he missed the curve of her hips under his hands and the way she kissed.

He was going to get her back, when he was done with this. With everything that was happening. He was going to get her back and take her away for the remainder of the summer. They were going to do Route 66 just like they'd planned. No more manipulating.

They were going to be happy. And he was going to visit his sister. For real this time. His father wasn't going to stop him.

She was his true reason for doing this. Most everyone had forgotten about her. Almost everyone had moved on to new juicy topics of conversation and let her rest. Now she was something that people whispered about behind their hands at fancy dinners, when there was nothing else to talk about. She had all but disappeared into urban legend—the Sano Daughter Who Fell.

If Stratford's murder was pinned on Cade, he'd be in the spotlight. Online. On the front page of newspapers. On TV. Maybe in magazines. "Millionaire's Son Convicted of Murder." Because of his father, he had the most potential for clicks and purchases, meaning news outlets would focus on him to get the most hits.

And then, by proxy, Jeni would be back in the spotlight too. They'd figure out where she was and ruin her all over again, because she'd be a perfect addition to the story. They could tear Cade apart, and then Jeni, and then his father, because there was nothing the American public loved more than seeing a powerful empire collapse. As long as it wasn't the empire of American Imperialism, of course.

Cade couldn't let them do that. He couldn't let them have Jeni again, to pull her to pieces the way they had when she'd fallen from grace. She was there to get better, away from their father and everything it meant to be a Sano. He could deny that he was doing this for himself, because he was *really* doing this for her.

And that meant taking the pressure off of the Sano family and putting it on someone else.

He picked up the phone and held it two inches away from his ear, because ear-print impression science was supposedly an actual investigation technique. Then he typed in a number he knew by heart from the countless television commercials and news stories.

A robotic female voice picked up.

"Thank you for calling Crime Stoppers. Please wait while you are transferred to the appropriate location. Have the details of the crime you are calling to report ready. Remember, if your crime leads to an arrest, you could be eligible for a prize of up to a thousand dollars."

The line went silent. Cade wanted to laugh. A thousand dollars. Like that would fix his problems. While he waited, his eyes strayed to the traffic light on the corner, flashing from yellow to red. A lone car—a beat-up yellow pickup with the bumper barely clinging on—chugged to a stop.

Did the traffic light have a camera? And if it did—could the lens capture him? Could the Crime Stoppers line track where the call came in from? Could they track the line and pull the film? He should have checked into traffic cameras.

Cade pulled the phone a little farther from his ear, ready to hang up, but a bored female voice answered. "Thank you for calling the Crime Stoppers anonymous tip line. Would you like to leave your name or remain anonymous?"

"Anonymous." He pitched his voice just a little lower than usual and forced himself to speak slowly, to adjust his normal rhythm to a more relaxed pace. He was going to do this. It was for Jeni. He forced himself to calm down.

The line buzzed with static, and then cleared. "And to what does this call pertain?"

"Dr. Anthony Stratford. I know who killed him. His name

is Tyler Green. He murdered Professor Stratford. I saw him dragging the body out of the school. He wrapped him in plastic and put him in the trunk of his car."

"What—sir—please stay on the line while I transfer this call to our lead detective—"

Cade dropped the phone, letting it dangle at the end of its metal cord.

He walked away, shedding his coat as he went. He hadn't wanted his DNA in the booth, but he didn't want to draw attention to himself, either.

The police would come later. They would have to investigate further. And if the operator was a local, she would probably know Tyler's name . . . or one of the detectives would. They would know Tyler's background, and look into it because his story sounded *plausible*.

There was a chance that when they picked up Tyler, he'd give them all up. But between Tyler and Cade, Cade felt pretty sure that the cops would be eager to pin it all on Tyler.

Exactly as Cade had planned.

Ivy

Ivy hated her brother in a whole new way. Not like she had thought she hated him when he used to pinch her and tease her when she was little. Or the time when he'd ruined her new stereo by putting Cheez Whiz in the headphones slot. Not even like the time when he'd dumped tampons all over her during a sleepover.

This was a new kind of hate. It was fueled by fear. And truth.

She glared at him from the other side of his messy desk. He had an office about the size of a closet, and it was a disaster. Folders spewed papers everywhere. Wrinkled files. Documents covered in 3 Musketeers wrappers. Papers that had slid off the packed desk and onto the floor. A tall bookshelf, empty except for a copy of *Helter Skelter* and a lone metal bookend, hunched in the corner and half covered a tiny square of a window that looked out onto the sparse grass of the lawn in front of the police station.

Ivy sat in the chair across from him. Her knees hit the desk and the back of the chair was already shoved against the brick wall.

"We need to talk, Ivy. Really talk."

Her phone buzzed. It was her father, wondering if she'd pick up milk on her way home.

Milk. What an odd, normal thing to think about.

At the police station. Be back soon.

Her phone buzzed again, but she ignored it.

"I need you to really talk to me, Ivy. I feel like you know something you're not saying. Something that might be important. And obviously, Mrs. Stratford thinks so too."

Daniel rested his elbows on his desk and folded his hands, like he was praying for something. And for a moment, she wanted to give him exactly what he was looking for.

Who would miss her, anyway? She had no friends. She'd turned Garrett away. Her parents were annoyed with her constantly—they liked Fun, Popular Party Ivy, the girl they'd raised. They didn't know what to do with the Sulky, Homebody Ivy who spent most of her time at home, underfoot. They were constantly bugging her to get out of the house, to get away.

She supposed that prison would qualify as "out of the house."

And it would feel good to finally tell someone. To get it off of her chest and just let everything sort itself out. The right way. The way it should have been from the beginning. She should never have let the others bully her into keeping the secret.

Ivy leaned forward too, and looked to her left and right. "Can we close the door, Daniel?"

Daniel barely had to stand up to swing the door closed. It nipped Ivy's sleeve as it shut.

"Do the other officers know why I'm here?"

Daniel shook his head. "I wanted to talk to you first. I want to know why Mrs. Stratford thinks you know something."

Ivy swallowed hard. Here was one question she could answer. "I don't know, Daniel. I was driving Mattie home after class, and—"

"Who?"

"Mattie Byrne. He's living next door with his aunt in that crazy-big mansion."

"Really?" Daniel raised his eyebrows. "I've never seen anyone come in or out of that place besides the help."

"Well, he's there now. He's nice." For some reason, she wanted to defend Mattie and his aunt. Mattie felt almost like a friend to her now. Maybe even something a little more. And he was definitely the only one who understood her, even a little.

"Is there something going on between you two?"

"He has a boyfriend, Daniel."

"Uh-huh." He considered her. "Now—what can you tell me about Mrs. Stratford's initial contact with you?"

Ivy rested her hands on her knees. Her movements felt purposeful. Uncomfortable. Wrong.

"Well, I was giving Mattie a ride home, and she stopped us to ask questions. She seemed—really . . . upset. Or maybe she wasn't. She said she and Professor Stratford had been in a fight and he'd taken off."

"Uh-huh. Did she expand on that?"

"Um. Well, we told her to call him. And she said he wouldn't answer anyway. It almost sounded like maybe they get in these sorts of fights a lot."

Daniel began rolling a pencil across his desk. Back and forth, between two stacks of papers, on the only tiny bit of wood that was actually visible. "Did she seem concerned?"

Ivy tried to remember. Had she? "She must have been, I guess, since she was actually looking for him. But no, she didn't seem really worried. At all. Like I said, she mentioned that if he had his phone, he wouldn't be answering her calls anyway."

Daniel paused.

"So why did she zero in on you, then? Why isn't she at Mattie's?"

"Uh, maybe because she'd have to get in the front gate? Can you really imagine Janice Byrne letting that car into her drive?"

Daniel chuckled. "No." But then he squared his shoulders, and the smile dropped off his face. He looked at her sternly.

"What?" Ivy asked.

Daniel hesitated. "Look, Ivy. I don't want to waste time here. Are you going to tell me if you know something, or not? Because if you do, if Mrs. Stratford's little hunch is right, I'd rather you tell me now than have it come out later. The hard way."

Ivy tilted her head. Was her brother actually trying to Bad Cop her? She'd almost been ready to spill her guts, and now he was practically threatening her? She was his *sister*. "Excuse me?"

"I'm saying that Mrs. Stratford has her eyes on you. And I've known you long enough, Ivy, to know when you're not telling the whole truth. And frankly, I don't think you are."

"Are you kidding me right now? I think this detective bullshit is going to your head, Daniel. I told you I don't know anything and I don't. If you haven't noticed, I've been having a rough few months, okay? Things haven't exactly been easy. And you dragging me down here like . . . like some sort of *criminal* isn't exactly helping."

Her phone buzzed in her pocket again, but she didn't reach for it. She leaned forward and looked hard at her brother.

"What, exactly, do you think I'm guilty of here, Daniel? Because I'd really, *really* like to know."

Daniel pushed back in his chair, which banged into the bookshelf behind him. "I—I think—"

But before he finished his sentence, the door crashed open and Mr. McWhellen stormed in. He slammed it shut behind him and stared at his son. His face was bloodred and a vein in his forehead was pulsing.

"What," he said, his teeth gritted, "in the ever-loving hell are you doing to my daughter?"

"I—I'm questioning her."

"Your own *sister*?" her father roared. "I thought you had morals and values, son. Are you so desperate to solve your first case that you're willing to consider your own sister as a suspect?"

Daniel opened and closed his mouth, his eyes wide. Sweat dribbled down his forehead. "She's not a suspect, Dad."

"Good," her father shouted. "Then we're going. He grabbed the door and ripped it open. It slammed into the wall, and her brother's degree from the local university fell off the wall and shattered on the floor.

"Don't bother coming home for dinner," Mr. McWhellen added. "Come on, Ivy."

Ivy had thought she was too old to be rescued by her father, but she was wrong.

And while the whole police station watched, she followed Mr. McWhellen out of her brother's office and into the sunlight.

But her relief was mixed with pain. Because her brother's instincts were good. Leaving with her dad . . . well, she knew she was choosing herself over Daniel.

She was selfish like that.

Sometimes, at night, she felt like she had changed from the Evil Queen Bee who ruined others for her own gain. She felt the way the things she said hurt in her chest and turned her stomach. She felt like she could never be that horrible again.

But in moments like these, she knew she was the same evil bitch that she always had been.

And she never hated herself more.

Mattie

It was the first time he'd ridden the bike since it had appeared back at the house.

It still felt new. Whoever had taken it clearly hadn't ridden it much. He tried not to think of where it had been. Who it had been with.

Who was watching him.

Even so, the bike felt better to him than the new car. It was weird, but he knew he didn't deserve the car. Every time he got behind the wheel, he felt worse. The guilt was everywhere. On the fancy navigation screen. In the leather-wrapped steering wheel. In the engine.

He didn't deserve it. He deserved nothing.

No, that wasn't it.

He deserved to be in prison.

And he was going to confess. (He really was.) He just needed to figure out how. What he was going to say. When he was going to say it.

And for now . . . now, he was heading over to Kinley's, on the other side of town. It was a half-hour bike ride. She'd called him, and she'd sounded nervous. Scared.

He remembered how calm she'd been that night. How utterly in control of the situation.

Something had her bothered now. She was really, truly scared. And he didn't like that.

It had to be something big.

He wasn't friends with Kinley, or anyone else involved besides Ivy, really. She wouldn't just call him and ask him to come over for fun. He'd never been that guy—the one people wanted to hang out with.

He pedaled hard. His leg muscles were tight, and they screamed at him to slow down. He didn't. He couldn't.

What if someone had been messing with Kinley, too? Maybe he wasn't the only one.

Maybe someone was screwing with all of them.

Mattie knew one thing with certainty:

He had to confess.

They all did.

But until then, he was going to show whoever was messing with him that he wasn't scared. And that meant riding the bike. That meant acting like nothing was off.

He crossed the railroad tracks in the center of town, his tires bumping over the rails. The bike rode a little differently now, like something had been changed in transport. It wasn't bad, per se—it was just *strange*. He'd tested his brakes, but they were fine. His pedals were moving smoothly. Maybe it was the seat, since his feet had to stretch to reach the pedals. (But why would anyone have taken the time to mess with the seat, just to return the bike?)

Behind him an engine rumbled, heavy and loud.

He moved to the left side of the road, to allow the car to pass.

He looked over his shoulder. It wasn't just a car; it was a truck. It was a huge gray pickup truck with a thick chrome grille. It was lifted, with an extended cab.

It was a monster—the kind of truck that smashed smaller cars.

And it was coming toward him. Fast. Down the middle of the street.

He eased his bike a little farther to the left.

The truck sped up and veered with him, the engine revving.

It was following him.

Mattie looked back and saw the truck was closer, the engine roaring like some sort of wild animal. He couldn't see the driver. The windshield was tinted heavily, making the machine seem less like it had a human behind the wheel and more like it was some sort of creature come to life to kill him.

And it would. It would squash him like an insect, leave him flattened and dead on the street.

Mattie pedaled faster. Harder. He was almost to Kinley's

house—could he make it there before the truck caught him? Or should he try to hop the curb, to go somewhere the truck couldn't? The engine roared louder in his ears, and the sweat beading on his forehead began to fall into his eyes. He blinked quickly, his vision blurring, and used his forearm to wipe the moisture away.

The truck advanced, the chrome glinting sharply in the hot sunlight. Mattie could almost feel the heat of the engine. The fumes of the exhaust reached his nose.

It was after him. The truck was *trying* to kill him.

And Mattie couldn't outrun it.

He jerked the handlebars sharply.

His bike tire hit the curb and skidded. Mattie slammed on the brakes hard. Too hard. The back wheel of the bike popped up, propelling Mattie over the handlebars.

He hit his head on the sidewalk.

The last thing he saw before everything went dark was the black tires of the truck, bearing down on him.

Kinley

Monday, June 29

"Holy shit, Kin. Holy shit." Tyler stood at the front window, his mouth slightly open.

"What?" she asked. "What is it?"

Tyler didn't answer. He threw open her door and sprinted outside. She followed him, her braid bouncing against her back.

He knelt down at the sidewalk.

Beside Mattie.

She rushed to the street. Mattie lay there, sprawled out next to his bike, his hair matted with blood.

A lot of blood.

It was more than his hair. A wide pool of red was spreading out beneath him, and his face was white.

As white as Stratford's face had been.

"Is he alive?" Kinley asked, her heart racing. "Is he okay?"

"He's not okay," he said. "But he's alive. Kinley, call 911. Now."

Kinley sprinted into the house. It crossed her mind that her parents would probably find out about this, and that meant they'd realize Tyler had been here, but for once, she didn't care.

She couldn't have someone else die.

"911, what is your emergency?"

"I'm at 1452 Brooklyn Terrace Drive. My friend—he fell off his bike and he hit his head, and he's hurt really badly." She hurried back outside. "There's a lot of blood."

"Okay, ma'am. Please stay calm. We're sending an ambulance now, okay?"

"Okay." Kinley pressed her hand to her chest. "What do I do?"

"Is the young man breathing?"

"I think so." Kinley peered over Mattie. His chest was rising and falling. "Yes. Yes, he's breathing. But he's white—like, really white. He looks dead."

"It's good that he's breathing. Now stay with him, okay? Do not move him. If he has injured his spinal column, it could cause more damage."

"What about the bleeding?" Kinley fought to keep her voice calm. "Should I stop the bleeding?"

"Can you do it without moving his head?"

"Maybe. Tyler, we need to try to stop the bleeding without moving his head."

"Yeah." Tyler nodded. He pulled off his shirt and pressed

it to Mattie's head. "Shit. It's too much blood. How long until they're going to be here, Kinley? They need to get here. Now."

"How much longer? Do we need to keep him warm? What more should we do?"

"Ma'am, can you take a deep breath for me, please?"

Kinley sucked in air through her mouth. "Yeah," she said, breathing out hard. "Yeah."

"Someone should be there in minutes, okay?"

"Okay." She nodded. "Sure. Okay."

"I am going to ask that you keep watching his chest, okay? When people are unconscious, they can't clear their throats, so their airways can get blocked. That means it's your job to make sure he continues to breathe, okay?"

"Yeah. Sure." Kinley knelt down beside Tyler on the sidewalk and watched Mattie's chest. It moved slowly, but he was still breathing.

In the distance, she could hear sirens.

"Now, I'm going to stay on the phone with you until paramedics arrive. Okay, sweetheart?"

"Thank you," Kinley said. She put her hand on her chest. "Thank you, thank you, thank you."

"He's bleeding through the shirt!" Tyler yelled. There was blood all over his hands. His wrists. There was a smear of it across his forehead.

"Hang on, Mattie," Kinley whispered. "Please, hang on."

And then, the ambulance was there. It came screaming up

to the sidewalk, and two EMTs leaped out. Kinley stood back, and Tyler held her tight to his chest while the paramedics carefully moved Mattie onto a stretcher and buckled him in.

"What—what just happened?" Kinley whispered.

"I don't know," Tyler whispered. "I just looked out—and there he was." He looked at Kinley "Did you hear anything?"

Kinley shook her head. "You don't think . . . maybe—someone—"

"No." Tyler cut her off. "He probably just hit a . . . a rock or something. And his tire skidded."

The EMTs moved Mattie into the back of the ambulance. "Where are you taking him?" Tyler asked.

"Saint Mary's East," one EMT said.

"Is he going to be all right?" Kinley asked, but the EMT ignored her.

Neighbors up and down the street were peering out of their windows. Mr. and Mrs. Richardson were actually standing by their mailbox, pointing and whispering. Kinley wanted to scream at them. How long had they been there? Why hadn't they helped?

She looked down at the sidewalk, at the wide pool of blood and Tyler's yellow T-shirt, stained crimson, at the edge of the puddle.

She was the reason Mattie had gotten hurt. If he hadn't been on the way to her house, he would have never fallen off his bike. She clutched harder at Tyler. "This is my fault," she whispered.

"And mine." He hesitated and looked down at her. She noticed, of all things to notice in that moment, his eyelashes. They were full and thick, and resting on the edge of the left one was a single tear. "Was this a bad plan, Kin?"

She shook her head as a car pulled up. Ivy. "No. We still need to do it."

Ivy climbed out of the car, her eyes wide. "Wh—what happened? What happened?"

The female EMT poked her head out of the back of the ambulance. "Are you coming or not?"

Kinley looked at Ivy. "Follow us, okay?"

Tyler and Kinley climbed into the back of the ambulance and found seats beside the stretcher, just out of the way of the EMTs, who were punching buttons on machines. One fixed a blood pressure cuff to Mattie's arm; the other turned to him and fit a breathing bag and mask on his face, which she pumped steadily.

Tyler found Kinley's hand and squeezed it, but it did nothing to comfort her. She looked up, into his eyes, and saw what was reflected in hers.

Everything was going wrong.

They'd invited Mattie—along with Cade and Ivy—over for one reason: to talk things over.

In other words, to get a recorded confession. From someone. Anyone who wasn't them.

And instead they were in the back of an ambulance.

Kinley wondered, for a moment, how different her life would be if they had just called an ambulance when Stratford fell. He'd still be dead—she was sure of that—but would she be in juvie? Prison, perhaps? Or would everything have been okay? Would the police have understood it was an accident?

She put her head in her hands, blocking out the scene in front of her. Mattie's too-pale face. The grim expressions of the EMTs. The sight of the machines, all working to save him.

But she couldn't block out everything. The endless chirps of the machine wormed their way into her mind, and the strong, coppery scent of blood was everywhere.

Tyler tapped her shoulder. "Kin," he hissed. "Kinley, look!"

Kinley sat up.

He was awake.

Mattie was awake.

His eyes were glassy and unfocused. He tried to move, but an EMT stilled him. "It's okay," she said. "Just stay still. It's going to be fine."

Kinley grasped Tyler's arm, her fingernails digging into his skin. Mattie blinked, and his chin moved slightly.

"He's trying to say something!" Tyler said.

The taller EMT pulled the breathing mask away. "Stay calm, okay?" she said, her voice low and soothing. "We're gonna take care of you." She touched his shoulder gently.

Mattie tried to focus. "Someone's following us," he said.

And then his eyes closed, and he started sucking in this

giant breaths of air, like he had just crested the surface of the ocean after nearly drowning. His chest rose and fell too rapidly, and Kinley wanted to hide her eyes again but she forced herself to watch.

This was all her fault. And now, she had to deal with the consequences, no matter what they were.

"Calm down," the male EMT soothed, grabbing Mattie's hand. "Just relax, okay? Can you count down slowly from ten? Good. That's it. That's it."

The female EMT turned to them, frowning. "What did he say? Something about . . . following?"

"Didn't catch it," Tyler said without meeting her eyes. "Sorry."

"Me neither." Kinley's grip tightened further on Tyler's arm, but he didn't seem to notice. "Maybe he'll say it again when he wakes up."

The EMT stared at them for a second longer. And then she turned away. "Listen a little closer next time," she muttered.

Before she could say anything else, they pulled into the emergency entrance.

Tyler

Tyler watched as Cade closed the door of the hospital room very quietly. They all stood around Mattie's bed—Tyler and Kinley, who had ridden in the ambulance, and Ivy, who had followed closely and cried until they'd let her into the room. "Ivy texted me about what happened," Cade said, holding up his phone. "Is he okay?"

He would be, they said. The doctor had called it a severe concussion. They were going to monitor him overnight to be sure there was nothing further wrong, but so far, it looked like he was going to be fine.

Tyler was almost a little jealous. Mattie had, for a few minutes, been able to escape into unconsciousness. Had been able to escape the screwed-up shit they'd all done together.

"I called his aunt," Ivy volunteered. "She was in Brunswig for the day, antique shopping, but she's going to call his parents and let them know what happened." Ivy checked her phone. "She'll be here in a half hour. We should probably all clear out by then."

For a few moments, no one said anything. They just stood around Mattie's hospital bed, watching him. He didn't look fine. A large white bandage was wound around his head, which was misshapen due to the swelling.

"He said something," Tyler said. "He woke up for a little bit in the ambulance, and he said something." He swallowed. "He said that someone was following him."

"What? When?" Cade asked. "When he fell? Did he fall? What happened?"

Tyler shook his head. "I don't know, man. All I know is that I looked out the window—and he was just lying there. Blood was everywhere." His hands started shaking at the memory. He shoved them in his pockets.

"Why would someone be following Mattie?" Ivy asked. "What did he ever do?" Her hands gripped the metal rails on the side of the bed.

"I think we all know." Cade met her eyes, his mouth set and grim.

"What did any of us ever do?" Kinley asked dully.

A knock at the door made them all jump. It opened, just a foot, and a man stuck his head into the room.

A man Tyler knew very well.

Emile Harkins.

His parole officer. He scanned the room, and his eyes landed on his charge. "Tyler," he said. "I need to speak with you. Now."

In the time it took Tyler to reach the door, a million differ-ent thoughts ran through his head.

Was this about Jer?

Or had Jacob finally ratted him out, like he'd been prom-ising?

Or even worse—was this about Stratford?

And how had Emile known he was at the hospital?

Keep it together, he told himself. *Don't lose your shit before he even says anything. That's how criminals get caught.*

Tyler had been caught enough. He should know. He left the room and let the door shut quietly behind him, as if a sound would wake Mattie.

Emile put a hand on Tyler's shoulder. He was a small man, but he had presence—at just five foot five, he seemed to stand six feet tall. His dark eyes held a deep intelligence that bor-dered on intimidating. "Come with me, Tyler. We need to find someplace to talk."

Tyler ignored the odd feeling in his stomach and followed his parole officer to a waiting room that was empty except for an old man in a brown cardigan, asleep in a chair. A line of glistening drool leaked out of the corner of his mouth.

"Sit," Emile said, motioning at a chair. He took the one across from Tyler, and steepled his fingers. "Look, man. I hope you don't mind that I'm bothering you. I know your friend is hurt, but your mom told me you were here, and we really, really need to talk."

Tyler leaned forward, resting his elbows on his knees, striving for casual. "Uh, okay. What about?"

Emile ran a hand through his messy hair. "I know you're going through a lot. Hell, we both know you're going through a lot. Can we agree on that?"

Tyler gave one curt nod. What was Emile talking about? Tyler's heartbeat was loud in his ears. So loud, he wondered if Emile could hear it.

"You're in a tough spot, dude. And believe me when I tell you—*I already know what's going on.*"

"You do?" Tyler's voice came out a little higher than usual.

Emile nodded. "Yeah. I figured it out. It wasn't all that hard—I've been working with you for, what, three years now? It's not that hard to pick up all the pieces and put them together."

Tyler cocked his head. Was Emile just trying to get him to fess up to something? He'd never said anything like this before. Never did anything like this. He never showed that much trust. Or faith.

This was a different Emile. It scared Tyler a little bit.

"So what?" Tyler finally said.

Emile looked left and right, and leaned in. "I can help you, Tyler."

"What do you mean?" Was Emile offering him a way out? Was a parole officer allowed to do that? Or was this some screwed-up new way to pin his ass to the wall?

Emile looked into his eyes. "Tyler. I already know what's going on. I know you get blamed for a lot of stuff, and I know that not all of it is really your fault. Guys like you get a lot of crap dumped on your lap. Some of it you ask for, and some of it just happens. Just ask me for help—tell me everything that's happening—and I can fix this."

Something twinged in Tyler's chest.

But no.

It couldn't be this easy.

It couldn't.

"You don't know," Tyler said. "I wish you did, but you don't know."

Emile laughed softly. "Tyler, I used to think that exact same thing when I was your age. But listen. I'm going to give you a little time to think about it, all right? But sooner or later—it's going to come out. The easy way or the hard way."

Tyler stood up. He wanted to get away from here. He had to get away from Emile.

He had to get this all figured out. And he had to do it now.

"I'll give you two days," Emile said, standing too. "Just remember, Tyler: I know everything. And I can help protect you."

"I wish you could."

Emile stuck his hand out, and Tyler shook it, feeling oddly like they'd just concluded some sort of business meeting.

"I'll be hearing from you soon," Emile said, and then he

left Tyler alone in the waiting room with the old man, who had just woken up and was wiping his chin on his sleeve.

Tyler walked back to Mattie's room. When he opened the door, Mattie was propped up, and his eyes were open.

"You guys?" he said. "I just talked to my parole officer."

The room was silent.

Tyler took a deep breath. "I think he knows—I think he knows everything. And we need to figure out what we're going to do."

Tyler looked at Kinley.

She knew what the look meant.

And then he reached into his pocket and quietly pressed record.

Cade

"This changes nothing," Cade said. Something was rocketing around in his head, some idea, and he couldn't quite get ahold of it.

This was not happening. He had been smart. He had been careful.

This was their fault. If someone had screwed up, it wasn't him.

Other than today. He hadn't meant for today to happen. Not like *this*.

"Hold on," Ivy said, her palms up. "What exactly . . . what just happened? I need to know what happened."

"Everyone calm down!" Kinley said. "We can't have Mattie upset." But she actually looked like she was trying really hard not to cry.

"Well"—Tyler dropped into one of the chairs—"it's time to get upset." He pushed his hair back and rubbed his neck. "He said he wants me to tell him everything. That he can help me. So what do I do? Cade, do I mention that you punched Stratford and he just happened to die?"

Cade made a deep, guttural noise in his throat. "If anyone mentions that, I swear to God I will hunt you down and kill you myself."

Kinley laughed. It was a harsh, cold noise, like jagged glass rubbing together. "Well we all know you're capable of that, Cade."

Cade's face darkened further. He had to put the brakes on this now. "Stop," he said. "Just stop. Don't act like you didn't all have a part in this. Before you revert to narc-land, Kinley, don't act like you didn't trip the guy. You killed him as much as I did."

Kinley shot a panicked look at Tyler. "You threatened me!" she said. "And I never meant for him to trip over my shoe."

It was Cade's turn to laugh. He couldn't have Kinley turning all Goody Two-shoes on him and going to the police. Out of everyone, she had the most credibility. He had to scare her. "I know who you are, narc. Don't think we've forgotten, either. Or that we're not watching your every move. We know what happened with the captain of the basketball team. Or Sarah Larson, the co–head cheerleader? Oh, or maybe Alera Samuelson, when she stole half of her paper off the Internet? It's your nature to do the 'right' thing." He made air quotes. "Don't think that if you make one wrong move, we all won't rip you to shreds."

"She's not going to say anything, Cade," Tyler said, a little defensively. "Let's just . . . find out what Mattie knows before we make any rash judgments here."

They all turned toward Mattie, who had been watching them quietly, his eyes as wide as saucers.

Ivy put her hand over his. "Hey, Mattie? Are you feeling up to telling us what happened?"

He closed his eyes for a long moment. So long, Cade wondered if he'd gone back to sleep. But then they fluttered open.

"Someone was following me," Mattie said. "Someone in a truck. I was riding over to Kinley's and heard someone behind me. I don't know for how long, but he ran me off the road. My bike hit the curb, and I thought he was going to run me over. When I passed out, I thought I was dead. But whoever it was . . . they must have hit the brakes hard."

They all exchanged glances, and for a few moments, the only sound in the room was the buzz and hum of the machines and the quiet murmur of voices in the hallway.

"Tyler," Cade said finally, pacing the length of the room, "the cops are watching you. I don't think they're watching us, yet."

Ivy shifted uncomfortably.

"The parole officer said he knew what you did, right? Not what *we* did."

"Excuse me?" Tyler blinked at Cade.

"I'm saying that . . . well . . . it sounds like the cops are going to bring you in for the crime. And like it or not, Tyler, you were part of it. You're going to get in trouble either way. I think the noble thing to do is take the fall."

Tyler stared at Cade for a one full second. And then he started across the room, his first raised.

If there was one thing Cade had never lost, it was a fight. But he knew that Tyler wasn't exactly a slouch either. He fell back into a defensive position, both fists raised. He didn't want to beat Tyler's ass in a hospital room, but he would.

"Stop!" Mattie cried, but Tyler ignored him.

Kinley jumped between the two, her hands raised. "Tyler didn't do anything wrong, Cade!" she yelled. "Tyler, stop!"

Cade stood on the other side of Kinley, his hands clenched into fists and his chest puffed out. "You want to go, Green? Bring it. I know you want one more thing on your record. But don't worry. I'll kick your ass and *then* my dad will sue your family. And he'll win."

"What the hell is wrong with you, man?" Tyler said, his hands on his neck. "You are the whole reason we're in this mess."

Cade's head started to get clouded and fuzzy. He remembered this feeling.

It was the same feeling he'd had right before he'd punched Stratford.

And killed him.

And all of a sudden, the fight went out of him. He bent

over and rested his hands on his knees. "I'm sorry, man," he said, breathless. "But we all had a part in this. All of us." He looked up, at all of them. "But don't think I wouldn't hesitate to kill any of you if you try to pin this shit on me. We are in this together."

His head spun, and the air in the room felt thick. He stalked out, pushing through the door. He almost knocked into a nurse wearing blue scrubs and holding a big stack of papers. "Sorry," he grunted.

"Oh, honey," she said, setting the papers at the nurses' station and grabbing his arm. "Don't you worry about it, okay? I know you're upset about your friend."

Cade just looked at her. She had a wide, trusting face, lined with years and years of hard work. "I didn't mean to," he said.

"I'm fine!" she said. "Don't worry! See, I didn't even drop the papers." She smiled at him. "And listen, I'm on duty tonight so I'll look in on your friend myself, but I can promise you he'll pull through. Okay?"

Cade nodded and gave her a smile. She wouldn't be so kind to him if she knew the truth.

He walked down, through the emergency entrance. He was parked in the lot closest to the emergency room. The one where they'd tow after four hours.

He wasn't worried about the towing. His stomach was roiling for another reason.

Cade clicked the lock on his black Lexus. It wasn't what

he'd been driving earlier today, when he'd borrowed his father's embarrassing monster truck from the garage and taken it out for a spin. His father hadn't ever actually driven it—he'd won it in a charity auction for some tragically rare disease. It had been tucked away in the back of the garage. No one would even notice it had been moved. Probably.

After all, he had only wanted to scare Mattie. To make him believe someone else had been following him.

But then, he had seen the bike.

The same bike Cade had stolen. The bike that was supposed to still be tucked away in Cade's garage.

And he had realized that maybe, just maybe, someone was messing with him, too. And he'd gotten a little carried away with frightening Mattie.

So carried away that he had nearly committed murder number two.

He'd yanked the wheel away just in time.

Ivy

"How are you really feeling?" Ivy reached between the top and bottom rail and took Mattie's hand. She squeezed it, very gently, hoping that her hand wasn't shaking. He didn't need to see how upset she really was.

Mattie tried to smile at her. "I don't feel much of anything, now. Maybe just . . . oddly shaped." He motioned to his head.

"Well, it looks like a giant potato." Ivy smiled. "So if that's the look you're going for, then you're golden." She made the okay sign with her free hand.

Mattie laughed. "I'm glad you stayed."

She smiled. "Yeah, me too. My parents always get super excited when I'm out of the house. If I stayed out all night and partied, they'd probably give me an award."

"So I'm basically doing you a favor right now."

The side of Ivy's mouth pulled up. "Hey, yeah, I forgot to thank you for getting stalked and almost dying. You did me a real solid there."

Mattie laughed again, and then winced.

"Hey. You okay?" Ivy's brow furrowed.

He shrugged. "I'm not great. And I'm . . . I'm scared."

Ivy nodded. "Want honesty?"

Mattie started to nod, then stopped. "Yeah."

"I'm scared too. And I really, really don't want to be alone right now. So thanks for staying here with me."

Mattie motioned at his hospital bed. "Best choice I've made all week."

Ivy smiled at him. Really smiled. And for the first time since she'd started spending time with Garrett, her heart felt warm.

She could see how pretty, popular, party boy Derrick had ended up with Mattie. He was really cute. He was shorter than her—that part sucked—but he was actually, well, kind of hot. His hair was cut into this stylish, shaggy 'do that accentuated his strong jawline. And he had stubble all over his cheeks for once, which was actually pretty attractive.

He's not even straight, Ivy reminded herself. *And he has a boyfriend. Sort of.*

Mattie cleared his throat. She was pulled abruptly out of her reverie and realized Mattie was staring at her, too.

"You know," Ivy said, "other than the whole Mr. Potato Head look you're currently rocking, you're really cute. And if Derrick doesn't realize that, it's his loss."

"I always thought so too!" Mattie said.

Ivy laughed. She really liked Mattie. He was a good friend.

He was kind. And maybe the concussion had rattled something loose in him, or maybe that was what getting stalked and nearly killed by a stranger did to a person, but he seemed . . . relaxed.

"Everything's going to be okay, you know," she whispered.

"I do?" Mattie tried to smile.

"Sure," Ivy said. At least she wouldn't be dragged into the police station again. It would be harder now, since her brother had brought her in without her parents' knowledge and without a real reason or evidence. That was apparently a Big No-No in the police world, even when it was your little sister.

Especially when it was your little sister.

"You think Tyler's going to narc on us?" Mattie asked.

Ivy shook her head. "No. He's not like that. Kinley . . . if she hadn't actually tripped the guy, I'd be worried about her. But no." Ivy looked down at him. "Mattie, do you have any idea who was following you? Any guesses at all?"

He shook his head. "No."

It was then that Ivy finally gave voice to what she'd been thinking all night. "It wasn't . . . it wasn't Mrs. Stratford, was it?"

Mattie shrugged. "It wasn't her car. And if she's driving that piece of junk, I don't know where she'd get such a nice truck. It was really, really swank."

"Oh." Ivy sat back a little, her only theory deflated. Who else had reason to suspect them? Had someone else been there, watching?

"I'm scared to leave here," Mattie confessed. He squeezed her hand tighter.

"Me too."

He shifted. "And I'm afraid . . . I'm afraid we're going to get caught, Ivy. With people following me, and Tyler's parole officer saying he knows what happened . . ." Mattie shook his head. "Maybe we should come forward."

"No." Ivy shook her head. "No way. If we were going to confess, we should have done it the first night. It's too late now. And maybe . . . maybe Tyler's parole officer was just trying to get him to confess to *something*. Cops do that, you know."

Her brother did that, at least.

Plus, if she confessed, she couldn't bear to think of the way her parents would look at her after they had stood up for her before.

What her brother would do after the way she had embarrassed him.

"This isn't going to turn out well," Mattie whispered. "One of us is going to turn up dead, Ivy."

Ivy drew her hands away and crossed them over her stomach. She rocked back and forth, a leftover nervous habit from when she was a little girl.

"What do you think we should do?"

Mattie paused. "What if . . . what if I just took the blame?"

"What?" Ivy's heart did a funny flip. Like she cared. Really cared. "No, Mattie. No. Why would you do that? You did nothing. You were pulled into the classroom. *Pulled.*"

"I helped ditch the body, same as everyone else." He shrugged a shoulder. "I could do it, easy. Besides, I'm the one being followed. Maybe, for whatever reason, whoever did it only suspects me. If I turn myself in, maybe it'll all go away."

Ivy stood up. "No, Mattie. I'm not going to let you do it. Out of all of us, you're the only one who deserves better."

"Maybe not," Mattie said very quietly.

"If you confess, I will too." Ivy stood up and put her hands on her hips.

"No way. I'll say you weren't involved."

"I'll say *you* weren't involved."

It was then that Ivy did something completely unexpected. She leaned over the railing and kissed Mattie.

She kissed him on the lips.

She kissed him harder than anyone was ever supposed to kiss people who had recently been admitted to the hospital.

And he kissed her back. He kissed her back a lot more passionately than someone in a relationship should have been kissing someone else.

And they most likely would have kept at it—if the door to the hospital room hadn't swung open, and if Mattie's aunt hadn't walked in, tears streaming down her cheeks, her face as red as a ripe strawberry.

She stopped in the middle of the room and gasped, her pudgy hand over her heart.

Ivy jerked away from Mattie. "Sorry, Ms. Byrne," she said,

backing away. "Um, Mattie, I'll . . . I'll catch you later, okay? Uh . . . feel better."

"You don't have to leave," Ms. Byrne said kindly, but she was already looking at her nephew. "I see you're feeling much better, young man."

Her cheeks burning, Ivy grabbed her handbag off of a chair and rushed out of the hospital room.

It was only when she walked out the emergency room exit to the nearly empty lot that she remembered she was scared to be alone.

Mattie

Monday, June 29

Mattie knew one thing in his heart: he deserved to go to prison. And maybe it wasn't for an actual crime that he deserved it (if you didn't count dumping a body, of course). It was for something else. Something so low he could never, ever forgive himself.

Cheating on Derrick.

Twice, now.

Twice.

Yes, Ivy was hot, but so were a lot of people. And yes, he was fuzzy from the concussion. But he's sworn it up and down, every single day. He would never cheat again. Not on a test— which was why he was in this mess in the first place—and not on his boyfriend.

His aunt was busy fluffing his pillow, which she had declared "too flat for hospital use" (as if that were an actual thing).

"You like that girl?" she asked, a little smile sneaking around the corners of her mouth.

"We're just friends."

"Mmmmm." She chuckled. "Looked like a good friend."

"Yeah. I guess." Mattie felt like he had swallowed lead. His whole body was weighed down with guilt.

She stopped fidgeting with his pillow and grabbed his shoulders, pushing him back onto it. "I was on the phone with your mother and father on the way here. Do you want them to come?"

"No." Mattie said it quickly. "Please, no. I don't want them here."

"Can I ask why?" His aunt sat down in the chair next to his bed. She crossed her legs and folded her hands over her knees. Mattie wondered when she'd become so perceptive.

"Because I'm fine," Mattie said. "I mean, look at me. I'm good. And because we both know my mother likes to make a bigger deal out of things than necessary."

His aunt looked at him sternly, her fingers tapping on her lips, and then her face split into a smile. "I'll give you that. Your mother does like to make something of a scene. Well, okay. Let me step out to call and let them know you're okay."

Mattie nodded. "Thanks." His aunt pushed herself out of the chair and disappeared into the hallway, leaving Mattie alone with his thoughts.

And his guilt.

He had kissed Ivy. Tonight. And why? For what? Nothing was ever going to happen with Ivy. He liked her, sure. He actually liked Ivy a lot. Behind her mean girl exterior, she was actually pretty decent. And she was beautiful, sure—he was definitely attracted to her. But he could never be with her—because every time he saw her, he saw Stratford's lifeless body.

Murder was not a foundation on which great romances were built, unless you were Dexter or something.

And there was Mattie's other . . . transgression.

Well.

It had been a party.

A party he was supposed to go to with Derrick.

But Derrick called five minutes before he was supposed to be at Mattie's house to pick him up, and he said he was sick. Only Derrick didn't sound sick. He told Mattie he needed to stay in. That he'd catch up with him tomorrow.

"Okay," Mattie had said. "I hope you feel better."

Derrick had coughed, twice. "Thanks."

But Mattie had a feeling, a dark, twisted feeling, deep in his gut, and it was reaching up to curl around his heart. And he decided to go to the party anyway, to see if Derrick was there.

So he'd walked in. Without Derrick.

It was a vacation home near the woods, one that had been boarded up for some time. The entire place had the strange, sick smell of spilled beer and vomit that had never been properly cleaned up. Instead of carpet, the living room had AstroTurf. Loud music pounded through the house, rattling the glass in the window frames. A shattered television was perched precariously on a skinny bookshelf never meant to serve as a TV stand.

It had not been Mattie's scene.

Jayla, a girl he halfway knew from his history class, got him a shot called "Panty Dropper" that was a pale red and tasted like fruit punch. He took two. He hated the party already.

And then Jayla had started doing this weird dance, out of nowhere. Like she was trying to distract him.

So he'd turned around. And he saw Derrick, his shoulders hunched, tiptoeing through the crowd like he was trying not to be seen.

"Derrick!" Mattie shouted. "Hey!"

But Jayla had grabbed on to him and spun him back to face her. "Space!" she had said, waving her hand in front of his face like she was trying to hypnotize him. "Give the boy some space!"

Mattie's heart had crumbled into a million pieces.

She poured two more shots, spilling the liquid all over the counter. She clicked her glass against his, and they took them together. It left a burning trail down Mattie's throat, like a race car in a movie that left flames in its tread marks.

"What's in these?" Mattie asked. He frowned at the orange cooler someone had probably jacked from the football field.

"Kool-Aid and Everclear!" She pulled an empty glass bottle from the counter and shook it at him. "Do you want another?"

He had needed another.

(And another after that.)

His memory got fuzzy about the whole thing then, but somehow, he'd ended up in the backyard with Jayla and there had been some sort of tree house and there had definitely been kissing and probably, if he was honest with himself, something else.

And that was the first time he cheated on Derrick.

He had tried to rationalize it. Tried to say that Derrick had lied to him. Derrick was hiding from him. But what was wrong with a little space? And why hadn't Mattie just given it to him? But no. He'd gotten trashed . . . and Mattie never got trashed.

And instead of talking their problems out and trying to fix stuff, Mattie had cheated.

It was why he deserved to be punished.

And now he was. Whoever was in that truck—whoever was driving—had gotten awfully close to killing him. Maybe someone actually was trying to kill him. Maybe the truck had just missed.

His eyes burned, and before he realized it, tears were falling down his cheeks. Everything was coming apart and it was all some sort of giant karmic paycheck that the universe was cashing, all at once.

The door opened, and his aunt bustled back in. She slipped her cell phone into her front pocket before she noticed Mattie's face, which he hastily wiped.

"What's wrong?" she asked. "Are you in pain? Should I get

the nurse?" She turned back to the door and Mattie reached out a hand. "No," he said. "Please. It's not that."

"Then what is it?" she asked. "Mattie, what's wrong? Are you unhappy? Or are you shaken up from your bike accident?"

"I just fell," Mattie said. It was the story he'd repeated, over and over. He just fell. There was no truck. There wasn't someone following him.

No one was trying to murder him.

He just fell.

He hadn't killed anyone.

Dr. Stratford had just fallen too.

More tears escaped. They rolled down his cheeks and onto his faintly blue hospital gown.

"What is it?" she asked.

"I'm a terrible person," Mattie told his aunt. "I'm a terrible, terrible person. And I need to tell someone."

"Mattie . . ." his aunt said. "You're talking crazy. I should have never bought you that new bike."

Something clicked in Mattie's head.

"What? My dad bought me that bike, right before I came here."

His aunt ducked her head, and her tiny pin curls fell in her face. "I noticed that you didn't like the car very much, so I found a bike exactly like your old one. I was going to surprise you with it, but the day I had it delivered, you were just leaving— so I stashed it, and you . . . well, you found it." She shrugged.

"Did you think some Good Samaritan had returned it?"

Mattie shrugged. "Something like that." His mind spun. Had he been—wrong? Had his bike really just been stolen that night?

Did it really not have anything to do with Stratford?

"Did something go wrong with the bike?" his aunt asked.

Mattie shook his head. "Uh, no. I think I just hit a rock, and the tire skidded. It was just one of those things, you know?"

His aunt reached forward and patted his hand. "Listen, Mattie. I know we haven't spent a lot of time together this summer, but I know you're a good boy. A good person. But you're like your mother, aren't you? You're probably thinking this accident is some sort of punishment."

Mattie ran his hands over the cotton sheets, not meeting her eyes. "What if it is?"

"Mattie." His aunt's voice was gentle. "That isn't how life works. You're a good kid. Start acting like you deserve good things and they'll come to you." She squeezed his knee. "Now, do you want me to stay, or what?"

"Yeah. If you would. It would make me feel better."

"Sure."

His aunt buzzed a nurse to bring her an extra blanket, and she was asleep in minutes, her head rolled back. She snored faintly.

She was the good person.

Not Mattie.

Mattie hated that she was so wrong about him. She thought he deserved good things.

Which was why, when he got out of here, he was going to the police.

The only way to make things right was to save everyone else.

Kinley

Kinley's hand shook as she stretched out another piece of tape. She wrapped it around the bubble wrap. It had to be secure.

"What are you doing?"

Arms encircled her from behind. Tyler kissed her on the cheek.

She did not want to be touched. She just wanted . . . she didn't know. She didn't know anymore.

"I have it," she said stiffly. "I have it all here. It's the confession. It's where Cade threatens us all and it's clear that he is the one behind the killing."

"Whoa." Tyler reached around and took both of her hands in his. "Slow your roll, baby. What's going on?"

"The confession. We have to do this." She wrenched his hands free. "Do you have a manila envelope? Or, like, a bubble mailer? I think we need to drop by the police station with this today. Or maybe you could give it to your parole officer?"

"You were lucky to get tape from me," Tyler said. "You

— 594 —

need to slow way down, Kin. Why are you in such a hurry to send that?"

Kinley looked at her shoes and leaned back against the desk. "Tyler, I just want this to be over. I just want to be done and I want to wash my hands of it and I want to go to college really far away and—"

Tyler grabbed Kinley and held her tight to his hard chest. "Calm down, Kin. Calm down. You're freaking out, okay? You're in a tough spot. We're in a tough spot. But you need to breathe for a minute. Just breathe."

She felt herself relax against him, just a little bit. He guided her over to the bed. "Turn around."

"What?" she said.

"Just do it, please."

Kinley turned away from Tyler, her pulse speeding up. She wondered if Tyler was going to play some sort of weird sex game. She wasn't ready for that.

She felt his hands grip her shoulders, and he began to rub in a slow, circular motion.

"Lie down," he whispered.

She obeyed, and he slid up on the bed. His hands kneaded her back. She felt Tyler lift the hem of her shirt and slide his hands beneath the stiff cotton.

It felt delicious.

"You're stressed, Kin. And we can't rush into anything here, okay?"

"Oh. Okay." For a moment, she wanted to dissolve into the mattress. She wanted to fall into a deep, forever kind of sleep. And suddenly, she didn't mind Tyler touching her.

"We need to stop and think. Do we throw this at the police immediately? Or is this our ace-in-the-hole move?"

If there was one thing Tyler knew more about, it was how to handle the police.

"I just . . . I just . . ." She paused, swallowing hard. "I don't feel right anymore. I feel like the outside frame of a person, and like inside there's just this hollowness and I need to do something. I need to do something to make something happen. I can't take much more of this."

Tyler moved his hands up, and rubbed the skin under her bra strap. "Yes, you can. You can because you deserve better. We both do. I am going to figure out what my parole officer knows. If it's too much—we give him the flash drive, and then at least it's clear that Cade instigated the situation. And if he doesn't know as much as he says, then we're not in a bad place. Okay?"

She nodded, her head half buried in his pillow. Funny how he considered their current situation to be "not a bad place." Because it was bad. It was horrible.

Maybe he didn't have as much of a life to ruin.

"It's not a perfect confession, Kin. We give that to them and there's going to be questions. And some of those are going to be about us. It's a good card to play, but it's not exactly the get-out-of-jail-free card, you know?"

"Yeah." Kinley sighed. "Yeah, I know." She paused. "Hey, Tyler?"

"Mm-hmm?" His fingers pressed into her skin, smoothing the deep tension from her muscles.

"Why haven't they found him yet?"

His hands paused on her back, and then resumed, a little more stiffly. "I don't know, Kin. They should have had him by now, I would think. Someone should have happened upon it. Or something."

Kinley found it funny how *him* had become *it*. Like murder was easier to deal with if the victim was dehumanized.

"Do you think they will?"

"Yeah." Tyler didn't hesitate. "It's just a matter of time."

"And do you think they'll find out that Kip didn't really see him that night?" Kinley asked. Kip was their safety. And as soon as he went away . . . everything would blow up.

"I don't know, Kin."

Kinley stayed very still on the bed, letting Tyler knead her body.

"So," Tyler said. "I needed to ask you a favor."

Kinley felt herself tense, and she knew that Tyler felt it too. "What kind of favor?"

"I need to borrow your recording system for, like, a day."

Kinley rolled out from under his hands and sat up on the bed. "What for, Tyler? I can't just lend it out. What happens if someone finds it? What if it's traced back to me and my dad?"

Tyler bent his knees and straightened them, shoving his hands in his pockets. Kinley tilted her head. He looked so awkward. Not Tyler-like at all. "Is it that big of a deal, Kinley?" he asked. He removed his hands and rubbed them on his jeans.

Kinley almost felt for him. But she also realized, watching him moving shiftily around his room, that maybe she didn't trust him.

And he hadn't found the flash drive yet. So maybe . . . maybe he didn't trust her, either.

"Why do you need it, Tyler?" She patted the bed beside her, wanting him to stop pacing.

He sat down awkwardly, his back ramrod straight. "Honestly?"

She turned toward him on the bed, one leg pulled up and tucked beneath her. "I think we're at that level with each other, don't you?"

Tyler looked at Kinley for a long moment, as if searching her face for something.

"I'm being threatened, okay? And I need to make it clear to someone that I'm not exactly going down for something he's blackmailing me for."

Kinley touched his leg. "Does this have to do with Stratford?"

Tyler shook his head. "You know from time to time I get involved with other shit."

She knew.

Everyone knew.

He turned to her and ran his fingers along her chin. "I understand if you can't part with it."

Her mind raced, but she kept her face neutral. He had the other flash drive. She had to keep him on her side. She needed it back. If it was with Tyler, it was like one million percent more likely to be discovered by the police. Or at least his parole officer.

"Sure," she said finally. "But you have two days. And then you give that back to me . . . along with the other flash drive."

Tyler fidgeted for a moment. And then he held out a hand. "Deal?"

She ignored his hand and kissed him. Hard. "Deal," she agreed.

They sat together on the bed, staring at the wall.

"Psych class starts in twenty minutes," Kinley volunteered after a long pause. "Do you want to go?"

"No."

"Yeah. Me neither."

Tyler

The flash drive was almost weightless—practically nonexistent, like a stick of gum. It was smaller than the last one he'd used.

"It's more than a flash drive," Kinley had explained. "It's more advanced than that. Just have it on your person when you're going to record, and press this button here. It will activate the microphone, which is actually going to be taped to the inside of your collar."

That's where it was now. The tape scraped at his skin. He watched his brother root through the freezer and come out with a large vat of strawberry ice cream.

"You're so lucky," their mother said, tweaking her son's nose. "I wish I could eat like you."

"It's all that swimming," Mr. Green said. "I heard that Michael Phelps eats, like, twelve thousand calories every single day." He chuckles. "Tyler, you should take up swimming."

Tyler wasn't totally sure how to take that. Yeah, he ate like crazy too, but he was fit as hell. Maybe he wasn't as buff as his brother, but he had muscles.

"Running from the police is enough of a workout." His brother looked at him pointedly.

"That's not very nice, Jacob," Mrs. Green said, but she gave his shoulder an affectionate little pat all the same. "Now, your father and I have an art show downtown. We'll be back in time for supper. All right?" Her mother tucked her hair behind her ears and checked her reflection in the mirror that hung in the entranceway leading to the kitchen. She was an art consultant for some of the more affluent dealers in town, and she was obsessed with looking fashionable.

Jacob dug into the carton and came out with a huge spoonful of pink ice cream. "Have fun."

His parents kissed Jacob on the head. His mother kissed Tyler, too, and his father gave him a quick cuff on the shoulder.

"We'll bring home pizza!" his mother called as she shut the door behind her.

And then it was just Jacob and Tyler in the kitchen. Jacob hopped up onto the counter and took another sloppy spoonful of ice cream.

"No one's going to want to eat that when you're done with it," Tyler said. He was sweating. He could feel it on the back of his neck, creeping down into the collar of his shirt. He hoped it didn't make the tape unstick. He should have asked Kinley how it worked for her.

Maybe she didn't get nervous. Other than yesterday, she was nearly unshakeable. It was a little creepy.

Jacob hopped down off the counter and peered out of the kitchen window, toward the driveway.

"Checking to see if they're really gone?" Tyler asked.

"Well, I can't talk about your drug dealing in front of them, can I?" Jacob smiled and put a tiny smidge of ice cream on the tip of his spoon and shoved it in his mouth. With the handle of the utensil hanging out, he opened the freezer and jammed the carton back in amid frozen tater tots and Lean Cuisines.

"I told you," Tyler said, gritting his teeth. "I don't do that anymore. I don't want to do that anymore." He loosened his jaw. He needed to speak clearly.

His brother removed the spoon with a *pop*. He tossed it into the stainless-steel sink, where it clattered against the plates waiting to be loaded into the dishwasher. "I think you've missed something."

"And that is what?"

His brother smiled. It was a victorious one, like he knew he had Tyler already. "You don't exactly have an option. Remember, I'll tell your parole officer."

Tyler felt the muscles in his shoulders tense. "Then why haven't you yet?"

"Maybe I have." He moved away from the freezer. "Or maybe I will."

"And why would they believe a piece-of-shit drug addict?"

Tyler asked. "Are you that anxious to ruin your career?"

Jacob shook his head. "A champion drug addict who was unknowingly poisoned by his well-meaning brother and eventually grew addicted. It's a sad, sad story, you know. But I'll get the help I need, I think. And so will you."

"You're evil." Tyler's voice was too quiet. He repeated it, loudly. "You're evil. And I'm done with this. I'm done with you. Tell whoever you need to tell."

"No. I'm smart." Jacob laughed. "It's always been this way. I'm smart—and you're the asshole." Jacob turned away.

"Jacob, can't you just stop?"

Jacob looked over his shoulder. "Why would I?"

Tyler flew forward, and before he realized what was happening, his fist collided with his brother's jaw.

Jacob stumbled back a few steps, and his hand flew to his cheek. He stared at Tyler. "You . . . you hit me."

Tyler's chest seized. He had never, in his entire life, hurt his brother. Not until now. He'd just hit Jacob. The good brother. The brother he'd sworn to protect.

"Jake, listen, I'm sorry. I just—"

Jacob made a noise, deep in his throat, and drove at Tyler, knocking him out of the kitchen and into the dining room. Tyler fell into the chairs, a sharp bolt of pain rupturing through his back where the wood collided with his spine. "Jacob! Calm down!" he said, but Jacob pulled back his arm and threw a wild punch at Tyler, hitting him hard in the eye.

Tyler's vision exploded in a billion tiny sparks. He fell back onto the table, and his head slammed into the wood. Jacob jumped on top of him, roaring, his voice too high and too loud, and started hitting Tyler with both fists: his head, his chest, anywhere he could reach. Tyler held up his arms, trying to block the blows, but his brother was stronger. Tyler's sinewy build was no match for Jacob. His head and body took blow after blow.

Tyler's head swam, and he couldn't think or see. Instead, it was just black, and then those white, blinding sparks, and pain. Pain exploding all over his body in what would be great bruises, as dark and purple as ripe grapes.

"Jacob! No!"

Suddenly, the beating stopped, but Tyler didn't move. He was still on the table, his face and body hot and sticky with blood and his mind still swimming in and out, in and out, in and out. He tried to blink, but his eyes wouldn't work, and very, very faintly, he could just make out the outline of his father holding his prick brother back. "Stop, Jacob!" his father said. "Just stop! Calm down!"

His mother raced toward Tyler, her hands outstretched. "Oh my gosh. Oh no, baby. Oh no. Are you okay? Can you see?"

"He hit me first!" Jacob was screaming again and again, his voice high-pitched.

Tyler tried to grit his teeth, but a sharp lightning bolt of pain shot through him. "Yeah," he said, but his voice sounded muffled and strange. "I'm fine."

The pain of even speaking was too much, and before he realized what was happening his parents were shuffling him into a car, and his brother was left at home while his mother held ice to his eye and cooed to him about leaving her purse on the entryway table.

That was why they'd come back.

They'd saved him.

"What happened, Tyler?" his mom said. "What set him off?"

"I hit him." Tyler's voice sounded like he was speaking through a mouthful of gumballs.

"But why?" his mother asked. "Tyler . . . why?"

Tyler tried to shake his head, but it sent pain through his body like a rocket. So he stayed still and let his mother hold a little bag of ice to his eyes. First one, then the other, as if that would make any sort of difference.

His father kept glancing at him in the rearview mirror and making concerned noises in this throat. He said things like, "You'll be all right, champ," and "Really just a few good shiners you got there."

And, as much pain as he was in, Tyler almost enjoyed the ride to the hospital.

It was the most kindness his parents had shown him in a really, really long time. Maybe since he was a little boy.

His father pulled up to the hospital, to the same emergency room entrance where he'd gone with Mattie just days before, and helped him out of the car. He leaned on his parents and hobbled in.

The microphone was dangling down, somewhere near his belly button. He tore it away and stuffed the cord in the pocket of his jeans.

An hour later, he was sitting on a hospital bed while a doctor stitched a cut along his cheekbone. The doctor was a jolly, fat man with a red face and steady hands.

"He got you good, didn't he?" asked Emile. He stood in the room, watching while they cleaned Tyler up. They'd also given him a healthy dose of Vicodin. He hardly felt anything. The swelling in his eyes had gone down enough that he had some of his vision back, albeit a narrow split of what was normal.

"Pretty good," Tyler admitted. It still hurt to speak. Jacob had split his lips in two places.

Emile watched the doctor stitch him up. His parents were waiting just outside with the promise that they would be updated after Emile had a chance to speak to his charge.

"You should have told me, Tyler. I could have helped you."

The doctor gently pressed a bandage along his cheek. "We'll butterfly these other ones, okay? Sit tight. I'll send a nurse in and she'll take care of it."

He stripped off his gloves and washed his hands at the sink. "Try not to get in any more fights while I'm out, okay?"

The door closed behind the doctor. Emile stepped closer to the examination table and put a hand on Tyler's back. "I know about your brother," Emile said. "And I know about his problem."

Tyler nodded. Though the painkiller was starting to clear away most of the pain, it was leaving him groggy and strange. "How?"

"I'm good friends with your swim coach. He's been suspicious for some time, and some traces showed up in Jacob's last drug test. He spoke to me. And this behavior, from a normally shy, kind boy, just confirms it."

Tyler's blood froze in his veins. Emile had said he knew what was going on . . . was he referring to all the shit with Jacob? Was that possible?

"I tried to get him to stop." Tyler's voice was halting. "I told him I wouldn't get him any more."

"Your brother is beyond your help, Tyler. His behavior . . . it was erratic. He was calling me. Making wild accusations about you. And when he didn't get the response he wanted from me, he went further. We think he may have even submitted bogus information to Crime Stoppers."

Tyler looked down at the floor, a lump rising in his throat. His parole officer moved his hand to his shoulder. "Am I . . . What's going to happen?" Tyler asked.

Emile shook his head. "We'll figure something out. But I've got your back on this, okay? I'm not going to let you go down for this when you tried to do the right thing." He smiled at Tyler. Really smiled. "We're getting somewhere together, aren't we?" He patted his shoulder again.

Tyler gripped the edge of the table. Something like relief coursed through his body.

And for some reason, he felt a lot like crying.

Cade

Cade paced in the game room, his phone pressed to his ear. The doors were locked, but it was a precaution he hadn't needed to take. No one ever used the game room. They hadn't for a long time. The room had died when his mother and sister left. Even the maids didn't come in here often, and a fine layer of dust lay over the pool table and the vintage pinball machines. A massive television hulked in the corner. An old one. The kind of monster that had been popular before flat screens had been invented, that took four men to even lift.

The line continued to ring.

They used landlines, overseas. At least they did where his sister lived. They didn't abide cell phones. There were rules. Rules and rules and rules, and that was the price she had paid.

Freedom was a funny, funny thing.

The landline crackled and buzzed, and for a moment Cade was afraid the call had been cut, but then the static cleared, and there was someone at the other end of the phone.

A female voice answered the call politely.

"Hello?"

It was a voice used to getting messages from strangers. It was not primed for familiarity.

"Hey, Mom."

There was a long pause. "Cade?"

"Yeah, it's me." He wasn't sure who else she might think was on the other end of the line; she'd only had two children.

That he knew of. There were plenty of secrets hiding between all of the dollar signs. Secrets that no one dared even whisper about.

"Does your father know we're talking?" she asked, her voice hushed, as if he might be listening in somehow.

"No. I just hadn't talked to you in a while. Or Jeni." He paused, suddenly nervous. "How is Jeni? I got her letter."

There was a long, thick pause that told Cade everything. "Great. Jeni is . . . she's great. She's happy here, I think."

His mother should have been a better liar. But she wasn't.

"Are you okay?" she asked.

"Uh, yeah." Cade sat down in one of the theater-style recliners his father had installed back when they were a real family. A puff of dust rose from the chair. "I'm taking a class. Psychology. I'm going tonight, actually. I think I'm going to get an A."

"Good for you, sweetheart." He could hear his mother trying to smile. But it was as if the air had gone out of her, like a week-old birthday balloon with only enough helium left to keep it bouncing along the floor.

"Can I talk to Jeni?" Cade tried to sound less hopeful than he was.

"She's not having a good day, Cade."

"Please, Mom. I miss her."

His mother sighed heavily. "Just a minute." He heard shuffling on the other end of the phone, and his mother's voice, gentle and low, like she was soothing a hurt animal.

A moment later, a voice that was familiar and strange all at once was on the line.

"Hello?"

"Jeni? It's me, Cade."

"Cade?" She sounded far away. Lost. He was reminded of the time they'd been separated in a Nordstrom, and she'd fallen asleep inside a clothing rack.

Their father had been furious. But he'd almost upended the entire store, just looking for her.

"Yeah. Cade. Your brother." Was he reminding her? It hadn't been that long. It wasn't as if people just *forgot* they had siblings.

"Hi," she said. "Hi."

"Hi." Cade cleared his throat. "Uh. I got your letter."

"My letter . . ." She trailed off. "Oh. My letter. Right."

"You said you were working in a restaurant?"

"Not today." She was matter-of-fact about this.

"Why not today?" he asked.

"I don't work when they give me . . . It's a shot. It's a special shot. Special medicine. It keeps me."

"It keeps you?" Cade repeated. His heart sunk. His mother was right. She wasn't well today.

"It keeps me calm. It's Zen medicine." She giggled, but the sound was loose and strange, like whatever had been holding her together was undone.

"Do they have to put you on so much medicine, Jeni?" Cade asked.

She stopped laughing. "Yeah."

"Yeah," he repeated. His sister wasn't his sister anymore. It was just like the last time they'd spoken. And the time before. And the time before that. She was an echo. An empty shell with the same name and the same voice.

But it wasn't her.

"Cade?" Her voice was mouse-tiny.

"Yeah, Jeni?"

She sounded muffled and tight, and he realized she was crying. "I'm sorry. Please forgive me."

Cade swallowed hard. "I still love you, Jens."

"I love you too."

But then there was some shuffling, and his mother was on the line again. "Cade, you know you can't upset her like that! The doctors say emotional trauma is what triggers her episodes. Now she'll have to miss her shift tomorrow in the kitchens. We have to go."

"Okay, um, can you tell her that—"

But it was too late.

The line was already dead.

Cade stood up and threw his phone angrily into the couch cushions. It bounced off and hit the floorboards, but he didn't move to pick it up. He crossed to the opposite side of the game room, where there were two large dartboards. A few rogue darts lay along the bottom of the baseboard. He picked them up, collecting seven before returning to a thin blue line painted neatly onto the floorboards.

He threw one. It stuck in the outer edge of the board.

It hadn't just been a phone call.

He threw another. It bounced off and hit the floor.

The third got the slightest bit closer. It stuck, precariously, along the very edge, and then fell to the floor.

He was looking at his future.

Cade had been there when it happened. He had been there when his sister killed their cousin. He had tried to stop her, but she had a knife and there was blood. A vast, incredible amount of blood that was spilling out of Andrew's chest, and his sister, screaming and screaming and screaming while his cousin convulsed on the floor.

And died.

Just like Stratford.

Angrily, he threw another dart. It hit the target near the center.

The next two were even closer.

Money was his family's legacy. But now so was this. The rage. The insanity.

And the murders.

One minute his sister was fine, and then she was odd, looking at movements in the air, taking pills from plastic prescription bottles, and then she was a killer.

That was why she was gone. The choice had been prison or a hospital for the criminally insane, and Jeni was in no shape for prison. She was manic, wild with happiness one moment, weeping the next, and practically shivering with rage in the space of an hour. And then she would have days where she was happy. Kind.

Normal.

And now Cade was her. She was the reason why his father was so harsh with him. Why he had been sent back to the psychiatrist. She was the reason his family had split into two separate units of perpetual disrepair.

And now he was doing the same thing.

He had killed someone.

He was a murderer. And he had been a prisoner in his own family for some time.

For the first time, guilt seeped through the walls he had erected and found its way into his brain. It seeped slowly through his blood until it found his heart and made a nest there.

For the first time, Cade wanted to tell someone.

He threw the last dart.

It didn't make it to the board. It bounced off the wall and clattered to the floor.

Cade didn't pick it up.

Ivy

Ivy strolled down the street, watching the black car trail her.

When she went into the coffee shop for a chocolate chip frappe, it parked and waited for her. When she sauntered into the clothing store, it did the same.

She knew who was in the car. She knew who was behind the dark windshield. She recognized it by the state license plate and the small white scratch on the hood where someone had keyed it.

It was her brother's car.

Daniel.

She pretended not to notice him following her. It wasn't until she sauntered down to a café, ordered a piece of Red Velvet Cake with Cream Cheese Frosting, and opened a book that he finally left the vehicle, looking left and right repeatedly as he crossed the street, like he was afraid of being followed.

Inside the café, he sat down at the little table across from Ivy.

"Hey, Ivy. Happy Fourth."

"Hello." Ivy was very polite. She carefully cut off the tip of the triangular piece of cake. It was sweet and moist and thick and perfect, and her favorite since she was a little girl. She'd tried to get the recipe many times, but the restaurant owner claimed it was a family secret.

"Can we talk?" Daniel put his right ankle on his left knee. His foot jiggled. It was what their father did when he was nervous. Daniel had inherited the habit.

"We're talking."

Ivy took another bite of cake. She had been to the café four times in the past week. It was new for her. Before, she had allowed herself two slices of the red velvet per year, and even then, she had only half.

Now, she'd clean her plate, and she would lick her finger and sweep it around the plate to clean up the crumbs.

"We can't talk here." Daniel looked left and right again. He leaned forward. "It's important."

Ivy considered him, and a heavy blanket of guilt wrapped itself around her shoulders. "Is it as important as my little visit to your place of work?" She cut off a large wedge of cake and stuffed it in her mouth, but suddenly, she couldn't taste it. It weighed on her tongue like thick kindergarten paste.

"Yes. More. I need to apologize. So can you just come with me? Please? I'll buy you more cake."

Ivy eyed the last few bites, but pushed it away. She dropped five dollars on the table. "It's fine. Let's go."

She followed her brother to his car, and they pulled away from the restaurant. For a moment, her heart sped up. Was he taking her to the station? Did they find something? But then he turned left, toward the park instead of the station, and her heart slowed.

"I'll drop you back at the café," he promised. "Or wherever you were parked."

"I wasn't."

"Excuse me?"

Ivy fiddled with a thread coming loose from her shorts. "I walked."

He blinked at her. "That's, like . . . almost four miles, Ivy."

"Yeah, well. I needed to work off the cake I was going to eat."

That was a lie. She didn't care about eating cake anymore. She walked often. She hadn't liked driving before, and she especially didn't now. Mattie used to drive her, sometimes, in his new car before the accident. But she hadn't spoken to him much since the kiss. She knew it didn't mean much, but she was afraid she'd just messed things up more by kissing him.

And, deep down, she knew she'd only complicated things so she had something else to worry about. Something else to concentrate on.

Something besides Stratford.

It wasn't that she wasn't attracted to Mattie, because she was. And it wasn't that she didn't want him, because she did. It was that in that moment, she had needed Mattie, and he had needed her, and they had needed each other. She'd needed someone to understand her. And now, she missed him fiercely, and she hoped he missed her, too.

Daniel cleared his throat. "We needed to talk about something."

Ivy gripped the seat belt, her nails biting into the smooth material. "Sure." Her blood was hot-cold. She closed the air-conditioning vents.

"I needed to, well . . . I needed to apologize. And I needed to clear something up, okay?" He put on his blinker and the car moved into the park.

"What?" She watched the trees pass by the window. A group of girls jumped rope in a patch of grass, ponytails swinging. She half smiled.

"I never really thought you had anything to do with it."

"Then why did you bring me in? Why did you try to scare me and embarrass me?"

His fingers tightened around the gear shift. "Can this stay between us, Ivy?"

She nodded.

"I was trying to draw out Mrs. Stratford. I believe, I *know*, she had something to do with it. I just can't prove it just yet. And I knew she was watching you. So I thought if I brought you in, maybe she'd make a mistake. Say too much."

Ivy suddenly felt hot. She flipped the air-conditioning vents back open. Ivy didn't want him to discover the truth, but she didn't want him blaming Mrs. Stratford, either.

"How is the case going?" she asked breezily as they drove around a small duck pond. A little boy tossed bits of bread to a few floating ducks and their ducklings.

He shook his head. "It's been hard, Ivy. We're not getting a lot of leads. Your classmate, Kip, was the last one to see him, as far as we can tell. But now we're wondering if he saw him at all. Apparently, a neighbor cuts through the parking lot most nights to get home—and we think he may have seen this neighbor instead. The police chief wants to question the rest of your class."

Ivy's hands started to shake. She tucked them beneath her legs. "Dad will be mad if you bring me in again."

Daniel paused. "Can you keep a secret? It'll cost me my job if this gets out." He shifted awkwardly.

Ivy nodded, keeping still. "I'm a steel trap." Her voice quavered.

"We found the body."

Suddenly, Ivy began to shake. She began to shake so hard she couldn't stop it or hide it. "He's . . . dead?"

"You're upset." Her brother touched her shoulder.

"I've never known anyone who's died before. I thought he was just missing. Or maybe he ran away from his awful wife or something." She wrapped her arms around herself as the lies fell from her mouth, just like she'd rehearsed. "Where was he?" she asked. "Was he at his home?"

He shook his head. "The river. About twenty miles downstream from downtown, in a very rural area. It looked like he'd been trapped between a couple rocks beneath the water for a while. He was battered. It was bad."

"Accident?" Ivy could barely get the words out.

Daniel shrugged. "Could be. We haven't released word that we've found him yet. They're rushing an autopsy. It will get out, though. Soon, everyone will know he's been found. I just hope we have the results by then. There'll be questions. Lots of them."

"Daniel."

"What?"

"Daniel. Danny. Pull over."

But before he could stop the car, Ivy opened the door and heaved red velvet cake all over the road.

It was the last time she'd ever have it.

Mattie

Mattie wasn't better. He didn't feel better, at least. His head pounded whenever he moved, but he wasn't sure if it was in his head or real or anything else, really.

(He didn't know if he'd ever be *better*.)

But he was good enough that he no longer had the fuzziness of painkillers. Nor did he have the solace of the hospital bed, and while Ivy had visited him at home a couple of times, things had been different with them since the kiss. Part of him actually wanted to kiss her again, but he couldn't let himself do it.

Still, he missed her. And he owed her this.

Now, all he had left were his promises. His promises to himself. And that was why he was driving the car today. He didn't want to ever see his bike again.

He stopped by Ivy's house first. Rolled the Audi out of the long driveway and over to her mailbox. It hadn't been a long note, but when she realized what he was doing, she'd understand.

Ivy, he'd written.

I like you. And I really, really wish things were
different. Because maybe I'd be writing this note to ask
you to dinner or the movies or something. But they're
not different. And I hope you understand.

You mean a lot to me.

Mattie

He had slipped it into a white envelope and left it in her
mailbox. He hoped she read it before her mom or her brother.
He hoped it would be enough.

And then he had driven away. He had more to reckon with.

There were the texts from Derrick, who hadn't even cared
that Mattie was in the hospital. It was a barrage, really, of
Confess now and I know what you did and Fess up. There
had been at least three a day, and today he'd woken up to one:
You aren't being honest.

Mattie had stopped answering. He wasn't sure what to say.
Derrick knew. Mattie could feel it, in the very bottom of his
stomach, where all of his bad feelings collected into a fetid pile
and rotted. He could feel it, when he moved the wrong way—a
sharp, frightening pain that almost doubled him over.

Mattie drove carefully, safely. Nothing could stop him.
Nothing would stop him. He prayed, over and over, that this

would all disappear by the time he got to the police station. He closed his eyes at red lights and made promises and deals in his mind. But then he'd open them and the light would turn green, and he would be a moment closer to the police station.

He neared his destination, but there was a sawhorse in the road.

It was closed. The road was closed.

And up ahead, a ton of people amassed in front of city hall, which was next to the police station. They were all looking toward the building and whispering to each other, like they were waiting for something. What was going on? A Fourth of July parade, maybe?

For a moment, Mattie wanted to turn back. He wanted to turn his back on his promise to himself. He didn't need to come clean. He didn't need any of it.

The street was lined with cars, anyway. He'd have to back-track a couple blocks to find a space. There was absolutely nowhere to park nearby.

Ahead, a green Suburban vacated its spot. It left enough space that Mattie wouldn't even need to parallel park (something he wasn't very good at).

Mattie swallowed hard and pulled into the vacant spot. He opened the door and set his feet on the ground: one, and then another.

And then he began taking his last steps as a free man.

They'd arrest him on the spot. That was how it worked with confessions (as far as he knew).

He trudged toward the police station, but the doors were almost completely blocked with officers, all looking to the steps of city hall, along with nearly everyone else.

"What's going on?" Mattie asked a woman who was standing with a tall man, whispering.

"Didn't you see it on television?" she asked. "They found Dr. Stratford's body. The autopsy results were rushed, and they're delivering them today."

Mattie's body went rigid. The police found the professor. They found his body.

It was over anyway. If they hadn't already, they'd come looking for them.

Before he realized what he was doing, he was pushing through the crowd, toward the front steps of city hall. He recognized Daniel McWhellen, Ivy's older brother, who had been a detective on the case. He assumed the other man was the police chief.

In his pocket, his phone buzzed. He removed it.

Derrick. Again. He unlocked his phone.

I know everything, you asshole!!!!

Mattie, feeling wild and reckless and racked with pain, texted him back. What do you know!?

You are a big cheat and we are over! I know you were cheating on me that night! Consider us done!

Mattie stared at the text message. He looked, and he realized he felt . . . glad.

Lighter.

Derrick had never known. He hadn't heard enough to know. Derrick knew about the cheating, and that was it. That was everything.

And they were over.

Finally, finally over. After a half summer of ignored phone calls and tense conversations.

Done.

Mattie didn't have to worry about him anymore.

If that is how you feel, I respect your decision. Mattie pressed send on his text. There was no reason to be mean. Even if Derrick hadn't always been perfect, Mattie had messed up. He'd messed up big-time.

He had ruined things. And it was best that he had no further involvement with Derrick.

And now he was going to make it right.

Feedback echoed from the microphone at the lectern. Mattie looked up from his phone. The police chief cleared his throat.

Detective McWhellen stood behind him, his hands by his sides, a silent guardian.

"Good afternoon. I am Police Chief William Nolanski and I am here to report on the state of the missing persons investigation for Dr. Anthony Stratford, a professor at the local university."

Beside Mattie, a man with a large camera snapped photos. Up on the steps, two news cameras rolled, capturing the footage.

Mattie's heart was thunder in his chest. In his ears. In his feet.

If he collapsed, would they stop the press conference?

The police chief paused. "We have determined the cause of death as a brain aneurysm."

A collective gasp went through the crowd. Mattie stared, his mind racing. What? A brain aneurysm? How was that possible?

"Although there were suspicions of foul play, the body was recovered from Loop River last week. While there was damage to the eye socket and some bruising around the back of the skull, we have determined it occurred after the aneurysm. The bruising was likely caused as the victim fell. He would have been dead almost immediately. Forensics has determined that Dr. Stratford has been dead roughly three weeks, but the state of the body has allowed for some speculation around the time frame. Dr. Stratford's health records show he suffered from polycystic kidney disease, which greatly increases the likelihood of brain aneurysms."

"What impeded the recovery of the body?" a reporter with tousled red hair called.

The police chief coughed. "Excuse me. The body was trapped underwater between two large rocks and was only found when the water levels were low enough for the body to be visible. It was recovered twenty-three miles south of the town, on farmland. A local farmer saw the body when he took his son swimming."

"Why was the professor by the river in the first place?" another reporter called. Mattie strained, but he couldn't see who it was.

"We have several reports from family and friends that he enjoyed long, solitary walks, particularly after arguments. He had recently engaged in an argument with his wife."

Another question was shouted, but Mattie didn't hear it. His own blood rushed into his ears, along with an ecstatic, wild happiness that he hadn't felt in what seemed like forever.

His mind buzzed. Was it true? An aneurysm had killed Stratford? Not the punch, or the fall?

A forensic scientist should be able to determine all of that.

Was it possible they'd all been in the wrong place at the wrong time?

Had all of this worry—all of this pain—been for nothing? He felt shaky. His head swam with vertigo, and he steadied himself against a trash can that had been dragged over toward the crowd.

He thought of Stratford—his uneven gait. His dropping face. Were those . . . symptoms?

Mattie forced himself to turn his back and walk through the crowd. He didn't stop at the police station. He walked past, deliberately and slowly.

For the first time in weeks, he felt . . . free.

Mattie climbed inside his new car, and cried. He cried big, happy tears that hurt his head and healed his insides. He cried like he'd never cried in his entire life, great, racking sobs of relief that evaporated some of the rot from his stomach and made him feel a million times lighter.

He called Ivy from his cell phone.

"Mattie?" she answered, breathless. "What is it? Is everything all right?"

Mattie put his hand on his forehead and tried to find the words. "Ivy?"

"Yeah?"

And then he said the words he in no way expected to ever say again.

"I think—I think we're going to be okay."

Det. Daniel McWhellen

It had been a long day.

But then, they all had been long lately. Paperwork was the worst part of police work, and he had a long way to go on the Stratford case. Still, he was about to go home for the day. His fiancée had rented *The Godfather* and *Goodfellas*, his two favorite movies, to celebrate his first real case being closed.

He was going to pick up a case of beer on the way home. And maybe some Pall Malls. He used to smoke. Started in high school. But now he'd cut down to the occasional celebratory cheap cigarette, which he relished like some people relished fine wines or fancy chocolates.

Colin, the new guy at the station who handled some of the easier administrative tasks, pushed the mail cart by Daniel's office.

And then he rolled the cart back. He was always doing that sort of thing: missing bits and pieces here and there, running into things with his cart, spilling coffee and mugs of hot tea on important papers . . .

"Sorry, Detective McWhellen. Almost missed you." He handed Daniel a package and two envelopes, neatly rubber-banded together. "Have a good night, okay?"

He pushed the squeaky cart farther down, stopping at the next office.

Daniel tossed the bundle on his desk and grabbed his brief-case. The mail could wait until tomorrow.

But it was only three things. It would be easier to get it over with.

He slid the rubber band off his mail. The package fell onto the floor, but he ignored it in favor of the other envelopes. The first was a credit card application. He tossed it into the shredder. The second was an invitation to the summer ball. Grudgingly, he tucked it into his pocket for his fiancée. She would be upset if he didn't tell her about the department's annual soiree. She lived for that sort of thing.

He knelt down and picked up the package, and then sat down in his chair.

It was a plain bubble mailer. It had been sent July 3. He slipped a finger beneath the flap to tear it open, and a small flash drive fell out. A flash drive and a typed note on the plainest of papers.

Everything you need to know about Stratford.

He stared at the paper. He set his briefcase down on the floor. And then Daniel plugged the flash drive into his computer.

Acknowledgments

I would like to thank Michael Strother, for being an incredible, insightful editor who took a chance on me.

Thank you to my parents, Steve and Kate, for supporting my wild dream. Thank you for encouraging my love of books and telling me never to give up. To my brother and sister, Ryan and Lindsay, thank you.

To Landon, Barrett, Henry, and Lily, well, maybe someday you'll think it's cool to have your names in a book.

Thank you to Laurisa for answering my super-weird forensics questions.

To Bethany Griffin and Suzanne Young for being incredible friends (and amazing writers). You are invaluable.

To Melissa Edwards, for all your hard work. You are so appreciated!

To all my writing teachers: thank you.

To the musers, a most wonderful group of friends.

And to Ogallala, Nebraska, my wonderful, supportive hometown, which still takes care of me.

About the Author

Amanda K. Morgan lives in Nashville,
Tennessee. She is the author of *Such a Good Girl*
and *Secrets, Lies, and Scandals*.

BELIEVE IN YOUR SHELF

Visit RivetedLit.com & connect with us on social to:

DISCOVER NEW YA READS

READ BOOKS FOR FREE

DISCUSS YOUR FAVORITES

SHARE YOUR IDEAS

ENTER SWEEPSTAKES FOR THE CHANCE TO WIN BOOKS

Follow @SimonTeen on

to stay up to date with all things Riveted!